Praise for *Flight*

Standalone Prequel to *Between Worlds*

'An adventure story that encapsulates both a physical and spiritual journey... interesting and original with some startling contrasts between the ordinary and the extraordinary.'

Bookseller & Publisher

'Dub writes evocatively about a beautiful landscape but, in the end it is the touching love story between Fern and Adam that truly compels.'

Sydney Morning Herald

'A mesmerising tale of the real, unreal and surreal...'

Weekend Gold Coast Bulletin

'*Flight* contains all the elements of a Gothic romance: the villain the persecuted heroine, the damaged hero and the forbidding mansion. Dub has a firm handle on action and pacing but in the end the realistic details of this novel: the Tasmanian wilderness, the shambles of Fern's mother's house... enable Flight to take off on what proves to be an enjoyable voyage.'

The Sunday Australian

'The sharp depiction and the emotional force of the narrative are impressive. Still more striking is Dub's ability to maintain the reader's fondness for her eccentric characters... *Flight* is an effective, well-written and glimmering novel with well-drawn characters, a good sense of place and a satisfying number of twists along the way.'

Flinders Indaily.

'This tightly written contemporary gothic tale grips readers from the first page…'

Busselton Dunsborough Times

'*Flight* is propelled by passion and sincerity as well as the rapid trajectory of the story line. It's a novel that will speak particularly to those who find themselves troubled by a sense of powerlessness over their lives.'

Tasmanian Times

Other Works by Rosie Dub

Fiction

Gathering Storm
Flight (standalone prequel to *Between Worlds*)

Dr Rosie Dub is a novelist, and her short fiction and creative non-fiction articles are published internationally. Her writing, teaching and mentoring are deeply rooted in the role story plays as a vehicle for psychological and spiritual transformation. This was the subject of her PhD, and her *Alchemy of Story* newsletter on Substack continues this journey into the heart of story. She also runs a range of *Alchemy of Story* workshops in Australia and the UK, which fuse big ideas with practical techniques for creating stories that reimagine ourselves and our world. Rosie lives in Hobart, Tasmania.

Alchemy of Story
www.rosiedub.substack.com

Rosie Dub
www.rosiedub.com

First published in Australia by Alchemy of Story, 2025

Cover design by Jason Anscomb
Formatting by Streetlight Graphics

ISBN: 978-0-6481227-4-6

Between Worlds

Rosie Dub

Your task is not to seek for love, but merely to seek and find all the barriers within yourself that you have built against it.

Rumi

Part One

Tasmania

Chapter One

Fern woke abruptly. Something felt different. Instinctively she reached across to wake Adam but her hand found only an empty space. After a befuddled moment, she remembered that he'd left for the forest the previous day and by now would be asleep on a platform perched amongst the tree tops. Still uneasy, Fern looked through the window, trying to gauge if dawn was approaching but it was the time of the new moon and the night was engulfed in a darkness her eyes couldn't penetrate. The stars too were blanketed with cloud and in this remote part of Bruny Island there were no street lights to illuminate the sky.

She lay on her back, cocooned in the warm winter duvet, her ears alert to every sound: the distant hoot of an owl, the rustle of a possum in the tree outside, and the regular but gentle folding of waves onto sand, because for once there was no wind to whip them into a crashing frenzy. The shack usually creaked and groaned its way through the night, the boards juddering in the wind, the galvanised roof snapping and cracking as it cooled. But tonight, it was quiet. Tonight, everything was silent and still, as if an enchantment had been cast upon the world.

Fern pulled the duvet even closer around her, wishing Adam were here to help lull her back into sleep but he was out there in the wilderness, embraced by the forest, his first love. Fern smiled ruefully to herself, wondering if she were the only person in all of history who was jealous of a forest. Freya perhaps, because at three years of age she was old enough to feel the empty space when her father was away.

Resolutely shutting her eyes, Fern turned on her side, tucked her knees into her chest and willed sleep to come, but just as she felt herself slipping into its seductive realm, a sudden shriek pierced the stillness, sending her hurtling out of bed.

'It's okay, Freya,' she called, stumbling through the dark into the next room. 'I'm here,' she added gently as her fingers found the switch on the bedside lamp, sending a play of light and shadow onto the wall, and revealing an empty bed, the duvet tossed aside, the sheet below crumpled by restless sleep.

Worried, Fern called out for her daughter then paused, listening for a response, but aside from the sound of her own breath, the house was silent. Panicking now, she raced downstairs, flicking on lights as she went, her mind already going over the worst possibilities. But there was Freya, standing barefoot on the cold flagstones in the kitchen, her blonde hair and flannelette pyjamas dishevelled, her face blank, her eyes focused on the back door as if willing it to open.

Fern felt a surge of relief that Freya was safe, that she was still too small to reach the doorknob and escape outside. 'Freya, it's me, it's Mama,' she said, trying to keep her voice calm as she knelt down to embrace her.

But Freya held her body stiffly in Fern's arms, her eyes open and unseeing. 'Mama,' she screamed, struggling to get away from Fern. 'MAMA.'

'Mama's here sweetheart,' said Fern, rubbing Freya's arms, trying to get some warmth back into her. 'Mama's here'.

But still the child stared right through her. 'Mama, Mama,' she called, struggling to free herself.

Fern felt a gnawing fear that this time she wouldn't be able to reach through to her daughter and bring her back. Night terrors, Granny Iris called them. 'Lots of kids get them,' she'd said when

Fern had described Freya's sleepwalking. 'Don't worry, it will pass.' But months later it still hadn't passed and Fern couldn't shake her growing disquiet.

She scooped Freya into her arms and carried her up the stairs, all the while talking to her gently, trying to bring her back to herself. 'Daddy's in the forest, darling. We'll visit him soon. Perhaps he'll take you up onto the platform at the top of the world. You'd like that, wouldn't you?' Fern paused, hoping Freya would nod her head eagerly, her eyes shining with excitement at the prospect. But there was no change; her body was still stiff and her eyes far away.

Fern tried again. 'Nanny Iris is coming tomorrow, and Michael. He wants you to help him plant the spring seedlings. You can dig over the soil with him and find some worms. Would you like that?'

Again, there was no response.

Feeling herself being drawn in to Freya's fear, Fern switched on the lamp next to her bed and climbed in, still holding her daughter. She tried to cover them both with the duvet but Freya shook it off and sat up in the bed, staring wildly around the room.

Desperate now, Fern started to sing Freya's favourite lullaby - *rock a bye baby, on the tree top, when the wind blows the baby does rock.* She sang it over and over until eventually the tension within Freya softened and Fern knew she'd returned.

'Mama,' said Freya, pleased to find herself in her parents' bed. She smiled and cuddled up close, her icy cold feet finding their way under Fern's pyjama top and warming themselves on her belly. 'Dada's in the tree tops,' she added contentedly, her thumb slipping into her mouth and her eyes closing.

Chapter Two

Fern spooned tea leaves into the pot then glanced through the kitchen window at Michael and Freya who were working together in the vegetable patch. Freya was squatting comfortably on her solid toddler legs with her stuffed wombat, Wombie gathering dirt beside her, while Michael dug the patch, loosening the earth in preparation for the spring planting. Fern filled the pot with boiling water then paused, kettle in hand, watching as Freya showed her uncle a worm wriggling in the palm of her hand. Michael smiled and they studied it together before he gently put it back and covered it with soil.

'They get on so well together,' said Iris, joining Fern at the window, a wistful look on her face. 'I wish he could marry and have his own one day. But that's not going to happen is it!' She sighed. 'You'd think I'd be used to it by now.'

'Michael's happy,' said Fern. She reached over and gently took Iris's hand, the joints livid and swollen with arthritis. 'You need to give yourself some time off. You're exhausted.'

'Pah, I'm used to hard work, it's what keeps me going.' Iris paused, an anxious look settling on her face. 'Though I do worry about what will happen to Michael when I'm gone.'

'You'll be around for a long time yet,' said Fern, looking affectionately at Iris. 'And when you're not, he'll live with us.'

Iris smiled and squeezed Fern's hand. 'Thank you,' she said. 'That helps. More than you could imagine.' She sipped her scalding mug of tea and glanced through the window again, further out this time, at the sea with its turbulent shades of grey, the clouds scooting across the sky, pushed by an icy wind. 'I'm fed up with winter,' she said, rubbing her swollen knuckles.

'That reminds me,' said Fern, picking up a jar filled with dried herbs from the kitchen bench. 'This is for your arthritis, just steep a couple of teaspoons in a pot for a few minutes. It's a little bitter, so you might want to add some honey.'

'What is it?' asked Iris looking at the jar suspiciously.

'A mix of ginger and nettle.' Fern paused and smiled, anticipating the response. 'With a touch of milk thistle.

'Milk thistle! Do you realise how much time I spend trying to get rid of that stuff?'

Fern smiled. 'It has its uses.'

'Well, that's a blessing! No seriously, why don't you do this for a living?' asked Iris. You've been studying all this time, surely you can put it to use.'

'Where? There's not exactly a large clientele on Bruny.'

'Set something up in town? Or at least start selling your herbs. Place an ad in the local paper and put some notices up here and there. I could put something in the shop down the way from ours.'

A familiar anxiety surged into Fern's stomach, fuelled as always by the thought of practising what she'd learned. She had no idea where it came from but the fear was there, gnawing at her insides, the certain knowledge that something bad would happen if she did. 'I just don't feel ready yet,' she said, then changed the subject abruptly. 'Next week I'm taking Freya up to see Adam for a couple of days. Shall I take Michael too? He loves it in the forest.'

Chapter Three

As they drove down the Southern Outlet into Hobart, the sun glistened on the water before them, its choppy surface dotted with billowing sails. It was a beautiful day and Fern felt her spirits lift as they approached the city. She loved the isolation of Bruny but sometimes living at the farthest end of a tiny island off southern Tasmania, felt too much.

'Shall we stop for a drink?' she asked.

'Yay,' shouted Freya from the back seat.

Next to Fern, Michael nodded enthusiastically. 'Need the toilet,' he said.

'Me too,' shouted Freya.

Fern took the turn-off to Salamanca, where they found a toilet and then went looking for a cafe. The air was chill with the remnants of winter but in Salamanca Square they were sheltered from the worst of the wind. Fern found an outside table in the sun, remembering her first day in Tasmania when she and Adam had sat in this very spot. They'd met only a few days earlier and were just beginning to find their way together, but even then, it was as if they'd recognised each other from some other time and place. That was four years ago and she still felt the same irresistible tug towards Adam, though the contradictory foreboding that accompanied it had thankfully faded. Now she simply felt grateful that they'd found each other.

'Beattie wants to sit down,' announced Freya.

Fern sighed. Sometimes this invisible friend of Freya's was a pest.

Michael jumped up and found a chair for Beattie, then scanned the seating area again. 'Need another one,' he said.

Fern put her hand on his arm, restraining him gently. 'It's okay, Michael, that's enough chairs.'

Michael frowned and pulled his arm away. 'Need another chair,' he said.

Knowing it was pointless to argue, Fern shrugged and let him go.

'It's alright Mama, Unci Micki has a friend too,' said Freya.

Fern ordered iced chocolates and muffins for Michael and Freya, and a latte for herself, then she leaned back in her seat and watched the café fill with customers. The hum of chatter blended with occasional bursts of laughter, the hiss of the coffee machine inside and the clatter of cups and plates, forming a cacophony of noise that was so different from back home on Bruny where every sound was distinguishable. For a moment, Fern felt the noise closing in on her but with an effort, shook herself free of it and focussed instead on the sunlight and the fountain in the centre of the courtyard where they were sitting. I need to get out more, she thought. Four years on Bruny and I'm practically a hermit.

The drinks came and Fern took a sip of her latte, enjoying the luxury of a treat they normally couldn't afford. On Bruny they lived cheaply; most of their vegetables were grown or foraged and they rarely ate meat, though sometimes Adam would catch fish. But fuel was expensive and there were other costs: the ferry across the channel, electricity, the car … Adam got some money from track maintenance in the national parks but it was casual work so they could never count on having enough. Fern was a qualified herbalist though, and was nearing the end of her homeopathy degree. Iris is right, she thought. I ought to use my skills to bring in some extra income. So why aren't I practicing?

Fed up with her indecision, Fern resolved to put a notice in the shop when she returned to Bruny. Immediately she felt the twisting anxiety inside her belly, but resolutely turned her thoughts elsewhere. Since when did fear become an excuse? she wondered.

Freya was chatting away to Michael and sucking intermittently at her iced chocolate. She'd broken a piece off her muffin and put it on the table in front of Beattie's chair. Michael had already finished his drink and muffin, and now he was looking hopefully at Beattie's. Then, forgetting the muffin for a moment, Michael stood up and waved excitedly at a late middle-aged man, who was immaculately dressed in a tailored grey suit and open necked shirt. The man nodded and began weaving his way through the tables toward them.

'Sit here,' said Michael, pointing at the empty chair.

'Thank you,' said the man, and glanced at Fern. 'I'm not intruding?'

No, no, said Fern, 'sit down.' She paused, puzzled. 'Do you two know each other?'

'Not directly,' he said, taking a seat. 'But Michael recognised me.'

Michael smiled and patted the man's shoulder. 'Good to meet you,' he said. 'Good to meet you.'

'Good to meet you too,' said the man. 'And you also,' he added, smiling at Freya, who smiled back at him, untroubled by the stranger.

Fern's initial surprise had turned into suspicion. This was an impromptu coffee stop so they couldn't possibly have planned this meeting, yet Michael had been expecting someone.

'How did Michael recognise you then?' she asked.

'Michael and I have never met and yet we know each other,' said Ahmed. 'Whether or not you accept my word on that is up to you.'

Fern shifted uncomfortably in her chair, aware of the prickle at the back of her neck that signalled something unusual was happening. A few years earlier, at a low point in her life, her normal world had suddenly shifted. The membrane between the physical and the metaphysical world had thinned for a time and she'd found herself stepping between one and the other. In the space of a moment her life had become filled with mysterious possibilities. Thinking she was mad, Fern had refused to believe it at first but in the end had chosen to trust her own senses. Since that time there'd been no magic, at least nothing Fern considered out of the ordinary. Instead, she'd found all the magic, the mystery and the miracles she needed in Freya and Adam, in her garden, and in the healing skills she was learning. For the past four years, she hadn't stepped through the veils between worlds, seen visions or even dreamed vital dreams. And she hadn't met any strangers like this.

'My name is Ahmed,' said the man, holding out his hand.

Fern placed her own hand in his and immediately felt the pulse of his energy. In his well-pressed grey suit, with his hair neatly cut and his clean-shaven face, he looked like one businessman amongst many but there was clearly much more to him than that.

'Who are you?' she asked.

The man laughed and let go of her hand. 'You're right. A name is not everything. Would it help if I tell you that I'm a friend?'

'Come on Unci Micki,' said Freya, already bored with sitting. 'Beattie wants to play.' She leapt up and ran towards the fountain.

Seeing his opportunity, Michael quickly grabbed the rest of Freya's muffin, then gave Ahmed a friendly thump on the back and looked intently at Fern. 'He is a good man.'

'Hurry up Micki,' called Freya.

'A good man,' repeated Michael. He waited until Fern nodded, then satisfied, turned away.

Fern watched him lumbering over to Freya. 'He likes you,' she said after a moment. 'He's usually shy with strangers.'

Ahmed smiled. 'It's a privilege to be liked by such a man.' He paused as the waiter placed an espresso in front of him. 'Thank you.'

Fern watched him spooning in sugar; a surprising amount for such a small cup. He stirred it slowly, the teaspoon clinking against the porcelain, then looked up at Fern who found herself unable to turn away from his eyes. Deep brown, almost black, they seemed bottomless and Fern felt as if she were falling into them as he spoke.

'At any one time there are four thousand people living on earth who are pure carriers of the light. For the most part they go unrecognised and yet they act as anchors; without them humanity would not have lasted as long as it has.' He paused and glanced again at Michael and Freya playing by the fountain, the glistening droplets enveloping them with darting sparks of light as they splashed each other, shouting with glee.

'Michael is one of the four thousand. His mother knows it, though she isn't aware of that knowledge. Aside from you, she's the only one and that's how it should stay.'

Michael? A carrier of light? A part of Fern wanted to laugh; she could feel it rising up inside her, a spell breaker that would turn Ahmed's assertions to a joke. But watching Michael galumphing bear-like around the fountain as he chased Freya, she could almost believe it. He lived each moment with such enthusiasm, radiating joy. There was something about Michael that made people feel easy in his presence. Intentionally or not, he'd already given Fern many lessons in how to live and she knew from experience that he had healing hands.

'Yes, he's special,' she said, turning back to Ahmed. 'Is that why you're here?'

'While it's a pleasure to meet Michael, it is Freya I am interested in,' said Ahmed.

Fern tensed, immediately suspicious. 'Why?'

'You know that Freya is a walker between worlds?'

'What?' Startled, Fern opened her mouth to tell Ahmed this was ridiculous but something held her back. She didn't like his message but she felt its ring of truth.

'Freya sees things, if that's what you mean,' Fern said, thinking of Beattie, her imaginary friend.

Ahmed nodded. 'Freya is a sensitive. It's both a blessing and a challenge for her.' He paused. 'And for you.'

'But it could easily be the imagination of a child,' protested Fern. 'She hasn't got anyone her own age to play with.'

Ahmed looked at Fern, one eyebrow slightly raised. 'It isn't wise to denigrate the power of the imagination as it plays a decisive role in all of creation. Freya's vision isn't mere fantasy. The veil between worlds is thin for all children but few can walk confidently on both sides.'

Fern sighed. Ahmed was right. She'd always known that Freya had access to something else. She'd seen Beattie herself; just a glimpse here and there, a flash of a lilac dress and dark hair tied loosely at the back. And Michael spoke to Beattie as if she were real. But then Michael would.

Ahmed leaned forward and spoke quietly. 'Freya carries a great spirit but there are forces that wish to destroy a spirit such as hers.'

Instinctively Fern glanced over to the fountain where Freya was shrieking happily and splashing Michael. 'That's ridiculous. No one would want to hurt Freya.'

Ahmed drained the black coffee from his cup and placed it carefully back on its saucer, before turning to Fern once again. 'If you wish to keep her safe you must resolve what stands between you and your daughter because the weight of the past is creating division.'

Fern felt a shiver of fear run along her spine. 'I love her,' she said defensively. 'Isn't that enough?'

'No, it's not. The past must be resolved.'

Fern shifted restlessly in her chair, fighting a sudden desire to flee. 'I've already dealt with the past,' she said eventually. 'If there's anything left it can stay there.'

'Do you truly believe that?' Ahmed leaned back in his chair and let his eyes rest on Freya who had now collapsed giggling on the grass near the fountain. 'A new body does not help you escape history,' he said.

The fear deepened inside Fern and it seemed that the shadows around her were somehow darker. She shuddered, remembering Freya's night terrors. The fear in her eyes as she called for Fern but couldn't see her. What was she seeing instead? What lay between them?

'You know this already,' said Ahmed. 'You know I am speaking the truth.'

'Things are good for us now,' said Fern, a pleading tone creeping into her words. 'I don't want to change anything.'

Ahmed studied Fern's face, his eyes penetrating hers until she was forced to look away, her gaze coming to rest on Freya, who was running around the fountain again, squealing with delight as Michael chased her. Freya seemed so happy and Fern wanted to keep it that way but deep down she recognised the truth of Ahmed's warning. Something wasn't right.

She turned back to Ahmed. 'What should I do?'

'Learn how to walk through the veils and into the past. Then remedy what needs remedying.'

'How do I do that?' she asked, aware that she had no skills in stepping through the veil, let alone navigating between worlds. Her past experiences had arisen spontaneously with no help from her.

He smiled. 'You'll need help.'

'Any ideas?' she asked, suddenly irritated. 'I can't exactly phone someone.'

'You too are a sensitive. You'll find the right person.'

'Great,' said Fern, her tone brittle. 'That's not exactly helpful.'

'Sarcasm doesn't suit you,' said Ahmed. 'It's like cynicism, closing down possibilities and reinforcing the barriers between worlds.'

Fern shrugged and scraped out the last of the froth from her latte. She was getting fed up with this man who assumed too much.

'Remember that no one is innocent,' said Ahmed. 'We've each lived many lives in many roles; in some we have chosen our path well, in others not so well. You will soon discover … a darker side.'

Despite her impatience, Ahmed's words made Fern shudder. She grabbed her bag and stood up abruptly. 'It's getting late. We've got a long drive ahead of us.'

Ahmed nodded. 'It is always your choice but it is usually more effective to face your fears. If you run from something it will find you eventually.' He pushed back his chair and stood up, then reached over and took Fern's hand once more. 'We will meet again, when the time is right.'

Chapter Four

The narrow road snaked its way through dense forest for mile after mile, the trees encased with a fine mist that made them appear ghostlike. It wasn't raining but the air was thick with a moisture that threatened to become fog.

Fern yawned. The driving was making her sleepy and her thoughts kept drifting back to Ahmed, whose unexpected appearance had cracked open the protective veneer she'd encased herself in for the past few years. She was content with her life, happier than she'd ever been and she wanted it to stay that way. She wanted to live in the real world with Adam and Freya, not immerse herself in something intangible that might threaten their peace. Fern glanced in the rear vision mirror at Freya sleeping peacefully in the back seat, a picture of an innocent child, not the walker between worlds that Ahmed described. But he was right. There was something between them and it was becoming difficult to ignore. A tension, a discomfort … but nebulous, not anything she could pin down.

A heavily laden log truck burst suddenly through the mist, turning the corner on the wrong side of the road. Instinctively, Fern swerved to avoid the truck but there was nowhere to go except off the road. The car skidded in the mud as she braked heavily, and then came to an abrupt halt with one wheel in a shallow ditch.

Fern was thrown forward but aside from a sudden tug on her neck, the seatbelt prevented the worst of the shock. Numbly she looked over to Michael who looked shocked but unhurt. Then she turned to Freya who was strapped tightly into her safety seat and didn't appear to be injured. Behind Freya, Fern could see the log truck hurtle into the mist. 'Bastard!' she shouted as it disappeared from view.

The shock had drained the energy out of Fern's body, a kind of internal crumbling that made her feel as if she were folding in on herself. Thank God I'd slowed down for that corner, she thought.

Confused by the sudden jolt and her mother's angry outburst, Freya started to cry.

'It's okay sweetheart,' said Fern, attempting a smile. 'We just had a little accident.' Fern tried to get her own seatbelt undone but her hands were shaking so much that by the time she managed it, Freya's crying had turned into an all-out wail and Michael, who hated loud noises, was humming to himself and covering his ears with his hands.

Fern lifted Freya onto the front seat and cuddled her until the sobbing stopped. Soon after, Michael's humming stopped and he cautiously took his hands away from his ears. Still holding Freya, Fern checked the mobile phone reception but as she expected, there was none. This car had better start, she thought grimly. It was a quiet road and the prospect of being stuck here wasn't appealing.

Pulling herself together, she strapped Freya back in her car seat then opened the door, letting in a rush of damp cold air. 'Come on Michael, let's get the car out of this ditch.'

The ditch was boggy, the muddy water seeping into their shoes as they pushed the car back onto the side of the road. There was very little external damage, just a slightly twisted mudguard. The tyres looked okay too, which was a relief. Fern held her breath as she turned the key in the ignition but it started first time. Gratefully, she pulled back onto the road.

It was mid-afternoon when they arrived. Fern parked the car just off the road and stretched her legs with relief; her muddy jeans were clammy against her calves and her wet feet were icy cold in her boots. Michael jumped out and relieved himself in the bushes while Freya scampered off to explore the Forest Information Booth, a rickety wooden structure stamped with posters and covered in blue tarps in a bid to keep out the persistent rain.

The atmosphere was heavy with moisture and the scent of eucalyptus. Fern breathed deeply, letting the air clear her nose and her chest. It was good to be back. When she'd first visited the forests in Tasmania, she'd felt the trees closing in on her and found herself struggling to breathe. But now she was used to the densely packed trees, and had learned to treasure the intense stillness and silence of the old growth forest, so different from the spinning, pervasive electromagnetic radiation and white noise of the city, and quieter even than their shack on the southern part of Bruny Island where the waves etched their way into the shore in a soothing rhythm that stilled her mind.

Fern treasured the forest but she respected it too. A few steps in the wrong direction and you could become irretrievably lost. She knew the terror of being alone out there, the panic that can set in, the discomforting sense of being watched by unseen eyes. But the forest was not out to get her, certainly not in the way the loggers were out to get it, clear-felling great swathes of old growth forest to lay claim to the land for plantations. The forest bore no malice but it certainly wasn't benevolent either. She would never take it for granted.

A path led into the forest and above it, strung up between the trees, was a fabric sign painted with the words, SAVE THE FOREST, the brushstrokes rough but clear.

Somewhat lower was a network of ropes that reminded Fern of the cat's cradles she could never get right as a child. At ground level was a smaller warning sign.

Forest Rescue in Progress
Exercise caution,
people's safety/lives attached to ropes. Thanks.

Fern glanced up uneasily at the platform sitting high in a treetop, the ropes holding it in place, stretching out in all directions. She hated to think of Adam up there each night, vulnerable like that.

'Dada,' Freya shouted joyfully when she spotted Adam walking along the path towards them. Arms spread she ran towards her beaming father, who scooped her up and swung her high into the air before smothering her face with kisses. Fern looked at Freya's face all lit up, and felt a twinge of envy. Why doesn't she ever look at me like that? she asked herself, as she always did when she saw them together. Adam said it wasn't important. He insisted that Freya took her for granted because they were together so much, but Fern had always felt there was more to it, and today Ahmed had confirmed it.

'Adam,' boomed Michael, reaching out and encompassing his brother in his massive arms.

'How's it going mate?'

'Good Adam, good,' said Michael nodding his head.

Adam disentangled himself from his brother's bear hug and reached for Fern, kissing her lightly on the lips.

'We had axdent Dada,' said Freya.

'An accident? What happened?'

'A log truck on the wrong side of the road,' said Fern. 'We landed in a ditch.'

Adam scowled. 'Jesus. You'd think they'd learn … Are you all okay?'

'We're good,' said Fern.

'You could've been killed,' said Adam, still scowling.

Smiling, Fern reached up and kissed Adam, her face brushing against his sharp stubble. 'But we weren't.'

Adam stared at her for a long moment, taking her in, before shaking himself free of his fear. 'Come on, I'll stoke up the fire and get some water boiled for tea.'

They followed the path down to the main building. It was raining now; not heavily, just a familiar drizzle. With no wind to buffet them the raindrops were vertical and so close together they looked like long silver filaments. They'd been exposed to the weather for only a few minutes but already Michael and Freya had become creatures of nature, caring nothing about the rain. Michael ignored the main building and swerved off into the forest, disappearing quickly amongst the trees.

'What if he gets lost?' asked Fern anxiously.

'Michael lost?' Adam shook his head. 'Not possible.' He smiled fondly. 'It's always been like that with him. He'll spend hours in the bush and then reappear when he's ready. It's like he's got some kind of inner radar.'

The kitchen, storeroom and sleeping area were ramshackle too, built by the protestors with mostly found material. Aside from the roof and some makeshift partitions, they were open to the elements and the wildlife so everything was stored in sealed barrels. Behind the kitchen was a small room with a hammock where Adam, Matt and the others took it in turns to sleep when they weren't up on the platform.

Stepping into the shelter, Fern sniffed the air contentedly. Underneath the smell of smoke which pervaded everything, was a damp reassuring earthy smell like freshly turned soil, and underneath that was the smell of strong tea. Just what she needed.

Matt was sitting by the fire, reading, his ragged dreadlocks held back from his face in a neat pony tail. Hearing them approach, he looked up and smiled. 'Hey,' he said. 'How's it going?'

'Matt!' shouted Freya. Squealing with joy she leaped onto his back. 'A piggy back. A piggy back.'

Matt laughed and put down his book. 'What do you say?'

'Pleeeaase,' said Freya, giggling.

Obediently, Matt stood up and began skipping around the fire with Freya clinging on behind, her arms wrapped tightly around his neck.

'Faster, faster.'

'Okay sweetheart, you asked for it.' He winked at Fern and then galloped off down the path.

'That girl's got Matt wrapped around her little finger,' said Adam as he put a fresh log on the fire.

A large iron pot sat on a metal grate above the fire, its outsides blackened by the flames. Adam poured some water into it from a plastic drum and it sizzled angrily for a moment. Fern sat down on one of the slabs of wood laid out around the fire, and began unlacing her wet boots. Then she peeled off her socks and draped them over her shoes before stretching out her legs to warm her feet which were pink and wrinkled from the cold. A single leech clung to her left ankle, gorging itself on her blood. She reached down and carefully pushed her fingernail under its sucker to disengage it before flicking it away. Once she would have squealed and made Adam do it but motherhood had toughened her up in ways she hadn't expected.

Adam handed Fern a mug of strong black tea. She held it close to her face, feeling its steam tickle the pores on her skin, her hands gradually thawing. When Adam sat down next to her, she leaned her head against his shoulder, breathing in the smell of him. He'd been out here a week and he smelled smoked and unwashed but fresh too, as if he was part of the forest.

'Freya wants to sleep up on the platform with you.'

Adam smiled. 'She's a little monkey. I'll take her up for a look like I promised but we'll sleep in the tents tonight. Matt said he'd do a shift up there for me.'

Fern was relieved. She wasn't good with heights at the best of times but this platform was designed to collapse if the forestry workers pushed their bulldozers or trucks through the ropes. Every time the protestors went up there, they were gambling that their lives were valuable enough to stop the clear-felling. Unlike the protestors, Fern didn't have the same kind of faith in human nature.

'Maybe she shouldn't go up at all.'

'Nah, there's safety ropes. She'll be fine. The logging trucks aren't around today so there's no threat.' Adam reached his arm around Fern and pulled her closer. 'You should come up too. See what it's like on top of the world.'

Chapter Five

Matt gave a final tug on Adam's and Freya's safety harness then began winching them towards the platform. Oblivious to any danger, Freya was rapt, chattering away as they rose slowly up the massive trunk. Then she peered down and waved. 'Mama, look at me,' she called.

Fern forced her mouth into a smile and waved back. She wanted to look away but was frozen in place by fear, unable to take her eyes off the dangling figures above. Holding her breath, she watched them make their way higher and higher until finally they were standing safely on the platform and she could breathe a temporary sigh of relief.

Five minutes later, Matt was strapping Fern into the safety harness and checking all was secure. 'Ready?' he asked.

Fern nodded nervously and instantly felt a tug as the rope tightened and her feet lifted off the ground.

'Don't look down,' Matt called as Fern rose into the air. Obediently she fixed her gaze directly ahead.

At first it was okay. Quite pleasant really, hanging suspended in the forest. But as she rose higher, Fern couldn't help glancing down and immediately she felt dizzy. The ground surged upwards in a wave of motion and she felt herself fall spinning downward. She could almost sense the moment of impact, the thud that would break her body. Yet in reality she was still here, suspended in a harness, intact and safe. How could she be in two places at once like this?

Adam had told her that we draw to us whatever we're most afraid of. If that was true, then she needed to take control of her imagination and stop it from dredging up these awful possibilities. Determined now, Fern closed her eyes and shut off her thoughts. Breathe, she told herself. Inhale, exhale, one, inhale, exhale, two ...

Adam reached out and pulled Fern onto the platform where she stood shakily, her eyes still tightly shut.

'You're safe,' said Adam. 'We're all strapped on.'

'Look Mama, look. We're on top of the world.'

Cautiously, Fern opened her eyes and gasped at the beauty of the tree-lined valley framed by mountains. The mist rose and fell in a graceful rhythm, back and forth, obscuring then highlighting the trees. Fern imagined it was the forest breathing, in and out, in and out ... As she watched, her own panicked heart settled to a gentler pace.

Above the distant mountains, the setting sun glowed red, its rays finding their way through the mist and turning the tree tops a golden hue. For a moment Fern thought she saw a different mountain range behind these, also tree-lined but much higher, their jagged tops somehow more familiar. When she blinked, it was gone, leaving her disoriented once again. She turned her attention to a bird of prey hovering above the forest, unmoving for what seemed an age, before rising and circling, higher and higher. Forgetting her fear, Fern imagined herself up there, feeling the freedom, feeling her back twinge, the muscles tweaking as if she had her own wings.

'So, what do you think of my other home?'

Fern forced her eyes away from the eagle and took in the flimsy-looking platform covered by a clear plastic tarpaulin, the only protection against the wind and the rain. She shivered. It was cold up here, much colder than below. And the platform itself was so tenuous. She shivered again and rubbed her arms, trying to warm herself. Adam was waiting for her to respond but what could she say? That the platform made her anxious? That she knew his strength was drawn from the earth and he shouldn't be separated from it, not even for this?

Instead, she smiled and reached over to kiss him. 'It's got a great view.'

'Best view in the world,' he said. 'Come on then, we'd better get down before dark.'

Michael was sitting by the fire, wet and muddy but content, with his treasures around him – cast off boughs of myrtle, beech, sassafras and mountain ash … some that Adam had collected for him, were dry, but the rest were freshly gathered, dark and heavy with moisture from the forest floor. As he worked on a piece of dry sassafras, cutting and scraping away at the wood, Michael was humming to himself, an unrecognisable tune that sounded almost like an invocation or a blessing. Watching him, Fern caught herself wondering what magic he filled his tiny wooden sculptures with. Perhaps it changed with each one.

Feeling her eyes on him, Michael looked up at Fern and smiled, then once more focussed all his concentration on the creature he was freeing from the wood.

Freya ran up to Michael and threw her arms around his neck. 'Unci Micki, we've been on top of the world.'

Michael smiled good naturedly at Freya, then quickly shrugged her off.

Adam handed out beers but when he offered one to Michael, he shook his head tersely. Surprised, Adam raised his eyebrows. 'You alright?'

Michael nodded impatiently.

'Hey Michael, what you making?' asked Matt.

'Don't know,' he grunted, his tone making it clear he thought Matt's question stupid.

Matt shrugged and turned his attention to the blackened pot hanging over the fire. He lifted the lid and a rich steaming scent of vegetables, lentils and herbs emerged.

'I'm hungry,' said Freya and yawned.

'Ah then, let's eat.'

Ten minutes later, Fern put down her empty bowl and stretched her feet out closer to the fire, savouring the warmth licking her bare toes. Thumb in mouth, Freya was nearly asleep on Adam's lap. Michael was still concentrating on making his wood creature, his food going cold beside him, while Matt was playing a plaintive melody on his guitar. Fern pulled her pipe out of her backpack and began playing along with Matt, improvising as she went; the two instruments seeking out each other, responding to every nuance and changing cadence, creating between them something harmonious.

Adam was gazing down at his sleeping daughter, the blond waves of his hair falling in disarray around his face and shoulders. Watching him, Fern felt a familiar surge of love. When it came it was always unexpected like this, triggered by something small yet opening her heart into an expanse so vast it felt as if she were embracing the entire earth. Only this time it was counteracted by a sudden sense of unease that thrust her back into her body and out of balance with the music so that she hit a wrong note and stopped in mid flow. Disconcerted, Fern removed the pipe from her mouth and wiped it dry on her jumper. Out here in the peace of the forest and surrounded by the people she loved most in the world, she should have felt content, and usually did. But something was askew. Perhaps her nerves had been rattled by the near miss on the way here or that strange meeting with

Ahmed. She yawned. This day had stretched so long that the conversation with Ahmed felt unreal, as if it had happened only in her dreams.

Fern took a mouthful of beer and stared at the sculpture which was beginning to take shape in Michael's hands. She still couldn't make out what it was, except that it had four legs, so it wasn't a bird, which was unusual. Michael loved birds. He'd carved an owl for her once. 'See in the dark,' he'd said as he handed it to her. Now she couldn't remember where she'd put it.

'Reckon, I'll turn in,' said Adam.

'Me too,' said Fern, yawning again.

Matt nodded and carried on strumming; his melody following them to bed.

In the tent they settled Freya, then lay down next to each other, their bodies touching and the tension between them building. When Freya's breathing had regulated once more into a deep sleep, Fern drew Adam closer, inhaling his earthy scent, then ran her hands up under his T-shirt, the softness of his skin belying the taut abdominal muscles that lay underneath. Lifting his shirt, she found a nipple and bit it gently. Adam gasped and tried to send his own hands roaming over her body but she pulled them away. Taking control, she lifted herself onto him and sat still, savouring the feel of him inside her. As the tension increased, she began to move gently, so as not to disturb Freya. Their love making made all the more exquisite by the need for silence.

Afterwards, Fern lay her head on Adam's chest and listened to the strong thud of his heart and the amplified gurgles of his stomach. She knew with a deep certainty that Adam was a part of her, long lost but finally found again. They were closer than close but sometimes it didn't feel enough. Fern wondered now if it was transcendence she wanted, a love that would turn two into one. There were times when it seemed they'd succeeded and yet now she caught herself wondering if rather than a spiritual union of sorts, this desire for unity was simply greed. Another wrong note.

Tonight, she felt frustratingly separate from Adam, and knew it was her fault; she should tell him about Ahmed and the cryptic things he'd said but something was stopping her. Adam would dismiss it. He'd say Ahmed was crazy, he'd reassure her about her relationship with Freya, and Fern would almost believe him. But talking about Ahmed would somehow set their meeting in stone and then she couldn't pretend it didn't happen.

She rolled off Adam and lay at his side running her fingers through his blond chest hair, straightening it then letting it spring back into tight curls. 'Please come home with us.'

She felt Adam's body tense a little. 'I can't leave Matt here by himself.'

'He'd manage.'

'Come on Fern. It's only a week before replacements arrive. I've got to protect the forest.' He paused. 'You know I have to.'

'What about us?' Even before the words left her mouth Fern knew they were unfair.

Adam pulled Fern closer and kissed her. 'There will always be us. We're not under threat. These trees are.'

We are under threat, Fern wanted to say but then she would have to explain how and why and she simply didn't know. There was nothing concrete to grab onto, only the knowledge that if she said it, everything and nothing would change. Instead, she blamed the forest. 'I know it's under threat.' she said. 'And I care about it but it's been going on for so long. When's it going to end?'

Adam shook his head sadly. 'I don't know. We have to stay until the trees are safe. What choice do I have?'

Fern sighed, defeated, and stared up at the curved contours of the tent. 'You're lucky to have a purpose.'

Adam looked at Fern in surprise. 'What do you mean?'

'You're not tugged between things. You just know what's important.'

'So do you.'

Fern shook her head. 'I've got you and Freya and a degree in herbalism. But is it enough to be a mother? A lover? A healer who doesn't heal?'

Adam propped himself up on an elbow and peered at Fern through the darkness. 'I thought you were happy.'

'I was … I am … I don't know. Suddenly I feel as if I've lost my way.'

'Start practising. It's what you were called to do.'

'Was it?' When she'd started her degree, Fern had thought healing was her calling but now she wondered if she'd been wrong. Perhaps her life purpose was something else entirely.

Adam looked worried and Fern felt suddenly mean. He was a solid force, a man of the earth and well rooted. He didn't need Fern digging up those roots and threatening his happiness. She leaned over and kissed him 'Don't worry. I love you and Freya just as much as ever … I just feel restless. As if I have to do something but I don't know what.'

'You'll find it,' said Adam, the certainty in his voice grounding Fern all over again.

She smiled at Adam's trust in life. It was one of the many things she loved about him. Feeling calmer now, Fern closed her eyes but it was only when Adam's breath became more regular that she was able to let go of her thoughts and follow him into sleep, cocooned within his arms.

In her dream Fern was in a dark passageway. The thick stone walls felt damp and cold as she brushed their rough surface with her hands, and a musty earthy smell permeated the atmosphere. At first she thought it was night time because it was so dark but then a little way ahead Fern noticed a dim source of light. As she drew nearer, she could see dust motes dancing in the beam of light and realised that daylight was finding its way through a narrow slit in the wall. She paused and peered through, shivering at the blast of cold air and dazzled by the light blue of a cloudless winter sky, broken by the silhouette of mountains. Below her was a dizzying vertical drop that seemed to go on forever.

Walking on, she came to a heavy wooden door and felt compelled to open it. Stepping inside what could only be a monk's cell, Fern closed the door behind her and peered around, taking in the slit high up in the wall that allowed a little light through, the pallet bed against one wall and the small table alongside it, on which sat an unlit candle.

Drawn back to the door she began inspecting it curiously, noting the strong ironwork that held it in place and the way the wood had rotted back at the bottom, leaving a large uneven space between it and the floor. She didn't notice the sound of footsteps striding purposefully down the passageway outside until the door flung open and a man burst through. Startled, Fern drew back and tensed, waiting for the inevitable blow as his body met hers. But the blow never came because the man walked right through her, oblivious to her presence.

Fern woke with a jolt, feeling queasy and confused. The light was dim inside the tent and for a moment she couldn't remember where she was. Then she saw Freya, asleep on her back, arms thrown above her head as if in surrender. Adam was curled in close to her, one arm flung across his face. They both looked so peaceful, no shadows crossing their faces, nothing to sully their perfection. Fern studied them, taking in every detail and filing the memory away to draw on later. It was something she did in peaceful moments like this, moments where she was reminded of how lucky she was. Gratitude welled up within her, blurring her vision but as always, behind this gratitude lay something else - a suspicion that she didn't deserve it.

Fern closed her eyes once again. She had no idea what time it was but knew there was no hurry. At home Freya would usually be up at first light or before, throwing herself into the day, but here she always slept on, shielded by the peace of the forest from which she instinctively drew sustenance. For a moment Fern pondered her dream, trying to understand its meaning. A man had walked right through her as if she were a ghost, which was certainly strange but it didn't appear to mean anything. The dream had felt real though, the textures and smells, the atmosphere … an unusually solid dream in which she was the only thing lacking in substance.

Unable to slip back into sleep, Fern eventually admitted defeat and pulled on some trousers before crawling carefully across Adam and Freya and unzipping the tent as quietly as she could. Outside, the drizzle had paused but everything was wet through, past saturation point, so when she walked into the forest each footfall squeezed little pools of water from the moss beneath her. In the tree tops the shrill cry of a cockatoo broke the silence.

Back in the camp area Michael had built up the fire and was putting water on to boil. He grinned at Fern but when she tried to speak, he held his finger up to his lips and shook his head. Fern nodded, understanding Michael's need to stay within the silence of the forest. When the water had boiled, Fern made them both cups of strong black tea and they sat together sipping it while the soft drizzle began once again around them, shrouding the forest even more deeply in silence. Michael picked up the wooden creature he had carved the previous evening and inspected it carefully then satisfied with what he saw, he began polishing it.

Curious, Fern looked at the carving more closely. It was intricately detailed and with a ferocious expression on its face, mouth open, snarling, its sharp teeth visible inside the strong jaw.

'A Tassie Devil?' she asked.

Michael nodded, 'For Adam.'

Chapter Six

A week later and back in her own bed in their little shack on Bruny Island, Fern once again woke abruptly into the pre-dawn darkness. She stared uneasily at the glowing numbers on the bedside clock. It was 5.33am. Tomorrow Adam would be here, she told herself. She would make lasagna the way he liked it with eggplant and mushrooms, and home-made sorbet with the leftover raspberries from last summer, while Freya would laugh and dance around Adam and he would smile and meet Fern's gaze with a promise in his own eyes. Stepping forward in time, she imagined that moment late in the evening when Freya would fall reluctantly into sleep and Adam would tuck her into bed before turning to Fern. Closing the bedroom door behind them they would undress, and remember each other's bodies all over again.

Just as Fern's imagination reached out to embrace Adam, something hit her in the guts, the force of it knocking all the air from her lungs and sending searing pain through her body. She sat up, gasping and struggling for breath, telling herself that it was only an echo from her dreams. It would fade as these echoes always did. And moments later the pain did fade, leaving behind it the same shadow of unease that had stayed with her since her trip to the forest. Only now the shadow had deepened.

Fern got out of bed and opened the curtains. The sun had just risen above the horizon and was sending its golden rays across the ocean and the sky, banishing the night. The water was calm and the sky almost clear, with only the occasional streak of soft cloud, flushed red in the dawn light. Feeling the chill rising through the soles of her feet, she turned away from the window and pulled on her lambswool boots then tiptoed past Freya's room and down the creaking circular stairs to the kitchen for her first coffee of the day. Even with the coffee in her hands she couldn't settle and instead paced back and forth from one end of the kitchen to the other.

Half an hour later, Freya walked into the kitchen, thumb in mouth and pulling her blankie along behind her. 'Where's Dada?' she asked sleepily.

Fern reached down to give Freya a kiss and then brushed some hair from her eyes. 'He's in the forest. You know that.'

Freya looked puzzled. 'I saw him.'

Now it was Fern's turn to look puzzled. 'Where?'

'In my room.'

'You must have had a dream,' Fern said.

Freya's face screwed up in fury. 'He's here. I know.' She turned and ran back through the house, calling for him. 'Dada, where are you? Dada … Dada.'

Fern let her go and forced herself to get breakfast ready. Mechanically she pulled eggs and bread from the fridge, a saucepan from the cupboard, filled it with water, put the eggs on to boil and the bread in the toaster. These mundane tasks brought some comfort but already she needed a second coffee, a further burst of caffeine to match the edginess of the morning. She poured the cold dregs of her first coffee down the sink and put the kettle on for another, then went upstairs to find Freya.

Fern found her peering in the cupboard. 'He's not here, sweetheart,' she said, then lifted Freya into her arms where she struggled briefly before bursting into tears.

'I want Dada.'

'Daddy will be home tomorrow. Come now and have breakfast. I've done you a boiled egg from Gran's hen and toast soldiers to dip in it.

Red-eyed, Freya sat at the table, halfheartedly dipping soldiers into her runny egg and sucking the golden yolk from the toast. Unable to face her own egg, Fern poured herself a coffee and continued her pacing. When the phone rang, she picked it up on its second ring, her fingers trembling.

It was Iris, her voice laced with worry. 'Sorry it's so early. I thought you'd be up. Something's wrong with Michael. He's howling and beating himself in the head. I can't stop him and I can't get a word out of him.'

With this, a further weight settled in Fern's heart. 'I can feel it too,' she said.

'Is Adam home yet?' asked Iris.

'He's due back tomorrow.'

'Do you think something's happened … to him?'

'I don't know.' Her voice caught in her throat as she whispered. 'Freya saw him.'

'Saw him! Where?'

Fern opened her mouth to respond then heard a car approaching up the dirt track. 'Hang on, someone's here. I'll call you back.'

She got to the window just as a police car pulled up in front of the house, and watched in dread as the local policemen stepped out of the car, pausing for a moment to stare at the ocean before turning resolutely towards the shack.

Fern reached the door before him and stepped outside, closing the door behind her to keep out of Freya's earshot. 'Is it Adam?'

The policeman nodded, surprised. 'He's been in an accident.'

Fern felt the breath leave her body in a rush.

'He was in the forest, sleeping on a platform up in a tree when it collapsed.'

Fern saw it then, the platform tilting at an impossible angle, falling, Adam with it … 'Collapsed?' she repeated, her brain shutting down with the shock.

The policeman nodded. 'He fell.'

Fern leaned against the door frame for support. 'Is he … ?'

'He's alive but unconscious.'

'He's alive?' Fern felt a sudden rush of hope. Adam was alive. She hadn't lost him.

The policeman nodded. 'They've taken him to the Royal. He's in intensive care. His wounds are extensive.' He paused and looked at her with eyes full of regret. 'I'm sorry.'

Chapter Seven

Fern ran along the hospital corridors towards the intensive care ward. The heaviness in her heart had been replaced with a sense of urgency and a strange clarity she hadn't expected. After the policeman left, she'd rung Iris and told her the news, then she and Freya had driven to the ferry. It was never a quick journey but this time it seemed to take forever; she'd found herself stuck behind a tractor, her foot hovering over the accelerator but never finding the right moment to pass. They'd missed the ferry and had to wait another forty minutes for the next one, with Fern holding back tears of frustration as she paced back and forth beside the car.

Iris had been waiting at the other side, and Fern had left Freya with her. Iris, Michael and Freya would follow, but Fern needed to see Adam first.

'He's unconscious,' warned the nurse as she showed Fern into the intensive care ward.

A sob caught in Fern's throat when she saw Adam lying there, his face ghostly white, his eyes closed, his body criss-crossed with tubes and wires attached to beeping machines with flashing lights.

'Let me know if you need anything,' said the nurse before quietly shutting the door behind her.

Alone with Adam, Fern felt shy for a moment, uncertain what to do. Suddenly he seemed a stranger, lost to her in a sea of bandages and blipping machines. She reached out and touched his face gently with the tips of his fingers. His skin was warm, his heart beating, there was hope.

'Adam?' Tentatively she lifted the blanket a little until she found his hand. She clasped her fingers between his, feeling the perfect fit once again. It was his hands that had drawn her to him in the first place, the strong fingers and the rough course skin speckled with golden hairs. She'd always felt safe with those hands.

'Can you hear me, Adam?' She waited a moment, watching his face for signs but there was nothing. Then the words came all in a rush. 'I'm here. You're not alone. I'll stay with you … I love you Adam … I love you … You must get better … I need you… We need you.' She stopped as another sob rose into her throat, then reached over and touched her lips to his.

The door opened and a doctor stepped into the room. He was young and clearly exhausted, with dark rings under his eyes, a worry line that extended along his forehead and a name tag that read, Dr Harris. He held his hand out to Fern. 'I understand you're Adam's wife?'

'His partner,' she said, taking his hand. 'Fern.'

The doctor nodded. 'I'm James. I was on duty when Adam came in early this morning.' He hesitated and glanced uncertainly at Adam. 'Perhaps we could talk outside.'

Fern nodded and followed him into the corridor.

'Adam's taken a very bad fall, I'm afraid.' He consulted his notes. 'What we've ascertained so far is serious concussion with some brain swelling, a collapsed lung, broken ribs, internal bleeding … and his spine is fractured in two places.'

'His spine?' Fern felt the alarm growing inside her.

Doctor Harris nodded. 'At present we don't know the full extent of the damage but he may well be paralysed. There's also the possibility of permanent brain damage but that's something we won't know for some time.' He paused and ran his fingers through his hair. 'At the moment all we can do is try to keep the swelling down, drain the fluid and keep him sedated. We've done our best to stabilize him but it's touch and go. He's unconscious now which is probably a good thing but there's the danger that he may sink further into a coma.' He hesitated for a moment. 'I'm sorry. I wish I was the bearer of better news.'

Unable to trust herself to speak, Fern nodded, feeling suddenly weak. It was *touch and go*. Adam might die. She might lose him. Panicking, she stepped back into the ward and closed the door behind her, shutting out the doctor but not his words. It was impossible to equate all that damage with the Adam lying on the bed looking peaceful and perfect. If only she could place her hands on him and let her life force knit his broken body back together. She'd done something of the sort once when Adam had been bitten by a Jack Jumper ant and had an allergic reaction. They were out in the bush, miles away from any help and he was sinking into a coma, his throat swelling and blocking off his breathing. In desperation she'd put her hands on him and felt the life force flowing. It had worked once, maybe it would again, though she'd been unable to use it since then. Perhaps occasionally she'd eased one of Freya's bruises or slightly calmed a fever but there was never anything to prove it was her hand that had done it rather than the simple comfort of a mother's touch.

Tentatively, Fern reached out her hand and placed it lightly on Adam's chest, making sure she didn't nudge the tube that was draining his lung. She tried to empty her mind, open up her heart and allow the life force through but instead of the calm focus she needed, her mind was racing over possibilities, her was heart thudding too fast and she was forgetting to breathe. Underneath her fingers she felt nothing but the texture of fabric and a slight warmth. Frustrated she took away her hand, knowing it was useless while she was in such a state.

Since escaping her intensely religious childhood, praying had rarely been a part of Fern's life but now she reverted to it instinctively. 'Please God, please, let him live. I'll do anything. Just don't take him away from us. Please God … '

A nurse stepped through the door, stopping Fern's prayer mid-sentence.

'The doctor thought you might need this,' she said, handing Fern a cup of tea. 'Shock can play strange tricks on you and a hot drink helps no end.' She pulled a chair up close to the bed. 'Here, sit down. You look a little shaky.'

Fern's legs suddenly gave way underneath her and she sat down abruptly, splashing hot tea on her jeans. The nurse mopped at her with a cloth, worrying about burns but Fern hardly noticed the searing heat on her skin. When the nurse left, Fern sat quietly, her gaze fixed on Adam, the tea forgotten in her hands. He was so still; as if he was here but somewhere else too. She watched the gentle rise and fall of his chest, forgetting to breathe herself, as she waited each time for him to take another breath. If only she could find Adam and bring him back. If only she could convince God, the universe, whatever it was that gave life to everything, that there was more for him here.

'Where's Dada?'

The door opened and Iris peered in anxiously, a frightened expression on her face as she fixed her eyes hopefully on her eldest son. 'Can we bring Freya in?'

Fern nodded. 'She needs to see him,' she said, her voice heavy with sadness.

Freya peered around from behind Michael's giant frame. 'Dada!' she cried. She dashed towards the bed and tried to climb on but it was too high.

Fern scooped her up so she could see Adam but Freya was incensed and struggled to free herself, wiggling and twisting her body. 'Let me go. I want Dada. Let me go.'

'Daddy's not well sweetheart,' said Fern as she struggled to calm Freya. 'You can't climb on him … See, he's asleep. You can give him a kiss but you'll have to be careful not to touch any of those tubes.'

Freya stopped her wiggling and looked closely at Adam, her eyes widening and her expression becoming solemn.

'Do you want to give Daddy a kiss?'

Freya nodded.

Fern leaned forward until Freya could reach her father and then fought back her tears as she watched Freya brush Adam's cheek with a gentle kiss. Then she leaned back against Fern and began quietly sucking her thumb, her eyes fixed on her father.

'Oh Adam.' Iris took her son's hand and stroked it gently. 'My darling boy,' she said, her voice cracking with grief. She looked at Fern with a question in her eyes. 'Is he … ?'

Fern shook her head quickly and pointed at Freya. 'The doctor will explain.'

Iris nodded abruptly and turned towards the door.

Fern looked over at Michael who was staring at Adam, his big shoulders sagging, his face infused with grief. If she couldn't heal Adam then surely Michael could. She'd watched him fix broken creatures time and again. He'd even fixed her once, drawing out the chains that were keeping her heart closed.

'Michael.' When he didn't respond, Fern tried again. 'Michael.'

Reluctantly, Michael took his eyes from Adam and looked over at Fern.

'Can you heal Adam?'

Michael stared at Fern for a moment, uncomprehending.

'Please try,' she begged.

Michael hesitated and for just a moment Fern felt some hope. 'Too far,' he said eventually, his voice cracking with pain. Then he turned his eyes back to Adam and began rocking backwards and forwards, consumed by his grief.

When Iris returned, her eyes were red and her face dull. She took Adam's hand and held it tightly.

'When will Dada wake up?' asked Freya.

'Not yet, sweetheart,' said Fern, struggling to form the words. 'He's not very well.'

The door opened suddenly and a man with a camera stepped in and took a photo, the flash blinding them momentarily. 'A tragedy,' he said, shaking his head. 'You must be furious with that forestry worker.'

'What?' asked Fern, confused.

'The one who pulled down the platform.' Surprised, he noted Fern's blank face. 'He put his foot down and drove his log truck through the barriers. The industry's trying to distance themselves. A rogue worker they're calling him. But he's saying the protestors drove him to it.'

As if from a great distance, Fern watched the man talking. 'Get out,' she said.

'I understand this is a difficult time but perhaps you could answer a few questions for our readers.'

'I said, get out.'

Ignoring her, the man raised his camera to take another picture but Michael suddenly seemed to notice him. 'Go,' he shouted, drawing himself up to his full height and sweeping the camera from the man's hands.

The camera landed with a thud and bounced once before coming to a halt. The man picked it up and cradled it gently in his arms, then cowering before Michael's fury, he backed towards the door just as the nurse burst in with two security guards behind her.

'I'm sorry,' said one of the guards as they escorted the man out, 'the press are everywhere and I didn't see this one sneak through.'

The nurse turned to follow them through the door, then paused. 'Oh, I almost forgot. We found this in his sleeping bag.' She held out the wooden Tasmanian Devil, Michael had made for Adam.

Shocked, Fern stared at the sculpture in the nurse's hand. Only last week it had been freshly carved and perfectly formed but now it was broken, a leg and its tail snapped off.

Michael reached out and took the carving from the nurse, his face forlorn. 'For keeping Adam safe,' he said and burst into tears.

So that's why he carved it, thought Fern. Michael had also sensed something wrong.

'You tried, Michael. It isn't your fault.' Still holding Freya in one arm, Fern reached out with her other arm and hugged this bear-like figure of a man who was, in a sense, her brother. She let her face rest on his heaving chest, feeling it shudder with each sob. Iris was crying quietly, her hand on Michael's shoulder, while Freya simply stared at Michael, her eyes wide and frightened.

'Adam, oh Adam,' cried Michael between each sob. 'My brother … I love you, Adam.'

When his sobs began to subside, Fern took a tissue and reaching up, gently wiped Michael's eyes and nose. Then his great arms, which had been hanging loosely by his sides, reached out and wrapped themselves around Fern and Freya, and Fern wanted to cry too but she couldn't find any tears inside her, just a hollow emptiness that nothing could fill, and alongside it a growing sense of guilt. She'd known. She should have trusted her uneasiness, just as she would her other senses. She should have made Adam come home. She should have insisted.

Chapter Eight

The hospital room was dimly lit and between the slats of the venetian blinds thin strips of darkness were visible, so morning hadn't yet arrived. A few hours earlier, Iris had taken Michael and a protesting Freya back to the house in Kettering but Fern had stayed on, unable to leave Adam's side. She'd eventually fallen asleep sitting on the chair while leaning her upper body on the bed, her head between her arms, one hand clasping Adam's.

Fern woke with a start when a nurse came in to check on Adam. She sat up in the chair and rubbing her neck, watched bleary eyed as the nurse efficiently checked the instruments and swapped an empty drip bag. When the nurse had gone, Fern took Adam's hand and kissed it. His fingers were cool against her lips so she rubbed them gently, trying to pass some of her own warmth into him.

As she rubbed his hand, Adam's eyes opened and Fern felt a surge of hope. 'Adam,' she whispered. 'I'm here. It's okay, you're going to get better.'

Adam looked at her steadily for a moment, then his lips moved ever so slightly as he whispered something Fern couldn't hear. She put her ear close to Adam's mouth, and this time there was no mistaking it. 'Love you,' he whispered.

'I love you too.' She gently squeezed his hand. 'You're going to come through this. You hear me. It's going to be okay. You mustn't leave me. We've only just found each other.'

Adam looked steadily at her for a moment longer before his eyes closed again. Fern waited and watched and listened but there was nothing more from him, no flicker of life except for the regular rhythm of his heartbeat, traced on the screen by his side. She could feel the tenuousness of the thread that was holding him here and wanted desperately to take him away from this impersonal hospital ward, back to their rickety shack on Bruny or even to the forest, somewhere familiar that would help him to hold on.

'Do you remember when we first met?' she asked. 'How much I hated you? You were drunk. Remember? In that bar. The Underworld. But even then, I knew. We were meant to be. And we still are Adam. You have to hang in there.'

Fern talked on and on, reminding Adam of the things they'd done together, telling anecdotes about Freya, Michael, Iris, Matt, anything to stop him from slipping away. After an hour or so, her throat was parched and her spirits lower than ever.

'I'm just getting a drink, 'she said, releasing his hand. 'I'll be back in a minute.'

In the bathroom she took a long drink from the tap, then stared at herself in the mirror, hardly recognising the pallid skin with dark rings under her eyes, or the scruffy hair, standing in all the wrong directions. Her mirror image reminded Fern of a time she wanted to forget, when the world had unraveled around her, the monsters in her dreams had stepped out into reality and the rest of the world had thought she was mad. Except Adam. He hadn't understood but he'd trusted her and that had been enough. He'd helped her find her way and now it was her turn to help him.

When Fern stepped back into the corridor, a red light was flashing outside Adam's ward. Two nurses rushed past her and disappeared through the door, closely followed by a doctor. Fearing the worst, Fern raced after them, only to find that the quiet room she'd left minutes before was now filled with a harsh light and a grim urgency as they worked on Adam. Fern stood just inside the door and watched helplessly as the line on the screen zigzagged up and down in a crazy panic before suddenly settling into a single straight line. For a time they continued their efforts but the line didn't move and gradually the urgency abated. It was over.

'I'm sorry,' said one of the doctors, shaking her head. 'We did everything we could.'

The nurses removed the drips and unplugged Adam from the monitors. 'We'll give you some time with him,' one said as they were leaving. 'I'm sorry we couldn't save him.'

Slowly Fern approached the bed, her eyes fixed on Adam who still looked so alive despite the blank screens and awful silence. She reached out her hand to touch his face; he was still warm but something was missing. Panicking, she clasped his hand again, and held it as the warmth gradually seeped away. Then she knew Adam was gone. She would never wake up again with him sleeping by her side, he would never go into the forest again or surf off Bruny or cuddle Freya or tell Fern he loved her. I failed him, she thought. Just when he needed me most. I shouldn't have left him. Not even for a minute. Not here or in the forest. As Fern stood holding Adam's hand, a jagged hole began to form inside her, the emptiness settling into place, a howling loneliness that would haunt the rest of her life.

Chapter Nine

After the service, Iris drove them from the church to the cemetery where Adam was to be buried. He'd always said he wanted to be returned to the earth and Iris had a plot waiting there. 'It was supposed to be for me,' she told Fern, the sobs rising into her throat and almost stifling her next words. 'No child should ever die before their mother.'

It was a beautiful sunny day, which only made it worse somehow because Adam was all closed up inside the coffin, encased in darkness. Fern couldn't bear thinking about it as she walked with Iris, Michael and Freya along the paths, past rows of gravestones, some well-tended, others neglected and forgotten. Adam's grave was a gaping black hole in the lush green lawn, the soil rich and dark and laced with worms.

Fern looked away, her gaze settling on two journalists who stood slightly apart from the gathering crowd. She sighed. At least they weren't being intrusive. The media had waited outside the church, taking photographs but otherwise not insisting, and only these two had followed them to the cemetery. That was an improvement on the past few days. The papers, the radio and the television had been full of the supposed battle between protestors and forestry workers, some trying to apportion the blame squarely on Adam's shoulders. But after his time in the army, Adam had abhorred violence. When Fern had met him, he'd sworn that he wouldn't fight any more battles. He didn't want to fight, just to share his love for the forests, and in the end he'd found the right balance. Staying up in the tree was a simple protective action that didn't throw blame and shouldn't have incited violence. Instead, it drew public attention to the forests, creating a space for others to understand the value of what they were destroying before it was all gone.

Fern turned back to Adam's empty grave as one of the journalists lifted his camera. A part of her was relieved that the story would now begin to fade but another part was appalled at the fickleness of the media and the speed with which stories were forgotten. She was torn between wanting Adam's death to stoke debate and force some real change, as some of the protestors did, and wanting to be left alone to her grief.

She watched as Matt, Michael and two more of Adam's friends carried the coffin towards its resting place. Sensing the importance of the occasion, Freya stood quietly next to Iris, holding Wombie in one hand and wearing the new pink lacy dress Iris had made for her.

Since the accident, Fern had felt numb through and through and hardly able to do anything or speak to anyone, so Iris had organized the funeral saying the activity helped her to take her mind off things, while Matt organized the speeches and the gathering afterwards. Fern had decided they should try to make sure this act of violence didn't ignite further violence, so she'd insisted on three things. The funeral would not be hate filled; there would be no talk of 'us and them' or of revenge, no dark words to add to the awful shadows already hanging over Adam's death. Secondly, the guests would wear colourful clothes. And finally, instead of flowers each person was asked to do a small act of kindness for another. It was what Adam would have wanted and the result had been a church filled to overflowing, with friends, family and supporters, the service a powerful, moving and peaceful outpouring of love and grief.

The brightly dressed group was gathered around the coffin, watching it being lowered into the ground, when unexpectedly a large truck pulled up on the road outside the cemetery, the sound of its brakes momentarily drowning out the priest's voice. Fern felt the nervous ripple move through the mourners as they realised it was a log truck. She felt it too, the dread of further violence when there'd already been too much. She couldn't believe these men could be so hate-filled they would disrupt Adam's funeral, and yet here they were. Responding to the growing nervous tension in the group, the priest stopped talking, a look of concern on his face. Tension continued to build as another truck pulled up behind it, and then another and another until there were eight trucks.

The mourners braced themselves for trouble as sixteen men walked towards them, weaving their way along the paths that led to the grave, but the men stopped a short distance away, standing back nervously as if uncertain what to do next. It quickly became clear to everyone that they weren't here to make trouble, but still there was an awkwardness as the mourners eyed the loggers distrustfully. Minutes passed and the stand-off between the two groups seemed to become immutable, until finally Matt stepped forward and shook each one by the hand, drawing them closer in to the circle and easing the tension.

After a nod from Fern, the priest began talking again and the coffin finished its journey into the ground. Then the spade was passed around and each person threw some dirt onto the coffin. Fern helped Freya hold the spade and toss some soil in, then took a turn herself, carefully skirting the thought of Adam's body in there forever, lost to her.

She stood for a moment looking down at the coffin, then handed the spade to one of the forestry workers who shook his head, clearly feeling it wasn't appropriate.

'Please,' said Fern. 'Adam would want it.'

The man hesitated for a moment more before nodding abruptly. He took the spade and to the click of the journalists' cameras, tossed some soil onto the coffin, before handing it to the next man who repeated the gesture to more camera clicks. Politely refusing an invitation to attend the gathering at Iris's house, the men left as quietly as they'd arrived. Fern watched them leave, seeing for the first time what Adam had always seen - their humanity, the hopes and dreams and fears they carried, and their roles as partners, parents, siblings and friends. Unlike her, Adam had always recognised this humanity in everyone. He'd believed in the innate goodness of the human race. He'd never felt hate for the loggers, only frustration at what they were doing. And now he was gone. The extent of the unfairness hit Fern once more. How could it have happened to him? she kept asking herself. The world needs bridge builders like Adam.

The gathering grew and grew, each person bringing a plate of food and drinks until the benches and tables were covered and the bath full to overflowing with ice and bottles. Mutt their ancient dog had died a year ago and although Iris said she didn't want another, Michael came home one day with a blue heeler puppy under his arm and Iris had fallen head over heels for the mischievous dog. Now it yapped excitedly at the ankles of the guests as they arrived, running around in circles and herding them into Iris's vast front room where they sipped on their drinks and stared uncomfortably through the floor-to-ceiling windows that overlooked the harbor, the anchored yachts and fishing boats tipping gently in the wake of the ferry, their masts singing in the breeze. Fern had never tired of this view; she loved the dizzying effect it had on her, with its unexpected angles and its calm domesticity, unlike the breathtaking wildness of the view from their shack on Bruny, with the ever-changing ocean before them.

Sipping on one of Iris's home-made ciders, Fern moved through the gathering, pausing sometimes to accept a hug or speak a few words here and there, but the numbness remained and she felt as if all this were happening somewhere else and to someone else. From a distance Freya watched Fern curiously but stayed close to Iris, knowing instinctively that she would find more comfort from her grandmother.

As the sun set over the hills beyond the harbour, the air grew cooler. Michael and Matt had built a great bonfire and they lit it now, the guests moving outside to watch it burn, the flames flickering shadows of light and dark across their faces. Fern looked around for Freya but couldn't see her. Worried, she went inside to find her trembling and sobbing in Iris's arms.

'What's wrong?' she asked, stroking Freya's hair.

Iris shook her head. 'I'm not sure. I think the bonfire scared her.'

Fern lifted Freya out of Iris's arms. 'Look,' she said. 'It's only a fire. It won't hurt you if you don't go too close. See how beautiful it is.'

Cautiously Freya lifted her face away from Fern's shoulder and peered through the window at the flames licking the sky, the sparks shooting out into space. Her face was troubled but she didn't look away again and she nodded uncertainly when Fern suggested they go outside.

They sat down next to Matt, and Freya immediately scrambled onto his lap, leaving a fresh hurt inside Fern. *Why does she always turn away from me?* Fern knew that Freya was hurting too. She was too young to understand death but she sensed what was happening and she missed Adam terribly. Fern was trying to fill the empty space but she was failing miserably.

The mood changed as people began telling stories about Adam; school anecdotes and close shaves from their surfing days, stories that Fern sometimes knew, sometimes didn't. She looked over at Freya who was listening solemnly to each story, her eyes wide, the flames reflected in them. The stories were building a picture of Adam for them all, something to hold on to, but Freya was so young, probably too young to remember.

When the story telling had run its course, a silence settled on the gathering, with everyone lost in their own thoughts. After a while, Matt handed Freya back to Fern, then picked up his guitar and began playing Leonard Cohen's *Hallelujah*. Fern joined in for the chorus, her voice reaching out over the crackle of the fire. Slowly others joined in too. At the end Fern's voice rose and she sang 'hallelujah' over and over, the blessing lifting above and beyond the gathering and into the heavens.

Afterwards there was a silence. Freya snuggled in closer, her thumb finding its way into her mouth, her eyes firmly fixed on the fire. Fern kissed the top of her head, winding soft strands of Freya's hair around her finger then letting them go and watching the blonde curls bounce back just as Adam's had done. When Matt started playing another song, Fern joined in again, the words reaching into her and cracking open the numbness. As she sang, her voice began to tremble and then for the first time since Adam's death, she cried, the silent tears dripping down onto the crown of Freya's head and dampening her curls.

Part Two

France

two years later

Chapter Ten

Fern stood on the vine shaded verandah looking out over the now deserted town. In the heat of the afternoon the streets were empty and silent except for the steady hum of crickets and the wild dance of the swallows darting and diving above her as they scooped insects out of the air. She and Freya had arrived only an hour ago, after catching a bus for the final leg, then walking through the narrow, cobbled streets that wound into the oldest part of the hilltop town.

Freya had been hungry and fretful from the sudden heat and the confusion of jet lag, while Fern was exhausted from lack of sleep and the responsibility of getting them there. The proprietor of the guest house, Madame Fournier was efficient and kind but spoke no English, so Fern had been forced to draw on the vestiges of her school French.

'Elle a faim,' she'd said, pointing at Freya and hoping the woman would understand her dreadful accent.

Madame had looked puzzled and then anxious before emitting a stream of sounds, punctuated with gestures. When Fern couldn't distinguish a single word they'd reverted to charades, and finally Fern had understood that everything was closed until later in the afternoon.

'Attendez,' said Madame. Then she disappeared into what must have been the kitchen before reappearing almost immediately with a baguette and a chunk of cheese. 'Voilà,' she said triumphantly and smiled at Freya. 'Pour la petite fille.'

The room Madame showed them into was small, just space for a double bed and an old wooden cupboard, but it was clean and the verandah added space and light and the barest hint of a breeze through the grape vine that shielded them from the ferocious sun. The bathroom was shared, which wasn't ideal but no doubt helped with the price. Even so, they couldn't afford to stay here for long. Three weeks, maybe four if she was careful with the food budget. But what then? Fern had pondered over this question as they ate the baguette and cheese. What if it didn't work out? The worry had crept through Fern's defences, sending her heart racing with an anxiety she struggled to hide from Freya's eagle eyes.

When they'd finished eating, Fern had gathered up the crumbs from the baguette, wiped Freya's hot face with a cold flannel, and then laid down next to her on the bed until the sound of Freya's breathing had steadied and deepened into sleep. But despite her tiredness, sleep had eluded Fern, so she'd stepped quietly onto the verandah to wait out Freya's siesta.

The loud ringing of the church bell broke the silence, startling Fern from her thoughts. She glanced back into the room to see if the ringing had disturbed Freya, but she slept on. Relieved, Fern reached out and plucked a grape from the vine, its sweet sun-warmed juice exploding in her mouth as she chewed. Then she picked a bunch and sat down at the little wrought iron table to devour them one by one. She was exhausted, hadn't slept for at least two days, but sleep felt impossible, with the worry surging inside her chest and the heat wrapping her like a heavy blanket.

Fern wished with every part of her being that Adam was here with her, sitting in the other wrought iron chair, chewing on warm grapes. The yearning in her was so strong that it became almost a summons and for just the briefest of moments she felt him – a presence, a breath on her neck, a scent of sweat and sandalwood – then he was gone, his absence a physical wrench. She stifled a sob and instinctively turned to check on Freya once again. It struck her then that if Adam was still alive, she wouldn't be sitting here on this terrace in France.

The rooftops were uniform in colour with their distinctive terracotta tiles, but they weren't uniform in shape; angles protruded in all directions as if the town itself was constructed from the imagination, giving it a topsy turvy quality that belied its ancient origins. The Pyrenees mountains that surrounded this town were all richly wooded, their jagged contours cutting into the sky, row upon row, receding into the distance. They were so much bigger than she'd imagined. Already she loved these mountains but there was more to it than love; Fern felt a stirring of recognition too, as if she were remembering them … as if she'd been here before. But the memory was eluding her, hovering just outside of her consciousness, like a forgotten word sitting on the tip of the tongue.

It was still ferociously hot when they set off to walk to Dr Leveque's house. Madame had given them directions. Up, was the gist of it. *De plus en plus*! Up and up! But first they had to go down into the centre of the town. They followed the narrow streets that wound their way into the town square. Here in the old part the houses were crowded in, each one taking advantage of the tiniest spaces; balconies hanging over the narrow streets, tables and chairs squeezed into flat roof spaces. Fruit trees had found their way into even the smallest of gardens; grape vines framed doorways and balconies, creating shade and food, while colourful geraniums filled window boxes.

Fern paused under the cool shade of a giant fig tree, heavy with fruit so ripe they were bursting with sticky juices. Unable to resist, she picked one, split it down the middle, turned it inside out and ate it. The taste was divine. The food of the gods.

She picked another and handed it to Freya, then picked a couple more to eat along the way. Progress was slow. First a cat emerged from a window and walked around Freya, rubbing itself against her legs while she stroked it gently as she always did. Then they passed an old woman sitting on her doorstep shelling almonds.

'Bonjour,' said Fern.

'Bonjour,' said the woman, her face crinkling into a smile as she spotted Freya. She scooped up a handful of freshly shelled almonds and offered them to the child. 'Prends-en.'

'Go on, take them,' said Fern but suddenly shy, Freya backed around behind her mother.

'Merci,' said Fern, taking the almonds for her daughter.

The kindness of the woman, the sweet flavor of freshly hulled almonds and the beauty of this town moved Fern in a way that nothing had for the past two years, igniting a tiny spark of hope within her. Surely she'd done the right thing coming here.

As they wound their way down the narrow streets into the central square, they were accompanied by the sound of running water. It was flowing off the mountain and gushing alongside them in deep ancient gutters, the sound and the scent of the water creating a refreshing feeling of lushness in the midst of the searing heat.

The square had been empty when they'd arrived earlier that day but now people were beginning to emerge again, drinking mineral waters and coffees at the cafes that surrounded it or sitting and passing the time under the shade of trees. Clouds were building on top of the mountains around the town. In the distance Fern could hear the occasional low rumble of thunder. Perhaps there would be a storm to cool them later but for now the clouds seemed to make it hotter still, adding an edge of humidity that made Fern sweat even more, until her shirt was wet through and plastered to her skin.

Once they'd left the town the sound of the cicadas became so deafening it drowned out all other noises. With no footpaths, they were forced to walk on the road, Fern holding Freya's hand and pulling her closer to the edge as cars sped by.

'Look, Mama, a butterfly,' said Freya, laughing with pleasure. She stopped and held out her hand, laughing again as the butterflies fluttered around her; large copper-coloured ones spotted with black, a luminescent green one and a tiny delicate blue one that settled briefly on her arm.

There were more butterflies than Fern had ever seen in Australia. There were bees too; honey bees, wild bees, bumble bees … an abundance of insect life, which could only mean that the environment was healthier here, up in the mountains away from heavy agriculture and spraying. As in the town, there were fruit trees in every garden; the stone fruits had already finished, but there were apples, pears, figs, grapes, olives, almonds and walnuts, ripe or ripening on the trees.

They carried on up the hill, stopping occasionally in the shade of a tree to catch their breath and take a drink from the water bottle. The trees and shrubs, the pale, dry soil, the rocky landscape and the tall rugged Pyrenees mountains with their craggy contours were overwhelmingly strange and yet it all felt like a long-forgotten memory. Fern didn't know the history of this part of France, but the atmosphere felt heavy, burdened with an unresolved weight. She shivered suddenly despite the heat, then struggled to reign in her imagination; after all, the rustle she heard in the tall grass was simply a lizard and the shadow in a copse of olive trees, just a misshapen branch.

'Beattie's tired,' announced Freya.

With a sigh Fern lifted Freya onto her shoulders and set off again up the seemingly endless hill, her concentration now entirely focused on the struggle to reach their destination.

The thunder was more frequent now. It sounded angry as if the mountains were grumbling a warning. Fern had insisted Freya wear a sun hat and sunglasses and she'd plastered sun cream on them both but without a cooling breeze she could still feel the sun burning her skin. It was a relief when the dark clouds finally obscured the sun.

The house looked old, ancient even, and a fusion of more than one building. A church or chapel by the looks of it, thought Fern. But then it had a section attached that looked like a house, with its uniform shuttered windows and terracotta tiled roof. Momentarily she wondered if this was the right place but a sign at the end of the drive was clearly marked, *Dr et Mme Leveque*.

Fern lifted Freya off her shoulders and they walked together down the short drive to the front of the house. The window shutters were closed and the pot plants on the window ledges and by the front door were untended, the flowers long faded and suffocated by weeds. Above the front door a small niche in the stonework held a carved figure of a woman wearing long robes. Disconcerted, Fern stared at it, mesmerized by the serene expression on the woman's face. The woman's eyes stared into Fern, as if she could see every facet of her, leaving Fern feeling discomfited and strangely vulnerable.

'Look Mama,' called Freya, freeing Fern from the statue's spell. 'A lizard. Just like at home.'

Fern spotted the back end of a gecko darting to safety under one of the pots. She smiled and turned back to the door. The ancient, dark stained wood was held together by iron bands and even without touching it Fern could feel the weight of its history.

The sound of the door knocker reverberated through the house. They waited but there was no answering sound of footsteps. Fern tried again, louder this time but again there was no response.

'He's not home,' said Freya matter-of-factly.

'No,' said Fern, wondering why she'd assumed he would be.

As she stood there trying to decide whether to leave a note, a passing cyclist paused on the road above the house. The man's face was ruddy with exertion and his voice out of breath as he shouted something at them, a stream of words from which Fern caught only one word. *Jardin.*

'Le jardin?' she called.

'Oui,' he shouted and pushed off again on his bike.

Fern grabbed Freya's hand. 'Okay, let's find the garden.'

They walked the length of the house but even after the house itself had ended, a tall stone wall continued further along before turning at a right angle. They followed it around to the back of the house where they were faced with an overgrown meadow dotted with trees. Beyond the meadow was a river lined with weeping willows and beyond the river, a forest climbed the lower slope of a mountain. Fern surveyed the scene before them. It was beautiful but she still couldn't see a garden or Dr Leveque.

As they retraced their steps around the wall, Freya stopped in front of a wooden door. 'Here,' she said matter-of-factly.

Fern was not so certain but she tentatively turned the handle and pushed the door open, revealing a secret walled garden. Paths crisscrossed through hedged garden beds and further on, fruit trees stood amongst uneven paving stones. This had once been a well-planned and well-loved garden but now the hedges had grown out of shape and become flowering bushes, the fruits trees were unpruned, the fallen fruit rotting around the base of each tree, their smell permeating the garden along with the heavy scent of rosemary and lavender. The unpicked herbs were going to seed and competing for space, and weeds were taking over the paving stones on the path.

On this side of the house, it was clear that the renovations weren't finished. The old house was crumbling in places, the windows of the rooms in use, framed with wooden shutters; the others, open to the elements. Just outside the shade of the terrace stood a number of citrus trees housed in giant ceramic pots, while a grape vine threaded up each of the terrace posts and along the roof, its bundles of grapes hanging heavy and low. Running along the length of the terrace was a row of overgrown lavender bushes, their scent rising into the still warm air. And behind them, in the shade of the verandah, a man was sitting on a wicker chair, reading. Fern studied him for a moment. Even seated it was obvious that Dr Leveque was tall, with elongated limbs and a long thin neck that reminded Fern of a heron. She guessed he was in his seventies, balding only slightly, his clothes unironed. About him was an air of deep sadness.

Before Fern could call out a greeting, Freya broke the silence with a gleeful shout and ran into the garden. At this, the man looked up, startled.

'Bonjour,' called Fern, noting the sharp contours of his face that even from a distance, exaggerated his features. She stepped through the doorway and made her way towards the man.

'Qu'est-ce que vous faites ici?' he barked as she approached, clearly furious at the interruption.

His unfriendly words sent Fern into a panic. What was she doing here? She didn't really know.

'I'm sorry, I knocked. There was no answer.' Realising she was speaking English, Fern tried again. 'Excusez-moi … she paused, frustrated, then tried again. 'Parlez vous anglais?'

'Non,' he said gruffly.

'I wrote … ' she said, acting it out in charades before remembering the French. 'J'ai ecrit.'

He stared at her for a long moment. 'And you think writing gives you an invitation?' he asked, switching suddenly to English.

'No, I'm sorry.' Fern looked away from his penetrating stare and gazed instead at the ground, noticing it was swarming with ants, all scurrying about bumping into each other instead of following their usual straight line. It's going to rain, she thought just as the first drop landed at her feet, followed by a flash of lightning. She'd been an idiot trusting Ahmed, a man she didn't even know. *Learn how to walk through the veils and into the past,* he'd said and on the basis of those few words she'd travelled half way around the world.

Dr Leveque was still staring at Fern, his face a mask of irritation. 'Get out,' he said, waving his hand dismissively. 'You are not welcome here.'

'Je suis désolée,' Fern said, turning to go. 'I can see this was a mistake.'

Oblivious to the conversation, Freya had been following the trail of a bumble bee flitting across the lavender plants. Fern took her hand and gave it a tug. 'Come on, we have to go.'

Freya scowled, not wanting to leave the garden. 'Bye bye bumble bee,' she said sadly.

At that moment the rain began bucketing down. Pulling Freya along behind her, Fern made a dash for the door but Freya suddenly slipped free. 'Wait Mama.'

Puzzled, Fern watched her daughter staring at the empty space under an apple tree as if she was listening intently. A moment later, Freya nodded then ran back to the man and grasped his hand. 'Don't be sad,' she said. 'Maddy is close by. Can't you see her?'

Shocked, Dr Leveque stared at the child for a moment, then looked beyond her, scanning the garden. Disappointed, he shook his head. 'No,' he said, 'I can't. Tell me, what do you see?'

His voice had taken on a greedy tone which frightened Freya, who pulled her hand away and ran back to her mother. At the gate, she stopped and shouted. 'She says don't be scared.' Freya paused as if listening again, then spoke hesitantly in French, 'Laisse-moi partir, mon amour.'

Chapter Eleven

Fern finished the last mouthful of her salad and helped herself to the left-over frites on Freya's plate. They were sitting in a café in the town square. It was dusk and the café's lights had just come on, dim at first but gradually brightening as the sky darkened. The rain had long since stopped, leaving the world washed clean. A brass band was playing and in the centre of the square the men and women of the village were performing a traditional circle dance. Freya had joined a couple of other small children who were running in and out of the circle of dancers, adding their own spontaneous dance to the traditional one going on above them, the faces of the adult dancers smiling good naturedly at their antics.

The restaurant was becoming noisier as the evening progressed. If she concentrated, Fern was able to catch a word here or there. If she tuned out then it became simply a stream of sound that parted around her. Fern's stomach was full of good food and the wine she'd ordered, which was cool and refreshing, but a bit tart. She should have felt content but it was at times like these that she felt her loneliness most acutely. If Adam had been here, he would have been alert and excited, pointing out things to them both, making them laugh. But he wasn't here. Two years had passed since Adam's death but Fern still couldn't grasp the idea that he wasn't coming back. She still saw him here and there or at least fragments of him: a shock of tangled blond hair, a head held at a particular angle, a set of shoulders, a hand, even a smile. If Adam had been here tonight, she would have danced along with the locals, not minding if her feet stumbled or she looked foolish. But Adam had gone and her spirit had followed him. Now all she could do was watch as others lived out their lives.

To make matters worse, Fern felt like an idiot. It had felt right at the time but now it seemed stupid to have travelled all this way without agreeing anything with Dr Leveque. Unable to sleep one evening she'd been googling randomly, had clicked an unlikely link and suddenly found herself reading about Dr Jacques Leveque, a psychologist and expert in past life therapy. Immediately she'd been flooded with a calm sense of clarity, a moment of inspiration that had given her what felt like a glimpse into her future. Feeling certain she should find Dr Leveque and ask him to help her, Fern had searched the internet for more information on him. There wasn't much: he'd retired a few years ago, was living with his wife in the Languedoc region of France, and had published two books, both now out of print. Disappointed but still caught in the thrall of certainty, she'd sent a letter anyway. Dr Leveque had never replied, which was an answer in itself, so she'd dismissed the idea, but then the message had come from Ahmed. *Just go.*

But Ahmed had been wrong and her intuition had been wrong. In fact, the whole trip had been a waste; of money she didn't have, and of time too, though she had plenty of that; she could feel it stretching ahead of her into a long and lonely future.

Freya ran back to the table, her face pink, her expression eager. 'Come and dance, Mama,' she said imploringly.

'No,' said Fern, 'I don't know that dance.'

'Pleeeaase?' asked Freya.

When Fern shook her head decisively, Freya sighed and the eagerness drained from her face, leaving in its stead a tired child. She cast a wistful glance at the dancers then sat down at the table and turned her attention to her lemonade, amusing herself by catching the liquid in the straw with her finger and then dropping it into her mouth from the other end.

Fern watched Freya drinking her lemonade. Ahmed might have been wrong about Dr Leveque but he was right about the tension between Fern and her daughter. It was getting worse every day. I have to pull myself together, she thought. If only for Freya's sake.

'When are we going to see Granny and Unci Micki?' asked Freya

'I don't know sweetheart, maybe in a few weeks.'

Perhaps even sooner than that, Fern thought, wondering once again what she should do now their trip had lost its point. A holiday, she supposed, days lounging around the town's public pool or walking up into the mountains, swimming in rock pools and visiting the hilltop monasteries.

'I want to see Granny Iris,' announced Freya, her voice suddenly wobbling with emotion.

Fern braced herself for an outburst but just then she was rescued by the waiter.

'Voilá,' he said, placing a bowl of ice cream in front of Freya and a crème brûlée before Fern.

The crème brûlée had been so glorious, Fern hadn't noticed the elderly man approach their table and was surprised to see Dr Leveque towering above her. He was even taller than she'd imagined. Earlier he'd reminded her of a heron but now he resembled a stick insect, his long skinny legs draped in baggy cotton trousers, his shirt, hanging off a concave chest.

'May I join you?' he asked.

'Oui,' said Fern, gesturing to the empty chair.

He sat down abruptly, his long legs only just fitting under the table. Catching the attention of a waiter, in a burst of rapid scowling French, he ordered wine. Then he turned to Fern. 'You should have gone to the restaurant across the road. The service is better.'

Fern shrugged. 'Maybe next time.'

'Have you got money?' he asked abruptly.

'Pardon?'

He was impatient again. 'Money? Do you have it?'

'A little,' said Fern, a defensive note creeping in to her voice.

'So you can't pay me. You came all this way, with no money and expected me to teach you?'

'It was the only thing I could think to do.'

He stared at Fern for a moment, assessing her. Then he nodded towards Freya. 'Where's the father?'

'Daddy's dead,' said Freya matter-of-factly.

Dr Leveque looked at Fern, a question in his eyes and Fern nodded and looked away.

The waiter arrived with a bottle of wine and poured a glass for them both.

'Here,' said Dr Leveque, handing her a fresh glass and pushing away her old one. 'Try this. The house wine is shit. He picked up his own glass and swirled the wine around, looking at the light through it. Then he took a sip. 'C'est bon.'

Freya watched him intently, then swirled the lemonade around in her own glass, managing only to spill it on the table cloth.

Embarrassed, Fern grabbed the glass from her and dabbed at the white tablecloth with her napkin.

'Don't snatch,' said Freya, her eyes filling with tears. 'Daddy doesn't snatch.'

'Daddy's … ' Fern bit her lip and turned away, focusing instead on the band members who had finished their playing and were now packing up.

'Where are you staying?' Dr Leveque asked abruptly.

'We have a room in a house near the church.'

He winced. 'Ah, those bells!' He drained his glass and refilled it. 'How long can you afford to stay there?'

'Why are you here, Dr Leveque?' asked Fern, changing the subject.

'Because of this one,' he said, gesturing impatiently at Freya. 'And please call me Jacques, it is easier than this doctor business.'

He leaned back in his chair, lit a cigarette and inhaled deeply, all the while staring at Fern, making her even more uncomfortable. She took a sip of the wine. Jacques was right, there was nothing tart about this one. He might not know how to conduct a polite conversation but he certainly knew about wines.

'Why are *you* here?' he asked.

'Because I want to learn,' said Fern.

Jacques brushed aside Fern's response scornfully. 'That much is obvious. I want to know why you want to learn.'

'I'm interested in past life therapy,' said Fern.

Knowing there was more to it than this, Jacques scowled again then decided to let it go. He filled his glass before turning back to Fern. 'Why then have you come to France? To me? It is easy to find courses in this therapy, even ones on the internet.'

Fern felt herself squirming again under the intensity of his scrutiny. How could she explain that incredible certainty she'd felt when she found his name on the internet?

'It felt right,' said eventually.

'Ah,' said Jacques, relaxing his scrutiny. 'It is written.'

Fern looked at him, searching for a sign that she was being teased but there was nothing to show either way. She pondered the words Freya had spoken earlier. *Laisse-moi partir, mon amour*. It was puzzling. Freya knew no French and even if she did, why on earth would she call Dr Leveque *my love*? The other words remained a mystery. *Laisse-moi partir*. She would have to look them up in her phrase book.

'I'll teach you,' said Jacques suddenly.

Startled, Fern reached for her wine but instead knocked over the glass.

'Naughty Mama,' said Freya, shaking her head in a perfect imitation of her mother.

Fern laughed despite herself and dabbed at the puddle with a serviette, her heart beating fast at this sudden turn in her fortune.

'On one condition,' said Jacques. 'No two conditions.' He paused and gulped down the rest of his wine. 'You will have to learn French. I do not want to speak this English for long. It will corrupt me. And number two, you, and this one will stay with me in my home.' He held up his hand as Fern began to protest. 'This is not an act of generosity. The villa is too big for me.' He hesitated before going on sadly. 'And it is not a place where one should be alone.'

Chapter Twelve

Fern inspected the heavy wooden door, concentrating on the roughly eroded line of its base. There was a slight breeze blowing underneath it and she knew the stone floor was icy cold but oddly the chill had no effect on her. Suddenly the door burst open and a man stepped through. Fern braced herself for the inevitable collision but to her amazement it never came. Instead, she felt just a slight ripple of energy as he passed right through her. I'm insubstantial, like a ghost, she thought, puzzled, then realised she was in a dream she'd dreamed before. Not knowing what to do next, she stood near the door, watching and waiting. Once or twice the man glanced in her direction but his gaze didn't register her presence. And anyway, he was busy pacing back and forth across the small room, only a few steps from one wall to its opposite, back and forth, fast and furious, reminding her of a caged wild animal, face taut with tension, body charged with misery. Then he abruptly stopped his pacing and emitted a groan of agony, before kneeling down by the side of the bed where he began rocking backwards and forwards on his knees, chanting something over and over again in a language Fern couldn't fathom. Some sort of penance, she imagined because he looked like a tormented man.

'Mama.'

Finding her courage, Fern crept closer until she could smell both the unwashed odour of his body and his fear. Startled, she slipped back into the shadows when the man suddenly tore off his robe, leaving only a light undergarment. Still chanting, he took up a stick with a knotted rope on one end and began lashing himself on the back.

'Mama.'

Freya's call entered into Fern's dream, so loudly she was sure the man would hear, and perhaps just for a moment he hesitated, before finding the rhythm of his penance once again.

'Mama!'

Fern opened her eyes. Light was streaming into her room as the morning sun found its way through the window, illuminating the stark white walls. She looked around, still adjusting to this different, lighter room she found herself in. The walls were almost bare, but directly opposite the bed hung a framed picture of Saint Jeanne d'Arc, clad in armour, carrying a heavy sword in one hand and in the other a banner on which the words, *Jhesus Maria* were written.

'Look Mama.'

Fern turned her head and saw Freya standing next to the bed, awkwardly clutching a ginger cat in her arms. Considering how it was being handled, the cat seemed remarkably relaxed but cats always were with Freya.

'Her name is Saint Jeanne,' Freya said, her mouth tripping awkwardly over the name.

'Really?'

'Yes, Jacques told me. He said she was a holy cat and can see things that no one else can but I'm just going to call her Jeannie.'

Fern smiled and patted the bed. 'Come and give me a cuddle.'

Jeannie chose that moment to wriggle out of Freya's grasp. She jumped up onto the window ledge and began putting her disheveled fur back into place.

Freya leaped onto the bed, gave her mother a quick kiss and leaped off again. 'Come and have breakfast,' she shouted, as she disappeared through the door. 'There are yummy things called crussonts and Jacques is making me a big bowl of hot chocolate.'

Still yawning, Fern followed the smell of freshly brewed coffee and found Jacques and Freya in the kitchen, sitting at one end of the long table. Freya was dipping her croissant into her bowl of chocolate and stuffing it into her mouth, never letting it halt the stream of words pouring out. There were crumbs everywhere and a growing puddle of spilt chocolate. Fern noted that despite Jacques apparent patience, his eyes kept straying to the unread paper in front of him.

'Bonjour,' she said, taking a seat opposite Jacques.

Jacques winced. 'Good morning,' he said, moodily. 'We will speak English until you can pronounce these things in a way that does not inflict injury to my ears.' He gestured to the coffee jug. 'Take some, it is still warm, though the croissants are not. Jacques pointedly picked up the paper and began reading.

'You slept in, Mama,' said Freya accusingly.

'Freya is correct,' said Jacques, looking up from his paper. 'In this season, it is best to wake early in order to conduct our business in the cooler parts of the day and rest in the heat of the afternoon.'

Fern sighed and poured herself a coffee. 'I'm sorry,' she said. 'It won't happen again.'

'It's alright, Mama. We've forgiven you.'

Fern caught the ghost of a smile flitting across Jacques' face before disappearing under what seemed a permanent mask of irritation.

Freya finished her drink and smacked her lips together, her mouth framed with chocolate. 'That was yummy,' she said, then promptly climbed off her chair and darted for the door.

'Wait,' called Fern.

Freya stopped in her tracks and looked back, a question in her eyes.

'You have to clean up after yourself.'

'I don't want to.'

'Well then you won't get another hot chocolate tomorrow.'

Dragging her feet, Freya returned to the table and carefully carried her bowl to the sink. Then she took a dripping sponge and wiped at the chocolate puddle and crumbs, only succeeding in spreading the mess around.

Fern winced and took the sponge from her. 'Here,' she said. 'Like this.'

Freya watched for a moment then darted to the door once again, singing loudly to drown out any protests from her mother.

'I'm sorry,' said Fern. 'She's a bit messy. I'm trying to teach her.'

Jacques waved aside her apology. 'She is a child. You should let her run free. Duty is not for small children.'

'Freya has to learn,' said Fern. She went to the sink, washed out the sponge and wiped the table down properly.

Jacques watched her for a moment then folded up the newspaper and proceeded to outline the program for the day. 'This morning, I am out on business so you will have time to settle in but usually we will have our training sessions at ten o'clock each morning.'

Fern had never actually thought about the logistics of studying with Jacques and now she felt a wave of anxiety. Freya was five now and fairly self-sufficient for her age but there was little doubt she would run in and disturb them.

'We will eat lunch at around noon,' said Jacques. 'After lunch I rest. So you will have free time each day to do as you please. At four o'clock on certain days we will resume training for one hour.

Fern was afraid to ask but she needed to know. 'How much will it cost?'

Jacques looked at her intently for a moment, 'You have no money and I am not short of money. I will not charge.'

Fern was taken aback by his unexpected generosity and simply stared at him.

'What is the matter?' Jacques asked. 'You are not offended by this offer?'

'No, no,' said Fern. 'Just surprised … and grateful. But I'm not penniless, I can give you some money towards the lessons.'

Jacques waved his hand dismissively. 'I need nothing from you.'

'What about shopping?' asked Fern. 'We should contribute to meals.'

'There is no need. I have my routines and will stay with them.'

'But I need to give you something in return,' Fern insisted, uncomfortable at the thought of being so much in his debt.

Jacques opened his mouth as if about to utter a retort, then changed his mind and looked out through the open doors to the overgrown walled garden buzzing with bees and butterflies. 'D'accord. I ask that you work on this garden.' Jacques turned his gaze to a framed picture perched on one of the kitchen shelves. 'Madeleine would like that,' he said his face softening.

'Madeleine?'

Jacques stiffened. 'My wife,' he said shortly then turned back to his paper, making it clear their conversation was over.

With Jacques gone, a different mood descended on the house, as if it had taken a deep breath out and relaxed its shoulders. Fern found Freya in the garden and called her in. 'Let's explore,' she said.

First they stepped into a large well stocked pantry lined with shelves from floor to ceiling. The jars of preserves were covered in a thick layer of dust, and Fern wondered how long it had been since anyone had replenished the contents. A musty smell and small black droppings suggested there was also a problem with mice.

Freya crinkled her nose and stepped back out into the fresh air of the kitchen. Caught up in the excitement of exploration she tugged Fern's hand and pulled her through another door into the entrance hall with its giant wooden front door at one end. 'Which way, Mama?'

Fern hesitated. There were three ways they could go; up the stairs where their own bedrooms were, or along a ground floor hallway dotted with doors, or into the chapel near the front of the house. 'Let's look at the chapel,' she said.

The chapel turned out to be a sparsely furnished living room, with a giant stone fireplace at one end and a slow combustion stove set within it. The parts of the house that Fern had already seen were quite different in style, with thick wooden beams across the ceilings making them feel top heavy but this room was light and uncluttered with arches and curved ceilings that blended smoothly into the walls and in places curved all the way from the ceiling to the floor. The windows were set into metre-thick walls and under one window a stone seat had been carved into the wall. A shaft of sunlight was coming in through an upper window, illuminating a statue that was set into the wall, not of a woman this time, but of Jesus on the cross. Fern felt his anguished eyes watching her as she gazed in through the door, suddenly reluctant to enter.

There were a number of carved niches in the walls, two holding candle sticks, another a small sculpture, while in one sat a glass lantern. The largest piece of furniture was a giant couch, its leather surface cracked with age. A thick-piled, ochre rug sat in front of the couch, with a heavy coffee table made from rough wood, standing on it. Opposite the lounge was a large screen television which looked incongruous in this setting. Still, it would be a lovely room to sit in, thought Fern. It was cool too, the thick walls keeping out the worst of the heat and the rough tiles cool under foot.

'It's pretty,' announced Freya. She ran in and leaped onto the couch, then bounced off and began inspecting the contents of the little niches in the walls.

'Careful not to break anything,' said Fern, still standing in the doorway.

Freya looked up. 'Come on Mama, come and explore.'

Fern stepped into the room and was immediately overcome by a swirling nausea in her stomach and a bitter taste in her mouth. Why me? she thought … It's not fair … these unexpected thoughts trapping themselves inside her head and repeating themselves like a stuck record, over and over. Why me? … It's not fair? … Why me?

Sensing the change in mood, Freya glanced over at Fern. 'Mama?' she asked. The room was getting colder around them and Freya shivered and glanced behind her before gathering up the courage to approach her mother. Then she reached out and took Fern's hand. 'Let's go, Mama. We don't like it here.'

At Freya's gentle touch, Fern became aware of her surroundings once again. Feeling a creeping sensation on the back of her neck, she shivered. It's the cold she thought, just the cold. She glanced once more around the room. On the surface nothing had changed and yet … it felt as if something had noticed them.

When Freya gave her hand a tug, Fern turned her back on the room and resolutely dismissed the idea.

Chapter Thirteen

As she unpacked, Fern wondered what had embittered Jacques so. Perhaps his wife. It was evident that Madeleine was no longer here but Fern didn't dare ask why. She sighed. Jacques was impossible; set in his ways, yet full of contradictions, impatient one minute, furious the next and then unexpectedly kind. Strangely enough, Freya seemed oblivious to his moods.

Fern pulled a few clothes from her suitcase and began hanging the dresses in a corner of the vast but empty wardrobe in her room. The chest of drawers was empty too, with just a few old sachets of lavender in each drawer, no longer smelling of anything but dust. The few clothes she'd brought would barely fill it.

As she placed a small framed photograph of Adam on the bedside table, Fern felt the familiar tug of grief in her chest. She stared at him for a long moment before returning to her unpacking. At the bottom of her suitcase was a small stone. For the past few years, it had sat untouched in a box in the bottom of her wardrobe back in their shack on Bruny Island, but when she was packing for this trip, Fern had felt a strong urge to bring the stone with her.

It had been given to her six years before by a man who, like Ahmed, had appeared suddenly in her life and then disappeared just as suddenly. 'Pietersite,' he'd said. 'A tempest stone because its nature is the storm. It will help you on your journey.'

Fern picked up the stone. It really was tempestuous, with its wild and windy tangle of seams and threads clearly visible on the surface. But its red and gold autumnal colours were earthy and there was a watery element too, in the way the colours flowed. The stone had done as the man had promised, showing her glimpses into other lives or other aspects of herself or even just her imagination. She'd never known which and in a way it hadn't mattered. But with each glimpse a patch of the stone would be drained of colour as if the fourth element, air, had found its way under the surface.

As she held it, Fern could feel a dizziness spreading up her arm. Outside, in the walled garden, Freya was laughing and chatting to Beattie as the sun rose higher into the sky, turning the coolness of the morning into a heat that would soon become too much, even for Freya. Her childish voice soothed Fern and its warmth and light resisted the coldness that had suddenly penetrated the room.

When Fern put the stone down next to her photograph of Adam, the dizziness quickly dissipated. Even so she felt it had marked her in some way, drawing something dark from deep within her that was now surfacing. She shuddered, then pushed the thought away and went to unpack Freya's things.

Fern would have been happy to share a room with Freya but Jacques had insisted there were plenty of unused rooms and Freya loved the cosy bedroom at the end of the corridor, with its tiny window looking out over the river behind the house. Fern straightened the sheets on Freya's bed, picked up the clothes strewn on the ground, finished emptying Freya's suitcase and put everything in the little chest of drawers. Then she went to the window and stood absorbing the view, still surprised at the sudden turn of events. Freya was the reason for Jacques change of heart and although she didn't understand why, she was grateful for it.

Realising she could no longer hear Freya chatting to Beattie in the garden, Fern headed downstairs to the kitchen.

'Freya,' she called, then paused, waiting for a response but there was none. She stepped out into the garden, calling again, but the garden was still and silent in the midday heat.

She was uneasy now. Had Freya found a way out of the garden and gone down to the river? Had she wandered along the street?

'Freya.' Her voice rose as she ran through the garden to check the wooden door. 'Freya. Where are you?'

The door was shut and the bolt too stiff for Freya to open. Momentarily relieved, Fern ran back through the garden to the house, remembering Ahmed's warning. Had someone taken her? Who was Jacques anyway? She'd been a fool to trust him.

Back in the house, Fern called again and again as she searched, the silence heavy and suddenly horrible, increasing her certainty that something terrible had happened. She tried the bathroom, the living room, Jacques' study and then upstairs, peering into each of the rooms until she reached her own room where she stopped abruptly. Freya was standing near Fern's bed, safe and sound, her back to the door.

'Freya,' she breathed, feeling the panic ebbing away. But the relief turned quickly to anger. 'Why didn't you answer? That was naughty. You frightened me.'

Fern expected some response from her daughter who usually couldn't keep still for a second; a laugh, a guilty apology, something, anything … but Freya didn't move. There was something odd too about the way she was holding her body; stiffly, as if she was playing a game of statues.

'Don't be silly, Freya. This isn't a joke.'

But there was still no response.

'Freya?' Puzzled, Fern crossed the room and looked into her daughter's face. It was passive and unmoving but the eyes held an expression of terror that sent a fresh sliver of fear through Fern. It looked like Freya was caught in a night terror, but in broad daylight.

Fern kneeled down and embraced her daughter. 'Come back sweetheart. It's okay, you're safe. I'm here.'

When Freya didn't respond, Fern kissed her on her forehead then noticed that Freya's fingers were clasped tightly around the tempest stone. She quickly peeled the child's fingers from the stone but in the brief time it took Fern to put the stone back on the bedside table, she felt something of the terror that was infecting Freya, a glimpse of flame and searing heat, a gasping for air.

Gradually Freya began to return; the stiffness in her body lessened and her face became a little more animated. But as she gazed at Fern, her eyes didn't lose their fear and when Fern reached out to hug her daughter, Freya backed away. 'No,' she cried. 'No, go away.' Then louder. 'Mama, help me.'

'Mama's here,' said Fern, reaching out once more but it only served to increase Freya's fear.

'No,' she cried, retreating further, her face turning a ghostly white. Then her eyes rolled upwards and she lost consciousness, falling heavily to the floor before Fern could catch her.

Chapter Fourteen

The shutters were closed against the heat of the afternoon, dimming the light in the bedroom. Freya was sleeping peacefully in Fern's giant bed. Jeannie had sauntered in soon after Freya fell asleep and now lay curled up on the duvet, fast asleep, one paw possessively resting on Freya's arm. Fern was sitting by the side of the bed, watching her daughter carefully for any signs. Of what, she wasn't sure, but she couldn't leave Freya's side. Not yet. Freya's face was still pale but the colour was beginning to return a little to her cheeks. The cut on her forehead was covered in a white bandage but around it, Fern could see the edges of a bruise developing. She would need to give Freya some arnica when she woke up.

Luckily, Jacques had returned while Fern was gabbling down the phone in a mixture of French and English, not understanding and not being understood. Grasping quickly that Freya was not well, he'd snatched the phone from Fern and emitted a stream of words into the receiver which resulted in a doctor arriving twenty minutes later.

The doctor cleaned up the blood and inspected the cut on Freya's forehead. 'Good,' he said. It is only a surface cut. She won't need stitches.' He looked at Fern. 'How did this happen?'

Fern hesitated for a moment, reluctant to mention the terror on Freya's face or the effect of the tempest stone, which the doctor and Jacques would dismiss as ridiculous. 'She tripped or fainted, I'm not sure … She looked strange, her face was pale and then she fell and hit her head. On the bedside table, I think.'

When Jacques translated, the doctor nodded. 'A faint. Did she lose consciousness?' he asked.

'I don't know,' said Fern. 'I think so. She seemed groggy.'

The doctor had checked Freya over, looking into her eyes with a torch and testing her reflexes. 'Let her rest for a few hours,' he'd pronounced. 'Call me if there is any confusion or dizziness.'

After the doctor had left, Freya had cuddled Wombie close to her, closed her eyes and gone straight to sleep. Three hours later she was still asleep and Fern was beginning to worry.

Jacques stepped into the room, carrying a coffee for Fern, who took it gratefully.

'How is she?' he asked.

'Still sleeping. Do you think I should wake her?'

Jacques shook his head. 'The sleep will help.' He paused for a moment before speaking again, more quietly this time. 'You said Freya's face was pale. Did she seem frightened?'

Fern glanced quickly at Jacques. 'I don't think so,' she lied.

'I see.' Jacques eyes strayed to the stone on the bedside table. He picked it up and turned it over in his palm. 'Intéressant.' He studied it closely for a moment. 'This is an unusual stone. Where did you get it?'

'A gift,' said Fern. This wasn't a lie, but there was so much missing from her answer that it felt like one.

Jacques placed it carefully back on the table. 'Keep it safe,' he said. 'It's too … ' He hesitated, searching for the right word. 'Valuable for little hands.'

The next morning it was as if nothing had happened. A few doses of arnica the previous evening had quickly cleared the worst of Freya's bruise and eased the shock. Now Freya was running about happily, though Fern could detect a slight reticence; an instinctive backing away, a stiffening of her muscles when Fern approached her. Adding to Fern's unease was the fact the tempest stone had gone missing the previous evening. Fern had decided to return it to her suitcase, out of the way of Freya's curious eyes but it wasn't where she'd left it on the bedside table. Out of sight, out of mind, she hoped, but still the memory of the stone kept intruding on this otherwise peaceful morning.

Having been roundly told off the previous day, Fern had managed to wake up soon after dawn and now found herself enjoying the relative freshness and cool of the morning. After breakfast, and with an hour or so to spare before her first lesson with Jacques, she had decided to begin tackling the garden. Alarmingly, Jacques had pointed out that there were scorpions and insisted she wear gloves. Swearing and swiping at the cobwebs, he'd dug around in a shed in the corner of the garden and eventually found a couple of pairs, stiff and old but thick enough to withstand a scorpion. Freya had insisted on helping so Fern had given her the smaller gloves, which were still many sizes too large. Armed only with a small trowel each, they were now tackling the herb bed closest to the kitchen door. Fern was freeing the sage bush from the weeds which had tangled themselves through and around it, while Freya was digging around a beautiful lemon thyme bush and telling Beattie off for being too slow.

With the morning sun on her shoulders and the pungent scent of the herbs permeating the air, Fern felt a sense of peace descending on her. It was good for them both to have their hands in the earth again. She thought of her own neglected garden on Bruny. She'd loved it deeply and for a time taken good care of it, slowly learning to read its patterns and eventually beginning to understand how those patterns were reflected in the larger world, in the shape of things and the relationships they bear to each other. A patterner, she'd called herself in those brief moments.

Then Adam died and she'd lost the flow, letting the garden go. Michael had felt its suffering and had tried sometimes to set it back on course but he had his own garden to care for and not much time for Fern's. He'd looked at her then, with frustration in his eyes as if he was trying to make her understand that she should pour her grief into living. But Fern couldn't do it, and she'd watched helplessly as the garden became a chaos of weeds. Like this one, she thought, straightening up for a moment and looking around at this once beautiful garden. It would take more than just trimming a few bushes and pulling a few weeds to get it back into shape. Once again Fern wondered about Jacques and what it was that was fueling his unhappiness. She tried to remember what Freya had said to Jacques that first day. 'Don't worry, Maddy is fine.' A simple phrase but powerful enough to change his mind about teaching Fern.

'Look Mama, I found a fig tree,' said Freya, who'd quickly lost patience with digging out weeds and gone off exploring. Her face covered in fig juice, she proudly held out a fig for Fern, who took it gratefully and dug her teeth into its sweet flesh.

'Freya, do you remember that first day when we met Jacques? You said something to him?'

Freya nodded solemnly. 'Maddy gave me a message.'

'A message?' said Fern, disconcerted. She looked at Freya more closely, wondering at the ease with which this tiny child walked between worlds and the way she just took it for granted. That level of sensitivity was both a gift and a curse and Fern hoped with all her heart that nothing bad would happen to her; no tragedies, no ridicule, no fear-filled influences in her life, acting to close her path or cripple her sensitivity.

'Where is Maddy?' Fern asked.

'Beattie says she died … Look Mama, this is like the one we have at home.' She pointed at the rosemary bush, then brushed her hand along a stem and sniffed her fingers. 'Smell, Mama, it's lovely.'

'Rosemary for remembrance,' said Fern, sniffing the bush and savouring its rich sharp scent. With it came a fleeting sense of déjà vu, as if a memory were hovering just on the edge of her conscience mind.

Chapter Fifteen

Jacques led Fern into a room on the ground floor adjacent to the chapel. 'I no longer have a treatment room, so we will work here.' he said. 'It was once the vestry for the chapel but now it has become my study.'

Fern looked around the study. Like the chapel it had thick walls, and curved ceilings, with rough tiles under foot, and like the chapel, the furnishings were heavy. With its back to the window sat a wooden desk, so large it made the laptop sitting on its surface look like a toy, and one wall was lined with dark wood bookshelves that were filled with weighty books. She scanned the books – history, philosophy, psychology, some in French, some in English.

'You may borrow what you wish,' said Jacques. 'I will guide you to the authors who will help you understand what you are learning. Jung is a good starting point for psychology. He was a man ahead of his time and for this he has been punished with ridicule by many – a form of torture that has more recently replaced the burning of heretics. Less painful but still most effective.'

'Did Jung believe in reincarnation?' asked Fern.

Jacques shrugged. 'He did not write directly about it but there are hints in his writings and his theories are easily extended in that direction.' He gestured at another section of the shelves. 'There are other books too, ones written specifically about past lives. These may be of more interest to you.'

'I'll have a look,' said Fern, trying unsuccessfully to sound enthusiastic. She could count on one hand the number of books she's read since Adam died. Jacques' study felt unused, the books encased in a layer of dust, the air slightly musty as if it had not been changed for some time. Fern wondered what else Jacques had lost his when his wife died.

Seeing her lack of interest, Jacques' mouth twitched into a smile which he quickly covered with a scowl. 'So, my student does not like reading.'

'No, I do,' said Fern, 'it's just … '

'That the words of the masters are not good enough for you,' finished Jacques.

When Fern blushed, Jacques gestured at the bookshelf. 'There is much that is of value here and you must read some of it in order to learn. However, you will be pleased to hear that most of your learning will come through direct experience.'

Surprised, Fern looked at him, a question in her eyes.

Jacques shrugged. 'Knowledge must be realised,' he said. 'Now, to business.' He moved his office chair out from behind the desk then sat down in front of Fern and stared at her so intently that after only a short time she had to look away.

Finally, Jacques broke the silence. 'I can understand why a homeopath might study herbal medicine or Bach flowers but past life therapy is a different tradition. It does not draw from the natural world but is based on a psychology that looks beyond the immediate to the source of deeper issues, ones that have been carried over from other lives. Most reputable past life therapists would have a background in psychology, not herbalism or homeopathy.'

Fern hadn't come here to add past life therapy to her list of healing therapies but rather to resolve the issues between herself and Freya, though she hadn't told Jacques yet. Maybe I don't need to, she thought, knowing that what she learned from

Jacques would deepen her understanding of the modalities she'd already learned. And hopefully help her and Freya.

'A homeopath needs an understanding of psychology too,' Fern said. 'We don't just fix bruises or colds; there are remedies and doses that work on a very deep level and we need to understand their nature and their function in relation to the patient. Which means we have to understand the physical, emotional, mental and spiritual aspects of their problem.'

Jacques nodded, pleased. 'Perhaps in the end all paths are one,' he said, 'though I have always found it useful to stay on one path.' He paused and stared sadly at a framed photograph of his wife that sat prominently on his desk, before returning his attention to Fern.

'Healing requires a rebalancing of energies. Whenever we search for the cause rather than the effect, we will find stories. These stories are held in place by scar tissue, and our lives form in reaction to them. Most patients are not aware of these stories so it is our task to help them make the necessary discoveries and release them. But not fix them. It is for the patient to heal themselves; our job is to show them the way. Do you understand?'

'Yes,' said Fern, surprised again at how similar Jacques' methods were to homeopathy where the patient was also encouraged to talk, expressing their stories and finding connections between events in their lives. Then the remedy would provide a helpful and sometimes deep rebalancing of the patient's energy.

Jacques lit a cigarette and inhaled deeply, then exhaled, filling the room with acrid smoke. When Fern coughed pointedly, he scowled at her then stood and pushed open the window.

'Better?' he asked, glaring at Fern.

The air outside was so still, it made little difference but Fern nodded anyway and stifled another cough.

'So, we begin,' he said gruffly. 'The first thing will be to take you back into the past.'

'Now?' asked Fern suddenly alarmed. 'Don't I learn techniques or something first?'

'It is no use me telling you what happens. You have to do it and then you have to understand what you have done. It is experience plus knowledge that brings understanding.'

Fern nodded. 'Okay. What do I have to do then?'

Jacques pointed at a chair 'First you must sit down.' When Fern had done as he requested, he went on. 'Past life therapy is a form of light hypnosis, triggered by suggestion and run by the imagination. You might call it a guided visualisation.'

Fern was confused. 'Isn't it more than just imagination?'

At this, Jacques scowled. 'You should not dismiss the imagination as mere fantasy. It is the source of all creation, the key to visualisation, the most powerful tool we have. With it we can access the unconscious and step into other worlds.' Jacques paused and drew on his cigarette. 'You must learn to harness and use the imagination and you must treat it with great care because where you take it will create your reality. Do you understand?'

Jacques second-hand smoke was now drifting up Fern's nose and making her eyes water. It was difficult to concentrate. She'd never thought much about imagination before but now she remembered something Ahmed had said that day in Salamanca Square. *Do not denigrate the power of the Imagination for it plays a decisive role in all of creation.* For a moment she was back there, sitting in the square bathed in sunlight and free of worries, knowing that in a few hours she would be in Adam's arms.

'Do you understand?' asked Jacques again.

'Yes,' said Fern, then sneezed three times running.

Jacques sighed and stubbed out his cigarette in the ashtray on his desk. 'Is there something you wish to discover about yourself? The source of a pain somewhere, an emotion that keeps returning, a phrase you tell yourself many times … ?'

Immediately Fern's mind filled with a barrage of possibilities but whenever she tried to look at them directly, they slipped away and the more she searched the less able she was to follow the threads of these fleeting thoughts to anything she could fix on. When Fern felt Jacques' increasing impatience, she lost any hope and shook her head.

'Nothing?' asked Jacques.

'I can't think,' said Fern.

Jacques sighed. 'You are surprisingly resistant,' he said, perplexed by her lack of response. 'You do not trust. It is as if you have erected a whirlpool of energy around you as a barrier of some sort. Like armour … It is as if you are hiding from something.'

Fern felt the truth of his words. What was it she was protecting herself from? Despite her unease, she felt the first real inklings of curiousity.

'Can we try again?' she asked.

Jacques nodded. 'D'accord.'

Fern closed her eyes and waited. This time she didn't try to pin down a story or look for a way in; instead she stared at the blackness behind her eyelids, simply letting the images flitter in and out until one settled and she found herself in a dark passageway, stone walls on each side. Her eyes were not used to the darkness and she could see only a candle flickering ahead.

'Where are you?' asked Jacques.

'I'm not sure,' said Fern. 'It's dark and cold,' she added, shivering suddenly. 'There's a musty smell and the walls are wet …'

'Look Mama,' cried Freya, cutting her off in mid-sentence as she ran into the room, bubbling with excitement. 'Look what I found.'

Fern opened her eyes, surprised at the brightness in the room and the warmth. The musty smell was gone, replaced by the acrid smell of cigarette smoke. She blinked and focused on Freya who was standing before her holding a small lizard in her hands.

'See,' she said. 'This is just like the ones at home.'

When Fern had dutifully admired the lizard, Freya ran happily back into the garden to release it.

'This is not going to work if we are interrupted,' said Jacques impatiently. 'You must tell her not to disturb us.'

'I have told her but she's too young to remember for long.'

'Well then,' said Jacques, 'we will have to find a solution.'

Chapter Sixteen

It was late afternoon and Fern was enjoying a rare moment of peace as she sat in the garden listening to the buzz of insects and watching dark clouds form over the mountain tops. The storms came nearly every day and she found herself looking forward to them, the rolling thunder sounded like the grumbling and roaring of the gods as they battled, the clash of their weapons evident in the crackling atmosphere and the blinding flashes of lightning. These mountains did feel sacred in some way; as if the veil between the physical and the metaphysical worlds was thinner here. And in particular the tallest one, Canigou. Even from here she could feel its power.

Fern took a deep breath and felt herself relaxing. She'd intended to finish pulling out the weeds from between the paving stones but when Freya had gone inside to help Jacques with the dinner, Fern had allowed herself to be defeated by the heat and the dense humidity. She closed her eyes and immediately her other senses kicked in; the buzz of insects grew louder and the many scents from the garden intensified. Her thoughts began to settle, and her breathing deepen as she slipped into a meditative state, garnering energy from the simple act of being, something she hadn't done for a long time.

Suddenly Fern sensed she was being watched. Assuming it was Freya creeping up on her, she smiled and prepared herself to pounce on her daughter. But when she opened her eyes, Freya was nowhere to be seen. Puzzled, Fern looked around the garden but there was no one there. She felt the skin on the back of her neck prickle and glancing back at the house, saw something in one of the windows; a silhouette of what appeared to be a man. He was staring out into the garden but the angle of the light meant that she couldn't make out any features. She counted the windows and realised that the man was standing in the window of her own bedroom. It must be Jacques, she thought. But why would he be in my room? And even if he was, why would he stand at the window like that? Distracted by the flutter of a bird nearby, Fern glanced away for a moment and when she returned her gaze to the window, the man had gone.

Before she had time to wonder further about the figure, Freya darted out of the kitchen.

'Mama, mama, I'm going to school,' she said, jumping up and down on the spot as she imparted her news.

'What?' asked Fern, confused.

'Jacques said I could go to school. Starting on Monday.'

As Freya's words took root, Fern felt a mixture of panic and fury rising in her. How dare he interfere like this. She stood up abruptly. 'Did he now?'

When she saw her mother's expression, Freya's smile disappeared and her shoulders slumped. 'He said I could,' she muttered.

'That's for me to say. Not Jacques.' Fern took a deep breath, trying unsuccessfully to quench her anger. 'You stay out here. I'm going to have a word with him.'

The delicious aroma in the kitchen almost put Fern off her mission. Jacques was grinding basil and garlic in a large marble mortar, while listening to the radio.

'You shouldn't have told Freya she could go to school.'

Startled, Jacques stopped his grinding and switched off the radio. 'Why not?' he asked. 'I need to teach you and she interrupts.'

'I can't just send her away because she interrupts.'

Jacques turned back to his pestle. 'I don't understand what the problem is. She wants to go to school. You want to learn from me. It is, as the young people say, a no-brainer.'

'She can't go to school here. It's a strange country.'

'It's France. We have schools and the autumn term has recently begun so the timing is good.'

'But Freya can't speak French.'

He shrugged. 'She will learn quickly. Children do. And in the mean time she will communicate without language.'

'She's too young to send to school,' said Fern, desperately searching for reasons.

Jacques looked surprised. 'You told me she is five. When do they start school in your country?'

Fern opened her mouth to retort then remembered that Freya had been eligible to start school in Tasmania the previous February but Fern had decided it was best to wait another year. Finding herself out of excuses, Fern played her last card. 'I'm her mother, you should have consulted me first.'

'And you would have said no.' He paused, not sure what he would unleash with his next words. 'Perhaps there is more to this than simple care for your daughter.'

'What are you suggesting?' asked Fern.

Jacques held up his hand. 'Let me explain … It is clear that you need her near you but she also needs the company of other children. You must ask yourself whose needs are more important?'

Fern was furious at Jacques for meddling like this and it didn't help that there was an element of truth in his words. Now she found herself backed into a corner. Jacques had won on every front.

'Yes, I'm protective of Freya but I'm Freya's mother and mothers are supposed to be protective.' She felt her eyes filling with tears. 'And she's lost her father. She needs me.'

Jacques nodded sympathetically. 'It is hard. And I see that you are afraid of losing her too.'

Rather than placate Fern, Jacques' words made her feel even less certain of herself. But just as she opened her mouth to retort there was a burst of wind and the clouds broke, sending rain pounding onto the tiled roof and saturating the garden once more.

Freya ran in to the kitchen; a dripping wet child encased in a whirl of excited energy. 'Can I go Mama? Can I?'

'Yes,' said Fern, glaring at Jacques. 'You can.'

By dinner time Fern's mood had settled into the 'foul' category and to make it worse, Jacques was in a playful mood for a change and Freya was bubbling over with excitement. She was asking an endless stream of questions about the school, none of which Fern could answer.

'I don't know,' she said again, her voice bristling with impatience. 'I don't know anything about this stupid school.'

'It's not stupid,' shouted Freya. 'It's my school.'

'Let's eat outside tonight,' said Jacques before Fern could retort.

Immediately Freya's face lit up. 'Yay,' she shouted.

'I will need your help,' said Jacques. He took some thick candles from a cupboard and filled Freya's arms with them. 'Here, you must take these out to the table in the garden.'

Solemnly, Freya carried them out as if they were sacred objects, and placed them carefully on the table. Then she ran back into the kitchen and collected the plates.

Fern watched Freya carrying the plates, taking one cautious step at a time, aware of their fragility and determined they would arrive intact. The joy and concentration on her face tore at Fern's heart; it had been a long time since Freya had been so excited by life. In her own grief, Fern had forgotten how to play and had lost her light heartedness, and now Jacques had forced her to see that she'd been unwittingly making her daughter live without joy too?

'Here Mama, Jacques said you should light the candles.' Freya handed Fern a box of matches, a peace offering.

As Fern stepped outside into the steamy post-storm atmosphere, she could feel her resentment ebbing away. After all, Jacques was only guilty of being a messenger. The air was still, making it easy to light the candles, which flickered hesitantly at first, before the flames grew roots and shone proudly, lighting up the darkness as dusk descended into night.

'Voilá,' said Jacques as he deposited the final item onto the table; a large bowl of spaghetti tossed with homemade pesto sauce.

Fern surveyed the table as Jacques filled their plates. Alongside the pasta sat a green salad dotted with cherry tomatoes, and alongside that a bottle of wine, a jug of water and a baton of bread. A perfect meal!

Jacques filled her glass with wine, then turned to Freya and poured a small portion into her wine glass before topping it up with water.

Fern was appalled. 'Freya's far too young to drink,' she protested. 'And she's certainly too young for that wine glass. She'll break it.'

Jacques looked astonished. 'It is almost all water and will do her no harm. In France we teach our children to have fine tastes in food and in wine. This means they must start as soon as possible.' He glanced at the glass Freya was holding reverently in her tiny hand. 'Children are naturally careful with things of beauty. This glass will survive the night.'

Fern sighed, feeling herself once again defeated by Jacques' reasoning.

'Now let us toast.' Jacques held up his glass. 'Bon appétit.'

'Bon Appetite,' repeated Fern, holding up her own glass before taking a sip of the fine wine.

Freya followed suit, made a face and put her glass down.

Fern began to eat and was immediately captivated by the flavours: crushed fresh basil, garlic, pine nuts, olive oil, parmesan cheese, fused together yet each still identifiable. 'This is wonderful,' she said.

Jacques looked pleased. 'I enjoy cooking, though I do not do it so much these days.' His face fell. 'It is not satisfying cooking for one person.'

They ate in silence, with Jacques lost in his own thoughts and Fern caught for once in the pleasure of the moment. Freya was twirling the spaghetti onto her fork and sucking up the longer strands with gusto, splattering her face with so much pesto that she began to look green.

Fern looked at her and burst out laughing.

'I'm a pesto monster,' said Freya, screwing up her face and snarling.

Jacques laughed then, a deep barking guffaw that startled them both because they'd never heard him laugh before. He filled up his own glass and Fern's, then proposed another toast. 'To laughter,' he said. 'It is good medicine.'

Jacques emerged from the kitchen, wielding a knife so large it looked like a machete. Tucked under his arm, was a giant melon. 'Watermelon for dessert tonight but tomorrow I will make you a lemon tart.' He sliced big chunks of watermelon and handed them to Fern and Freya. The deep pink flesh was speckled with black seeds.

Freya briefly inspected her slice then put it down. 'It's got seeds.'

'Just pick out the seeds and eat the flesh,' said Fern.

'No,' said Freya and crossed her arms obstinately.

'Ah, but the seeds are important,' said Jacques. 'They are for spitting. Watermelon must always be eaten outside and with it we must have a spitting competition.' Jacques took a bite, chewed the flesh, then worked a seed into the front of his mouth and spat it across the courtyard. 'That was a good one. You will not beat that.'

A moment later they were laughing and spitting and measuring and soon half the giant watermelon was gone. It was agreed that Jacques had won but he conceded that Freya was very good at spitting and was likely to win next time.

Fern began collecting the plates but Jacques stopped her.

'Sit down please,' he said. 'It is time for cheese and coffee. We will deal with the washing later.'

Jacques disappeared into the kitchen and Fern turned her attention to Freya whose pesto covered face now wore an extra layer of sticky pink watermelon juice. Her eyes were drooping and her thumb had found its way into her mouth.

'Time for bed, sweetheart,' said Fern.

'No,' said Freya, shaking her head stubbornly. But nevertheless, she climbed onto Fern's lap and snuggled in close. A few moments later, when Jacques returned with the cheese, she was fast asleep.

Fern carried Freya up to her little bedroom, feeling herself overwhelmed with love for this small child asleep in her arms. She placed her on the bed then wiped her sticky face and hands with a wet cloth. 'Sweet dreams my darling,' she whispered and kissed Freya on the forehead. She stood for a moment gazing at her sleeping daughter. There was so much of Adam in Freya; a gesture, a blonde curl, the shape of her ears … and each of these pieces hurt to see, and yet they were a blessing too. Fern sighed and turned away. 'Sleep tight little one,' she whispered and switched off the light.

Fern fetched her pashmina shawl and then returned downstairs. Outside the moonlight had illuminated the garden in a gentle silver light that highlighted the silhouettes of the shrubs and trees without picking out the details. The effect was an eerie deepening of the shadows.

A rare sense of contentment crept into her as she sat at the table with Jacques, eating slices of cheese, punctuated with grapes plucked from the vine that wove its way around the terrace, and sips of the bitter strong coffee Jacques had made. Underneath their feet the flagstones were warm from the heat of the day. The busy sound of insects rose into the night amidst the regular slap of moths seeking the light of the lamp by the door.

'How old is the chapel?' she asked.

'It is the oldest part of this building. Romanesque I am told, dating from the 11th century. It was only after the revolution that a farmhouse was added, so this part of the building is much younger. Even so, it was derelict when we bought it.'

'You've done a lot of work to it then.'

'Yes,' said Jacques, his voice filled with bitterness. 'It was our project but we did not have a chance to finish it.' He poured himself a fresh glass of wine and took a gulp. 'It will not be completed now.'

Fern wanted to ask what had happened but she found herself unable to formulate the words. In the end all she could say was, 'I'm sorry.'

They sat without speaking for some time, each lost in their own thoughts.

'I should not regret the time we had together,' Jacques said, breaking the silence. 'We finished much of the house and turned the chapel into something quite special. Do you agree?'

'It's beautiful. There's a statue over the front door, of a woman. Who is she?'

'Saint Marie Magdalene. This chapel was dedicated to her.'

'Mary Magdalene?'

'Oui.'

'But she was a … '

'Prostitute!' Jacques practically spat out the words. 'Pah! That is what the church would have you think, though they have now had to admit this was not the case. Now Marie Magdalene is worshipped as a saint, alongside Mary, mother of Jesus.'

Jacques paused and sliced himself some more cheese. 'This is a mysterious region, filled with heretical schools. The original Christian tradition was a mystical one and it has suffered through many centuries of persecution by the Church which did its utmost to stamp out dissent.'

Seeing Fern's blank expression, Jacques asked. 'Do you not know of the Council of Nicaea, held in 325AD?'

'No,' said Fern, thinking how strange it was that her childhood had been structured around the Christian religion and yet she knew so little about it.

'At this council the church decided on what should be included in the bible and what should be excluded.' Jacques stood up abruptly and began pacing along the terrace. 'From that time on, every dissenter and nearly every dissenting text was hunted down and destroyed, but despite this the mystical tradition has survived. In this part of France heresy has always flourished.'

'The Cathars?' asked Fern.

'That is not who I was referring to but yes, the Cathars were labelled heretics by the Church and were massacred.'

'Why?'

'For reasons both political and spiritual. But in essence it was because they were scornful of the excesses of the Church and the way that it did not allow direct contact with God.'

'Were the Cathars following the original mystical tradition.'

Jacques nodded. 'Oui, in part. Some of the beliefs the Cathars held coincided with the gnostic tradition. He paused and shook his head sadly. 'But much has been lost.'

'What has this got to do with Mary Magdalene?' asked Fern.

'There is an alternative history that is believed by many in this region, that after the crucifixion, Marie Magdalene fled to the southern part of France. She is revered here for this and because she was the favoured disciple of Jesus and the inheritor of his teachings. Her gospel, along with others was discovered just over a hundred years ago in Egypt. Some of that gospel has been made available to the public and it reveals a different perspective on the teachings of Jesus as well as the role of Marie.'

Fern smiled, imagining the horror these ideas would have inspired in the members of the church her family attended. 'What was this different perspective?' she asked.

Jacques' expression softened. 'Love.'

'Is that it?' asked Fern, disappointed.

Jacques nodded. 'Oui, but mystical love directed through the heart. This is the essence of gnostic teachings.'

'But Christianity is all about love,' said Fern, remembering the interminable sermons she'd sat through as a child.

'It should be.' Jacques frowned. 'But the Christian path of love is broken'

Fern plucked another grape from the vine and chewed it slowly, savouring its sweet juice. 'I still don't understand what this has got to do with Mary Magdalene. Why is the chapel dedicated to her?'

'Not just one, but many churches are dedicated to Marie because she represents the true teachings which are based on Love and which do not deny the feminine. The Church has always been intent on diminishing the feminine aspect of God, which has created a great imbalance in society. But here it is still recognised and revered.'

Fern was intrigued. 'If the Church wanted to deny Mary, why did it make her a saint?

'There is an old saying – 'keep your friends close but your enemies closer'. The Church has brought St Marie into its arms to weaken her power. For most Christians she is only an associate of Jesus.' Jacques smiled mysteriously. 'Many centuries ago, those who followed the mystical tradition hid the knowledge she represents - often within the church itself. There are clues, but only to eyes that know, because the truth must be hidden from those who would deny it or make bad use of it. Jesus himself said, "do not cast pearls before swine."'

Fern opened her mouth to ask another question but her words were halted by a sudden crash, followed by a scream.

'Mon dieu!' said Jacques. 'What is that?'

'Freya,' said Fern. She ran inside and then up the stairs, alert for more screams but there were none and the silence frightened her even more. As she ran into Freya's room she almost tripped over the cat which stood in the doorway, back arched, eyes wide with fear and the hair on its spine standing on end.

Freya was illuminated only by the light of the moon that streamed through the window. She was half sitting up in the bed, her face ashen, her expression terrified and her eyes fixed on a spot in the corner of the room.

'It's okay sweetheart,' said Fern, 'I'm here. You're safe.' She wrapped her arms around Freya whose body was rigid with fear.

Freya looked at Fern without appearing to recognise her. She whimpered quietly and tried to back away from her mother. 'I want Mama,' she whispered, the words forced out as if they were coming from the depths of a nightmare.

'Mama's here sweetheart,' said Fern. She tightened her hold on Freya and kissed her on the forehead. 'It's okay, you're safe,' she said again then suddenly remembered that she'd spoken almost exactly the same words to Adam just before he died. They're just words, she thought, they mean nothing. In reality, Fern had no way of protecting Freya from wherever it was she went in these night terrors. All she could do was hold her daughter and wait.

Feeling something wet under her feet, Fern looked down and saw a dark puddle forming on the floor. Then she remembered the crash they'd heard and realised this was more than a night terror. She tore the sheet away from Freya, searching for the source of the blood, her panic making her gasp for breath as she rolled Freya over, trying to see the injury through the darkness.

'She's bleeding,' Fern shouted as Jacques appeared in the doorway.

Jacques switched on the overhead light and the room was suddenly bright. He scanned the room then strode in, grabbed Fern's arm and spun her towards him. 'Ecoutez-moi,' he said. 'Listen, Freya is safe. This is your blood. You have trodden on broken glass.'

But his words didn't penetrate Fern's mind. 'Something's trying to hurt Freya,' she said trying to push Jacques away. 'He warned me. He said I had to protect her but I wasn't there when she needed me.'

'Be quiet, you'll frighten Freya,' said Jacques. 'You must take control of yourself. It is only glass. See.' He turned her face towards the broken vase. 'The window was open and a gust of wind has knocked the glass vase off its perch. That is all. The noise frightened Freya and you have cut your foot on the broken glass. Do you understand?'

Fern nodded.

'Bon.' He glanced at Freya who was now back with them, her body trembling and tears welling in her eyes. 'Now you must comfort your daughter. She is in shock.'

Finally able to control her breathing once more, Fern sat with Freya in her arms while Jacques ministered to her foot, swept up the glass and brought them hot drinks. The chocolate brought colour back to Freya's face and life back into her eyes, but as Fern sipped her own chocolate, she realised it wouldn't be enough to dispel her lingering fear. Jacques had said it was just a gust of wind and Fern wanted to believe him, but she couldn't help feeling there was something wrong with this explanation.

Chapter Seventeen

There was no visible path down to the river so Fern followed the line of poplars on the edge of Jacques' property, picking her way carefully through the long grass in case there were snakes. It felt strange to be alone like this and more than once she caught herself about to point something out to Freya; a golden beetle, a butterfly with wings the colour of fresh grass … but Freya was not here. She was at school.

Fern didn't know what she'd expected. More drama perhaps, a ritual she and Freya would work through together. But with so little notice, the moment of separation had happened almost of its own accord and without a hitch. Fern hadn't needed to buy books or stationery or even pack a lunch for Freya because all this was provided by the school. There was no uniform either, so Freya had simply put on her favourite dress and her sunhat, then grabbed her little backpack, into which Fern insisted on packing a drink bottle, even though Jacques assured her drinks were provided.

They'd driven Freya down to the school in Jacques' car, a tiny citroen deux chevaux which delighted Freya with its backward opening doors and bouncy suspension and the way it leaned dangerously every time they rounded a corner. At the school Freya had given Fern a distracted peck on the cheek and run off eagerly to join the other children. There'd been no tears from Freya but Fern had swallowed down a lump in her throat as she watched her daughter disappear into the building and re-alised she'd forgotten to take a photograph.

Jacques had stayed in town for an appointment so Fern was free for the morning. Feeling she should mark the occasion in some way, she'd sat in a café, dipping a croissant into her coffee and trying to feel something other than bereft. Then she'd walked back up the hill to the house, made more coffee and paced the kitchen, not knowing what to do with herself. She'd considered working in the garden but in the end decided to visit the river instead.

As Fern approached the river's edge, she felt tears welling in her eyes, and she let them flow. Something was over and she could never return to it with Freya. Their relationship would change irrevocably and while that was necessary and good, it was also tempered with sadness.

The river was lined with willow trees, their bows grace-fully brushing the ground and swaying gently in the hot breath of a gentle breeze. It was running fast, leaping over boulders and forming white water in its eagerness. Fern wiped her eyes and stood for a moment under the welcome shade of a willow tree, listening to the water's joyful progress and wishing her own mood could mirror the mood of the river.

It was cooler here by the water so Fern decided to follow the river for a while before the hot trek back up the hill again. A few minutes later she found herself facing a fence that ran up the hill perpendicular to the river. She edged carefully around it, won-dering if she was now trespassing on someone else's property, but Jacques had said she was free to go where she pleased. On the opposite side of the river the woods sloped all the way down to the water but on this side, there was a cleared field planted with raspberries. Past that was another field planted with vines and then a small stone-fruit orchard where the leaves were just beginning to turn. Beyond the orchard lay the woods; still and dark, they looked forbidding yet alluring too and Fern found herself drawn to them.

When she stepped in amongst the trees the atmosphere changed immediately. It was as if Fern had stepped out of time, or at least into a timeless space. Like the forests in Tasmania, these were natural woods and diverse but the trees could not have been more different. Fern could identify chestnuts, oaks and acacias, pines, plane trees, a few walnuts and the occasional olive tree, gnarled and weighed down with slowly ripening fruit.

She walked carefully, weaving her way through the trees, trying to tread lightly but still she felt out of place, an intruder, creating an unwelcome disturbance in the atmosphere. Her bandaged foot was hurting a little so she stopped beside a giant walnut tree and picked a nut. Unable to break it with her hands, she found a stone and cracked it then stared mesmerized at the perfect brain-like shape within. Was it just a coincidence that the walnut Bach flower essence worked with the brain? It was a pattern breaker, helping people through life's transitions, encouraging them to accept change and loss. Why had she never thought of taking some? Why had she never thought to treat her own grief? After Adam died, Iris had thrown herself into doing, wearing herself out with hard work to keep her mind off things. Michael's grief had been intense but short lived and he'd never claimed it as a part of him. He missed Adam, she knew that, and there were moments when she caught a fleeting sadness in his eyes. But he was someone who allowed himself to feel everything to its fullest and for him life was too good to waste. Fern, on the other hand had held her grief close until it had become a precious part of her, and now she had no idea how to let it go.

Fern dug out the walnut and savoured the tasty flesh, then picked another, not minding that they were still a little unripe. A rustle in the undergrowth nearby startled her and she remembered Jacques' warnings about wild boars. There were bears and wolves in the mountains too, he'd said, but they didn't come down this far. Even so, Fern walked on quickly, her heart beating fast.

The last few nights had been sleepless ones, with Freya refusing to come into Fern's bed but not wanting to be left alone. Instead, Fern had to climb into Freya's single bed and curl up with her and the cat, who was determined to stay close despite Fern's bad-tempered nudges. Freya would fall asleep easily but stir and cry out each Fern tried to slip out of the bed. In the end, Fern would give up and lie there trying to work out what had really happened that night and why it was still affecting her daughter.

Jacques' version of events was the most attractive and the neatest but there was one major problem with it. The air that evening had been still, no gusts of wind, not even a gentle breeze. The most likely explanation was that Freya had walked in her sleep, picked up the vase and dropped it on the other side of the room but it didn't make sense that she was in bed when Fern found her and she hadn't cut herself on the broken vase. The cat could have knocked it over, but cats were careful creatures so that seemed unlikely. Each night the possibilities would go around and around in her head, but nothing eased her mind because underneath all the rational explanations, she sensed that the real reason was deeply irrational. She was trying to guard her daughter from something she didn't understand.

When Fern did slip into sleep, her dreams were peppered with a confusion of images: blood and broken glass, a searing fire, screams of guttural terror, none of which explained what was going on.

The sleepless nights, the confusing dreams and the worry had left Fern tired and now the building heat forced her to slow her pace. The trees thickened, making the edge of the river impenetrable in places, and Fern soon lost sight of it. Without a visible path, she had to pick her way through the undergrowth and clamber over fallen logs, slowing her pace even further.

As she walked, Fern tried to piece together everything that had happened since she and Freya had moved into Jacques' house. First there'd been her discomfort in the chapel, then Freya's episode with the tempest stone and its disappearance. And the figure in the window of course; the broken vase had wiped it from Fern's mind and she'd forgotten to ask Jacques about it. While there was probably a rational explanation for each of these things, together they added up to something. But perhaps Ahmed's warning about keeping Freya safe was making her construct mysteries that simply weren't there.

In the corner of her eye, Fern caught a flash of movement and turned just in time to see a snake appearing from under a fallen log. She stopped and watched it, the forest uncannily silent around her, the silence broken only by the thundering of her racing heart. The snake stopped too then lifted its head and tested the atmosphere with its tongue as if it knew she was there and was trying to understand if she was a threat. And so they waited, Fern and the snake, each sensing the other, until finally the snake lowered its head and slithered away, disappearing into the undergrowth.

Fern breathed a sigh of relief and moved forward again, more cautiously this time, watching out for more snakes and wondering if they were as poisonous here as they were in Tasmania. While her own tension had eased a little, she could still feel the tension in the atmosphere around her. It felt as if something were poised to happen. Around her the density of the air seemed to shift, the atmosphere rippling so that nothing seemed quite real. Fern felt dizzy and realised she was probably dehydrated. She'd not had anything to drink aside from those early morning coffees.

Up ahead the trees were thinning and soon Fern stepped into a large clearing. She stopped and stared at the old cottage nestled into the far side of the clearing. Directly in front of Fern was an array of fruit and nut trees, some gnarled and ancient, others young and establishing their roots, none of them neatly pruned like the trees she'd seen in other properties. At a quick glance, she identified almond trees and olives, a walnut, a hazelnut and a variety of stone fruit trees. Hens were wandering freely amongst them, pecking in the dirt.

Deciding she would ask for a drink of water at the cottage, Fern stepped into the orchard and wound her way through the trees, the hens scattering before her. She passed an abundant vegetable patch, protected by a rough wooden fence. Lettuce was growing there, along with rocket and spinach too, which had mostly gone to seed. The tomato bushes were drooping under the weight of the late fruit. There were courgettes too and aubergines, broccoli, cauliflower and pumpkins. Amongst the vegetables stood tall sunflowers, their majestic yellow petals already faded and falling and their large heads beginning to bend low with weariness as their seeds grew heavier. Despite the hot day, these sunflowers were proof that the season was changing. Looking at them, Fern felt the first sensations of the precious melancholia autumn always brought, as nature shifted into old age and then death, before starting the cycle once more with the birth of spring.

As Fern approached the cottage, her dizziness returned, stronger than ever and she had to reach out a hand to steady herself. To her surprise the stone wall was icy cold. She pulled her hand away and stood for a moment waiting for the dizziness to pass. The house looked smaller than it had at first sight, a tiny cottage, probably only one or two rooms. It was well maintained but old fashioned, its rough stone walls daubed with mortar, its roof lined with clay tiles. A closer look revealed that even though it was a hot day, smoke was coming from the chimney and there were no electric wires attached to its roof or outer walls, at least not any that Fern could see. Intrigued, Fern stepped closer to the door which was slightly ajar. As she did so, the sun slipped behind a cloud taking with it the light and warmth from the clearing. She shivered and folded her arms across her chest trying to keep warm but even so there were goose bumps rising on her skin. The thirst she'd felt moments earlier had disappeared so now it was only curiousity that made her peer through the crack in the door.

'Entrez.'

It was the deep voice of a woman, the accent broader than she was used to but the meaning clear. Fern pushed open the door. 'I'm sorry,' she said. 'I was just passing and wondered who lived here.' By now the cold had encompassed her completely and she was shivering in her shorts and T-shirt.

'Come and warm yourself by the fire.'

At the voice's bidding, Fern stepped into the room. The open fire had a blackened metal pot hanging above it and in front of it were two chairs. One was empty and in the other sat an elderly white-haired woman, wearing a long skirt, patched in places but clean, and a shawl wrapped tightly around her shoulders.

The woman stared at Fern, her gaze sharp. 'I recognise you,' she said at last with a hint of satisfaction.

'Really?' asked Fern, surprised. 'I don't think we've met before,' she added.

The woman smiled then, revealing a gap where a front tooth was missing. 'No, not in the flesh,' she said. 'But you are familiar to me.' She gestured to Fern. 'Sit,' she said. 'The night is cold and there is little time.'

Fern sat down in the chair and savoured the warmth of the fire on her bare skin. 'Who are you?' she asked when it was clear the woman was not going to introduce herself.

'My name is Petrona.'

The pot over the fire was emitting the rich smell of a winter stew and Fern found her mouth watering.

As if reading her mind, Petrona asked, 'Would you like to eat?'

'No,' said Fern abruptly, suddenly uneasy. 'Thank you,' she added politely. 'I'm not hungry.'

The old woman nodded. 'So be it.' She leaned back in her chair and studied Fern again, apparently in no hurry even though a moment ago she'd said there was little time.

The silence deepened, broken only by the crackle of the fire and the howl of the wind outside. Fern shivered again. The fire was raging but most of the heat was escaping up the chimney while the freezing wind was finding its way in through the wooden shutters. Looking more closely she realised there was no glass in the windows. This was an unusual house.

Petrona's penetrating gaze was making Fern uncomfortable. Unable to meet the old woman's eyes, she inspected the room. A small table was set in one corner and near that a bench with some shelves above it. The shelves were packed with clay jars, an assortment of sizes. On the table sat a giant pestle and mortar for pounding and a straw basket filled with rosemary, its scent blending with the sweetness of the wood smoke and the rich smell of the stew bubbling over the fire.

Fern's bewilderment grew, yet she also felt strangely calm, taking everything in as she might in a dream, accepting the lack of logic, the fact that outside it was hot and sunny but inside it was a winter's night.

'Where am I?' she asked, breaking the long silence. 'Why is it winter?'

Petrona smiled. 'You have courage. Many would not be open enough to step through like this and if they did so without intention their fear would turn the experience into a nightmare.'

A ginger cat rubbed itself against Fern's calves, and she reached down to stroke its soft fur. It accepted her gesture then flicking its tail, turned haughtily away.

'You haven't answered my question,' said Fern.

'You are where you were but you have stepped through into another time. It happens. Time does not run in a straight line as we are taught, instead all times run concurrently.'

Fern nodded. She didn't understand what the old woman meant but a part of her sensed its truth. 'Why am I here?' she asked.

Petrona shrugged. 'Perhaps there is something you need to learn,' she said. 'But it is for you to understand the purpose of your encounter.'

'How do you know me?'

'Again, that is for you to discover.' She paused, as the cat leaped onto her lap, then grimaced as it massaged her legs with its claws before settling down, its green eyes fixed on Fern.

'You are an old soul, made heavy by your many lives,' said Petrona, turning her attention back to Fern. 'I can see that you are struggling to free yourself from this heaviness.

'You must remember that everything you need is within you. There are lives in which damage was inflicted upon you and others in which you have done great damage. You must befriend the darkness and call it your own. Only then will you be able to reclaim your power to live well.'

She paused and stared into the fire, one hand absently stroking the cat. 'You have also had many good lives,' she said, turning back to Fern. 'Some of them great. You have learned much and understood more. You have found wisdom and strength and it will soon be time to reclaim this knowledge and the skills you have learned. But first you must release yourself from the heaviness of a past life you carry and from unnecessary obligations to the negative imprints of your ancestors.'

'How do I do … ?' But as Fern spoke the air seemed to ripple once again and the dizziness grew as the scene gradually faded before her. First the walls disappeared, then the fire, then the figure of the woman. The last thing Fern could see were two sets of eyes boring into hers, one pair green, the other almost black. As the chair beneath her disappeared, Fern tumbled to the floor, completely disoriented.

Chapter Eighteen

The dim flickering firelight had been replaced by bright day-light and the bitter cold by a searing pervasive heat, but the cold had penetrated so deeply into Fern that she was still shivering and the cool tiles underneath her weren't helping. There was shock too, making her teeth chatter and her hands shake. The strange calm she'd felt when speaking to the old woman had fled, replaced by a sense of panic as she tried to understand where she'd been and perhaps more importantly, where she was now.

It was beginning to dawn on Fern that she was lying on the floor inside someone's house and that this wasn't a great place to be discovered. With an effort, she controlled her chattering teeth then forced herself into a sitting position and rubbed the painful spot on her back where she'd landed on the tiles. She was clearly in a kitchen, and a lovely one, but she'd never seen it before. This room was larger than the old woman's and quite different in style and atmosphere. To one side was a rough wooden table with six mismatching chairs each bearing a different brightly coloured cushion. To the other side was a row of benches and cupboards, made from wood so fresh she could still smell its sweet odour. On one bench was a vase stuffed with lavender and rosemary, the scent permeating the air and reminding Fern of that other room, with the old woman rocking on her chair in front of the fire, the cat's green eyes staring into her unblinking.

'Bonjour?'

Startled, Fern looked up and saw a woman standing over her holding a bulging straw shopping basket in each arm. To Fern's relief the expression on the woman's face was more alarmed than angry. Embarrassed, Fern tried to get up but her legs were trembling too much to hold her.

Puis-je vous aider? asked the woman with a hint of concern.

Puis-je vous aider? Fern desperately ran the words over and over in her mind but couldn't make sense of them.

When Fern didn't respond, the woman reverted to English. 'Can I help you?' she asked with a strong American accent.

'I'm sorry … I don't know what I'm doing here,' said Fern who had no idea how she could even begin to explain any of this.

The woman studied Fern for a moment, decided she didn't look dangerous and put her heavy shopping bags down. 'It's not every day I find someone sitting on the floor of my kitchen. Are you okay? You look like you've seen a ghost.'

'I'm fine,' said Fern. 'Just a bit shaky.'

'You're shivering. That's not right, it's thirty-four degrees out there. Perhaps you've got heat stroke.' She poured a glass of water and handed it to Fern who gulped it down gratefully.

'I'm Amber, by the way. What's yours?'

'Fern. It's nice to meet you,' she held out her hand and then laughed, suddenly aware of the absurdity of the situation. 'I'm staying in a house upriver.'

Amber gazed at Fern for a long moment then smiled, her face transforming in an instant as she took Fern's hand. 'So you're our *sort of* neighbor.'

Fern made another effort to sit up and this time found her legs had recovered some of their strength. She stood awkwardly, leaning for support on the kitchen table.

'Feeling better?' asked Amber. 'The heat can leave you feeling pretty dizzy if you're not used to it. Why don't you sit down? On a chair this time,' she added.

Gratefully, Fern sat on one of the dining chairs, then made a faltering attempt to tell Amber something of what happened, without mentioning the old woman.

'It sounds like you fainted,' said Amber. 'Not surprising if you were out walking in this heat.' She turned to the shopping. 'I'd better get this stuff into the fridge before it goes off.'

Fern watched Amber unpack the shopping. She had an imposing presence; tall, strong, sturdily built but graceful too, with long limbs and a swan-like neck. She was beautiful, but not in any traditional sense. Her features were exaggerated: a strong jaw, large nose, penetrating blue eyes and long fair hair held away from her face in a pony-tail. Fern guessed Amber was a little older than her, maybe in her late twenties or early thirties.

'I got some lovely goats' cheese from the market this morning,' said Amber. 'It's best fried so the middle bit gets all runny. And I made a raspberry sauce the other day. That will go perfectly, along with a green salad.' She laughed. 'Hell, anyone would think I was French, talking about food like that.'

Fern laughed and stood up. She had no idea what the time was but her stomach was rumbling so it must be lunch-time. 'Talking of food, I'd better let you get your lunch.'

Amber eyed Fern for a moment. 'You still don't look great. Why don't you stay and eat with me?'

'I've already imposed on you more than enough.'

'Don't be silly. There's plenty of food and it's nice to have someone to talk to. Kia's away for a few days and the solitude gets to me after a while.'

'Well, if you're sure.'

'Course I am.' Amber leapt up and opened the fridge door. 'We can have that cheese I was telling you about.' She unwrapped the cheese and sliced it carefully. 'Mmmm, that's glorious.'

'Can I help?' asked Fern.

'If you like. I picked some salad leaves and flowers this morning. You could put them in a bowl with some of the basil,' she added, pointing at the cut basil sitting in water in a glass jar on the bench. 'Bowls are in there,' she said, gesturing towards one of the cupboards.

Amber picked up a frying pan from the bench, poured in some olive oil and put it on the stove to heat. Then she paused and sniffed. 'Smell that?

'Rosemary,' said Fern, pointing at the vase on the bench.

'Yes, but much stronger, as if it's been pummeled into a paste, and there's wood smoke too.' She shook her head. 'Sometimes I think this place is haunted. Either that, or I'm losing my marbles.'

'Haunted?' asked Fern, suddenly alert.

Amber laughed. 'Well, not really. I've never seen any ghostly figures, things don't move around by themselves and there aren't any footsteps on the stairs. It's just the smells. Kai notices them too, though he always thinks it's the garden. But you know, garden smells aren't the same, they're pungent but not overpowering. Sometimes there's a smell in here as if someone's been boiling up potions or making essential oils. It's only ever in this room but that would make sense because it's the original part of the house.'

Amber sliced the cheese and put it in the pan, where it sizzled in the oil, sending out new aromas into the kitchen. 'I never get spooked though, even when Kia's away. It's as if the spirits want us to be here.' She smiled. 'I like to think the house approves of us.'

'Do you know much about the history of this place?' asked Fern.

'A bit. We bought it a few years ago for next to nothing. But it needs masses of work. The kitchen's great. That's the first thing we did. But the bathroom's still pretty basic as are the rest of the rooms. There's been a house here forever but not all of it was built at the same time.'

As she tossed the salad leaves, Fern looked around the kitchen trying to see if there was anything that pointed to it being the same as the strange room she'd sat in with Petrona. The renovations had been carried out tastefully, preserving the sense of history while making it lighter and bigger, with floor-to-ceiling glass doors that looked out over the garden and the river beyond. The wooden furniture was roughly designed, not finely cut or highly polished, and it suited the house well. The only things that seemed familiar were the fireplace, which now held a giant wood-burning stove, and the shelves on one wall that were filled with jars, preserves, jams, chutneys and cordials.

'The builders said that was an original feature,' said Amber, noticing Fern's interest in the shelves. 'They were cut into the wall when it was built, not added later. We decided to leave it. Most of our preserves go in the pantry over there so this is really only for display,' she added. 'But it looks pretty.'

'How old is the original part of the house?' Fern asked.

Amber shrugged. 'Not sure but it's pretty old. The locals say it was in the same family for centuries. About fifteen years ago it passed out of the family and since then there's been a few owners. None of them lasted long. No one's saying anything but I think the spirits drove them out.'

Amber flipped the cheese over in the pan, then spooned the raspberry sauce into a bowl and placed it on the table next to the salad Fern had made and a fresh baguette. 'Before we bought it the locals told us some of the stories. They said it was a witches' coven and strange things happened here. I guess they were trying to see how we'd react.'

'A witches' coven sounds unlikely,' said Fern.

'Yeah, though there's usually an element of truth in these stories. Someone else mentioned that a wise woman had always lived here. It couldn't be the same one over all that time so I guess the role and the house was handed on to a daughter or an apprentice. Wise women … witches, there's not such a big difference.'

'Do you know the name of the family who owned it?'

Amber paused in the middle of scooping out the fried cheese. 'Can't remember, though I think I've got it written down somewhere. 'Here, can you grab those plates and the cutlery?'

When the food was on the table, Amber took a bottle of white wine from the fridge. 'Yeah, I know, it's still early but let's do it the French way.' She poured them both a glass of wine and raised her glass in a toast. 'To unexpected meetings on kitchen floors.'

Fern smiled and clinked glasses with Amber then took a cautious sip. It was cold and fresh, with a strong bouquet. 'Wow. That's really unusual.'

'Lovely isn't it,' said Amber. 'Some friends of ours have got a vineyard in the next valley. They've only been there a few years but they're already getting a name for themselves. So you'd better make the most of it, I won't be able to afford it for much longer!'

'How long have you been here?'

'Full time, only two years but we bought this place six years ago. It took us four years to move in. This house is like a money vacuum cleaner, sucking up everything we earn. We had to base ourselves back in Seattle with proper jobs just to make it habitable. Now we're eking out a living and doing the renovations ourselves. At least we don't have to wash in the river anymore, though there's still a way to go on the bathroom. Here try this,' she said placing a slice of goat's cheese on Fern's plate.

As Fern cut into it the warm insides spilled onto the plate.

'Whoops, might have overdone the heat on that,' said Amber laughing.

'No, it's lovely,' said Fern. The white cheese was fragrant and strongly flavoured which perfectly balanced the raspberry sauce. 'Great sauce too,' she said.

Amber nodded. 'I'm proud of that sauce. It's from our first ever batch of raspberries.'

Fern took a forkful of the green salad, savouring the sweet sharpness of the balsamic vinegar, the earthy dark olive oil and the pungent flavor of fresh basil leaves. 'Did you grow all this too?' she asked.

Amber nodded. 'Well only the salad leaves and basil. We've got some olives but we're a bit high here to get a great crop so we did a swap with some friends further down the hill who are farming olives; gave them a few cases of stone fruit in exchange for a few litres of oil.

Fern polished off the last of the cheese and spooned more salad onto her plate. 'Are you pretty much self-sufficient then?'

'Nowhere near, but there's a network of people here who live off the gift system and we've plugged into that. What we've got too much of we swap for what we need. It's great and means we don't have to spend much money.' She looked around with a mock expression of despair. 'Except on this bloody house of course!'

Fern felt a stab of envy when she remembered the life she and Adam had been building together. All the plans they'd made for the future. Then one stupid act of violence and it was all gone.

'So where are you staying?' asked Amber.

'With Jacques Leveque.'

Amber raised an eyebrow. 'Him! Bloody grumpy old man. Always shouting at me when I go out picking on his land.'

Fern laughed. 'That would drive Jacques mad.'

'I just wave and carry on regardless. There's a traditional way here. People collect what they need, gathering up the wild plants when the season's right, and no one's allowed to stop them.'

'In Australia you'd get shot. Private property means keep off.'

'Same in America,' said Amber. 'I prefer it the French way.' She stood up and put the kettle on. 'Time for a coffee. One glass of wine and I'm knocked out.'

Fern stood up too and picked up the plates. 'I'll help you with these then I'd better get going. You've probably got things to do.'

'Not at this time of the day, I don't. It's way too hot out there to do any harvesting. I'll do it later and then make my deliveries early evening. It's the only way. Though it's officially autumn now so the heat has got to give soon.'

'Where do you deliver?' asked Fern.

'We've got a few local restaurants that take our produce. It's organic and that's getting more popular down here. We sometimes have a stand at the market but I don't like doing it by myself. Kia's French is better than mine!' She held up the coffee jug. 'I'm better at coffee though. Want one?'

Fern laughed, 'I'd love a coffee.' She rinsed the plates while Amber set the coffee on the stove. It felt so natural being here. There was a sense of ease between them that Fern hadn't felt with anyone for a long time.

'You know,' said Amber. 'I feel as if we've known each other for ever.'

'Me too,' said Fern, surprised to hear her own thoughts voiced out loud.

Amber poured the coffee then offered Fern a square of dark chocolate. 'My favourite sort. It's got chilli in it.' She popped a square into her mouth. 'So how do you know Jacques?'

Fern hesitated. Once again she found herself with a story to tell that would sound strange to most people's ears. 'He's teaching me,' she said cautiously, not knowing how else to put it.

Amber raised an eyebrow. 'What? How to be a grumpy old man?'

Fern laughed. 'No. How to be past life therapist.'

Amber looked truly shocked. 'Really? Is that what he does? I don't believe it.'

'He's retired now but he was pretty famous in his time.'

'God, that's so interesting. Wow. So why past life therapy?'

Fern hesitated. She couldn't exactly tell Amber that she was doing it to keep her daughter safe. 'I'm trained as a herbalist,' she said. 'And a homeopath. Well, I'm qualified in one and nearly in the other.'

'So how does past life therapy relate to being a herbalist or homeopath?'

'It doesn't really, though I'm beginning to see how all the healing modalities fit together, feeding each other. Past life therapy's all about understanding the patterns we're stuck in - mental, emotional, and even physical sometimes. So is homeopathy. I need to be able to respond to each patient's needs on every level and that means drawing on elements of different therapies.' She paused and then laughed. 'Maybe I'm just greedy. I want to collect them all.'

Amber shook her head. 'No, that makes sense to me.' She drained her coffee. 'What did Jacques see in you? I've heard he doesn't let anyone visit. He's been a recluse ever since his wife died.'

'Well, he did say no but then changed his mind. It wasn't me he fell for in the end. It was my daughter.' At the mention of Freya, Fern suddenly realised she'd lost track of time. She leapt up, panicking. 'What time is it? I have to collect Freya from school.'

'Don't panic,' said Amber. 'It's still early and I was planning to drive you home anyway. You can't walk back in this heat, not after fainting like that. We'll just make a detour to the school.'

Chapter Nineteen

Fern grabbed the hand rail and pulled herself up into the passenger seat of Amber's landrover defender.

'It's old,' said Amber, 'but it's sturdy and just keeps going. Touch wood,' she added before releasing the handbrake and chugging up the drive.

They arrived just as the children were pouring into the school yard. Almost immediately Fern spotted Freya holding the hand of a small boy with long hair and scruffy trousers. She waved and Freya ran towards her, tugging him along.

'This is Henri,' said Freya. 'He's mon ami.'

'Bonjour Henri,' said Fern and held out her hand

The boy smiled shyly then ran away, shouting goodbye to Freya over his shoulder.

'Henri likes Beattie too, though the others say she isn't real.' She paused and looked at Amber curiously. 'Who are you?'

'This is Amber,' said Fern. 'She's our sort-of neighbour.'

'Hey Freya. How'd you enjoy your first day at school?'

Freya smiled. 'It was great. Are you American?'

Amber leaned down close. 'Only a little bit. My blood is French.'

Freya's eyes widened. 'What's my blood, Mama?'

'Oh you're pure Tasmanian!' said Fern.

Freya smiled. 'Like Unci Micki.'

'Well then, we'd better get home.' Fern turned towards Amber. 'Thanks so much for the lift.'

'No problem. I'll give you a lift up the hill if you like.'

Freya took one look at the battered old landrover and nodded eagerly. Fern gave her a leg up and she sat in the middle chatting about school as they slowly chugged up the hill.

As Amber pulled up outside the house, Jacques appeared in the window, looking indignant and Fern remembered suddenly that there'd been a teaching session planned for after lunch.

'Oh God,' she said. 'I'm in the merde!'

Amber laughed and blew Jacques a kiss. Scowling he turned away from the window.

'Come and visit again,' said Amber as Fern lifted Freya out of the van. It's much quicker by road.

When they stepped inside the house the air was filled with the smell of burning. They found Jacques in the kitchen banging dishes.

'Pew!' said Freya. 'It stinks.'

'Did you burn something?' asked Fern.

Jacques paused and glared at her. 'The tart,' he said, shortly. 'And now I must make another.'

'It's okay, we can just have some fruit,' said Fern.

'It is not okay.' He began opening and closing drawers. 'You have moved everything and now I can find nothing.'

'What are you looking for?'

'That is not the point.'

'I'm late and I'm really sorry but … '

'Sorry is not acceptable,' said Jacques.

'I know. It was just … '

Once again Jacques cut Fern's explanation off in mid-sentence. 'I am teaching you against my will and you do not turn up to my teaching.'

Feeling her mood sinking, Fern took a deep breath. 'Against your will? You were the one who came and found us. You asked us to come.'

Jacques waved away Fern's protest. 'Instead of coming to class you disappear and then return with this American hippie woman who sneaks onto my land and takes the wild mushrooms, the asparagus, everything… '

'Isn't that the tradition here, Jacques?'

'She is not part of that tradition. '

'Why not?'

Jacques shrugged impatiently. 'Amber is not the point of this conversation. It is you I am … ' he paused, as if looking for the right word.

'Telling off,' said Fern, finishing Jacques' sentence. 'I've already apologized. What more do you want?'

'Mean it.'

'I did mean it,' said Fern, suddenly furious. 'You're impossible. I know you're still grieving over your wife's death but that's no excuse to take it out on everyone else.'

Jacques reacted as if he'd been slapped. 'How could you possibly understand?' he said.

'I lost my partner,' said Fern quietly.

It was as if Jacques hadn't heard. 'Madeleine was the other part of my soul.'

'And Adam was my soul mate,' said Fern.

'You were together for how long?' asked Jacques.

'Four years. What are you insinuating?'

'Madeleine and I were together for fifty-three years.'

'For fuck's sake, this isn't a competition.'

'Casse-toi,' shouted Jacques, gesturing at the door.

'Don't worry, I'm going,' shouted Fern. She stormed passed Freya, who stood frozen at the door, then ran up the stairs and into her bedroom where she pulled the case from under the bed and started hurling clothes into it.

A few minutes later, Freya tugged on Fern's dress to get her attention. 'Why were you shouting Mama?'

Fern paused in her packing for a moment. 'Because Jacques is a selfish stubborn old man.'

'Why are you packing everything up?'

'We're leaving.'

'But my school?'

'You can go to school somewhere else.'

'I want to go here,' Freya said, her bottom lip trembling.

'I'm sorry Freya but Jacques doesn't want us to stay any longer. We'll go back to Tassie and see Uncle Micky and Granny Iris. How does that sound?'

Tears welled up in Freya's eyes and the confusion was evident in her face as her loyalties tugged her in opposite directions. Seeing this, some of the blind fury left Fern and she softened a little. 'I'm sorry sweetheart but Jacques doesn't want us to stay.'

Fern gave her a hug and wiped away her tears. 'Why don't you go and start packing your things for me,' she said.

'No, I'm not going.' Freya shouted. She ran out of the room then paused at the door and shouted back at Fern. 'It's your fault. You made Jacques angry.'

Fern sighed and turned back to her packing. It seemed she could please no one. As she pulled the last of her clothes from the drawers there was a clunk and something landed on the floor at her feet. She bent over to retrieve it and with a shock realised it was the wooden owl that Michael had carved for her years ago. She hadn't packed it. She hadn't even seen it for a long time. Perhaps Michael had slipped it into her case or it had found its way in of its own accord, caught up in something else. For a moment she held the owl in the palm of her hand where it fitted snuggly then she tucked it into the side pocket of her bag just as Jacques appeared in the doorway.

'May I come in?' he asked

'It's your house,' said Fern, not looking at him.

'But you are my guest so I must ask permission.'

'I am no longer your guest so there's no need,' said Fern. Abruptly she tossed the rest of her clothes into the case and began zipping it up. Immediately the zip stuck and no matter how much Fern tugged, she couldn't shift it. 'Bloody thing,' she said, giving it another tug.

Jacques stepped into the room. 'Let me,' he said.

'I don't need your help,' said Fern.

'But I need yours. I have come to ask you to stay.'

Startled, Fern stopped her struggle with the zip and turned to Jacques, who looked distinctly uncomfortable.

'Sorry is not a word that comes easily to me,' he said. 'But I must ask your forgiveness. I see that I have become protective of my love for Maddy and now I have denigrated your love for your partner. I am sorry.'

Fern's fury dissipated immediately. She let go of the zip and the suitcase sprang open once again, tipping out some of its contents.

'When Maddy died, my life lost all of its colour,' said Jacques, his voice cracking with grief. 'I don't know how to live without her. There seems no point. Everywhere I look, she's there and yet she is not there.' He attempted a smile but it looked more like a grimace. 'And you are right; I have turned into bad tempered old man.'

Fern's anger subsided. 'Do you remember the message Freya gave you on that first day?' asked Fern. 'Laisse-moi partir, mon amour. I didn't know what it meant but now I understand.' She hesitated, uncertain whether it was safe to go on. 'She wants you to let her go.'

'Oui,' said Jacques, his eyes filling with tears. 'But I don't know how to do it.' He paused as if considering his next words. 'But I am aware that you and Freya are helping me. Will you stay?'

Freya's voice rose from the garden below as she talked to Beattie, bringing with it the spicy sweet scent of over-ripe figs. Freya had been fond of Jacques right from the start and now as Fern looked at him standing awkwardly there, waiting for her response, she realised that she'd also begun to care for this grumpy old man. Half expecting to be slapped away, she reached out tentatively and put her arms around Jacques. His body stiffened momentarily and then relaxed a little.

'We'll stay,' she said.

Chapter Twenty

The season was turning faster now, the leaves flashing gold on the poplars bending in the breeze. The extended heat wave had suddenly passed and now there was a slight chill in the mornings, not enough yet to warrant a jumper, just a hint of something different, a melancholy that suited Fern's mood. Today she was cutting back bushes, searching for a shape to each one. The gardening was doing her good, grounding her and she could feel herself getting stronger. For a few days there'd been no more strange events, nothing out of the ordinary to alarm any of them. It was as if the house had accepted the newcomers but despite this, Fern wondered if this peaceful time was merely a hiatus before this something, whatever it was, revealed itself.

A couple of days earlier, Fern had remembered to ask Jacques if he'd been in her room the day she'd seen the figure in her bedroom window.

'Mais non,' he'd said, puzzled. 'Why would I go in there?'

'Then who could it have been?' she'd asked.

'I do not know, perhaps it was the light playing tricks.' But the expression on Jacques' face said otherwise.

'Is this house haunted?' Fern had asked.

Instead of assuring Fern that it wasn't, Jacques' answer had been enigmatic. 'Every house is haunted,' he'd said. Then realising this was not enough for Fern, he'd backtracked. 'Sometimes

I wonder if there is something but it is only ever in the background, just a sense.'

Jacques' reticence and his obvious discomfort with the subject reminded Fern of something he'd said about his house in the restaurant that first evening. *It is not a place one should be in alone.*

Fern battled with a stem too thick to snip, then tried a different tactic, sawing at it with her cutters until finally it gave way and the bush settled into a new, neater shape. She'd always preferred planting to cutting back, but pruning was needed too, bringing with it the possibility of renewal.

Despite the cooler air, the sun's rays were still fierce. Fern peeled off a glove and wiped a dribble of perspiration from her face then sat down on the edge of one of the garden beds, too tired to persevere. It was Friday and they'd almost made it through Freya's first week of school. The second day, Fern had walked down to meet her and they'd gone to a café then walked back up the hill but Freya had been so tired that since then Fern and Jacques had driven down to collect her.

Freya still loved going off to school in the mornings but every afternoon came home exhausted and overwrought. At home she'd run into the kitchen demanding to be fed, then she would either play out in the garden while Fern weeded or sit inside watching a movie. She didn't seem to mind that the films were in French but she flatly refused to watch them in the chapel even though the large screen television was in there. Instead, Jacques brought out his laptop and set her up in the kitchen, where she would sit in the big armchair, then inevitably drop off to sleep before waking in a bad mood, too tired to eat her dinner. Then would come the bedtime battle and finally a story and a moment of peace together before Freya slipped into sleep too tired even for a night terror.

It was a relief for Fern, that Freya was sleeping peacefully, but her own dreams had begun to plague her. Each night she found herself back in the monk's cell, replaying the same scene over and over. It was as if she'd become a ghost from the future, an invisible visitation. But last night something had changed. She'd been watching the monk rocking back and forth on his knees, mumbling an incantation, when suddenly he'd turned his head and looked right at Fern, a puzzled expression on his face. Instinctively she'd shrunk back, trying to blend into the shadows but her eyes had met his and she'd glimpsed a ferocious anger in them. It had been enough to scare Fern out of her dream and into a sleepless night of tossing and turning as she tried unsuccessfully to erase the man from her thoughts.

The dreams were the only shadow in what had been a good week. She and Freya and Jacques were finding ways of accommodating each other and developing a routine that suited each of them. Fern had begun to enjoy her time alone each day. She would visit the early morning market, read books on past life therapy or work in the garden before her session with Jacques. Then they would eat something simple together, before going their separate ways until it was time to pick up Freya.

In the distance the town church bell rang ten times. Fern stood up and stretched, then went inside to find Jacques for her class. She was still at the introductory stage, Jacques said, insisting she needed a grounding in the different philosophical and psychological approaches to past life therapy. He was also explaining the distinctions between the mental, physical and emotional effects of past lives on the present, giving her examples to compare so she could begin to understand how the symptoms manifested in each level.

Fern was beginning to find the theory fascinating but she was still uncomfortable with the practical exercises Jacques insisted on. Each time he would regress Fern to a past life, so she could experience the strange sensation of being someone else, feeling the other person's feelings, their pain and their joy but still being aware of herself in the present. So far nothing particularly shocking had happened in her sessions. She'd identified a life where she'd been a seamstress in Germany and another one in which she had been a mother of four, only to die giving birth to her fifth child. That had been an uncomfortable regression but she'd felt a lightness afterwards. Despite that, Jacques said Fern's defences were still up and he was getting frustrated with their slow progress.

Fern sat down in the chair opposite and studied Jacques as he worked on his laptop. Today he looked more than ever like a bird, with his narrow, elongated face and his beaklike nose.

'Okay,' he said eventually. 'We will try something different today. It seems to me that there is something you are avoiding. Perhaps you are not telling me or perhaps you do not even know it yourself. So today I will take you through what is sometimes called journey work, where we will find what is lurking inside.'

'I don't think there's anything lurking inside me,' said Fern, alarmed.

Jacques smiled. 'Okay then, we will find what is hidden. The shadow, if you like – it is something that is within each of us, and within it lies the key to balance.'

Fern nodded, already familiar with Jung's notion of the shadow.

'If we clear those elements of the past that are inhibiting your ability to live well then you will eventually learn to live through action rather than reaction. You will become an integrated person.'

Jacques stood up and Fern noted an expression of sadness pass across his face as he turned to look through the window. 'This is easier said than done,' he continued. 'Most of us are not even aware that there is a problem but for those who are willing to work, it is a long road and one in which there is no room for complacency or self-congratulations because there are many traps along the way. Each time you release something that is blocking you, an emotional wound or conditioned thinking, there comes a sense of exuberance and peace, followed by an empty space that must be filled with a new way of living. Then of course there are more blocks that only become visible when enough has been cleared around them. It is like being trapped in a cave and digging your way out. Sometimes there will be a hint of air, and sometimes a beam of light but to get there we must work hard and suffer many scrapes.'

Jacques turned back to Fern. 'It is not an easy road but I would like to think that it is a worthwhile one.' He sat down in a chair in front of Fern and looked at her intently. 'Today, I feel will not be easy for you. But that is the way of it.'

Feeling a wave of fear but also a resolute sense of determination, Fern shrugged. 'C'est la vie,' she said.

'C'est la vie,' repeated Jacques, smiling. 'Now we will begin. I want you to close your eyes and then direct your attention to a point of tension in your body. It might be a place that you are holding tight or a pain that is persistent.'

Fern dutifully closed her eyes and found her attention directed towards her upper back where the muscles felt as if they were raw and burning. This was a pain she had become so used to that she rarely noticed it now. An osteopath had once told her that each person stores their tension in a certain place in their body and her place was the upper back. He'd given her exercises to help her relax the muscles there but she hardly ever remembered to do them.

'You have found something?' asked Jacques.

Fern nodded.

'Good. Now I want you to direct your attention into the pain, allowing yourself to settle deeper and deeper into it until you pass through the pain and into its source.'

Fern concentrated, and as she did so, the pain became a red and angry spot before her closed eyelids.

'What does it feel like?' asked Jacques.

'Angry,' said Fern. 'And kind of thick, like treacle but not sweet.'

'Keep focused on the anger,' said Jaques. 'Try to go through the feeling.'

Against her instincts, Fern tried to penetrate the anger. She felt herself sinking into and through it and suddenly found herself inside the dank cold space of her recurring dream. But this time something had changed. She was no longer a visitation, instead she was inside the man's mind and body, bombarded by a flurry of emotions and overwhelmed by an image of a woman pervading her senses. The stone floor was icy cold beneath her knees and she shivered underneath the scratchy robe as she rocked back and forth reciting a prayer.

'What have you found?' asked Jacques.

Fern opened her mouth to speak but the image of the woman filled the man's mind, blotting out everything else as he impatiently discarded his robe, picked up a knotted rope and began whipping his back, lashing viciously at his skin and tearing its surface, in a futile effort to evict the woman from his mind. The pain was intense and Fern winced and jerked as each lash met his back.

'Who are you?' asked Jacques, concerned.

To Fern, Jacques words were only a distant echo not the life jacket she needed to keep her from drowning in this man's mind. She tried to mouth an answer but the rope landed once again as the image of the woman penetrated his senses and fixed itself immutably inside him: her scent, the freshness of her skin, the silken softness of her hair, the sensual gleam in her eyes. His body was tormented, his need for her beyond his control. She cannot be innocent, he told himself as the rope bore down on his back once again. She must be of the devil, sent to test my devotion, he decided through gritted teeth as the rope lacerated the skin of his back, reopening his older wounds and seeking fresh ones, the blood seeping to the surface and overflowing …

'Fern,' Jacques called. 'Fern!'

Fern was suddenly jerked out from inside the man and found herself watching once again, a separate being with physical boundaries, appalled at the pain this man was inflicting on himself. In the distance she heard Jacques calling her again and seconds later she was back in his office. The shock of the transition was so strong she leaped out of the chair, sobbing, the pain as immediate as the memory of its infliction, her mind needing time to catch up with this sudden change in setting. She gazed around the room desperately trying to anchor herself and was surprised to see that nothing had changed, the sun still shone through the window, everything was in order, the books sitting neatly on the shelves, and Jacques sitting in the chair opposite, watching her intently, his eyes alight with curiousity.

'What happened?' he asked.

'Didn't you see?' she asked, surprised. It had been so vivid he must have seen.

Jacques shook his head. 'I get only glimpses and not always that. I often have a sense of what is happening, a form of intuition that is enough to guide a regression but this time you did not hear my questions. You went too far and almost lost yourself in the past.'

Alarmed at the thought of losing herself in that man, Fern sat down abruptly and tried to gather her thoughts. With the other sessions she'd been able to talk her way through the experiences, sensing the feelings of the women she'd been while staying detached enough to answer Jacques' questions. But this monk had pulled her right inside of him and she was hugely uncomfortable with what she'd found there.

Jacques was waiting impatiently as Fern searched for a way to describe the experience. 'I was a man,' she said eventually. I was in his body. I was him … ' she looked helplessly at Jacques. 'It didn't feel right.'

'Why not?'

Fern hesitated, remembering the intensity of the man's sexual desire. She blushed. 'Because I'm a woman. I don't know what it's like to be a man.

'If you are an old soul, you will have experienced life many times over as a male and a female.' Jacques paused and lit a cigarette, then seeing Fern's expression he sighed and opened the window.

'He can't be me,' said Fern and the vehemence in her tone made Jacques look at her once again.

'Why not? What was the man doing?'

Fern haltingly explained what had happened, though she couldn't bring herself to tell him the sexual details.

'Mmm,' said Jacques, 'at last we are on to something. We need to understand this man. What else do you know?'

'Nothing. He was a monk or a priest, and it was a long time ago.'

Jacques stubbed out his cigarette impatiently. 'If you were in the mind of the man, you would have known much about him. Where he lived, how old he was, his name … '

'But his mind was full of this woman,' said Fern who now had a vivid and detailed image of her etched into her memory. 'There was no room for anything else,' she added, uncomfortable at the thought.

'That is strange,' said Jacques. 'We must find out more about this man.' Noting Fern's shaking hands and pale face, he reluctantly added. 'But it is clear that you have had enough for today.'

Relieved, Fern stood up to leave then hesitated for a moment. 'This isn't the first time I've seen the man.'

Jacques looked at her intently. 'Where have you seen him?'

'In my dreams.'

'Ah, that is not so unusual, said Jacques. 'How long have you been dreaming of him?'

'For years now but only occasionally, until this week. Now I'm dreaming about him most nights.

'Do the dreams vary?'

'No, it's always the same room, the same monk, like a film replaying over and over. He's always upset, as if something terrible has happened … but something changed in last night's dream.'

'What?' asked Jacques, leaning forward eagerly.

'He looked at me,' said Fern. She shuddered, remembering the man's puzzled expression as he'd searched for her in the shadows, and the dreadful moment their eyes had met and she'd seen something of his torment.

'Impossible,' said Jacques, clearly disappointed.

Chapter Twenty-One

Jacques had finally entrusted Fern with some of the shopping so she and Freya were wandering around the small Saturday market, inspecting the stalls. They paused at the wine stall where a ruddy faced man offered Fern a taste of a dark red Corbiere but it was too early for her. They moved on past the fish stall, then past the roasting chickens skewered in rows and dripping their fat on the potatoes turning golden below.

As the crowd grew in the tiny square, Fern reached down and took Freya's hand in hers but Freya shook it free then held her arms stiffly by her sides, inaccessible to her mother.

'Suit yourself,' said Fern, 'but stay close. I don't want to lose you.'

Freya just looked away. All morning her face had been set in a frown, and nothing had shifted it, not the pain au chocolat in the café across the road, not the cheese tasting from the cheese man and not even a visit to the bee woman who had let Freya sample the honey.

They stopped at the olive stall where Fern bought olives marinated in herbs and garlic, and some olive pesto for a quick pasta dish. They passed a stall selling woven Balinese bags, their scent strong and exotic, then paused before a display of hand-made jewellery, where Fern wistfully fingered a stone necklace she couldn't afford. Hearing her name called, Fern turned around to see Amber standing behind one of the stalls, the table before her laden with jars of raspberry sauce, jam and fresh organic vegetables.

Fern smiled and made her way over to the stall, 'How's business?

Amber shrugged. 'So so. The tourist season's over now so it's pretty much just the locals and not all of them trust us yet.' She reached over and mussed up Freya's hair. 'Hey Freya, want a walnut?'

Freya nodded and quickly devoured the one Amber broke open for her then held out her hand for more. 'Golly,' said Amber, handing her another. 'You'll eat me right out of walnuts!'

Fern laughed. 'And all that on top of a pain au chocolat, a hot chocolate and half a baguette! School's giving her an appetite.'

'Well then, have as many as you like,' said Amber, breaking open another couple for her. 'You're a growing girl.'

While Freya chewed contentedly on her walnuts, Amber turned to Fern. 'I have a proposition for you.'

'For me?' asked Fern, surprised.

'Yes … Hang on a second,' she added as someone stopped in front of the stall. 'Bonjour Madame,' she said, smiling at the woman who was inspecting a jar of jam.

'I'll leave you to it,' said Fern, when another potential customer joined the woman. 'We can talk another time.'

'Hang on a moment,' said Amber. She filled a paper bag with a mixture of salad leaves and handed it to Fern. 'Here. On the house. Come over tomorrow night for dinner. You can meet Kia and we can talk over my idea.'

'Okay, that would be great,' said Fern, intrigued. 'And thanks for this,' she added pointing at the paper bag.

As Amber turned to the new customer, Fern took Freya's hand firmly in hers and made her way back through the crowd.

'Do you smell that?' asked Jacques when Fern and Freya returned with the shopping.

Fern put down the shopping bags and sniffed. 'Incense?'

'Yes,' said Jacques. 'But I am not burning incense.'

Fern followed the smell from the kitchen through the entrance hall and into the chapel where it was so strong she expected the air to be hazy with smoke, and yet it was clear.

'It's coming from the chapel,' she called, then jumped, startled when from the corner of her eye she saw a shadow flicked past. Heart pounding, she spun around but the shadow had gone and by the time Jacques joined her in the chapel, the smell had disappeared too.

He sniffed. 'It has gone.'

'What do you think it was?' asked Fern.

'Nothing … Just the imagination.'

'But we both smelled it,' said Fern, irritated.

'Ah, but that is simply an example of the power of suggestion,' he said and resolutely turned back to the kitchen.

Fern sighed. There was no point telling him about the shadow she'd seen. He would only dismiss it and maybe it was just a trick of the light after all.

In the kitchen, Jacques was inspecting the shopping. 'Bon,' he said, pulling out the bag of salad leaves. 'We will have this for lunch.'

'A gift from Amber,' said Fern.

Jacques scowled and put it down. 'Stolen, most likely.' He pulled out some eggs and looked at them suspiciously. 'When Maddy was alive we never had to buy these things. Our eggs were superb,' he added proudly.

'Why don't you have chickens anymore?' asked Fern, who'd noticed the empty chicken coop on her way down to the river.

'They died,' Jacques said. Then at Fern's questioning look, he reluctantly added. 'I forgot to shut them in at night.'

Jacques took four eggs and handed them to Fern. 'Boil these,' he said. 'We will have l'oef salade for lunch with this fresh baguette and those stolen salad leaves. And then I will take you and Freya out.

'Where are we going?' asked Freya from the back seat of the deux chevaux.

'That is a surprise,' said Jacques for the third time.

'Is it far?'

'Not far.'

Though they were not high up the mountain, the road down to the plains below was narrow and windy. Fern felt the beginnings of motion sickness coming on and wound down the window to get some fresh air.

Freya was more like her father, loving movement of any kind and the faster the better. 'Weeee,' she said every time the car turned a sharp bend, leaning onto its side. 'Weeee.' However, when they reached the plain and joined a traffic jam, Freya grew quickly bored. 'Are we nearly there?'

'No,' said Jacques, his patience clearly reaching its limits. 'Just wait.'

Fern smiled. 'Do you have children?' she asked.

Oui, two boys.' A shadow crossed his face. 'Now there is only one. Alain died six years ago from a tumour in his brain. He had just turned thirty and was not yet married.'

'I'm sorry,' said Fern.

'He was like me. Stubborn. He refused to see a doctor and then it was too late.' Jacques slammed on his brakes and honked his horn at a car that had pulled in front of him. 'Merde. The bastard idiot.'

'And the other boy?'

Jacques smiled fondly. 'Edmond is thirty-eight now and lives in Paris.'

'Do you have any grandchildren?'

'Non, there is little hope for children … Our line is at an end. Edmund and his partner, Alexis visit occasionally so perhaps you will meet them.'

'Are we nearly there?' asked Freya again.

'Yes we are!' said Jacques triumphantly as he swung the car off the suburban street and into a car park. The sudden transition from the busy road felt like slipping through a portal into another world. Before them stood an ancient stone wall surrounding a cluster of buildings. A single square bell tower rose high above the wall with circular buildings clustered at its base, their roofs topped with terracotta tiles. Behind the buildings were heavily forested hills, rising in gentle curves with the higher peaks of the Pyrenees visible in the background. Here too, the leaves were just turning, tinting the predominant dark green with a lighter golden hue.

'It's beautiful.' said Fern.

Jacques nodded. 'Welcome to Saint-Michel de Cuxa'

'A monastery?' asked Fern.

'An abbey,' said Jacques. 'You are visitors to France, so it is time you saw some of the special places in this area. And perhaps it will also jog your memory regarding the man in your dreams.'

As they walked through the gate and into the abbey grounds, Fern could feel the accumulated energy of centuries of focussed worship. This place is holding secrets too, she thought uneasily, not sure she wanted her memory jogged.

Subdued by the energy of the abbey, Freya stayed unusually close, slipping her hand into Jacques'.

In the entrance room, Jacques insisted on paying but Fern refused to allow him.

'You have little money,' said Jacques.

'But you're teaching me and we're staying with you.'

'You are my guests,' said Jacques, trying another tack.

'And as guests we shouldn't take advantage of you or your hospitality.'

Jacques sighed and retreated. 'If you must, then you must,' he said grumpily and paid only for himself. Then he ushered them through the door and into the information room where there was a model of the original monastery.

'Built in 878,' Fern read aloud. 'And consecrated in 975. It's ancient!' This was the oldest building she'd ever seen. She was fascinated by the history and would have stayed longer but Freya, who had recovered her spirits, was impatiently tugging her toward the door.

Outside was the cloister, a covered walkway supported by rose coloured marble columns that were topped with astonishing carved figures – lions, plants, monkeys and fabulous beasts. The central lawn was bright and sunny, compared to the cool dim light of the walkway, its floor lined with the same mottled rose marble as the columns. The place was deeply silent. A silence broken only superficially by the voice of a tour guide in the far corner who was gesticulating at the group gathered around him.

'Here,' said Jacques, as they approached a door. 'You must see the crypt of the Virgin of the Creche.'

They descended a few steps into an underground chapel then passed through two chambers, which Jacques explained were dedicated to the archangels, Gabriel and Raphael. The crypt itself was circular and made from rough stone, the vault supported by an enormous central pillar.

Freya's eyes widened as she looked around. 'Look,' she said, tugging Jacques' hand and pointing at a statue that was suspended in a large curved niche and lit with a diffuse golden light.

'Oui,' said Jacques, looking at it affectionately. 'This is my favourite statue of Mary and Jesus.'

The ancient wooden statue showed Mary, dressed in dark red and seated on a throne; on her knee sat the child Jesus, holding a bible against his heart. What was unusual about the statue was that Jesus had a child's body but his head was that of an adult. And its presence was made even more significant by the fact that it was the only decoration in the crypt.

Freya disengaged her hand from Jacques and approached the statue. 'Hello,' she said. After a while she smiled a gentle secret smile then nodded, and Fern had the distinct impression that Freya and Mary were having a conversation. Then Freya blew the statue a kiss and ran off to explore the rest of the crypt.

Fern stood still and reached out her senses to feel the energy of this place. Christianity was very different down here in the south of France. It was softer somehow, more tender. As she stood studying Mary and the infant Jesus, she realised that the love Jacques said was the central message of gnostic Christianity, felt palpable in this chapel.

It was a simple crypt, with no intricate detail, no gold rendering or polished candlesticks. The Romanesque style walls and ceiling were rounded, creating a sense that this was a nurturing womblike space. Yet despite this, Fern began to feel uncomfortable. As Freya ran between the rooms, enjoying the space, Fern felt a familiar dizziness and her head began to spin. Suddenly she felt another presence inside her, filling the spaces that should have been hers. Panicking, she tried to push it away but it was too strong.

Then she felt her mouth open of its own accord. 'Forgive me. I have done my penance.' The unfamiliar voice was deep and raspy, its edges rough and ragged.

Jacques turned quickly and stared hard at Fern, while Freya stopped in her tracks and looked fearfully at her mother.

'I beg of you, forgive me.' Fern felt the desperation of someone trapped in purgatory, trapped and unable to release themselves. The atmosphere around her grew tight with anticipation and her dizziness increased as she stood staring at the statue of Mary and Jesus.

'You have only to forgive yourself.' The woman's voice carried such compassion that Fern began to sob as her knees buckled beneath her.

If Jacques hadn't anticipated something like this and caught her, Fern would have landed hard. As it was, he simply guided her to the floor where she sat, her head in her hands, confused and still sobbing.

'Here we have the Crypt of … ' Seeing Fern sitting on the ground and Jacques kneeling beside her, the tour guide stopped mid-sentence and rushed forward. 'What has happened?'

Glancing up Fern was confronted by a large group of tourists, all staring at her tear-streaked face. She looked away quickly and tried to stifle a sob.

'It is fine,' said Jacques. 'She became dizzy and needed to sit down for a moment.'

The concern left the guide's face. 'Ah,' he said. 'Perhaps she was overcome by the Virgin Mary. It happens to some.'

Jacques nodded. 'Oui, peut-etre.' He helped Fern to her feet and in an unexpected show of solidarity, Freya stepped tentatively forward and slipped her hand into Fern's as they exited the crypt.

In the bathroom, Fern stood for a moment and studied herself in the mirror. Her face looked unfamiliar, thin lipped, taut with anxiety, the eyes red rimmed and puffy. She knew this reflection was her own but she felt so distant, neither here nor somewhere else but rather stuck in between, as if she were two people at once. Even the contours of her body seemed blurred.

Fern turned on the tap and splashed her face with water, its coldness effectively snapping her back into this world, her vision sharpening and her face becoming familiar once again. She recalled the gentle compassion of the voice that had answered her. 'You have only to forgive yourself,' it had said, the words bursting through her defences, penetrating a secret place in her heart and sending her into a sobbing mess on the floor of the chapel. Fern had no idea what the words meant or if they were addressed to her or whoever it was who had spoken through her. But whatever the case, they'd been cathartic, emptying out something imprisoned deep inside.

She checked her face again and was relieved to see herself reflected back. Then she patted down her hair, took a deep breath and went looking for Jacques and Freya who were waiting in the grounds of the monastery.

'Did I speak out loud?' she asked Jacques.

'Oui.' He hesitated and glanced quickly at Freya to check that her attention was elsewhere. 'But not in your own voice and the words were in Latin.'

'But I understood what I was saying,' said Fern, confused. 'Do you think it was the monk from my dreams?'

'Perhaps,' said Jacques, clearly uneasy. 'That seems most likely. Just as in yesterday's session, it appeared that someone else inhabited you.'

'That's what it felt like.' Fern shuddered at the memory. 'But there was no sense of a different time or place, or even a different body. Something just talked through me.'

'Yes. It is clear that you are easily inhabited.' Jacques frowned. 'This is not something I have encountered before in my therapy.'

For the first time since Fern had met him, Jacques seemed uncertain. 'Does that mean he could talk through me like that anywhere?' she asked nervously.

'I think not. There is clearly some connection here for this man. He is a monk and this is an abbey. It happened very quickly so I was not able to catch all that you said. However, I did understand the words *forgiveness* and *purgatory*.'

'Yes,' said Fern. 'I … ' she paused, before correcting herself. 'He was begging for forgiveness.'

Chapter Twenty-Two

I t was just before dusk on Sunday evening when Fern walked
down the long driveway to Amber's house, carrying a bottle
of wine. She was nervous. It had been a long time since she'd
been out in the evening with or without her daughter, and tonight
she was alone. Freya had school tomorrow so Jacques had suggested she stay home with him.

'Non, non,' he'd said when Fern had protested. 'We will
have fun together,' he'd added, winking at Freya. In the end Fern
had agreed, knowing that Freya loved Jacques and would be on
her best behaviour for him.

When Fern had left, they'd been making chocolate eclairs,
Freya excited that they were having spaghetti too. 'Fruits de la
mer,' she said proudly when Fern asked what sauce they were
making. 'Seafood,' she explained patiently, when Fern pretended
she didn't understand.

'Take a jacket,' Jacques had warned as she left. 'The tramontane is coming and it is a merciless wind. The season will change
in a moment.'

Fern had brought her shawl but in the balmy late afternoon
warmth and with the air so still, it was difficult to believe she'd
need it. Amber's driveway was rough and rutted with deep chan-
nels and Fern stumbled and nearly fell, tightening her grip on the
bottle just in time. Heart thudding, she paused for a moment to
gather herself. Around her were woodlands, deep in shadow and

seemingly impenetrable. Careful where she placed her feet, she walked more quickly towards the house, the shadows of the trees around her lengthening across the driveway as the sun prepared to set.

Dressed in Khaki shorts and a grubby t-shirt, Amber was in the garden cutting bunches of spinach. Fern hesitated, worried suddenly that Amber had forgotten about the invitation to dinner but when she saw Fern she jumped up and kissed her on both cheeks, then stood back and observed her for a moment, taking in her petite form, the silk dress she was wearing, its abstract pattern reflecting the colours of autumn, her long brown hair streaked with red in the sunlight and brushed for a change, and the short fringe highlighting her eyes.

'You look beautiful,' said Amber. 'Like an autumn nymph.'

Fern blushed. 'No I don't,' she mumbled.

Amber smiled at Fern's embarrassment. 'Yes you do. And you should learn to accept compliments. They're a gift … Where's Freya?' she added.

'It's school tomorrow so Jacques is babysitting.'

Amber burst out laughing. 'Babysitting! The ogre has a soft spot after all.' She took Fern's arm. 'Come. I want you to meet Kia.'

Instead of going into the house, Amber led them through the orchard, stopping briefly to pick a few grapes from the vine that wound its way along the fence, before leading Fern towards the woods.

'Wait,' said Amber, taking Fern's arm as they were about to step in amongst the trees. Then she spoke, directing her words not at Fern but at the woods themselves. 'I ask permission to enter into these woods and for protection while we are within them. I thank you for granting us shade and warmth and oxygen and peace. I leave an offering for our entry.'

Amber reached down and put the grapes at the base of a tree, then stepped into the forest, tugging Fern in behind her.

'Why did you do that?' Fern asked, incredulous.

'It's only polite,' said Amber. 'On paper we own these woods but we can never truly own them, so we show our respect to it and the beings who live here and in return they protect us.'

Fern had never seen such direct communication with nature, though she knew that Adam had related to it in a special way. While she'd never seen him asking permission to enter the forests back in Tassie, he'd always treated them with respect. At this, Fern felt a sudden surge of anger. Then why hadn't they protected him?

'It's also a good idea to bring a gift when you make a visit, just as you did with that bottle of wine. A bit like knocking,' added Amber, giving Fern a significant look. She laughed and darted off between the trees leaving Fern to follow as best she could.

The atmosphere in the woods was different today. There was a sense of ease that hadn't been there the last time. Then she'd felt watched, as if something was lurking in the shadows. Today she felt safe, like a child at play but she also felt the sanctity of the woods. The energy was rejuvenating too, and despite the fact that Amber was nowhere to be seen, Fern felt suddenly light hearted and certain she knew her way.

'There you are,' said Amber. 'This is Kia.'

Astonished, Fern gazed at the man standing before her. Kia was wearing an old pair of jeans torn off at the knees and a pair of sturdy lace-up boots, but that was all. He was tall and slender, his torso and arms well muscled, the veins swollen from exertion. He was clean shaven but had long dreadlocks bundled into a pony tail. There was grime on his cheek and Fern caught herself wanting to reach out and wipe it away. For the first time in two years, she felt a surge of desire, but one she stifled immediately. This was Amber's partner.

She reached out and took Kia's outstretched hand.

'Pleased to meet you,' he said, smiling. 'So you're the one Amber found on the kitchen

floor.'

Fern smiled. 'It seems I'm never going to live that down.'

'Not if Amber can help it.' He looked up through the trees at the darkening sky. 'I'd better get on, the light's fading.'

'You'll remember to come back for dinner?' asked Amber.

Kia laughed. 'I'll be there. Just a couple more trees to cut.' He turned to a young sapling and began sawing at its base, and it was clear he'd already forgotten about them.

'Okay, we'll see you back there,' said Amber planting a kiss on his back. She took Fern's hand and gave her a tug. 'Come on. Let's get that bottle of wine opened!' As they made their way back through the trees Amber shouted back over her shoulder. 'We might leave you some.'

Darkness was descending, making it more difficult to navigate but Amber seemed to know exactly where to go. 'Kia would live in the woods if he could get away with it,' she said. 'If I wasn't here, he'd never bother to come in.'

'What does he do in here?' asked Fern.

'Kia's really into wood management. It's an ancient tradition.' She paused. 'Coming from Tasmania you'd know all about that, I guess.'

Fern grimaced. 'Not really,' she said, thinking about the way whole swathes of old growth forest were bull-dozed to make way for plantations. 'There's nothing selective about forestry in Tassie.'

'That's a pity,' said Amber. 'I'm not up on forest management but Kia says it's all about sustainability; getting rid of diseased trees, creating enough light for new ones to grow, thinning out the saplings, that sort of thing. We use the wood to burn in winter and for our renovations.'

By the time they returned to the clearing it was dark. While Amber checked on the hens, Fern plucked a stem from a rosemary bush then crushed it between her fingers, releasing an overpowering scent. All at once she felt the dizziness descend on her again. She reached out to steady herself on a fence post but it was no longer there. Instead, she was standing outside the old cottage, blinking in the sudden bright daylight. Apparently unaware of Fern's presence, Petrona was sitting on a stool carefully tying long freshly cut rosemary stems to a stick. When the broom was finished, she went indoors and began sweeping the dirt floor. Through the open door, Fern watched the dust rise as Petrona swept; the pungent scent of rosemary quickly replacing the stale indoor smell. Her hands were old but still strong, with thick working fingers, her wide hips and her long skirt sweeping back and forth in time with the broom as she brushed vigorously, filling the air with dust and rosemary. Finally satisfied, she put aside the broom and picked up an earthenware jar filled with lavender water which she sprinkled on the floor to settle the dust. Fern watched her intently, feeling strangely calmed by her presence. There was a steadiness within Petrona that she wished she could find within herself. The old woman clearly knew a good deal but had learned to say little, living with caution but without fear in a time of great fearfulness. It's this that keeps her safe, thought Fern.

For the first time, Petrona looked at Fern and smiled. 'Yes,' she said. 'Fear only creates more fear, drawing its object to you and making it a reality.'

'How do I stop being afraid?' she asked, frustrated.

'By imagining otherwise. You must take responsibility for your thoughts.'

As Fern pondered these words, Petrona began to fade, just as she had the last time.

'Wait,' called Fern.

Petrona turned her head to look at Fern, her eyes inviting a question.

'Am I you?' Fern asked, wondering if this was another past life she was remembering.

'No,' came Petrona's voice. 'But my wisdom is within you. It has many names: the wisdom of the feminine, the wisdom of nature … but names are secondary and limiting. It is enough to know that what you seek is within you already. You must face the shadows and release your fear in order to remember.'

Remember, remember; the words echoed in Fern's mind as Petrona disappeared and Fern found herself standing in the garden once again, surrounded by darkness, the stars brightening in the sky and the scent of rosemary fading.

'Wait,' she whispered again, but Petrona had gone and Amber was there instead, looking at Fern with a puzzled expression.

'Who were you talking to?'

'I'm not sure,' said Fern. Still feeling dizzy, she reached out and supported herself against the wooden fence. 'It happened again. The dizziness … It wasn't dehydration the other day. I didn't faint. I saw something … I don't know how much was imagination and how much was real.' She hesitated. 'You'll think I'm mad.'

'Try me,' said Amber.

Fern explained what had happened that day and also in her second meeting with Petrona.

When she'd finished, Amber simply nodded. 'So,' she said. 'You're a witch.'

'Me?'

'Of course. I'm not surprised. Witches are drawn to their own. This house and the land around it has a long tradition of witchery so it's welcoming you.' Amber gave Fern a hug. 'I already knew you had a strong aura but I never suspected you were so connected.'

'Connected to what?' asked Fern, confused.

'To the innate. It's the communal wisdom, the intuition if you like. It allows you to see in and through but it's as powerful and destructive as it's creative. Most of us are afraid of it and those who aren't, respect it.'

'How do you know all this stuff?'

Amber shrugged. 'I'm a witch.'

As her words echoed around them a silence grew, and Fern was suddenly afraid. Once that would have been a death sentence, she thought, shivering as Amber's eyes bored into hers.

Kia appeared suddenly from the orchard, breaking the spell. 'Where's that glass of wine?' he asked. 'Did you save me any?'

Amber picked up the unopened bottle she'd left by the vegetable patch and waved it at Kia. 'We got distracted,' she said, then added. 'Fern's a witch.'

'Really,' said Kia, eyeing Fern curiously for a moment. 'That makes two of you. I'd better watch out.'

Amber looked at Kia fiercely and he backtracked. 'Okay, three of us then. I'm having a shower,' he said, turning toward the house. 'The tramontane is coming,' he shouted back over his shoulder. 'Better batten everything down.'

'That bloody wind!' said Amber. She picked up a watering can and some gardening tools and put them into a small garden shed. 'That should do it, we'll just have to hope nothing gets shredded or smashed.'

Fern sat at the table in the flickering candlelight, sipping a glass of wine and watching Amber and Kia prepare dinner. There was nothing witchy about either of them. Kia looked the epitome of a hippy and Amber looked more like a Nordic goddess now that she'd changed from her shorts into a dress and let her blonde hair loose. They were an imposing couple and so was their presence in this house which they were making their own. Aside from the fireplace and the shelves there were few physical connections to the past but that didn't matter thought Fern, because the strongest link was in the atmosphere.

'Did you remember the name of the family who owned this place?' she asked Amber.

'Oh yes, I looked it up the other day. The first record we have is from 1255 and the woman's name was Petrona.'

'That's the name of the woman I met,' said Fern.

Amber's eyes lit up with excitement. 'That's all I could find. Those days they didn't always record surnames. But later, the house was listed as owned by the Soler family and it stayed in their name for hundreds of years, always in the name of a woman and unusually only a single name.'

When it was clear that Fern didn't understand the significance of this information, Amber explained. 'In France a house is passed down to all of the children and stays in their name. After a few generations it can be owned by so many people it becomes impossible to sell. But the Soler's never had more than one child and only ever a daughter, so there's no doubt this has always been a wise woman's house.'

Kia sat down at the table, holding a bottle of beer. 'That explains why the locals are still wary of this place.' He smiled at Fern and took a swig of his beer. 'No one can understand why we're still here.'

At Kia's smile an uncomfortable sensation pulsed through Fern's body. He was freshly washed with the grime gone from his cheek but wearing a crumpled shirt, the buttons done up crookedly. The feeling he inspired in Fern was confusing and she turned away relieved when Amber put a giant salad bowl on the table.

'Everything in there is from our garden,' she said. 'I still get a kick out of that.'

'That's why we're still here,' said Kia, kissing Amber's hand. 'This girl respects the place.'

'And we don't care about its reputation, added Amber. 'I'm envious though,' she added, pulling a face. 'I wish I'd met Petrona. Still, everyday I'm immersed in the collective energy of all those generations of wise women so I guess it doesn't matter if we have a face-to-face or not.' She looked at Fern, curiously. 'I wonder what it is about you that made Petrona reveal herself like that.'

Fern shrugged. 'I'm in a pretty weird place at the moment. Studying with Jacques means I'm going in and out of past lives all the time, so everything feels a bit unreal and there's nothing solid to stand on. Sometimes I don't know who I am.' Fern took a sip of wine then described what had happened in the monastery the day before.

"That's heavy,' said Kia, when she'd finished. 'Maybe you need to strengthen your boundaries a bit, otherwise you'll lose yourself. You know, do some auric self-protection?

'Some what?' asked Fern.

'If your aura isn't contained it becomes too open and that makes it easy for anyone to access. You've got to tug it back in towards your solar plexus.'

Fern stared at him for a moment, wondering if he was kidding her but he seemed completely sincere. 'Okay, so how do I do it?' she asked cautiously.

'Easy,' he said. 'Here let me show you. Stand up.'

Fern stood and Kia positioned himself behind her, putting his arms around her waist and then tugging the air in front of her with his hands as if he were pulling on a rope. 'Can you feel that?' he asked.

'Sort of,' said Fern, but it was Kia creating the tension in her. His sandalwood scent reminded her of Adam and she found herself engulfed in a yearning sadness once again.

'You have a go,' said Kia. He stepped in front of her, and watched while she half-heartedly pulled at her invisible aura, feeling like an idiot.

When Fern had finished, Kia stood back and studied her aura. 'That's better,' he said. 'But you'll need to practice. You don't want to let anyone else in.'

'Hey, don't frighten her,' said Amber. 'Fern's strong and she's got Petrona on her side.' She placed a bowl of couscous on the table. 'Let's eat.'

The stew was a rich blend of aubergines, almonds, honey and dates with garlic and a hint of cinnamon in a tomato sauce. 'This is lovely,' said Fern, savouring the perfectly balanced flavours and textures

Amber smiled happily and clinked glasses with Fern and Kia. 'Bon appetit.'

As Fern ate, she thought about Amber's claim that she was a witch. It was as if the word itself was a powerful spell that had set something off within her, something she found disconcerting. She had so many unasked questions: Why did Amber think she was a witch? What was a witch exactly? But she felt oddly reluctant to ask.

'Have some more,' said Amber when Fern finished. 'There's plenty there.'

Fern shook her head. 'I couldn't.' Feeling content, she sipped her wine while they took second helpings.

'So what's the proposition you mentioned?' she asked, steering onto safer ground.

'We want you to work with us on our herbs,' said Amber.

'Why?' asked Fern cautiously.

'Because you're a herbalist,' said Amber. 'We've inherited an amazing herb garden but all we do with it is add a few things to our cooking. I want to get it functioning properly again but I don't even know the uses or even the names of most of the herbs in the garden. We want to start value adding – making teas, flavourings, maybe even remedies at some stage but I don't know where to start.'

Fern was surprised to hear that Amber knew so little. 'But you're a witch. Aren't they supposed to know all about herbs?'

Amber laughed, embarrassed. 'Let's just say I was a lazy student … Will you help?'

They were both staring at Fern intently, waiting for her response and the pressure was making her feel more and more uncomfortable. 'I don't practice,' she said eventually.

'Why not?' asked Amber, clearly confused.

Fern shrugged. 'It just doesn't feel right.'

Amber studied Fern for a moment before responding. 'Even so, you've got all those skills. This is an opportunity to do something with them.'

'And give us a hand,' added Kia.

'Yeah,' said Amber, 'it would really help us.'

'I won't be here for very much longer,' said Fern. 'So I don't know how much I could do.'

'Where are you going?'

She shrugged. 'Home, I guess. I'm running out of money and I can't ask Jacques to put me up forever.'

'You can make some money this way,' said Amber. 'It wouldn't be much but you wouldn't be committed either. Once you've taught us how to use the herbs we could take over if you'd prefer.'

Fern hesitated. It did sound tempting. It wouldn't exactly be practicing and it would be good to spend more time with Amber and Kia. 'Okay,' she said. 'I could teach you which herbs are which and some of their properties. And I guess I could show you a few tinctures and tea mixes but herbs are potent things so you'd have to be careful.'

Amber smiled. 'Right, nothing medical then. Just a few concoctions we can sell at the market. She paused. 'Is it a deal?'

Fern nodded. 'Deal,' she said.

'Great,' said Kia. He pulled the cork from a new bottle and filled their glasses. 'Let's drink to that.'

Chapter Twenty-Three

F ern walked quickly up the driveway towards the road, trying to ignore the shadowy darkness of the woods, made even creepier in the moonlight, and wishing she'd accepted Kia's offer to walk her home. The air had been still all night, defying both Jacques and Kia's predictions but as Fern reached a bend in the driveway, everything changed. At first it was just a distant sound, like an approaching jet plane, the noise intensifying, the air thrumming with tension. Fern looked around fearfully, trying to identify the source of the disturbance but could see nothing. It hit the trees first, sending them into a wild dance, and then it hit Fern, almost knocking her off her feet. She steadied herself and continued up the driveway, struggling against the force of the wind, which was showering leaves on her like confetti. Beneath her feet, the trees' shadows stretched across the path dancing in the wind and making the ground look like liquid.

Sensing something behind her, Fern spun around, but there was nothing there. She walked on, resolutely keeping her eyes on the driveway, and telling herself it was just the wind. Then suddenly out of nowhere a hand grabbed hers. Terrified, she screamed and tried to tear herself free.

'Hey,' shouted Kia. 'It's only me.'

Fern laughed, relieved. 'You scared the hell out of me,' she shouted.

'Sorry, thought you might need some help in this wind.'

'Thanks,' shouted Fern, as the wind nearly knocked her off her feet again.

Kia looked up at the swaying trees then slid his arm through Fern's and pulled her close. 'Come on, let's get clear of these trees.'

Arms linked they walked on, impervious to the buffeting of the wind and not attempting to speak over its howling din. Fern felt Kia's proximity acutely. Something about him was cracking open a part of her that had closed down when Adam died. Suddenly she was back there in the tent with him on their last night together, reliving their love making, the roughness of the stubble on his face, the smell of sweat and sandalwood that permeated his skin and its softness as she caressed his chest. She remembered the cocoon-like feel of the tent, the forest quiet around them and Freya sleeping soundly beside them, safe and content. And she remembered laying her head on Adam's chest and listening to the strong steady beat of his heart.

The memory filled Fern will a new surge of grief and a howling unfulfilled desire. She was trembling and Kia must have noticed because he gave her a searching look before asking if she was cold.

'No. Just tired … I can go on from here,' she added as they reached the road but Kia insisted on accompanying her all the way to Jacques' house.

'Thank you,' said Fern when they arrived at the top of the drive.

'No problem. You're so tiny, Amber was worried you'd get blown away.' He bent down, took her shoulders in his hands and kissed her on each cheek. 'See you soon.'

Fern walked down the short driveway to the house, her cheeks burning where Kia had kissed them. Don't be an idiot, she told herself.

There was a light in the window of the old chapel so Fern assumed Jacques would be sitting in there watching television.

'I'm back,' she called as she stepped inside, bringing with her a swirl of dust and leaves. With some difficulty she pushed the heavy door shut against the wind then stepped into the chapel, but it was suddenly dark in there, with only the lingering smell of a recently extinguished candle. Puzzled, Fern flicked the light switch and scanned the empty room but could see no evidence that Jacques had been here. Following the smell, she walked further into the chapel and reached out to touch the antique lantern that sat in one of the wall niches. The glass was still hot and the candle wax inside still malleable looking. Feeling a chill running up and down her spine, Fern backed out of the room, eyes peeled for movement in the shadows. But there was nothing to suggest anything amiss.

She found Jacques in the kitchen, sitting on the couch with Freya asleep next to him, her feet on his lap and a blanket over her. It was evident he'd been there for some time.

'Ah,' said Jacques, his eyes flicking briefly to the clock on the wall. 'You're back. Good. I am in need of the toilet.'

Fern looked at Freya. 'Did she have a night terror?'

Jacques lifted his hands and shrugged. 'I am not certain. It did not seem like that because she was awake.' He hesitated, obviously reluctant to go on.' She says she saw a man in her room.'

'A man?' The fear hit Fern in the chest.

'Apparently he was standing at the end of her bed, watching her.' He hesitated again. 'She said he looked hungry.'

'Hungry? What does that mean?'

Jacques shrugged. 'She couldn't explain this but when I asked if she thought he wanted food, she shook her head.'

Hungry for her, thought Fern. *There are forces that wish to destroy her*. She shuddered. 'So where did he go?'

'She screamed and I raced up but there was no one there.' Noting Fern's expression, he went on. 'Yes, of course I checked. I searched the entire house but there was nothing.'

Fern thought of the freshly extinguished lamp in the chapel. There was either a man hiding in the house or a ghost living here, and she didn't know which was worse.

'Freya wouldn't go to sleep in her own bed so I brought her down here and gave her a hot drink. She fell asleep watching a cartoon.' He looked at the clock again and grimaced. 'That was some hours ago.'

'I'm sorry. I didn't realise how late it was. Thank you for looking after her.'

Jacques looked at Fern and nodded to himself. 'It appears you have had a good time.'

'I have. Now let me relieve you of Freya.' She reached down and heaved the sleeping child into her arms.

'Would you like me to carry her?' asked Jacques, seeing Fern struggling to lift her.

'I'll manage,' said Fern not ready to admit that Freya was becoming difficult to carry. As she struggled up the stairs with her daughter in her arms, she pondered the complexities of motherhood. Sometimes it seemed as if she were wishing Freya's childhood away, celebrating each new sign of her independence and yet she also mourned every step that took Freya away from her. Motherhood was both a joy and a torment.

Instead of taking her to the tiny room at the end of the corridor, Fern tucked Freya into her own large bed and drew a blanket over her. Then she straightened and stood for a moment gazing at her daughter. Even in the peace of deep sleep, Freya looked exhausted, her eyes red-rimmed from crying and her face pale, and yet she was likely to wake up brimming with energy and enthusiasm for life, all fear banished from her mind. Freya was a puzzle, tantalizing and mischievous but there was also something heavy, something that kept draining the energy from her. Was it the force that was trying to harm her, holding her back, stopping her from connecting with life fully? Fern shivered as the wind outside howled, battering itself against the shutters on the window and sending little tendrils of cold air through the tiniest of cracks. She gave Freya a gentle kiss on the forehead and made her way back down the stairs.

Jacques was pouring himself a drink, his face troubled. 'I thought she would be safe with me,' he said.

'She is safe with you,' said Fern. She sat down at the table and studied Jacques. He looked exhausted. And his pallor was greyer than it should be. For a moment she wondered if he was unwell but then remembered how exhausting looking after Freya could be. 'Freya tired you out. I'm sorry.'

He shook his head, adamantly. 'Non, non, but it is hard to face such fear in a little one.'

'She's not making it up. You know that don't you?'

Jacques looked uncomfortable. 'Perhaps it was a dream. She is so young and sometimes at this age it is difficult to distinguish between dreams and life.'

'When I walked down the drive earlier, I saw a light in the chapel window, but when I stepped inside the room was in darkness.

'A trick of the light,' said Jacques obstinately.

'But the lamp was still hot. Did you light that lamp tonight?'

Jacques shook his head, defeated. 'Non,' he said.

'Is there an intruder in the house?'

'No. I have checked everywhere.'

'Then it must be a ghost. Why won't you accept this house is haunted?'

Jacques shrugged. 'It is not a comfortable thing to admit.' He drained his drink. 'Perhaps it is because I am afraid you and the child will leave.'

'Why would we leave?' she asked.

'Because of fear,' said Jacques quietly. 'Many people are afraid of ghosts.'

Fern pondered this. Yes, she was afraid but despite the fear she didn't want to leave. Ahmed had said this trip would help, and earlier this evening Petrona had told her to face her fear – both good reasons to stay. She was also curious to find out more about this ghost.

'We're not leaving yet,' she said.

Jacques smiled. 'Bon. Then we must work on finding an exorcism.'

'How long have you known there's a ghost here?'

'It is not Madeleine if that is what you are suggesting,' said Jacques looking directly at Fern for the first time, his eyes challenging her to disagree. 'I may be reluctant to let her go but that is my problem not hers,' he added, his distaste for the subject clear in the tone of his voice.

'Of course it isn't,' said Fern. 'Freya said it's a man.'

Jacques nodded. 'There has always been a sense of something, the shuffle of feet, the prickle on the back of the neck. But we only ever felt it in the chapel and we soon became used to it. Since you arrived it has spread into other rooms and the effects are intensifying.' Jacques paused and drained the last of his glass. 'It is as if the ghost is excited or disturbed.'

Fern pondered this for a moment, unable to see how they could be disturbing the ghost. Perhaps it didn't want them here. But why? 'Do you know much about the history of the house?' she asked.

'That was Madeleine's thing.' Jacques' voice was filled with regret. 'I have to admit I didn't always listen to her pronouncements … ' He paused and looked wistfully at the photograph of his wife sitting on the kitchen dresser. 'I have had plenty of time to wish I'd taken more notice of Madeleine. When someone is gone, you wonder why they did not seem special every moment of every day.' He glanced at Fern. 'But of course you will know this.'

Fern nodded and looked away. 'It doesn't seem to get any easier.'

They sat immersed in their memories for a few minutes. Fern was just about to head upstairs to bed when Jacques returned to the subject of the ghost.

'Madeleine was intrigued by the idea of a ghost and did some research but this house has a long history and the chapel an even longer one. There has been much upheaval in this area over the centuries, from wars, disease and bands of robbers, and no doubt this place would have seen many deaths. I'm afraid my wife never discovered who our ghost might be, though she did believe he was associated with the chapel.'

'Did anyone ever live in the chapel?' asked Fern.

'It was not a monastery so that is not likely, but who knows, perhaps priests stayed here or travellers stayed on their way across the mountains … there are many possibilities.' He paused and when he spoke next, his voice was filled with sadness. 'But my wife is no longer here to explore them.' He stood up slowly, using his arms to lever himself out of the chair and grimacing as if in pain. 'Merde! Tonight, I feel like an old man.'

Chapter Twenty-Four

In the morning, the tramontane was still blowing, driving out the last of the warmth, and tearing the leaves from the trees. Freya hadn't woken brimming over with energy; her eyes had dark shadows underneath them and she was bad tempered, refusing to eat her breakfast. Fern's suggestion that she stay home from school had sent her even further into a temper and she'd insisted on going. Despite this she dragged her feet, refusing to hurry getting dressed and then refusing to walk. In the end, Jacques had given in and they'd driven her down the hill and then sat inside a café, seeking refuge from the wind that buffeted the empty streets, and recovering from the onslaught of Freya's bad mood.

The last thing Fern felt like this morning was a session with Jacques. She was on edge. The peace of the last week had been replaced with fear and anxiety. Jacques was right, they needed an exorcism but neither of them had any idea where to begin. To make matters worse, this morning Freya had refused either a kiss or a hug goodbye from Fern, and had resolutely walked into the school yard without even a wave. It didn't help that Fern had spent half the night awake, listening nervously to the wind battering against the shutters, her thoughts flitting between worry about the hungry ghost Freya had seen and worry about her own strangely intense response to meeting Kia.

Fern was nervous about doing another regression. She didn't like being in the skin of this tormented man and the sense of being one person and watching as another, was also disconcerting. She worried about the consequences, thinking again about the warning Kia had given her the previous evening. Perhaps she should create some armour for her aura, as he'd suggested. But she felt silly attempting it and anyway, she was supposed to be learning from Jacques so she needed to stay open enough for the regression to work. There might be ways to protect yourself and stay open at the same time, but she didn't know them.

'Voilá,' said Jacques as Fern reluctantly stepped into the room.

She seated herself in the chair opposite Jacques' desk and studied him. He still looked tired but at least he seemed in a reasonable mood.

'Let's begin. Now that you have accessed this life you should no longer have to concentrate on the pain in your upper back in order to find a way through.'

Fern was confused. 'What has my pain got to do with this monk?'

'There is often a linkage between chronic pain or physical weakness in a current life, and something that occurred in a previous life. Your link might be between the tension in your upper back and the self-flagellation of this man. No doubt you are still carrying the pain of his self-damage.'

Fern flinched at the memory of the searing pain the man had inflicted upon himself. 'I would never do that to myself,' she said.

Jacques raised an eyebrow. 'Most of us find ways to damage ourselves, though they are not always as obvious as the method of this man.'

Feeling the tension in her upper back intensify under his scrutiny, Fern rotated her shoulders, trying to release some of the pain. 'Will it go away now?' she asked, hopefully.

'It might ease but generally the release does not come fully until we find and undergo the death.'

'His death?'

'Yes, I am not sure why it helps,' said Jacques. 'It is a rule only because I have seen the relief it brings to many of my clients. If a death holds great emotion, this emotion can become trapped in the form of a phrase, a thought, a feeling or a physical wound that blocks out the experience of death and its aftermath. Instead, the emotion is retained and passed through subsequent lives.

'When a client relives the experience of death and more importantly the moments after death, they are able to understand that it is over. It is only through this understanding and detachment that they are able to separate from whatever pain, mental pattern or negative emotion is causing problems in their life.'

Jacques' explanation made sense to Fern though she didn't like the prospect of seeing this monk die. She steeled herself. 'Okay. What do we do now?'

Jacques leaned back in his chair. 'First you must imagine yourself back inside the same scene you entered on Friday and then I want you to lift yourself out of the monk's cell and into another period in the man's life. The scene in the cell is like a pattern that is caught in a time loop, repeating again and again, an intense moment of emotion that he couldn't escape but there must be other times in his life, times which are both happy and sad, from which we can glean some information that will help us to understand who this man is.'

'Why do we remember only the bad things?'

'The negative imprint creates wounds which then form into scars.' Jacques paused. 'When you break an arm, forever after it is likely to ache when the weather changes. So it is with emotional wounds which respond to triggers.'

'Can we ever free ourselves completely?' This was something Fern had asked herself throughout her training in homeopathy too, but she still didn't know the answer.

'There will always be triggers and most likely the scarring will also remain but we can make them less livid by releasing the trapped emotions within them. We can also learn to identify what it is that triggers our reactions and then retune our responses. This way we live consciously through positive action rather than unconsciously through negative reaction.'

'I'm guessing releasing the trapped emotions isn't a comfortable process,' said Fern.

Jacques laughed. 'No, it is not always easy. Are you ready?'

Fern closed her eyes. 'Let's do it.'

As Jacques had predicted, Fern entered the scene immediately. She slipped right into the man as if he was her but this time the shock was not as intense and she had time to notice the smells – damp walls and unwashed wool and burning wax. Despite the thick stone walls the air was chill and she shivered, drawing the robe closer around her and rubbing her arms. The raw wounds under the robe stung and throbbed as she paced with him and as him.

'Who are you?' asked Jacques.

As on the previous occasion, the man was immersed in thoughts of the young woman and images of her were flooding into Fern's mind, threatening to take over. However, this time she was able to push them back a little in order to stay focused.

'Hugues Pelet.' Fern gasped as a powerful image of the woman entered her mind, momentarily pushing away all other thoughts. 'I was betrayed. She went with another.' Hugues paced back and forth in the small cell, covering its width in only a few steps then turning abruptly at each wall, back and forth, the fury building inside of him. 'Roese promised herself to me. She is a whore and deserved to die.'

'Who is Roese?' asked Jacques

'My beloved.' Caught in his torment he groaned. The pain of the betrayal so strong it overcame the sting and throb of the festering wounds on his back. 'It is the anniversary of her death.'

'How did she die?'

Hugues groaned again but didn't answer. Once again, the image of the woman entered into his mind, overwhelming him.

'Go backwards or forwards to another time in your life,' ordered Jacques.

As if from a great distance, Fern heard Jacques' words. Pushing back the image of the woman, she searched for a different, more positive feeling. Suddenly the musty darkened room disappeared and she found herself in the countryside. It was a beautiful early summer's day and the air was thick with the scent of wildflowers and grass. As he galloped through the fields, his lanky wolf hound, Arnou, bounding along behind him, Hugues' heart was light. How could it not be for he was young and the days were warm and long. These were his last few months of freedom before he entered the seminary, and his father had given him room to play. So, play he would.

He turned his horse toward a low hedge bordering the field and leaped over it, the horse landing with a thud in the next field, where a young woman was balanced precariously on a boulder and reaching up to pick the first fruit from an apricot tree. His sudden appearance surprised her, sending her off balance, and she fell, dropping her basket and gasping as her ankle twisted beneath her.

Hugues pulled on the reins and drew his horse to a standstill then turned to face the woman who was sitting on the ground tentatively inspecting her ankle, the herbs and apricots she'd gathered, scattered around her.

'I'm sorry to have frightened you,' he said.

There was something vaguely familiar about her, as if he had known her from some other time and place. Disturbingly she was not as demure as he would expect a peasant girl to be. Instead, she met his gaze with an expression that was disconcertingly direct. She was beautiful, her skin porcelain smooth, her cheeks flushed with the heat perhaps but more likely embarrassment. Her dark hair was pulled back from her face but glistening strands had escaped and their thick curls framed her face, while her neck curved to her shoulders in a slender graceful line. It was difficult to gauge her figure under the simple loose gown she was wearing but this only increased his desire to discover it for himself.

It struck him suddenly that as she was a peasant he could do as his brother would no doubt have done. Take her and make her his conquest. No doubt his father too would approve of him sowing his seeds before he took his vows. But Hugues was destined for the service of God and knew this meant forgoing the things of this world; particularly carnal affairs. If he could not control himself now, he would suffer torture later. Then again, seeing her on the ground like this, powerless, her cheeks flushed, her eyes wary yet challenging, he could feel his desire dissolving the edges of his resolve.

Noting with alarm the lust in his eyes, the woman scrabbled to stand up, wincing in pain as she did so. At that moment Arnou caught up with Hugues, panting from the long run in the heat of the day. Curious he approached the woman, sniffing at her ankle then nuzzling her leg. To Hugues' surprise, instead of shrieking with fear as most women would have done, she reached out and patted Arnou, forgetting her fear for a moment in the joy of communion with the dog.

The dog had broken the spell and with an effort Hugues was able to seize control of himself. Unlike his brother, he was still a virgin and though he would claim it was for the love of God, truly it was because he did not have the courage.

'You are hurt,' he said, his failure to fulfil his desires evident in the slightly bitter tone of his voice. He dismounted and approached her. 'Let me see.'

'I am fine,' she said, drawing away.

Ignoring her protests, Hugues knelt before her and took her ankle in his hand. He was astonished by how slender it was, its gentle curve igniting another wave of desire within him, which he pushed aside. He inspected her ankle carefully, noting that the shadow of a bruise was already appearing. Without treatment it would soon swell.

'No doubt it is just a sprain,' he said, 'but you should not walk on it.' He reached out his hand to take hers. 'Come, I will take you home.'

Sensing she was no longer in danger, she laughed and shook her head. 'First we must retrieve what I have gathered for I will not waste an afternoon's work.' Her voice was a melody to his ears, the tone mischievous, as if she were flirting a little with him, and he smiled despite himself, knowing that he was falling helplessly under her spell.

When Hugues had collected the scattered apricots and the spilled herbs, she allowed him to take her hand and lift her onto his horse. Because of the nature of the saddle, she was forced to sit astride, her skirt lifting up dangerously free of her ankles. Hugues leapt up onto the horse behind her and took the reins. Despite his resolve, he could not ignore the penetrating warmth of her body in his arms or the rose scent that permeated his senses, and his own body responded of its own accord. Afraid that she would soon feel the evidence of his excitement he kicked the horse into action and began cantering in the direction she pointed, with Arnou racing along behind them.

As they rode it became quickly apparent that she knew horses well; her body moved easily with the cantering horse, surrendering naturally to its rhythm. This puzzled Hugues momentarily but her proximity was so overwhelming it quickly sent all thoughts fleeing from his mind.

Having assumed she was a farm woman, Hugues was surprised when she directed them toward Alet les Bains, the walled town a few minutes ride to the south. When they reached the bridge across the Aude River, he slowed the horse into a trot, and then to a walk, because once inside the fortifications, the streets were busy and their cobbled surface was not easy for the horse's hooves. They drew many curious looks from the townsfolk and one or two ribald comments, but a glance from Hugues silenced them quickly. He was angry at the insinuations but the woman only laughed and tossed her head.

She directed him to halt before a large villa that he recognised well. So she was a servant for this family. Claude de Bergier, a rich merchant, had often done business with his own father and Hugues himself had been a frequent visitor here as a child, until de Bergier died suddenly, leaving his business in disarray and severing the connection between the two families. Hugues had been good friends with their only child, Roese whose tomboy antics had gotten them both into trouble time and again. With the father dead and no son to carry on in his stead, Hugues wondered how the family fortunes were faring now.

He helped her off his horse, handed her the basket and bowed, forgetting for a moment that she was a servant. Then remembering that she had damaged her ankle, he took her arm, whistled to the dog, and leading his horse with his other hand, stepped through the gate into a spacious paved courtyard.

She directed him to a minor door which must have been the entrance to the servants' quarters. Having fulfilled his duty, he withdrew his arm and prepared to leave but she tugged at his sleeve. 'Come inside,' she said. 'You must have some refreshment for your trouble.'

The invitation in her voice excited Hugues again and in his hurry he fumbled to tie up his horse. 'Stay,' he commanded Arnou, who whined but sat down obediently to wait for his master.

As he stepped inside the house, his vision faded in the sudden dim light. When his eyes had adjusted, he saw her smiling mischievously at him but when he reached out to grasp her arm she twisted away, laughing.

'Maman,' she cried. 'Where are you, Maman?'

'In here.'

Hugues stopped dead in his tracks, his face flushing at his stupidity. This was a voice that he remembered well from his childhood.

Sensing he was no longer following her, she turned and looked at him, and seeing his expression, she smiled, delighted.

'If I had known … ' he stammered.

'You would have behaved better no doubt. Do not worry, your behavior was impeccable, if not your thoughts.'

'Why didn't you say?'

'Because I did not know. At least not immediately. It took some time to piece together your features and remember my childhood friend.'

'But you have … ' Hugues paused, helplessly looking for the right word.

'Grown up?'

Hugues nodded, still lost for words.

'And so have you,' she said, looking him over appreciatively. 'Do you remember, Hugues. We promised each other endless friendship and loyalty when we were nine.' A fleeting sadness crossed her face. 'Oh, the whims of children and the vagaries of fate.'

'Your father died. I am sorry.'

She nodded. 'Yes, that changed everything.' She gestured at the empty hall through which they were passing and when she spoke there was a new bitterness in her tone. 'Once this was filled with activity but now there is just myself and my mother and a few loyal servants. We get by. But it is not the same.'

She took his arm. 'Come, I need to find a chair to rest in.'

Hugues supported Roese once again as she led them into a comfortable sitting room. The walls were lined with tapestries, the stone floors softened with woven rugs and the afternoon light shone through the window, illuminating Roese's mother. The passing years and the trials of widowhood had brought lines to her face and added grey streaks to her once raven hair but even so Madame de Bourgiers remained a beautiful woman.

As they entered, she looked up from her embroidery, her face breaking into a smile when she saw her daughter then her expression changing to concern. 'What has happened?'

'Nothing Maman, I just hurt my ankle a little.' She gestured at Hugues. 'Look who I have brought. Remember Hugues? Monsieur Pelet's son?'

Madame Bourgiers put aside her handiwork and stared at Hugues blankly for a moment then gradually a look of recognition registered in her eyes.

'Yes,' she said, and laughed. 'I remember you well. My little girl had you wrapped around her tiny finger … My, you're a grown man now. And handsome too.'

Hugues smiled. 'And you, Madame are as beautiful as ever.'

She laughed. 'You flatter me.' Her face suddenly became serious. 'But I am aware that the years have not been kind.'

She turned to Roese and eyed her with a stern expression. 'Look at you. Grass in your hair like any servant girl who has been rolling around with her lover, your dress is in a state and no doubt you have been out again without supervision.'

'Mother!' cried Roese, her face flushing with embarrassment. 'Hugues is not my lover. I fell and he came to my rescue.' She cast a mischievous look at Hugues. 'Despite thinking me a servant, he refrained from taking advantage of me which is undoubtedly the mark of a true gentleman.'

Hugues is not my lover. He was surprised at how much her denial cut him. She would never be his lover, not now. If she had been a servant girl, he could have taken her but he had no claims over this young woman who would marry well and forget him in a moment. He wondered briefly if she already knew that he was destined for the priesthood.

For the first time Hugues truly understood what he would be sacrificing and a surge of bitterness rose within him. But there was no choice. His brother would take over the business which was not large enough to be divided. Hugues' character did not suit that of a knight so it had been understood from early on that he would become a priest. His mother insisted it was because he was a dreamer and had always loved the saints but he knew it was a political move, to placate the church and to position him in such a way that he would have power to direct policy in the future.

He stared at this girl who had been his childhood friend, remembering her skinny little arm waving the stick as if it truly were a weapon, the look in her eyes, intent and ferocious as she plunged in for the kill. She'd borrowed his hose more than once, hitching them up with string so she could run around freely without tripping over the hem of her robe. And to his eternal shame she had once beaten him in front of his scornful brother. At the memory his cheeks reddened with shame all over again.

The woman standing before him now bore no resemblance to the girl she had been. Except perhaps for the eyes which were lively and curious, and her lack of convention – something which had thrilled and shocked him, even then. He had taken more than one beating for her. His backside stinging with pain yet knowing he would do it all over again if she asked.

'Well, you could do worse,' I suppose, said Madame Bourgiers, looking him over as she filled pewter cups with the wine a servant girl delivered to the table by her side.

'Maman!' Roese laughed in spite of herself. 'What will Hugues think of us?'

'He will think we are forward and in need of a man to keep us in control.' She held a cup out to him. 'Here, the day is hot and you must be thirsty from the effort of rescuing my wayward daughter.'

'Thank you, Madame.'

'It is the least I can do,' she said. 'And please call me Elena. I feel old enough as it is, and Madame Bourgiers makes me feel ancient.'

Hugues nodded, knowing full well he would never be able to call this woman by her first name.

'I have never been able to control my daughter,' continued Elena. 'And it has become worse since her father died.' She sighed. 'She will go her own way, despite my warnings.'

Roese rolled her eyes. 'You know there is no one to supervise me and I cannot be a prisoner here day after day. It will drive me quite mad.'

'I know that you are my daughter and I wish to keep you safe,' retorted Elena. 'Let me look at that ankle,' she added and knelt down on the floor in front of Roese.

Roese lifted her skirt to reveal an ankle already livid with bruises. Elena tutted at the sight of it. 'It needs attention now.' She threw a quick wary glance at Hugues before encasing Roese's ankle in both her hands.

Hugues watched, puzzled by Elena's behavior. He could not see how grasping an ankle like this could help it. Roese needed a bandage not a caress.

After a few minutes, Elena took her hands away and kissed her daughter's ankle. It will be fine, my sweet. The bruising is receding already but I will ask Alays to prepare a poultice just to make sure.'

Groaning at the effort, she stood up once again and addressed Hugues. 'Stay and eat with us.'

Hugues did not know if it was an invitation or an order but there was something inside of him that was panicking. He felt uneasy at Elena's display. On the surface it was simply a mother inspecting her daughter's ankle but he could not deny the evidence of his eyes. The bruising had almost disappeared. This could only be coincidence, the bruise slight and receding anyway, the strength of a mother's love perhaps, but the alternative explanation was not one he could condone. He glanced over to the servant girl who stood waiting by the door; a Cathar by the looks of her blue robe and that scarf. When he scowled at her she withdrew further, a sudden wariness in her expression. He had heard the rumours that the church was planning to come down hard on the Cathars and believed it would not be too soon. Like his father and brother, he would welcome the opportunity to remove these heretics, for the Cathars were akin to weeds, taking root in every household and threatening to undermine the Christian faith.

'It is getting late,' he said. 'I must return to Limoux before nightfall.'

Elena smiled regretfully and held out her hand. 'Well then, I must thank you for rescuing my daughter and hope that you will visit us again.'

'It was a pleasure,' said Hugues, politeness overcoming his discomfort. He glanced at Roese once again and immediately wished he had accepted the invitation to eat.

Roese attempted to stand but Hugues waved her back down. 'Please, stay where you are.'

Remaining seated she smiled, her smile an open invitation that melted any remaining discomfort within him. 'Thank you for rescuing me, Hugues,' she said then added quietly, 'It is good to have found you once again.'

Unable to deal with his conflicting emotions, Hugues nodded stiffly and strode out of the room. His future was mapped out for him and he did not dispute the need for it or even its suitability to his nature, but Roese had shaken his certainty and his heart was suddenly filled with doubts. For the sake of his family and his future Hugues knew he must not see her again. He mounted his horse and rode out of town, then with Arnou running by his side he kicked his horse to a gallop.

Fern's eyes were stinging with Hugues unshed tears when she opened them to find Jacques regarding her curiously. 'So,' he said. 'Hugues was an enemy of the Cathars.'

Chapter Twenty-Five

' I 'm not going,' shouted Freya. 'I'm never going again.'
'I thought you loved school,' said Fern.

'I hate it,' said Freya, stamping her foot in fury.

'Did something happen yesterday?'

Freya bit her lip and shook her head.

'Nothing? Are you sure?'

Freya just shook her head again. Fern was too tired to bother arguing and a long weekend might help Freya calm down a little. 'Okay. You can have a rest day then. But if you have a problem you need to share it with me so I can help you.'

Freya nodded sullenly then began picking half-heartedly at her croissant.

Fern yawned and drained her coffee, hoping for a shot of energy. They were both exhausted. The wind hadn't let up for days and although the house itself was solid, the shutters and the roof creaked and groaned as each gust hit, rattling their nerves and sharpening their tempers. Since the episode with the hungry man, Freya had insisted Fern sit with her each night, and last night had been particularly difficult. It had taken over an hour for Freya to fall asleep, and then just as Fern felt it was safe to creep out of the room and into her own bed, Freya's night terrors had returned with a vengeance. She'd finally fallen into a peaceful sleep in the early hours of the morning but by then Fern was too tense to sleep. At dawn she'd come down to the kitchen and made herself a coffee only to be joined by a foul tempered Freya a few minutes later.

With Freya at home, there would be no session with Jacques so Fern decided to work in the garden instead. Jacques wouldn't be happy they were missing a session because progress was so slow but Fern was relieved to spend the morning with her hands in the earth.

Soon Freya wandered out into the garden and stood there listlessly watching Fern work.

'Do you want to do some weeding?' asked Fern.

Freya shook her head but soon reconsidered and knelt beside her mother. They worked side by side, clearing a patch of earth, though today Freya was impatient and broke the weeds off at the stem without bothering with the roots.

Soon Freya wandered off, weaving slowly between the garden boxes and stopping sometimes to inspect something before losing interest again. Fern glanced up occasionally, wondering if there was more to this mood than a sleepless night.

'No, I won't play with you,' said Freya, her voice stubborn.

Surprised, Fern stopped her weeding and looked at Freya, who had never before refused to play with Beattie.

'Everyone says you're not real, said Freya. 'Why didn't you show them?'

There was a long pause. 'Oh, alright,' said Freya with no trace of enthusiasm.

She began to play half-heartedly with Beattie but there was a new self-consciousness to it that tugged at Fern's heart. It was tempting to ask Freya about it but she knew from experience that it was better to wait until her daughter was ready to talk.

Fern kept at her weeding until her wrists ached and her knees felt bruised from kneeling on the paving stones. Then she dug over the patch before surveying her work. It looked good. The whole garden was looking much better. Jacques would need to get someone in to prune the fruit trees or do it himself but other than that she was managing just fine. And it was doing her good too, she could feel it strengthening her.

She gathered up the tools and put them away, then called Freya. 'Let's get some lunch and then visit Amber.'

The wind had died down a little as they walked along the road to Amber's house but the trees were still swaying as the breeze played a tune in their branches. It made walking easier and Freya seemed more settled.

They met Kia chopping up a tree that had fallen across the driveway.

'Hey,' he said, straightening up and smiling at Fern. 'Good to see you. And you must be Freya,' he said, holding out his hand. 'Nice to meet you, he added as Freya tentatively took his hand and gave it a solemn shake.

'Where's Amber?' asked Fern,

'In the veggie garden as per usual,' he said and turned back to his chopping. 'See you down there in a while.'

By the time they reached the bottom of the drive, the wind had stopped completely and the air was suddenly still. Fern spotted Amber digging over a section of the vegetable patch. Her overalls were covered in dirt and her face was red from the exertion.

'Phew,' she said. 'Nearly done. Just got to plant out these seedlings, she added pointing at some punnets near the fence. She stood up and looked with pleasure at the freshly dug earth.

'You'll have to give me some advice on what vegies to plant now,' said Fern. 'The seasons are all back to front here.'

'You're the one from down under,' said Amber, laughing. 'Hey Freya … Hey Beattie,' she added, looking at an empty space beside Freya.

'Can you see her?' asked Freya, astonished.

'Of course I can,' said Amber.

'But no one else can, not even Mama.'

'That's not true,' Fern protested. 'I see glimpses of her … And what about Henri? He plays with Beattie too.'

Freya looked down at the ground. 'Now he says he can't see her. He says it was just a joke.'

Fern suddenly understood what was going on. There was the ridicule of her class mates, which was bad enough but Freya also felt betrayed by her friend.

Fern squatted down in front of Freya and took her hands. 'Most people are like sheep,' she said. 'They follow the crowd, too afraid to go their own way. They don't want to stand out or be different … Henri is afraid. He thinks it's safer to run with the crowd.'

'And he's right,' added Amber, drily. 'That way you don't get noticed.'

'Can I run with the crowd?' asked Freya, hopefully.

Fern hesitated, remembering her own schooldays, the times she'd tried to fit in only to have them see right through her again and again. 'Sure,' said Fern. 'You can try but you'd have to turn away from Beattie.'

Freya's lip trembled. 'I don't want to lose Beattie.'

'Maybe you could find a middle way. Sometimes we have to keep certain things secret because other people don't understand. You won't be able to share Beattie with other people but that's not Beattie's fault. She's still your friend.'

Freya digested this new information then smiled. 'Okay.' She spotted the hens in the orchard. 'Chickens,' she shouted, and clamored over the fence.

'It's not easy being sensitive,' said Amber as they watched the hens scatter before Freya. 'God, I hated school.'

'Me too,' said Fern. 'Couldn't wait to get out of there.'

Amber turned back to the vegetable patch. 'I won't be long. Then we can take a look at the herb garden.'

''I'll help,' said Fern.

'Sure. You make the holes and I'll plant.'

'What are they?' asked Fern as Amber carefully separated the seedlings.

'These ones are spinach, and those are chard and kale. They all grow pretty well over the winter.'

Fern knelt on the damp earth and felt it seeping into the knees of her jeans. The earth was so soft and loose that she only needed her fingers to dig the holes. This was healthy soil; dark and rich smelling. It would produce good vegetables.

'Why did you come to France?' asked Fern as they worked.

'I don't know really. I just felt a call and when I got here it felt right. We didn't move straight away. It took years actually.'

'You're lucky,' said Fern. 'It must feel special to belong somewhere.'

Hearing the tone in her voice, Amber paused in her planting and glanced over, a question in her eyes.

'I've never felt that kind of connection with a place,' Fern explained. 'It's probably got something to do with being adopted. There's always been this yearning for somewhere else but I don't know where it is.'

'How about here?' asked Amber.

Fern thought about it. 'No,' she said, eventually. 'Here's closer than anywhere I've been yet. But it still isn't mine. I don't belong here.' She paused. 'Or at least, I don't like the part of me that does.'

'Sounds like you're a reluctant soul,' said Amber, as she patted down the earth around a seedling.

'What do you mean?'

'You're still yearning for home – your true home. But you're in a physical form for the time being so you need to find a way to ground yourself here.'

'So, I've got a bad case of homesickness.'

Amber laughed. 'Yep.'

'What's the cure?'

'If you want to live well, you'll have to accept you have a right to be here. Can you pass me that punnet of kale?'

'I do have a right to be here,' said Fern, handing over the seedlings.

Amber paused and studied her for a moment, then shook her head. 'You're carrying a strong sense of illegitimacy. Probably because you're adopted but who knows what you've brought with you: the burdens of the ancestors, the wounds of your past lives … all of it feeding your old stories and weaving a cage around you.'

As Fern dug the final row of holes she thought about Amber's words and wondered if she would ever free herself from that cage. What would it feel like to be free of fear, to walk the earth lightly? As she worked, she could feel the yearning inside her but there was no map she knew of that would take her there.

She finished digging the holes and stood up, brushing the dirt from her jeans. Amber was carefully separating the roots of the final punnet of seedlings. As she placed each of the seedlings in the earth and patted the dirt around them, Fern had a sense of something holy, as if the dull and sometimes painful task of planting had become a ritual that was a vital part of their growth. Iris would say that Amber had green fingers. She thought of Michael then and the sense of presence he imbued every activity with. Suddenly she missed him.

'Mama,' shouted Freya. 'Look Mama.'

Fern looked over to the orchard where Freya was sitting with a hen on her lap and two others pecking at the earth contently next to her.

'That girl's a natural with animals,' said Amber, laughing. 'Come on. I'll show you the herb garden.'

When Fern stepped into the garden she gasped. It felt ancient, as if the herbs themselves had been there forever. It also felt powerful, as if the qualities of each herb had been heightened in some way. She'd always been sensitive to plants and especially to herbs, and could never work in a garden without carrying some of its energy away with her. It was both grounding and unsettling. Somehow the plants imprinted themselves on her, so that for hours afterwards when she closed her eyes they were there in the darkness: leaves, stems, flowers, patterns of nature … even penetrating her dreams. In this garden the effect was greatly increased, as if each plant was jostling for her attention, showing off its properties, Shouting – 'LOOK AT ME!'

Amber was watching Fern intensely. 'You feel it too,' she said.

Fern nodded. 'These plants are powerful.' She shook herself free of their spell and focused instead on the garden itself with its overgrown bushes all going to seed. It hadn't been well cared for. 'You need to cut back perennial herbs,' she said.

'I've never been much good at cutting back,' said Amber. 'It always feels like I'm hurting them. Kia does all the pruning.'

'It does them good,' said Fern. 'See this lavender, it would have lasted much longer if you'd cut it right back to the woody bits. Now it's overgrown and will probably uproot itself or die off in the next year or two. I'd get some new lavender plants. Maybe a few different varieties and put them in for the spring. That way they'll be ready for harvest when these old ones give up.'

Fern reached out and picked a leaf from a bush. She crushed it in her hand and sniffed it. 'Mmm, lemon verbena.' She held it out for Amber to sniff. 'Do you know anything about herbs?

'A few things but I wasn't exactly talented in that area or, as my grandmother put it, I was crap.'

Fern laughed. 'Well among other things, verbena is used to ward off spells and keep witches at bay, so watch out. She walked on, stopping and inspecting plants as she went and pointing them out to Amber, different varieties of thyme, a purple sage and a couple of large green sages, comfrey gone wild … 'For knitting bones,' said Fern, 'St John's Wort,' she added, 'for depression and healing wounds.' Then noticing the nasturtium and dandelions spreading through the garden, she frowned. 'These are great plants, she said, but you have to keep them under control.'

Amber was watching her, surprised. 'Wow. You're a different person in here.'

Fern shrugged. 'I did a course.' She reached down and picked a pink flower. 'Hyssop,' she said, then continued as if reciting, 'useful for coughs, asthma, sore throats, rheumatism … '

'A course doesn't give you that kind of ease. This is the first time you've shown any certainty about anything since we met. You were born for this. You know that don't you?'

'It comes easy to me. But that doesn't mean it's what I should do.'

'I can't believe I'm hearing this,' said Amber. 'How can you be so blind?'

Fern reached down and picked some peppermint that was growing under the shade of a bay tree. Am I being blind? she wondered.

'Why don't we start by cutting and bundling some of the herbs,' she said, changing the subject. 'Then we can hang them up to dry for a few weeks before mixing some different teas.'

Realising she wouldn't get an answer from Fern, Amber sighed. 'Yep. That sounds good.'

'It's getting a bit late in the season but we could still get some rosemary. And the burdock looks good, though that's harder to work with and we need to keep it easy … and safe. We'll cut back the lavender too and next time I'll show you how to make a tincture. That should sell okay.'

As they snipped at the rosemary, the pungent scent reminded Fern of her second meeting with Petrona and the strange words the wise woman had left her with. *Remember,* she'd said. *You must face the shadows and release your fear in order to remember.* Fern paused in her snipping for a moment, only now making the connection. Rosemary was the herb of remembrance, but she wasn't sure what she was supposed to be remembering. She cut some string and wove it around a bunch of rosemary, ready for drying. Petrona had also said that her wisdom was within Fern but again she couldn't see how that was possible. None of it made sense yet she felt on the verge of understanding, if only she could step past her fear. It was as if she were standing on the edge of a precipice seeking the courage to take the necessary step and either fly or fall into the abyss.

Looking up, Fern noticed that Freya had lost interest in the hens and was now helping Kia measure some wood. She watched wistfully, as Freya solemnly held the end of the tape measure, her face a picture of concentration. Kia leaned down and said something to Freya, whose eyes lit up as she smiled proudly. At that, Fern felt the familiar pang; a fusion of sadness and anger, the two so bound up together that sometimes she couldn't tell them apart. Adam should have been doing this with Freya. He was missing out on seeing his daughter grow up and Fern was having to manage all this on her own. It was too much for her to be both a mother and a father to Freya, and it was becoming more and more evident to her that she wasn't doing either role well.

'Is she bothering Kia?' asked Fern

Amber glanced over at the pair and smiled. 'No problem there, he's enjoying her company.' She paused and studied Fern for a moment. 'You and Freya are so alike.'

'Really?' said Fern, surprised. 'Everyone says she's like her father.'

'Maybe, but you're there too. Look how fine her features are; the shape of her mouth and her tiny nose, those wide startled eyes, the way she holds herself and the way she sees into things. Just like you.'

Fern studied Freya for a moment longer, failing to see what Amber was referring to. 'All I see is Adam,' she said and turned back to her pruning.

'How long ago did he die?' asked Amber.

'How do you know?' asked Fern guardedly. She'd never spoken to Amber about Adam.

'Just guessing really. I can see the sense of loss, the heaviness around Freya's heart … and yours,' she added, studying Fern. 'You're carrying a load of grief.'

'Adam died just over two ago.' Tears welled up in Fern's eyes. 'He was protecting the old growth forest,' she said, then went on to describe what happened in a way she'd never done before, letting it all pour out, the anger and the helplessness, the injustice and the desperate need to find a way to forgive the forest worker who'd killed Adam. But she had to forgive Adam too, for putting the forest before her and Freya. And she had to forgive herself for not insisting Adam came back with them that day, even though she'd known, she really had; not in a way she could have put into words or proven to anyone, but she'd known, and despite that knowledge she'd kissed him and turned away.

'Sometimes I can't bear it,' she said, then stopped, her voice choked by the lump in her throat.

'Hey,' said Amber, reaching out and embracing Fern who promptly burst into tears, sobs wracking her body.

They stood like this until Fern's sobs subsided and even then, Amber didn't immediately release Fern from her embrace. 'Don't be so hard on yourself,' she said. 'It's tough being sensitive and sensing things but not being able to change them. You tried. You asked him to come home.'

'But I didn't tell him he was in danger,' said Fern.

'Do you think he would have believed you?'

Fern shook her head. 'No. He would have thought I was being an idiot.'

'If you'd insisted on bringing Adam back that day, he would have resented you telling him what to do and that would have created a crack in your relationship.'

'A crack we would have had a chance to mend,' said Fern fiercely.

Amber nodded. 'Possibly, possibly not. Every action has an effect and there are multiple possible futures. You can sense the future but you can't know it, and not many of us have the skills to tell which path is the most appropriate.'

Fern pondered Amber's words for a moment. If she were suggesting that Adam's death was for the best, then she was fundamentally wrong. 'This path isn't one I would have chosen,' she said, turning away from Amber and wiping her eyes. 'And Adam didn't get a choice,' she added bitterly.

Chapter Twenty-Six

'See where these words take you,' said Jacques. 'Purgatory, forgiveness.'

Fern drew her eyes away from the rain beating against the window and looked at Jacques. 'Why those words?'

'Because you spoke them at the abbey and I want to find out if what happened there is connected with this monk you are uncovering in your past or if you simply picked up on an entity located there. Words are often a good entry point into a past life. Recurring phrases such as *if only* or *I should have* or *no one cares* are like a scratch on a record; they reemerge any time life appears to follow a similar pattern to the event that established the problem. So, if you were a slave in a past life, in this life you might feel trapped in something such as a relationship, or a small space and your reaction will be the same. Sometimes the key to the story behind a reaction lies in the words we use to describe our feelings. Do you see?'

Fern nodded. 'It's like a password.'

'Oui,' said Jacques. 'Exactly. But you do not know where it will take you.'

Fern nodded. Then steeling herself for whatever was coming, she closed her eyes and began repeating the words to herself. *Purgatory, forgiveness, purgatory, forgiveness*, letting them lead her away from this room and into another, where Hugues knelt on a flagstone floor, muttering a prayer quietly to himself as he

rubbed his prayer beads. Before him was a statue of Jesus, cruci-
fied, his face a picture of pain and surrender, his head crowned
with thorns, his hands and feet pierced through, blood dripping
from his wounds. The violence of this image contradicted the
serene atmosphere of the chapel but reflected something of the
turmoil within Hugues who despite his prayer was unable to
focus his attention on God.

'Where are you?' asked Jacques.

'I am in Carcassonne, in a chapel within the cathedral,' said
Fern.

'Are you certain?' asked Jacques, clearly surprised.

'I am not a fool,' said Hugues. 'And even a fool would know
where he is.'

When the bells rang, he stopped his recitation and jolted into
action, standing up carefully so as not to trip over the formal
gown he had donned for the occasion. An occasion he had
almost refused. But in the end curiousity had got the better of
Hugues and he had agreed to the meeting. Only later, pondering
it in the solitude of his bedchamber had he realised that this was
a test from God, and one he must pass without error if he would
continue his rise through the ranks of the church.

Hugues tucked his prayer beads into a pocket then straightened his gown, tugging at the pleats to ensure they fell smoothly
to the ground. As he backed away from the statue of Jesus, he
kept his head bowed, his fingers touching his forehead and chest,
then right and left, forming the cross again and again until he
reached the steps leading into the main body of the cathedral.
Here he halted for a moment. He ran his fingers across his smooth
jawline, massaged the oiled skin of his freshly shaved head and
patted down the remaining circle of hair. Reassured that all was
well with his appearance he climbed the steps and hurried to the
visitor's room where she awaited him.

As he stepped into the room the sunlight filtering through the window blinded him momentarily and all he could see was her silhouette. He waited for his eyes to adjust, noting the thudding of his heart in his chest and the trembling of his fingers. Little by little her features became visible, until finally he recognised the woman standing before him; the source of the unbearable torment that had accompanied him these past ten years.

He studied Roese's face. She had aged, there was no doubt of that but if anything, her beauty had increased over time. Roese was now a mature woman, not the flirting girl who had threatened to turn him away from his calling. Nevertheless, she was still dangerous. Of that he was certain. Perhaps even more dangerous now that he had risen in the ranks of the church and was subject to the envy of those beneath him. And now she was here, standing before him, her eyes searching his, a need within them that Hugues had not seen before. He fought to keep his face expressionless and maintain his distance but just the sight of her made him aware once again of his ravenous hunger, and caught in her spell, he could not take his gaze away. Her gleaming black hair was held back from her face by a finely braided head-dress, a modest emerald taking pride of place on her forehead and making her eyes appear greener than he remembered. She was dressed modestly too, but not as simply as a Cathar, he thought, relieved, as his eyes freed themselves from hers, only to find themselves roaming across her slender form, laced loosely into a dress, its muted green tones further highlighting her eyes. Hugues noted the swell of her breasts and had to fight an overwhelming desire to reach out to her. Wrenching his gaze away, he found himself filled with hatred for this woman who had more power over him than the devil who no doubt she was in league with.

Reading the sudden anger and disdain in his eyes, Roese shrank back involuntarily before gathering her courage once again. 'Hugues,' she said, breaking the silence and stepping forward, hand held out towards him. 'It is good to see you again,' she added, smiling.

Hugues ignored the hand and nodded at her curtly.

Hurt, Roese withdrew her hand and her smile. 'I have brought some gifts,' she said, offering her basket to him.

Hugues gestured towards the table, not deigning to look at the basket. 'Why are you here?'

Shocked by his curt manner, she blushed then hesitated as if uncertain of the best approach. 'My … friend, Ramon d'Orion has been arrested.'

'I am aware of that,' said Hugues, noting the flash of surprise on Roese's face. Clearly she did not yet know his role in Ramon's arrest but it would not be long before she began to suspect. He could almost see the thoughts racing through her head, and it was evident that she was battling to keep her expression neutral.

Hugues tore his eyes away from Roese's face and turned his attention to the view through the window, the distant mountains still capped with snow. For ten years he had monitored Roese from afar and during that time he had fought a long and arduous battle with his nature as all those who serve God must do. For ten years, Hugues had stayed loyal to his love and she too, had appeared to remain loyal to him. Others wondered why Roese, a beautiful young woman, did not marry, blaming her independent spirit and the poverty the family had gradually slipped into since the death of her father. But he had always believed that she remained loyal to his memory. To that one stolen kiss in the meadow that day. The last time they had seen each other before he had taken his vows. Even now he could feel the touch of her lips on his.

'Please Hugues. You are a rising figure in the Church now. I hear that you have power.' She paused and drew her hands together as if in supplication. 'Please use your influence to have him released.'

A smile flirted at the edges of Hugues mouth as he drew his gaze back to Roese. The desperation in her face was evident and he yearned to reach out and slap it away as his anger rose. 'And why should I do that?'

'For the sake of our friendship,' said Roese.

'Friendship!' he exploded. Suddenly afraid of being over-heard, he paused and closed the door to the room then lowered his voice, though it was still laced with vitriol. 'You have be-trayed me with this man. This heretic! And you wish for me to go against God and the Church to have him released?'

Roese looked confused. 'How can I have betrayed you? We were never betrothed. And you have taken vows.'

'Our kiss,' he said, his face flushed. 'With which we sealed our love.'

'But Hugues that was a farewell kiss. We sealed nothing except our eternal friendship.'

'Friends do not kiss in this way.'

Roese blushed. 'No,' she said, 'they do not but the following week you took your vows.' She looked at him, her eyes search-ing his face for some indication of good-will. 'Perhaps if circum-stances had been different … her voice trailed off. 'But you are a priest. You have given yourself to God. I have taken no such vow and I am free to choose whom to love.'

Hugues flushed and turned away, his fury threatening to overcome him. He scornfully inspected the contents of the basket Roese had placed on the table beside them. Herbal concoctions, cordials, a tincture of wine made from the fruit of the local ber-ries. Useful items but bordering on dangerous. She should be more careful.

'Please, Hugues. You have influence. You must be able to have him freed.'

The desperation in her voice moved Hugues and he gazed at her for a long moment, his thoughts and emotions battling with each other as he remembered that last summer and how close to his heart he had held its memory all these years. The days he would find Roese in the fields and help her with her herbs, the meals he shared with her and her mother, filled with laughter and hints of possible futures. He had been aware of her mother's intent. How could he not have been? She hinted at it often enough and treated him like a member of the family. Yet all that time he had nursed his secret, never letting on about his future, allowing himself to believe he was free to choose. Then one day, he had arrived at her house and announced his presence, only to be shown into Elena's room from which Roese was notably absent.

'Why did you not tell us that you were destined for the priesthood?' she had asked, her voice empty of its usual warmth and humour.

Even now, just thinking about it, Hugues could feel again his heart thudding with fear and the awful knowledge that his pretence had been uncovered.

'You will not see my daughter again,' Elena had said, and with that he had been expelled.

Hugues had mumbled an apology and left the house forever. Yet he had found Roese again, waiting for him in the field, and she did not hate him for his subterfuge. Instead she had kissed him, a long and lingering farewell kiss that he had held close to his heart for all these years.

'Hugues?' Roese was looking at him, her eyes pleading. 'Please help Ramon.'

'Help Ramon?' For a moment he wondered what she was talking about but then he remembered and with the memory his fury returned. Ten years had passed and he was still a virgin, despite the many opportunities that had presented themselves in the form of willing women, mainly the wives of noblemen and merchants seeking favours. There were servant girls too who would no doubt have taught him what he needed to know but he dreaded their whispers and the knowing looks they would cast between them. Instead he had remained pure, obeying his vows and earning himself a reputation as a godly and moral man. It had not harmed him and he had risen quickly in the ranks, marked as one who would not be easily bought or bent. And all the time he had told himself that he was being true to his one and only love beside God. When he had discovered that Roese was in an alliance with this heretic, Hugues' fury had been immediate and intense. His love had betrayed him.

'Hugues?' whispered Roese. She wiped the tears from her eyes and continued, her voice breaking with grief. 'I love Ramon. I cannot see him die.'

Hugues wished with all his heart that those words of love were directed at him but they were not. A part of him wanted to reach out and wipe her tears away, to feel the tenderness of her skin beneath his fingers, to touch her lips with his own … but an even greater part knew she should be punished for her disloyalty.

'Ramon is a heretic. I have no power in this matter.'

To his satisfaction, Roese recoiled as if he had slapped her after all.

'I had thought better of you, Hugues. I had never taken you for a small-minded man. Ramon is no heretic. He is a man filled with the love of God.'

'A Cathar.'

'No, not a Cathar.'

'A Cathar sympathiser then.'

Roese hesitated. 'As a man of God, he protects those who are in need of protection.'

'He practices alchemy,' hissed Hugues.

'He is a man of science. A curious man who would explore great things,' said Roese controlling her voice with an effort.

'You would do well to leave him to his punishment or you may find yourself tainted by the stain of his heresy.'

Hugues words were a warning and Roese knew it well but her anger did not allow caution. Her temper had always been her weakness. She met his cold eyes with her own, blazing hot with a new hatred.

Hugues smiled, a chilling smile. 'You would also do well to learn your place as a Christian woman.'

Realising that she had failed in her mission, Roese threw on her cloak and stormed past him. 'I believed you were a friend and an intelligent man,' she said pausing at the door. 'But now I see that you are merely an unthinking pawn.'

'Wait,' called Hugues, as she disappeared through the doorway. When she reappeared, hopeful for a moment that he had changed his mind, he simply gestured at the table, 'Your basket.'

Furious, Roese spun around. 'Keep it,' she called over her shoulder. 'For it is tainted now with your righteousness.'

Faced with an empty door, Hugues's helpless anger overflowed and he swept the basket off the table, watching with a grim satisfaction as the bottles and jars smashed upon the tiles, the sticky cordials seeping onto the floor, the wine splashing red in a wide arc around the room.

Alerted by the noise a servant appeared at the doorway and nervously surveyed the bloody mess.

Hugues strode from the room. 'Clean it up,' he barked over his shoulder.

Fern was breathing rapidly, her fists clenched, the nails digging into the skin of her palms. She opened her eyes, struggling to find a way back into the safety of Jacques' study but all she could see were the stone walls of the cathedral.

Concerned, Jacques stood up and approached Fern, then gave her shoulder a gentle nudge. 'Fern, it is me, Jacques. You are no longer back there.'

'Roese has destroyed everything.' Fern spat the words out and Jacques was surprised at their ferocity. It was as if she'd brought Hugues back with her from the past.

He shook her shoulder again, a little more vigorously. 'Fern, you are here with me, Jacques. In my office.'

Gradually Fern's breathing calmed and the tension in her fists eased. She looked down at her body, relieved to see that it was hers and not Hugues' lumbering frame. Her palms hurt where her nails had dug in and there were spots of blood where one had pierced her skin. She shivered and looked up at Jacques, attempting a smile. 'He's not a nice man.'

Relieved, Jacques smiled. 'He is a torn man. Like many of us.'

'Doesn't it seem strange to you that Hugues lived so near? He was a priest in Carcassonne!'

'Strange, perhaps, but it does not explain what happened when we visited the crypt in St Michel. Was it Hugues who spoke through you? That is still not clear.

'It all seems like too much of a coincidence.' said Fern.

Jacques shrugged. 'What is coincidence but an outcome of intent? It is the product of invisible forces coming together to draw people to a time and a place and enable them to learn through experience.'

'We're just pawns then?'

'Yes and no. For example, I had always wanted to leave Paris and live in the south but ten years ago when I retired, I knew it was time to act. Madeleine loved history so she was drawn to this property and wanted to renovate it. You have a past life history in this area so when you saw that a past life therapist lives here you decided to visit him rather than seek training locally.

None of this might have occurred if one of us did not follow the prompts that led us to this place.'

'And if it hadn't occurred?' asked Fern.

'Then we would have missed an opportunity to learn but other opportunities would have presented themselves.'

Fern thought of all the events that had come together to cause Adam's death. If only she had made him come home with them. If only he had woken earlier. If only he hadn't swapped a night on the platform with Matt when she and Freya had visited him. But then Matt would have died and she loved Matt too …

'What learning could possibly come from Adam's death?' she asked.

'That I do not know,' said Jacques.

Chapter Twenty-Seven

Jacques was away for the day so Fern and Freya walked down the hill to the school. Now that she'd decided to leave Beattie at home, Freya had no qualms about going and ran inside without a moment's hesitation, leaving Fern wishing her own worries could be resolved as easily. She stopped for a coffee and managed a reasonable exchange in French then stocked up at the boulangerie before walking back up the hill to Amber's house. Half way there it started raining and by the time Fern arrived she was wet through and the baguette and pastries were soggy. Soaked and shivering, she stood on the doorstep and stripped off her muddy boots before stepping into the welcome warmth of the kitchen where Amber was bagging carrots for their stall.

'You look like a drowned rat,' said Amber as Fern headed, dripping, towards the fireplace. 'Come upstairs and I'll get you a towel.'

The smell of fresh cut wood filled the bathroom. 'Isn't it lovely,' said Amber, gesturing to the new cupboard fitted along one wall.

'Gorgeous,' said Fern. 'Kia's good at this.'

'Amazing at it. You know he's never learned. Didn't even have a father to show him. He just works it out in his head and gets on with it.' She opened one of the doors to reveal the hot water tank, surrounded by curved and slatted wooden shelves that fitted around it on both sides and were piled with towels. 'Look at that! And there are more shelves up top.'

Amber pulled a warm towel from the shelf and handed it to Fern then fetched her dressing gown. 'Here,' she said, 'you can wear this while your clothes dry.'

Fern gratefully towelled her hair dry then stripped off her clothes and wrapped herself in the dressing gown which was much too big for her, its hem trailing on the ground, and the sleeves reaching to her fingertips.

'You really are tiny,' said Amber, when Fern returned downstairs and hung her wet clothes by the fire.

'And you're clearly Amazonian.' Fern rolled up the sleeves and helped Amber bag the last of the carrots. When they'd finished, Fern reached into her handbag and extracted a bottle of vodka.

Amber raised an eyebrow. 'It's a bit early for that don't you think.'

Fern laughed. 'This is strictly for the tincture. We could do it with apple cider vinegar but I didn't know how to order that in French.'

'Okay, what do we do?' asked Amber

'Did you get hold of some large jars?'

Amber pulled three large preserving jars from the cupboard.

'Perfect. First we wash the lavender then we stuff it tightly in the jars. Usually the dilution is one to three parts vodka to lavender but this lavender isn't completely dried so we'll add a bit more vodka to stop the water in the lavender diluting the tincture.

They worked side by side at the kitchen bench, the heavy rain beating against the window and blurring the world outside.

When they'd topped the jars up with vodka, Fern screwed the lids on. 'There. We're done.'

'That was easy,' said Amber.

'Tinctures are pretty straightforward, not like essential oils, which need loads of equipment. Now we just have to wait for about three weeks until the liquid changes.'

'Right,' said Amber. 'Let's have a cup of tea.'

As they sat down in front of the fire, Fern was reminded of her first meeting with Petrona and smiled at the thought that the old woman was here with them, but in another dimension, rocking in her chair, a ginger cat curled up in her lap. She looked at Amber who was staring mesmerised into the fire. 'How did you become a witch?' she asked.

Amber smiled. 'It's not really a straight road is it, like studying engineering at university or doing a plumbing apprenticeship. I kind of inherited it though. My grandmother was a witch and my great grandmother, much to the horror of my own mother when she found out. I don't think she would have married Dad, if she'd known. She spent all her energy trying to create the perfect suburban life for us; shiny kitchen units, well-trimmed garden, meat and three veg on the table each night at six pm, that sort of thing. I did ballet and my brother did football and my dad went to work every day and got kind of smaller over the years.' Amber paused and sipped her tea. When she spoke again her voice was tinged with sadness. 'My brother always said it was my imagination but it wasn't his size that was shrinking, it was something inside of him.' She looked at Fern. 'Know what I mean?'

Fern nodded, thinking of the sterile suburban world she'd grown up in, the restraints, the constraints, and the fear which had permeated everything.

'Anyway, you can't control life for long because in the end it always steps in and does what it wants. Mum ended up having a nervous breakdown when I was about twelve, so Gran had to take over for a few months. When Mum recovered, she sent Gran home pretty quick, but by then I'd found out who I was.

'My parents wanted me to go to university and study law but instead I went and stayed with my gran for a bit and learned some skills.' She laughed. 'No, not herbs. I didn't have the patience for them.' Amber paused and topped up her mug with the remnants of the tea. 'My skills are mainly in scrying. I can sense things generally though, sometimes see what's coming. And I can talk with nature spirits. A channel, I guess you could say. But I only use it when I need to. You have to be careful who you allow to speak through you.'

Remembering the strange words someone had spoken through her that day in the crypt, Fern shuddered and changed the subject. 'Where did you meet Kia?'

Amber smiled fondly at the memory. 'We were both doing some volunteer work over here on an organic farm. Our eyes met and that was that.'

'And Kia's a witch too?'

'Of a sort. He trained as a shaman. Quite different but not in essence. They're both nature-based traditions'

Fern took a sip of tea. 'Why do you think I'm a witch then?'

'You're a herbalist for starters.'

'But I don't make spells, I don't scry into the future, I don't do any of that stuff.' And I don't want to, Fern added to herself, uncomfortable at the thought of it.

'Okay, I'm using the term witch pretty loosely,' said Amber. 'You've clearly got talents, some latent, others evident, and your reluctance to use them is a pretty big clue.'

'More likely it means I'm not intended to use them,' said Fern. 'We all have a path in life, a destiny ... ' she paused, gathering her thoughts. 'And we all have loads of talents. Some of them we have to ignore if we're going to settle to anything at all.'

Amber laughed. 'The talents that keep hitting us in the face are the ones that direct us on our paths. Yours are shouting and kicking for attention.' Her face grew suddenly serious and she leaned forward in her chair. 'Lots of present-day witches were persecuted for their powers in a past life, so chances are you're carrying the memory of being tortured and killed for your gifts. If it's not a personal memory then you're probably plugging into a collective one.' She paused and eyed Fern, 'though with you it's so strong it has to be personal. Maybe Jacques could help you find it.'

'Maybe,' said Fern, then shivered. Six years ago, the tempest stone had drawn her into the past, showing her flashes of a life where she'd been a healer with a young daughter and both of them had been killed for it. For a moment she saw it again; the command from the priest, the soldier's sword swinging, the shock, the sharp sting of grief as she realised her daughter was dead, then the gloating priest turning to her. Why had she forgotten it all over again? Had Freya been that child? Was that why she didn't trust Fern now?

'Are you okay?' asked Amber. 'You've gone pale.'

'I'm fine,' said Fern, sipping her tea. It felt good to be here in this house of a wise woman, sitting with her friend, the mug warm in her hands, the fire crackling. 'I think what Petrona is trying to do is encourage me to start drawing on the wisdom and the gifts I've inherited rather than the trauma.'

Amber nodded. 'That's the idea but sometimes we have to wade through some pretty awful muck to get there.' Amber stood up and pushed a fresh piece of wood onto the fire. 'More tea?'

'Please,' said Fern.

While Amber filled the kettle, Fern stared into the fire, mesmerised by the crackling flames that flared up to claim the fresh wood. She felt an impatience growing inside her. It was time to get on with life but at the same time she felt trapped; the heavy density of trauma and grief holding her in its chains.

'So how do we draw on the good stuff?' she asked when Amber had sat down again with a fresh pot.

Amber shrugged. 'Partly it's visualisation, I guess, applying your imagination to positive outcomes instead of negative ones. It just sort of happens as you release all the other stuff.'

'I've got a way to go then,' said Fern.

Amber laughed. 'Don't we all.' She filled their cups with the fresh tea. 'It isn't just our experiences in this life or in our past lives that we have to clear though, it's also ancestral trauma.'

'Petrona said something about the ancestors,' said Fern.

'I'm not surprised. You can't properly access the innate until you're free of any negative obligations to the ancestors. You know the severing of just one binding will have repercussions all the way back to its source and forward into your descendants.'

'Really?' asked Fern feeling suddenly sceptical.

'It's true! It's even got a scientific name now. Epigenetics. But really its ancient knowledge. It's the idea that trauma can be inherited and passed through generations. In shamanism it's thought of as bad energy trapped within you or bits of your soul that have been stolen and need to be returned.'

'And this process makes someone a witch?' asked Fern as she poured herself a second cup of tea.

Amber nodded. 'That and other things,' she said. 'Witches stay close to nature, they follow the way of the heart, but in order to follow this path you have to be willing to be free of everything that blocks your freedom. It's never easy.'

'There's no way I'm a witch then,' said Fern. 'I'm not free, I'm trapped in the past.'

'Ah, but you can walk between worlds, you're a sensitive and your gifts are already manifesting themselves; they're impatient for you to catch up.'

Fern sipped her tea and mulled over Amber's words. It seemed there were lots of labels you could apply to being sensitive. Jacques had told her about the gnostic tradition, saying its essence was love and now Amber was claiming witchery as the way of the heart. And then there was shamanism and probably lots of other wisdom traditions. She'd never wanted to commit to one path yet she needed skills, techniques and knowledge to help solve the problems in her life. Maybe it was important to choose a tradition and follow it, to accept the training of a teacher rather than fumble her own way to knowledge with all its wrong turns and its dangers.

She could ask Amber to teach her but that didn't feel right. And anyway, Jacques was already teaching her and he was definitely not a witch! In fact, she was pretty certain he'd sneer at the idea. Even so, he weaves magic, he works energetically. Isn't that the same thing? she asked herself.

The door burst open suddenly, letting in a blast of cold air and making them both jump.

Kia stepped inside and shook himself, droplets splashing brightly across the room. 'Hey. It's wet out there.'

'No kidding,' said Amber. 'There's fresh tea in the pot.'

'Great.' He paused, and looked at Fern, who blushed and drew the dressing gown more tightly around her.

'Wet clothes,' she said, gesturing towards the clothes rack behind her.

Kia nodded and turned to the preserving jars on the kitchen bench. 'These the tinctures?'

'Yes, but they won't look like that in the end. We'll have to strain them into smaller bottles.' Fern turned to Amber. You'll need to choose the bottles, and a name and design a label.'

Amber groaned. 'I'm useless at names and I can't design anything to save my life. Anyone think of a name?' she asked hopefully.

'How about *Amberosia,*' said Fern, plucking the word out of the air.

Amber's face lit up. 'Perfect!'

Chapter Twenty-Eight

The wind and rain had been replaced by a tranquil calm and the air was warmer again, so Fern was sitting in the late afternoon sun on the terrace, trying to read one of Jacques' psychology books, while Freya sat beside her on the sun-warmed flagstones, drawing.

Fern usually enjoyed reading but today she was going over and over the same paragraph. It was her fault, she knew. She was becoming obsessed with Kia. Just the thought of him was enough to send a trickle of excitement through her. But he was completely out of bounds and even if he'd been single, Fern wouldn't want anyone to fill Adam's place. Not for her or for Freya. Yet despite everything, Fern *was* wildly attracted to Kia and Freya *was* forgetting her father; only yesterday she'd looked blankly at Fern when she'd mentioned the way Adam used to carry her on his shoulders.

Fern gave up and closed the book, wishing she could simply imbibe the knowledge in it, instead of having to make sense of all those words. She sighed and closed her eyes, trying to steady her breathing and settle her mind but there was Kia gain, trespassing.

Jacques appeared at the back door. 'Why do you keep moving my things?' he demanded.

'I don't,' said Fern, bracing herself for one of Jacques' moods.

'Then where is the kitchen knife?'

Fern shrugged. 'No idea.'

'I give up!' Jacques threw his hands in the air in frustration and plonked himself down in the chair next to Fern. 'Nothing is where it should be. Nothing is as it seems. What are we to do? I cannot even cook dinner.'

'We could have something easy like scrambled eggs on toast.'

Jacques looked horrified. 'Eggs on toast. That is English food.'

Fern sighed. 'Okay, I'll make an omelette and we can have it with a baguette.'

Jacques looked at her suspiciously, reluctant to let anyone else take over his kitchen.

'I won't break anything,' said Fern. 'You look tired, that's all.'

Jacques sighed and sat down next to Fern. 'Okay,' he said, 'but I'm not tired just exasperated. Do you understand?'

'Perfectly,' said Fern. 'You also look like you could do with a drink.'

Jacques glanced at his watch. 'Oui,' he said. 'Why not? I am too old to drink myself to death.'

Fern smiled to herself and went searching for a bottle of red. Jacques stored most of his wine in a small room off the chapel, which was lined with wine racks. There were no windows in this room and with its thick stone walls, the air maintained a stable temperature, which Jacques had assured her was vital for storing wine. In an effort to create some kind of balance between giving and receiving, Fern had begun topping up the wine racks occasionally, though Jacques was mostly scathing about her choices.

Fern switched on the light and stepped into the tiny room. A single bulb glowed overhead but its low wattage did little to brighten the space. According to Jacques, wine preferred the darkness so this dimness was intentional. As she reached up and retrieved the bottle she'd bought the previous day, there was a sudden surge of air as the door swung shut and the light bulb exploded, showering her in glass. Encased in a thick impenetrable darkness, she froze and listened, her heart thudding in her chest.

'Jacques?' she called quietly. 'Is that you? … Freya?'

Just as she'd expected there was no response. This was not the sort of trick Jacques would play. Nor Freya.

Feeling a cold breath on her neck, Fern swung around quickly, wielding the bottle as if it were a weapon. 'Keep away from me,' she whispered, a sudden burst of anger overtaking her fear momentarily. Immediately the presence receded but she could still feel it there in the background, waiting.

In the pitch blackness, Fern had no idea where the door was and had to feel her way along the racks, her spine tingling and her skin raised in goose bumps as she felt the presence growing again, the air becoming colder by the second. She forced herself to keep moving until finally her hand found the door. To her relief it opened easily, releasing her back into safety.

Back in the kitchen, Fern struggled with the bottle opener and poured two large glasses of wine, her hands trembling so much she poured some on the bench. Then she took a few deep breaths, trying to ground herself once again.

'Merci,' said Jacques when she returned to the terrace with the glasses. He took a sip and closed his eyes, savouring the flavour. 'You have done well. If I am failing to teach you about past lives, then at least you are learning about wine.' Jacques paused and looked at her pale face. 'What has happened?' he asked. 'You look like you have seen a ghost.'

'I have,' Fern said quietly. She turned to Freya. 'Would you mind picking some herbs for our omelette tonight? Then you can help me cook it.'

'Oui Mama,' said Freya, jumping up excitedly.

When Freya was out of earshot, Fern sat down next to Jacques and described what had happened.

'Merde,' he said when she'd finished. 'This is becoming serious. It is almost as if this ghost is playing with us, leaving spaces between visitations so that we become complacent and forget that it is here.'

'It does seem to be getting stronger,' said Fern. 'We should do that exorcism you suggested.'

'Oui,' said Jacques. 'But how? I do not know any priests.'

'Maybe there are ghost busters around,' said Fern, half joking.

Jacques shook his head adamantly. 'I do not want strangers with machines sucking up our ghost. He deserves more respect than this.'

'We could do it ourselves.'

'How? Is there a recipe for the expelling of a ghost?'

Fern had asked Amber about spells and rituals. She'd wondered if the words were important and if a wrong one would create something completely different. Amber had told her that the words have power but the intent behind them was more important. 'The ritual grows around the intent,' she'd said. 'That's what builds bridges between worlds.'

When Fern had asked if a ritual works for anyone, Amber had laughed, 'No. Thank God! When a ritual becomes a recipe, it usually ends up empty, like a shell and then it stops working. The intent or the inner essence of the ritual has to stay true, but the outer form can change when it's needed.'

Fern topped up Jacques' glass. 'We could do a ritual of some sort; make up the words and do our own exorcism.'

'That would be no more effective than play acting,' said Jacques scornfully.

'Not if we create a strong intention that directs the words.'

Jacques looked at her for a long moment. Then he shrugged. 'Why not. It can do no harm.'

'Okay, let's do it after dinner. You can do the talking. It's your ghost.'

Jacques pondered this for a moment then nodded. 'Yes, that is for the best. However, you must join your intent with mine in order to make it stronger.'

'Come on Beattie,' shouted Freya, racing back through the garden, skipping over the uneven paving stones, her hands filled with herbs.

'Here Mama,' she said, dropping a mix of oregano, thyme, sage and parsley onto Fern's lap.

'Perfect,' said Fern. 'Let's cook.'

By the time Fern had finished with it, the omelette looked more like scrambled eggs but Jacques' mood had mellowed over his second glass of wine and to Fern's relief he ate it without complaint.

After dinner Fern put a film on for Freya and tucked her up on the couch in the kitchen. Then she and Jacques went into the chapel to do their exorcism. The overhead light felt too intrusive so Jacques lit the lamp and they sat side by side on the couch illuminated by the flickering light. As the silence grew in the chapel, Fern began to feel nervous as well as self-conscious and was relieved when Jacques finally began speaking hesitantly in French.

'Bon soirée a vous fantôme,' he said, politely greeting the ghost. Then he paused and looked at Fern, 'Merde, it is strange to speak like this to the air.'

'You're doing great,' said Fern.

Jacques gave her a wry smile and began addressing the chapel, his voice gradually gaining confidence. Fern could only understand the occasional phrase: *you are dead … it is time … seek freedom …* so she tried to focus on the meaning behind Jacques words, holding her intention steady and imagining the ghost free at last.

'Allers vers la lumière,' said Jacques finally, the words echoing around the chapel, replaying themselves over and over … *go to the light … go to the light …* Fern found herself holding her breath as the silence in the chapel deepened, until it seemed as if there was nothing beyond this room, as if the world itself had stilled.

Gradually the world began to move once again. The distant chatter of the movie crept into the room and an owl hooted outside. There was no sign of the ghost and nothing to show whether or not the ritual had worked.

'That is that,' said Jacques, looking exhausted. 'Now I would like a coffee.'

Feeling strangely deflated, Fern followed Jacques into the kitchen and sat down at the table while he made hot drinks. The house did feel different somehow. Perhaps it really had worked.

Jacques handed her and Freya a mug of hot chocolate then sat down at the table with his coffee and a bottle of whisky.

Fern raised an eyebrow as he tipped a good measure of the whiskey into his coffee. 'Scotch?'

'Yes, yes, I know. It is my only British trait.' He smiled fondly. 'I learned it from a teacher I once had. A good man. I miss … 'Jacques froze mid word, his coffee half way to his mouth as upstairs a door slammed, followed immediately by another and another.

As Jaques raced upstairs something crashed behind Fern. Turning she saw that Freya had dropped her drink, spilling it on herself before the mug smashed on the tiles. As it soaked through her trousers, Freya started screaming. Fern quickly peeled Freya's wet trousers off and carried her over to the sink, turned on the cold tap and began splashing it on Freya's legs while she struggled to get away.

'It's okay, sweetheart, It's just a spill. The milk wasn't too hot. You'll be fine,' said Fern, crooning the words over and over until they got through to Freya and she stopped struggling. Soon her screams subsided into sobs and then as Fern continued her crooning, the sobs settled into little gasps.

Jacques reappeared in the kitchen, his face red, his breathing heavy. 'Every door upstairs was slammed shut,' he said.

'The hungry man is angry,' said Freya. She threw her arms around Fern's neck, buried her face in her chest and began to cry again.

Jacques sat down heavily at the kitchen table and drained his whiskey-laced coffee then looked at Fern and shook his head. 'So much for our exorcism.'

Chapter Twenty-Nine

'I'm cold,' said Fern.

'Where are you?' asked Jacques

Fern struggled to concentrate. The world was on its side and her cheek felt frozen as she looked up at the late afternoon sun filtering through a window. Was she lying down? She couldn't tell. Then all at once, the window and the sunlight were gone, replaced by a montage of images: Roese laughing outside somewhere, a field perhaps, the sun in her hair adding a wealth of red, copper and gold amongst the brown strands, her eyes playful as she smiles at Hugues; Arnou, the wolfhound curled up before the fire, lifting his head and nuzzling his wet nose into Hugues hand; darkness; a knotted rope bearing down on Hughues back and the festering sores reminding him always of his torment; the love in his mother's face as she draws him into her arms and tells him he'll be a saint one day; the scorn on his brother's face as Roese defeats Hugues with a wooden sword; the soft warmth of Roese's lips on his, it's promise melting all his defences, a treasure held forever in his memory; and the fire, always the fire …

Hugues was lying on the floor paralysed by the terrible cold, a creeping numbness and a sharp pain in his head, as his mind roamed in and out of the past, playing hide and seek with the flames. It was dark now and all he could see was the outline of the window, framing a black sky sprinkled with stars.

'Fern? Where are you?' asked Jacques again.

Hugues shook his head, uncertain. 'I am cold,' he said. 'I cannot move. Please help me.'

'Fern, it is time to return now. You are here with me in my office and all is well.'

The concern in Jacques' voice filtered slowly into Fern's mind and she opened her eyes, blinking in the sudden daylight. She was shivering, her teeth chattering and her mind muddled. For a moment Fern wasn't sure where she was. It felt as if a part of her was in two places at once. She was too heavy, her joints aching and stiff, and there was still a pain inside her head but it was the remorse that was the hardest to bear; the remorse, the helplessness, the waste … and permeating it all, a furious sense of betrayal.

Jacques was looking at her with an expression of concern. Fern tried to smile and put him at ease but her features felt frozen in place. When she shivered again, Jacques fetched a blanket and covered her with it.

'What happened?' asked Fern.

'I'm not sure. I thought we were in your dying moments.' Jacques ran his hands through his hair, clearly worried. 'I hoped this was the breakthrough we had been looking for and that to-day's session would free you from the residue of this past life. However, there was something holding Hugues there. Do you know what it was?'

Fern thought for a moment. 'No. But it was pretty intense emotionally. A blend of fury and guilt and regret.'

'Ah,' said Jacques. 'Then there is something else in the lifetime of this man that is waiting to be looked at. We will have to seek it.' He paused and looked at Fern then sighed. 'But not today. You have had enough.'

Fern nodded, relieved. 'Is it always this hard?'

'No, usually there is a willingness to release what is trapped. Almost the opposite of what is happening here.'

Fern wrapped the blanket more tightly around herself, an idea beginning to form in her mind. 'When I visit him, does he know I'm there?' she asked, remembering the dream when Hugues had looked straight at her as if he could see her.

'No,' said Jacques. You are simply experiencing the past once again. As an onlooker but usually through the eyes of the past life.

'So am I possessing him?'

'I do not believe so. At least not in any way that he would understand.'

Could I go back and speak to him rather than be in him?

Jacques looked at her, uncomprehending.

'Kind of pass on a message,' explained Fern, suddenly excited. 'Like an angel.'

Jacques smiled at the idea but shook his head. 'I have not seen it happen in my many years of therapy.'

'But if I can visit Hugues in the past in order to understand something then why can't he receive a message from the future?'

'In the past you do not exist,' said Jacques. 'This is a conundrum I have pondered for many years. Is it possible to intervene in a life in some way, to pass on a message at a crucial time in the development of the past life? I don't know. But we could be changing the past and that would carry many implications regarding history.' He paused and lit a cigarette. 'And of course, there would also be many implications regarding therapy.'

Fern remembered Petrona's strange words that day. *You are where you were but you have stepped through into another time. It happens. Time does not run in a straight line as we are taught. Instead all times run concurrently.'*

'What if we're not stepping into the past but into another dimension?' Fern asked.

Jacques shrugged. 'There are many theories. Perhaps linear time is constructed. Perhaps we live all our lives at once, as fragments of a higher self so that when we experience a past life we are actually stepping between dimensions and connecting to another part of ourselves. But then some people say that it is not our own past we are experiencing; instead, we are plugging into the collective unconscious, where we link with something that parallels the issues within our life.' Jacques stood up. 'As I said, I do not know the answers. It is enough for me that it works as a therapy. 'Come, it is lunch time and you have an appointment with your hippy friend.'

That afternoon Fern decided to take the longer route to Amber's, making her way alongside the river, through the dying brambles, their leaves a vivid red and gold. It was quiet today, the cicadas long gone and the air still, only the rushing river breaking the silence. Her session with Jacques had been exhausting and now she was worried that Hugues was taking her over. She felt bigger somehow, and heavier. It was a bright day and the sun was warm against Fern's back but she still carried the cold within her, as if her experience that morning had penetrated her bones. She shivered, feeling the swirling anxiety in her chest forming into something almost solid.

Last night's botched exorcism was also worrying her. If anything, the ghost seemed to be gaining strength and focus, and although Fern had told Freya it was harmless, she was worried by her daughter's strangely certain pronouncement that the 'hungry man' was angry.

Amber had warned Fern that intent is never as straightforward as we want it to be, explaining that you can think one thing and mean another, wish for one thing but unconsciously wish for another. 'We blame the spell for backfiring or not working, but usually we're to blame,' Amber had said.

Fern wondered if she'd played a part in the failure of the exorcism. Was there some part of her that needed the ghost here? Or was it Jacques' doing? His wife had been fond of the ghost so perhaps he didn't want to release it after all.

As Fern approached the woods, the sun slipped behind some clouds and the shadows between the trees darkened. In the distance gun shots rang out and Fern looked around nervously. Jacques had warned her it was hunting season so she would be in danger from both the wild boar and the bullets.

Remembering Amber's ritual before entering the woods, Fern decided that she too would ask permission, though she'd not brought a gift. 'Hi woods,' she said, feeling a bit silly talking out loud like this. There must be a right tone, something serious and deferential but all she could conjure was something casual. 'It's me again … I'm sorry I didn't knock last time,' she added for good measure, then asked permission to enter.

'Thank you,' she said, after waiting for a moment. She stepped into the woods, her heart suddenly feeling lighter, the anxiety dissipating as the steadiness of the trees stilled the tension inside her. Today the woods felt different, not friendly as such but as if she were a part of them instead of an intruder.

As she walked, Fern caught herself hoping to see Kia working amongst the trees but though she listened out for the sound of chopping, the woods were empty of human sounds. When she stepped into the clearing, she was surprised there was no one in the garden. Perhaps Amber was inside. The land rover was missing and Fern felt a momentary disappointment that Kia was out, which was quickly counteracted by relief. If he was here, she'd struggle to hide her feelings.

Fern paused at the door and peered through the glass but the kitchen was empty. She knocked on the door and waited but there was no reply. Then she opened it a little. 'Hello,' she called. 'Amber?'

Puzzled, Fern wondered if Amber had forgotten their plans to make the rosemary tincture today. It seemed out of character. Perhaps something had happened. She called out again and waited but still there was no reply. Then just as she was about to turn away, the door opened.

'Hey,' said Kia. He looked sleepy as if she'd woken him from a siesta. Sleepy and more beautiful than ever, his t-shirt crumpled, his trousers sitting loosely on his hips, dreadlocks framing his square jaw.

'Hi. Is Amber around?' asked Fern, the inevitable blush rising into her cheeks.

'She's out,' said Kia. He yawned and scratched his chest, revealing the tight muscles of his stomach under the t-shirt.

'Oh, I thought we were making a tincture today.'

'She had something important to do. Come in. I'll make us a coffee.'

As Fern stepped through the door, Kia gave her a hug and for just a moment she felt herself melting into his arms. Pulling away Fern inspected the lavender tincture she and Amber had prepared. 'It's nearly ready,' she said. 'Next week we'll have to sieve it and bottle it, and then you can sell it at the market.'

'Sounds good,' said Kia, putting the percolator on the stove.

Fern sat down on the couch watching him in the kitchen, getting out the mugs, heating the milk, his movements so graceful and yet there was strength there too. She could look at him forever.

Kia sat down next to Fern on the couch and handed her a coffee, his fingers brushing her hand and making her blush all over again. Then he stared at her searchingly until Fern had the disquieting sensation that he was seeing inside her, uncovering all her secrets.

'I find you attractive,' he said eventually.

'Me? … Thank you.' Fern looked away, not knowing what else to say.

As the silence lengthened between them, Fern sipped her coffee, feeling Kia's physical presence more and more intensely. Outside the wind had picked up, reflecting the turbulence inside Fern.

When Kia leaned towards her, Fern forced herself to back away. 'I think I should go.'

Kia touched her cheek with his fingers and the shock of it raced through Fern. 'Don't go,' he said and kissed her.

Despite her doubts, Fern's body betrayed her and she responded, losing herself in the kiss, feeling herself melt into him.

Remembering where she was, Fern pulled away. 'I can't do this.'

'Why not? You want to.'

'You're with Amber. It wouldn't be right.'

'We follow our needs,' said Kia.

They kissed again and then he slipped his hand under Fern's shirt. She shivered at the roughness of his skin, her nipples reaching out to him.

Fern's mind was struggling to return her to her senses but her body had a mind of its own. She ran her fingers over the soft hairs covering his chest and felt the contours of his muscles, the hard buttons of his nipples. It had been so long since she'd touched anyone like this. The thought of Adam brought her back to her senses momentarily but then Kia kissed her again and her body forgot itself all over again.

He stood Fern up and peeled off her clothes, one layer at a time until she was standing naked. Then he stared at her, taking his time, his eyes roaming over her, absorbing every aspect. Instead of embarrassment, her body responded with desire.

'You're beautiful,' he said. Gently he sat Fern gently back on the couch then took off his own clothes and stood naked before her.

'You're beautiful,' said Fern. She reached out to Kia and pulled him towards her, wanting his mouth to explore every part of her, wanting him to penetrate deep inside of her, wanting life.

Chapter Thirty

T he narrow street outside the school was usually filled with smiling parents and grandparents, as well as swarms of children ecstatic at finding themselves freed from the bondage of the classroom, but today Fern was early and the street was practically empty. When she'd come to her senses Fern had dressed quickly, then grabbed her bag and rushed out of the house, mumbling something about collecting Freya from school.

Now she climbed up the steps into the empty school yard and sat down on a bench overlooking the street below. It was a relief to have some time to pull herself together before seeing Freya. The school grounds were small and covered in concrete, with only an occasional tree breaking up the grey monotony; unlike the street below where each house was decorated with pots of geraniums, different coloured shutters, pretty fly-screens hanging from the doors, stones and shells on window ledges, and vines draped over balconies or winding along clothes lines, their leaves turning a vivid red as autumn progressed.

It was a pretty sight and one that usually caught Fern's attention but today her body was still tingling with the memory of her love making with Kia and her mind was trying to grasp the implications. Despite her growing worry about what she'd done, something had changed inside her; she could feel it already, her armour dismantling, the pieces clanging to the ground. But she was also filled with remorse. It should never have happened and now it couldn't be undone. She'd betrayed Amber and lost a friend, but Amber had lost everything: her partner, her life here and the business she and Kia were building together. But I'm not the only one at fault here, Fern thought. Kia loves Amber, so why would he betray her? And why did I go along with it? For a moment she wondered if he'd cast a spell on her but she knew that was ridiculous. If it was a spell, it wasn't the magic sort, and she'd been the one weaving it ever since she'd met him in the forest that afternoon. Fern was an adult. She had a mind of her own. She could have said no but she'd wanted to say yes.

When the bell sounded, she stood up and scanned the children, searching for Freya who eventually ran outside with Henri, shouting and laughing and surrounded by a small group of friends. Fern marvelled at how quickly Freya had found her way back into the group. Was it that easy to divide your life like this? Perhaps at Freya's age, but there'd be more issues as she got older. She just hoped her daughter wouldn't turn away from her abilities the way Fern had, hiding behind cynicism and trying desperately to fit in.

Freya was talking in French, interspersing it with English and charades as was necessary. Listening to her, Fern wondered again at how quickly Freya had found her voice in this country which had effectively silenced her own. Perhaps language was not as important for small children who could communicate in so many other ways. How long could she expect Jacques to speak English for her convenience? But then, how long could they stay here now that this had happened? If the ghost didn't drive them out, then Fern's stupidity would.

Then it struck Fern that she no longer had a way of making money. Their small business venture was over even before it had properly begun. She couldn't work with Amber again and she couldn't tell her why. It would be best if they returned to Tasmania as soon as possible, she realised feeling her heart sink.

She and Freya were growing to love this place, and she hadn't finished working with Jacques.

'Mama,' shouted Freya, running up and throwing her arms around Fern's waist in an unusual display of affection. 'Can Henri come and play? Please. Please. His mum says she'll come and get him later.'

An hour later, Fern was standing at the kitchen bench preparing a plate of fruit for Freya and Henri who were playing outside in the garden.

'Have you gone deaf?' asked Jacques.

As the question penetrated her mind, Fern paused in the middle of slicing an orange and looked over at Jacques. 'No. Why do you ask?'

'I have been speaking to you and you are not hearing anything I say.'

'Sorry. What were you saying?'

Jacques opened his mouth to reply but was interrupted by a loud rapping on the door.

Certain it was Amber, Fern felt herself tense. Would Kia have told Amber what had happened? If he had, Amber would bring accusations and if he hadn't then she'd bring apologies for not being home earlier. Fern didn't know which would be worse.

'Ah,' said Jacques, heading for the front door.

Listening to Jacques effusive greeting, and the rapid exchange in French, Fern felt a fraction of her tension dissipate. It wasn't Amber. With trembling fingers, she finished arranging the fruit on the plate and called out for Freya and Henri who ran in from the garden, complaining of being thirsty. Fern poured them each a drink, put the plate of fruit on the table and watched it disappear in seconds.

Jacques reappeared, carrying a large cardboard box which he placed on the table.

Freya looked at it curiously as she stuffed a final slice of apple into her mouth. 'What's in there?' she asked.

'Ah,' said Jacques. 'That is a mystery.'

There was a scuffling noise from inside the box. 'It's moving,' shouted Freya.

'Would you like to have a look?'

Freya nodded eagerly and she and Henri climbed up onto the table to watch as Jacques opened the box. Freya gasped as a creamy coloured hen stuck its head out and looked around. 'Chickens, Mama,' she shouted. 'Three of them. Where shall we put them? Can we let them free in the garden?'

'We will put them in the hen house,' said Jacques. He picked up the box. 'Shall we go and settle them in?'

Fern followed Jacques and the excited children through the walled garden and into the back of the property. To her surprise the hen house was no longer derelict. The hinges on the door had been replaced and the wire mesh nailed back in place, fresh straw was scattered on the ground inside the house and the laying baskets were clean and filled with straw.

'Can we let them out?' shouted Freya when Jacques put down the box in then hen house.

'Shhh,' said Jacques. 'You will frighten them.'

'Can we?' whispered Freya.

Jacques nodded and Freya and Henri opened the box. Seconds later the hens poked their heads up cautiously before jumping out and shaking their wings.

'What shall we call them?' shouted Freya, sending the hens fluttering into the corners of the enclosure.

Jacques gave the children some seed to scatter about and moments later the hens were pecking it up, while the children looked on, trying to pat them and arguing over names.

Fern looked at Jacques, who was smiling at the scene before him.

'What?' he barked when he noticed her looking.

She raised an eyebrow. 'I thought you said hens were too much trouble.'

He shrugged and stifled a smile. 'It is wrong to buy eggs when we can make our own.'

Between them, Freya and Jacques lifted Fern's mood so by the time dinner was over, the world felt a little more manageable. Fern finished putting away the dishes and sought out Freya who was nodding off on the couch, a picture book propped up on her knees.

'Come on then, let's get you ready for bed.'

'Not yet,' said Freya, forcing her drooping eyes open.

'School tomorrow,' said Fern. 'You need to rest up for that.' She scooped up her reluctant daughter in her arms and kissed her on the nose. 'I'll sing you a lullaby,' she promised.

When the nightly routines had been completed and Freya was tucked in bed with clean teeth, a shiny face and fresh pyjamas, Fern bent over and kissed her. 'How about rock-a-bye baby? That used to be your favourite.'

Freya nodded eagerly so Fern began.

Rock-a-by baby

On the tree top,

When the wind blows

The cradle will rock.

When the bough breaks,

The cradle will fall,

And down will come baby

Cradle and all.

Fern reached over to kiss Freya on the forehead. 'Night, night, sleep tight.'

Freya kissed her back, her soft lips brushing Fern's cheek. 'Daddy fell too. Just like the baby,' she said sleepily.

Fern felt as if she'd been winded. She hadn't thought about the lullaby, hadn't made the connection, just sung it mindlessly. Yet Freya had seen it.

'Yes,' she said, struggling to form the words. 'Just like Daddy. Do you miss him?'

Freya didn't answer, her eyes had closed and her breathing steadied as she slipped into sleep. Fern watched her for a moment, wondering what was going on inside her daughter. Lately it had seemed as if she'd forgotten her father, which wasn't surprising given that more than two years had passed – a long time in the life of a child. But here she was reminding Fern about Adam, as if Fern were in danger of forgetting him. And she was. The memory of making love with Kia flooded back in and the world suddenly became unmanageable all over again.

Chapter Thirty-One

Sensing Jacques' frustration, Fern closed her eyes and tried again, but her thoughts were skipping around in her head and she couldn't fix on anything. Disparate images were flashing in and out of her vision too quickly for her to catch, and only exacerbating her fear. She was trapped in her mind following circuits that led back on themselves, rerouting, seeking a way out but finding only walls.

'What's wrong with you?' asked Jacques.

'I can't settle my thoughts.'

'Merde,' he said, his irritation spilling over. 'This is the slowest past life regression in the history of my practice!' He groaned and buried his face in his hands. 'And I am supposed to be teaching you how to do it! What sort of teacher does this make me?'

'How long does it usually take?'

'A few sessions at most, though some are more stubborn than others. This life that we are working on must be pivotal in some way. Something important hinges on it but we will not find it if you refuse to concentrate.'

'I'm trying,' protested Fern. She shivered suddenly, feeling her skin prickle and looked around fearfully, wondering if the ghost was making its presence felt. But the chill was inside her. Fern shivered again then crossed her arms over her chest, instinctively trying to sustain her body temperature.

'Are you unwell?' asked Jacques.

'I'm okay, just a bit cold.' More likely it was a hangover, she thought. She'd drunk too much last night. Too much for her, anyway. Jacques had matched her glass for glass and then some, and he hadn't appeared to feel it, either then or now. He never did and she envied him his iron constitution.

After settling Freya into bed, Fern had come downstairs, the lullaby repeating itself over and over in her head, reminding her of everything she'd lost. She'd quickly drained the glass of wine Jacques placed in front of her and poured herself another, finding the escape she was searching for in wine and conversation. Around two in the morning she'd cheerfully staggered upstairs, fallen into bed and immediately into a deep sleep, only to wake in the early hours with a fuzzy mouth, a headache and a gut churning with panic as the realisation of what she had done hit her harder than ever.

When Fern shivered again Jacques looked at her more closely. 'You are unwell.'

'No. I'm fine.' But even as she said it, Fern realised that her throat was stinging and the glands beginning to swell and ache. All her strength was draining away and even through the thick socks she was wearing, her feet felt icy cold on the tiled floor.

Jacques leaned over and felt her forehead. 'You are very hot. You must go to bed.'

Something hit Fern on the forehead and she woke abruptly, not knowing where she was. Light was streaming in through a crack in the blind so it was clearly daylight. But she'd been somewhere else and now she was between two places, neither here nor there. She could still feel the numbness, her body lying prostrate, her cheek resting on the tiles of a floor somewhere, the cold seeping into her. She touched the right side of her face and discovered it was icy cold.

Gradually the numbness began to recede and she was able to identify the familiar objects in her bedroom: the sturdy chest of drawers opposite, the bedside table beside her, the brass lamp with its tasseled cream coloured shade, a glass of water Jacques must have put there, and the framed photograph of Adam smiling into the camera. Unable to meet his eyes, Fern fixed her gaze instead on the portrait of Joan of Arc on the wall, which she found strangely comforting, just as she did the statue of Mary Magdalene above the front door of the house; two strong women, driven by love and true to their vision. If only she could take strength from them.

Fern rubbed the spot on her forehead where she'd felt something hit her in her dream, and found a tender bump which puzzled her. The dream had fled, leaving her with the familiar feeling that she was losing herself. It was as if the boundaries of her current self were not strong enough to keep out the other self from the past, or perhaps that self was already in her and only now was trying to break free. Fern wondered again if she should try the protective exercise Kia had suggested but it felt silly tugging at an invisible part of herself as if it were real. The thought of Kia sent Fern into a fresh panic and she groaned as the memory replayed itself all over again. She'd enjoyed it but now she couldn't find any trace of her desire for Kia. It was as if that one act of love making had set her free of him. But too late. The damage was already done.

Fern's mouth was dry so she leaned over and took a sip of water, but her throat was swollen and raw and it hurt to swallow. Shivering suddenly, she curled her knees tightly into her belly and pulled the blankets up close to her chin in an attempt to warm herself. At Jacques insistence she'd gone to bed and fallen into a deep sleep, but now she had no idea what time it was.

Worried that she would be late collecting Freya from school, Fern rolled over in the bed and sat up. As she did so, her hand touched something cold and she automatically clasped it with her fingers. It was the tempest stone. Puzzled, she turned it over in her hand, staring at its fluid beauty and wondering how it had found its way back to her. This must be what had woken her a few minutes earlier, landing on her forehead and snapping her free of her dream. But who had thrown it? A surge of fear raced through Fern and she tried to turn her eyes away from the stone but it had her transfixed. Liquid fire, she thought, her gaze caught in its gold and red veins.

As she watched, the veins in the stone began to flow and Fern felt the familiar dizziness descending on her. A moment later she saw fire. There were crowds too, jostling for position, most with their faces turned eagerly to the flames, some holding small children on their shoulders, only a few averting their gaze in disgust. Fern stood at a window, looking down on the crowds in the square outside but even from here the smell of burning flesh pervaded her nostrils. She grimaced, wanting to turn away but unable to move, her eyes drawn to the fire which had been lit only moments before. The wood was dry and there was little smoke, so the victims would not die a merciful death from smoke inhalation. Instead they would experience the agonising ferocity of the flames. Three of the victims were screaming for mercy, two were crying quietly, while one remained silent and digni-fied, her eyes scanning the crowd as if looking for someone. As Fern watched, the young woman's gaze lifted above the crowd and began scanning the building behind before settling on the window in which Fern stood framed. They remained this way, their eyes locked, until the flames rose around the silent woman, consuming her.

Fern lay in bed for three days, tossing and turning, her temperature rising and plummeting despite the pills Jacques insisted she take every few hours that were supposed to settle the fever. At times she wondered if Amber had sent this illness. She was a witch after all. Perhaps it was a curse, or a spell, she thought. But soon she stopped thinking and lost herself in delirium, slipping in and out of sleep, losing all track of time. The dreams were strange but repetitive too, and it felt as if she were trapped inside them, going around and around, seeking but never finding.

Amber's face kept appearing and the coldness of her expression made Fern shiver. For dream after dream Fern found herself searching her friend's eyes, going deeper and deeper into the patterns of her retina until she was immersed within them, shivers wracking her body. Then Kia appeared and she could see right through his skin. Fern watched, hypnotised by the blood pumping through him, her own body heating again until she had to toss her blankets away.

Sometimes she woke and Jacques was there, wiping her forehead with a wet cloth, cooling her. Sometimes Freya was there, sitting quietly on the chair by the bed, watching Fern, her face expressionless. Sometimes she woke and she was alone. Once Fern felt something next to her, a sense that there was someone else in the bed and she leapt up screaming until Jacques came, with Freya behind, staring at her with eyes wide. Then Fern slid back into nightmares and became Hugues, tormented, striding down darkened halls, slapping himself with the ropes, destroying himself, riddled with anger and guilt, his mind obsessed with Roese as he walked along endless dark passageways, seeking but never finding.

Fern woke to find herself bathed in sweat, the sheets wet beneath her, the pillow damp. She tried to push off the bed covers but they were too heavy. She tried again and then gave up, sinking back into a delirium. When she opened her eyes again a man was standing by the side of the bed. He smiled and asked her how she was feeling and then took her temperature and all at once she felt safe, knowing that a doctor was here, helping to pull her out of this nightmare. She tried to thank him but her mouth was dry and the words wouldn't come. Then his face became transparent and when he spoke again the movements of his mouth and the words it emitted were two separate things. Fern watched in horror as he hissed in her face. *We are one. You would do well to remember.*

When Fern opened her eyes again Freya was there, holding Jeannie. Fern smiled and reached out to stroke the cat but Jeannie hissed and arched her back, sending out a sharp claw which dug into Fern's hand, before squirming out of Freya's arms and dashing across the room as if a demon were chasing her. Fern stared at the blood on her hand and was suddenly overcome by the stench of effluent and rotting flesh. Then she was suddenly cold again, her body shaking under a growing mound of blankets as Jacques tried to warm her.

On the fourth morning, Fern awoke free of fever. She felt light and empty after days of sipping water when Jacques had insisted, but refusing all offers of food. The world had continued without her. Outside, birds were welcoming the morning just as they always did, and Fern could hear Jacques in the kitchen preparing breakfast for Freya. The smell of fresh baguette and coffee drew Fern out of bed and down the stairs, which she negotiated carefully, her legs trembling and weak.

'Ah,' said Jacques. 'You have returned to us.'

Fern smiled and reached out to hug Freya who was sitting at the table drinking her hot chocolate.

'You look like a witch,' said Freya, shrinking away.

Jacques laughed. 'Freya is right. You do not look your best.'

Disconcerted, Fern looked in the mirror, to discover that she really did look a mess; her face was pale, her hair had found its way into bird's nests sticking up all over the place in clumps, and her eyes looked somehow different.

Fern made herself a coffee and tore off a chunk of baguette.

'A good sign,' said Jacques, noting her appetite. 'But you must take it easy today. A fever like this leaves you tired.' He took Freya's hand. 'Come ma chérie, it is time for school.'

Fern blew Freya a kiss which was not reciprocated. Instead, Freya stared at her blankly for a moment, before following Jacques out the door. Fern was left alone in the kitchen, wondering what had happened to further damage her relationship with her daughter. Could Freya possibly resent her illness? Had Fern said something in her fevered delirium to upset her. Then it struck her that Freya had already lost her father and might have been scared of losing her mother too. But if that was it, why was she so withdrawn now? It didn't make sense but it did reinforce Fern's sense that they needed to return to Tasmania soon, to Freya's grandmother and uncle, and whatever memories remained of her father.

Carrying her coffee, Fern walked to the chapel and peered through the window as Jacques helped Freya with the seat belt and then ruffled her hair affectionately. She felt a surge of envy that a stranger could so easily win her daughter's trust yet the abyss between her and Freya seemed to be growing by the day. Ironic, considering she'd come here to find a way of healing whatever it was that lay between them.

As the car pulled out of the drive and onto the road, the air in the chapel suddenly chilled. Sensing something behind her, Fern spun away from the window and glimpsed a figure standing near the door. Startled, she jumped and dropped her coffee, the cup exploding on the floor. When she looked again the figure had gone.

As Fern bent over to pick up the pieces, she noticed that her hands were shaking, and this sent a surge of fury through her. 'Fuck off,' she shouted to the empty room. 'And stay away from Freya.'

Chapter Thirty-Two

Washed, dressed and hair free of tangles, Fern arrived at Jacques' office at their normal time. He was typing on the laptop, his face tensed in concentration and she hesitated at the door, not certain whether to interrupt him.

Sensing he was being watched, Jacques looked up, surprised. Seeing Fern, he frowned. 'Tu es malade. We will not work today.'

'I'm fine. Really I am.' It was the truth. Fern felt weak but well.

Jacques shook his head. 'This past life regression can be a tiring process. That is most likely why you became sick.'

'I need to finish this, Jacques.'

Surprised by the urgency in her voice, Jacques stared at her for a moment as if considering the pros and the cons. In the end he nodded. 'D'accord. But the session will not be a long one. Come, sit down.'

As soon as Fern closed her eyes she gagged.

'What is wrong?' asked Jacques, concerned.

'It stinks,' said Fern, covering her nose.

'What stinks?'

'I don't know. It smells like sewerage.' She hesitated. 'And death.'

'Where are you?'

Fern was walking along a dank and freezing passageway. 'In a passageway. I think it's a jail.'

Carrying a set of keys, a man in a ragged uniform was limping ahead on bowed legs. He stopped outside a door, turned a key in the lock and pushed it open, before gesturing to Hugues. 'All yours,' he said and winked, a lewd expression on his toothless face.

Hugues scowled and pushed past him. 'Leave me,' he growled as he stepped into the cell, then paused, shocked by the fetid smell.

'Hugues,' cried Roese, her eyes lighting up with hope. 'You came.'

Hugues stared at the filthy bruised figure, her hair laced with straw, her dress torn, her face pale and terrified. He could see little trace of his beloved.

'So this is what you have been reduced to,' he said, his voice cracking with a sudden surge of sorrow. 'For the love of a heretic you would sacrifice yourself?'

'Yes I would, for I cannot live a lie and I cannot live without him. Ramon was … ' she paused and corrected herself, her voice dull with grief. 'Ramon is my true beloved. He is my soulmate.'

'And yet you loved me.'

'As a child yes but not as a lover.' Seeing his expression, Roese hastened on. 'We were friends, Hugues, tied together by loyalty and a shared history.'

'Loyalty!' scoffed Hugues. 'I do not see any loyalty.'

Fire flashed in Roese's face, giving Hugues a glimpse of the old Roese, fierce and intelligent. 'You were the one who left me, Hugues. Maman had high hopes for a match between us and I would have welcomed a proposal from you.' She met his gaze, her eyes boring into his. 'But you were already pledged to the priesthood and you had not told us. As you know, Maman was livid when she discovered this, but I was willing to forgive you. If there has been a betrayal here, it was … ' She gasped in pain, tears springing into her eyes as Hugues slapped her hard on the face.

'Do not twist the truth, witch.'

Roese wiped her eyes and calmly met Hugues' gaze once more. 'I am truly sorry if the love you felt for me was not matched by my feelings for you. I did love you Hugues, but I pity the man you have become.'

Her words were like a dagger thrust into Hugues's heart. Roese was right. He had been greedy, wanting to live two lives, one with the church and one with this woman who could never have been his lover once he had taken his vows. Other priests had carnal relations, taking whores, village girls, even sometimes powerful ladies, but he had chosen not to follow this road. Despite the difficulties that arose from his decision he had held to his principles, buoyed always by his love for Roese, his motivations aligned with the highest good of the Church to whom he was wed. Yet Roese had succumbed to the love of another, making a mockery of his sacrifice. At this Hugues fury grew once again for it was evident that Roese and her mother had bewitched him all those years ago; using their skills to cast him under their spell and bind him to Roese.

Hugues looked at her closely. She had been roughly treated; tortured no doubt, most likely raped by the guards. At the thought of that stinking toothless guard having his way with her, Hugues felt an even greater fury. He would see to it that the man lost his job. Perhaps even his life.

Hugues knew that he held the key to Roese's life and death. That a word from him in the right place would enable her to live, but it would also provide ammunition to those who wanted to harm him. And there were plenty who were envious of his rapid rise within the church. Intervening would also go against his own beliefs which mirrored the official policy of the church towards heretics. They were a dangerous force and one that must be stamped out. It broke his heart that Roese had crossed into the camp of the enemy but it was his head not his heart that must decide the outcome.

'There is nothing I can do for you now. You will die in the morning.' As he pronounced her sentence, Hugues felt an unexpected sense of relief. Perhaps her death would liberate him from the spell she had cast over him.

Roese's body sagged in defeat for a moment before she drew herself up again, not willing to let him see her fear. 'So be it. Then I will walk into the light and join my beloved.'

'You will take confession now?'

The fear returned to Roese's eyes and she had to take a moment to gather herself again. 'Yes. And the last rites. I am no heretic Hugues and neither was Ramon. We follow the Way of Love but this does not mean that I have ever denied the Church.'

She knelt down before him and bowed her head. There was a moment's silence as she gathered her thoughts. 'Father, forgive me for I have sinned. I have had hateful thoughts against those who imprison me… And I have loved a man … ' Her voice broke and she paused, struggling to control herself. 'More than I have loved myself or the Church.'

Hugues stared down at the top of her head, bowed before him in a submission that gave him no pleasure. With each word she was condemning herself further but that no longer mattered as the damage had already been done and there was no turning back. Her hair was filthy, her bare arms bruised. She was hurt but not broken and for a moment he wondered what it would take to break a woman such as this. He looked away quickly, deliberately shifting his thoughts, not wanting to imagine what her torturers had done to her, for to do so would soften his anger and make it impossible for him to continue. Deliberately he turned his mind to the heretic, Ramon.

'You loved this man more than God?' he asked, his voice heavy with condemnation.

Roese looked up then and met his gaze. 'I love Ramon more than the *Church,*' she clarified.

The words of a heretic, thought Hugues. But this was no surprise. She and her mother had always been independent in their thinking and supporters of the Cathars. Even eleven years ago they had been veering dangerously towards heresy. It did not do to let a woman think for herself. Women were easily led, as had been proven from the beginning of time with the temptation of Eve.

'Have you given yourself to him?' he asked.

Roese hesitated before giving a quick, almost imperceptible nod.

'How often,' asked Hugues.

'That is not your business.'

'Yes, it is,' said Hugues, grasping her and pulling her to feet. 'Each time you have opened your legs to this heretic you have sinned and turned yourself into a common prostitute.'

Roese remained silent, her eyes fixed on his.

'Tell me,' he ordered. Then in the wake of her continued silence, he shouted. 'Tell me!'

Hugues grabbed her shoulders and shook her, amazed at how fragile she was. She did not fight back, just stood and waited, watching the battle rage within him. In a fury he tore at her dress, exposing her breasts and then stood staring at her, his breath coming too quickly, his heart pounding, excitement pumping through him.

Roese did not take her eyes from his face.

'Do not look at me,' he shouted, but her gaze remained fixed. He slapped her across the cheek again and for a moment she turned from him, only to turn back, her eyes searching out his. He watched as the red mark grew on her cheek, the stinging imprint of his hand on her pale skin.

In disgust, Hugues hurled her away from him, sending her reeling headfirst into the wall. Half-conscious she sank into the filthy straw that littered the floor.

'You are a whore and a witch and do not deserve the last rites.' Overwhelmed by the hatred he felt, Hugues spat on Roese. 'You will die in the morning and go to hell where you belong.'

When Fern opened her eyes, she was still shaking with anger. It was Hugues' anger, not hers, she reminded herself, horrified that this despicable man was a part of her. It was impossible to equate the awfulness of what she'd once been with her perception of herself now.

'What happened?' asked Jacques.

In a shaky voice, Fern summarised the regression. 'He's not me,' she said when she'd finished.

'No, he is not. But he is an aspect of you and your energy is connected so you are carrying his negative emotions.' He paused, noting Fern's trembling hands. 'You must release them after each regression.'

Remembering what Jacques had shown her, Fern took three deep breaths, concentrating on stilling her body, grounding herself once again in the present, feeling her energy connect itself into the earth.

'Good. You are learning,' said Jacques when she'd finished. 'As you know, most of us have lived many lives already, in every place, with different skin colours, genders and personalities. We have had lives of wealth and lives of poverty just as we have had lives of goodness and lives of evil.'

'Then why haven't we learned compassion and empathy. Why is it that we still can't live well together?'

Jacques shrugged. 'Who knows! Perhaps it is because we cannot remember our past lives despite the fact they are stamped within us and inform our present in many ways.'

'So we unconsciously react to the past rather than live our lives consciously,' said Fern.

'Yes, exactly. And we find ourselves in different circumstances but caught in the same patterns. I have always found it interesting that lives seem to take on reversals. We live a life of wealth and power only to find ourselves scraping together a living as a scorned peasant. We live a life of violence and disregard for others only to find ourselves working selflessly for others. Yet the qualities we have in one life, both negative and positive are carried through to another life, so the ruthless and powerful king becomes a powerless peasant who terrorises his children. There are lessons to be learned but most of us are slow to learn them. We must remember and in remembering we will liberate ourselves from the weight of living unconsciously.'

Jacques stood up wearily. 'You are right. We still have not learned to live well together and it seems we have a long way to go yet.'

Chapter Thirty-Three

Amber came to visit exactly one week after 'the thing with Kia', as Fern had come to think of it. Fern returned from picking Freya up from school to find her ensconced in the kitchen, chatting to Jacques as if they were old friends. Caught unawares, Fern froze in the doorway, uncertain what to do.

Freya had no such reservations. 'Hello Amber,' she shouted and ran into the kitchen, delighted to see her.

Amber bent over and kissed Freya. 'Howdy,' she said. 'Where's Beattie?'

Freya shrugged, looking unconcerned. 'Beattie doesn't come to school with me anymore. But she's still my friend,' she added.

'I have something for you, Freya,' said Jacques pointing at a paper bag on the table.

Freya's eyes lit up when she saw the chocolate tart inside. 'Merci, Jacques,' she said before settling at the table to eat.

Amber looked over at Fern standing in the doorway. She smiled, but Fern found herself incapable of returning the smile or even meeting Amber's eye. She was certain that Amber knew what had happened but she didn't have a clue how Amber intended to respond to that knowledge. Unable to delay any further, Fern reluctantly stepped into the kitchen.

'Ah, there you are,' said Jacques. 'Your friend has come to visit.'

'I can see that,' said Fern with an attempt at a smile.

Jacques glanced at Fern, surprised no doubt by her lack of warmth. 'We are getting on like… ' He paused. 'Like a house on fire, I think is what you say in English.'

'Great,' said Fern. 'I've got to finish in the garden so I'll leave you to it.' She fled outside, grabbed a rake from the shed and began raking up the fallen leaves. Her heart was thudding and her face hot with shame as she worked, and even the regular rhythm of the raking did nothing to calm her racing mind. How could she face Amber? And what right had she to avoid this confrontation? She'd destroyed any possibility of friendship with either Amber or Kia but the very least she could do was apologise.

'Jacques said you've been sick.'

Fern hadn't heard Amber approaching. Startled, she spun around to face her. 'Just a fever,' she said dismissively, her face reddening.

Amber studied Fern for a long moment. 'It's okay,' she said eventually.

Fern wondered what Amber meant by 'okay'. Surely she couldn't be forgiving her. They hadn't even discussed 'the thing'.

Seeing Fern's confusion, Amber continued. 'I asked him to do it.'

Mouth open, Fern gaped at Amber, unable to believe what she was hearing or work out where to begin understanding why.

'He didn't want to?' she asked, her pride hurt. Kia had been very convincing for someone so reluctant.

'He's a man,' said Amber, 'and you're beautiful. Of course he wanted to. He's not really into sleeping around. But he knew it was necessary.'

'What do you mean - necessary?'

'He had to wake you up.'

Anger began to rise within Fern, replacing her initial confusion. 'Wake me up?' she asked, struggling to keep her voice steady.

'Yes,' said Amber. 'You needed something and he gave it to you.'

So it was an act of charity, thought Fern, her pride stinging even more. She was furious that either of them would have the audacity to decide what was best for her. How dare they! Needing to get a grip on herself, Fern resumed raking again only this time more vigorously, while Amber watched silently. By the time she'd formed a second huge pile of leaves, she could feel her anger abating a little. Trying to get some perspective on this new version of events, she looked out over the wall to the mountains receding into the distance. If she were honest there was some truth behind Amber's words. Her body had come to life with Kia and though any desire for him had quickly fled, the feeling remained. But even so, it had been wrong to trick her like that.

'So it was planned?' she said, gathering the vestiges of her dignity and turning back to face Amber.

'Well, yes, you could put it that way.'

'And because of that everything's okay?'

Amber nodded.

'That's ridiculous.'

'Why?'

'Because planned or not, I didn't know, so it hasn't changed anything. I've betrayed you and I've betrayed Adam … and you and Kia have manipulated me.'

'Adam is dead,' said Amber. 'Do you think he would want you to live out the rest of your life without pleasure?'

'That's not the point.'

'Yes it is.' Her voice went suddenly cold. 'You think you're being loyal to Adam's memory, but it's just an excuse. You're terrified of embracing life again.'

The words hit Fern hard. Not wanting to deal with them she turned her back on Amber and resumed her raking.

'Look at me,' said Amber, grabbing Fern by the shoulder. 'I'm the one who should be hurt but I'm not. Why do you think that is?'

Fern shrugged and pulled herself free of Amber's grip.

'Because I love Kia, and I trust his love,' said Amber. 'True love is not binding and it's not easily broken.'

'I love Adam,' said Fern, fully aware of Amber's subtext.

'I know you do. But you can embrace life without giving up your love for him.'

Fern sat down on the garden bench and put her head in her hands. It was all so complicated. 'I couldn't protect him,' she said.

'No, you couldn't and you have to accept that. Let go of the guilt and find some gratitude for all that you have. You're alive for God's sake. You've got an amazing daughter. You live in one of the most beautiful parts of the world … Focus on life for a change instead of loss. That's the only way to free yourself from the shadow world.'

Fern was surprised by Amber's outburst but she had to admit there was some truth in it. How long since she'd felt grateful for anything? She'd become so attached to being a victim that it had become her identity and a convenient excuse to turn her back on living. Appalled at herself, Fern groaned. 'Oh God, you're right.'

Amber laughed. 'Of course I'm right. But don't you get lost in self-disgust either. It's just another excuse.' She sat down next to Fern and gave her a hug. 'It's okay to be afraid. It isn't easy stepping into life because you have to commit to everything it throws at you, good and bad.'

'Well it's throwing me a bunch of shit,' said Fern.

'Like what?' asked Amber, surprised.

'Like Freya being in danger and this freaky past life I'm trying to sort out and Jacques' ghost.'

'How's Freya in danger?'

It was only then that Fern realised just how little she'd told Amber. 'That's why I'm here,' she said, and explained what Ahmed had told her. 'He was right, we do need to sort out our relationship but it's got much worse since we arrived here and the hungry man hasn't helped.'

'Who?'

'Jacques' ghost. Freya calls it the hungry man.'

'Do you know who the ghost is?'

'No idea. Jacques hasn't got a clue either. It's got more active since we arrived, though for the past few days it's been quieter than … ' She stopped as Freya ran out to join them.

'Can I dress-up for the party, Amber?' Freya asked.

'Of course you can,' said Amber.

'Yay,' she said, skipping back indoors.

'Party?'

Amber nodded. 'For Samhain. We're having a bonfire.'

'What's Samhain?'

'You'd know it as Halloween,' said Amber, 'but its roots are ancient. Here it's called, La Fete de la Sorciere. The night when the veil between worlds is at its thinnest and we can communicate with the dead. It's a time to remember and a time to let go.'

A time to remember. Amber's words stayed with Fern as she broke off a sprig of rosemary and held it to her nose, savouring its sharp aroma. There were things she had to remember, pieces that needed to find their right place in the muddle her life had become. Petrona had said as much and Amber was saying it too.

'Remembrance. That's what this is for,' she said handing the sprig to Amber. 'So I'm invited to this party?'

'You're all invited,' said Amber.

'Jacques too?'

'Of course.'

'Is he coming?'

'Of course.'

Fern laughed, feeling suddenly lighter in the unexpected but supremely welcome knowledge that she still had a friend in Amber. 'How did you swing that?'

'Oh, I have powers of persuasion. And anyway, he's quite fond of witches.'

Fern raised an eyebrow. 'Really?'

'Believe me, there's more to Jacques than meets the eye.'

Chapter Thirty-Four

They were keeping him waiting. Hugues had been sitting on the stone bench outside the door of the meeting hall but his increasingly nervous energy forced him to stand and pace back and forth along the hallway, sweating profusely in the heavy formal gown he wore over his simple habit for the occasion. His mind was going over the possibilities, seeking something positive to cling to; surely they would take into account his loyalty, the sacrifices he had made over the past twelve years and the inexhaustible energy he'd spent on completing his duties.

Berenger, the current Bishop had died unexpectedly two nights previously. His heart had given way, which Hugues thought was not surprising given the recent events, however there were whispers that his death had not been as straightforward as was announced and some believed he had been helped into the afterlife. Berenger had been a fair man and a humane one who as a good Catholic had been opposed to the Cathar heresy, while making no secret of his abhorrence of the way the Crusade did not always distinguish between Cathars and Catholics.

Seeing Hugues' potential and the level of his devotion to the Church, the aging Berenger had quietly set about ensuring that Hugues would take over from him when the time was right, training him in the required duties and sending glowing reports on Hugues to the Vatican's representative. So now Hugues was doubly grieving his loss. With Berenger gone, his succession to Bishop was suddenly in doubt, but almost as importantly, Hugues had regarded Berenger as a second father and had come to rely on his guidance. He felt immense gratitude for Berenger's understanding of his torment after Roese's death just over a year before. Berenger had taken him aside and explained that God sent temptations to all who would devote their lives to him but that Hugues had shown the world that he'd resisted his temptation. In so doing his trial had become a triumph. Berenger's words had eased Hugues' heart but even so this triumph had taken its toll, for his dreams had become nightmares, filled with blood and fire and fury, the eyes of Roese haunting his every moment. As a result, he had not been fulfilling his duties as well as once he might have done, but the growing tension and fear in Carcassonne as the Crusaders had approached, meant that only a few of Hugues' fellow priests had noticed the shortfalls, and when necessary Berenger had spoken for him, dismissing their reports as simple envy.

Hugues paused at the window and looked out over his beloved Carcassonne, the once bustling streets empty of all but a few soldiers who were kept busy clearing the last of the stinking corpses from the streets and alleys and throwing them onto a great bonfire just outside the city walls. The stench of burning flesh was slowly replacing the stench of rot but both were smells that Hugues knew would haunt him for many years. In the end there had been little fighting. Instead, the city had been brought to its knees by thirst, the crusaders cutting off the water supply in the middle of a ferocious heat wave, bringing an agonising death to scores of people each day. Helplessly, Hugues had listened in distress to the dying cries of women and children and watched in disgust as vultures and ravens circled the city walls waiting for their feast.

For months Carcassonne had been heaving with people seeking refuge from the massacres, Christians and Cathars alike. The crusaders lack of discrimination between the two had shocked Hugues and many others who had believed the Church would care for its own. When he'd heard of the massacre at Beziers, he did not trust his ears at first, but it had quickly become evident that none had been spared, not children or devout Catholics, and not even the priests. It was whispered that Arnoud Amalric, the Papal Legate who had been charged with leading the crusade had advised the soldiers, 'Kill them all. For the Lord knows those that are His own.'

Hugues could only thank God that unlike in Beziers, the citizens of Carcassonne had been spared death, if not exile. After Viscount Raymond-Roger had surrendered himself as hostage, offering his life for the lives of the people, Hugues had watched as the doors to the city were opened and the citizens and refugees alike had flooded out into the ravaged countryside, dispersing in all directions, desperate for water and carrying nothing but the clothes on their backs. His heart had bled for the many decent Christians among them who had been forced to suffer because of their kindness towards the heretics.

Unexpectedly, the city had not been pillaged like the others. Instead Amalric had stood in the square and forbade the crusaders to steal or destroy anything. He had then pronounced Simon de Montfort the new Viscount of Carcassonne in place of Raymond-Roger, an appointment for which Berenger had perhaps already paid. In consequence, Hugues' own future was now being sealed behind these closed doors within the chateau, and both his reason and his intuition were telling him that the news would not be good.

Heart thudding, Hugues spun around when he heard the door opening behind him, then paused to gather his dignity and his nerves before stepping past the guards and into the vast hall. He strode along its length and bowed when he reached the table, at which sat three men. While he had not previously met any of them, Hugues recognised both the Abbot Amalric and the younger man sitting to his right, a bored looking Simon de Montfort. The third man was a stranger.

Please sit, said Amalric, gesturing at a seat opposite them.

Hugues sat and placed his trembling hands on his lap, hoping they had not already noticed. He hoped too that these men who held his fate in their hands would not imagine that the drops of sweat on his cheeks and brow were evidence of his fear rather than the heat.

'As you know my brother, with the death of Bishop Berenger and the appointment of the new Viscount there has been much upheaval in our ranks. Bishop Berenger … ' Amalric paused and bowed his head in, what Hugues thought, was a poor rendition of grief. 'Berenger spoke well of you and as you will no doubt be aware, made it clear to the Vatican that he thought you his best successor.'

Hugues felt a sudden thrust of hope. Perhaps all was not lost after all and Berenger had in fact died naturally in his sleep.

'However,' continued Amalric, 'we must take into account the scandals that have been attached to you recently, along with the reports from your peers who state that you have been more negligent in your duties than Berenger reported.'

Hugues swore under his breath. He had hoped the 'scandal' that had erupted after Roese's death would work in his favour but instead they were using it against him. Once again, he cursed Madame de Bourgiers who had spoken out against Hugues, insisting that her daughter had been a scapegoat for his thwarted lust. She'd tried to embarrass him publicly, much to the amusement of those, such as his brother, who thought him a dullard, and the distress of his parents who were concerned that this would reduce his sway within the church.

Hugues had dismissed their concerns at first but Madame de Bourgiers' efforts to muddy his reputation were more effective than he'd believed possible and soon his superiors, including Berenger, were forced to question him regarding the episode. He'd stood before them as they reminded him that scandal is not easy to dispel, even if disproved, and asked if there was any truth in the accusations. Hugues had hesitated for a moment, his gaze caught by the painting of Jesus on the cross, his expression serene despite the torture that had been inflicted on him. Jesus had sacrificed himself to save humanity. Hugues' own sacrifice had been modest in comparison but nevertheless important. 'We were childhood friends,' he had told them. 'It was not easy for me to turn my back on Roese but my allegiance to the Church and all that it stands for is greater than any childish affection.'

Evidently his answer had been the right one for they had smiled. 'Good. Then we have a way forward.' Relieved, Hugues had not questioned what that way forward might be until Madame de Bourgiers had been arrested and charged with heresy. He had felt the weight of her sentence on his shoulders but told himself it was fitting, for like her daughter, she was indeed a heretic. Hugues had been prohibited from visiting her but he would not have done so if it had been allowed, for he could not face her accusations. However, for reasons he could not explain he had stood in the window once more and watched her go calmly to her death, just as her daughter had done a few months earlier. Only this time, the eyes that had met his had been filled with hatred and her lips had moved with what some said was prayer, though he had known even then it could only have been a curse, for since her death he had been plagued by demons.

Hugues wiped his brow and forced himself to meet Amalric's eyes. 'The scandal that you refer to was fabricated by a heretic who was dismayed at the loss of her daughter, another heretic and an associate of Ramon de Cayeux, a known enemy of the Church.

Amalric glanced down at a paper before him. 'But you were in relations with the daughter, Roese.'

Hugues swallowed down his anger, knowing it would not do to lose his temper. 'I am a celibate,' he said, 'and I have kept my vows. Roese was a childhood friend. Nothing more. The result of the investigation confirms this was the case.' Hugues stopped, afraid that he was going too far.

Simon gestured impatiently. 'Come man, pronounce your verdict, I have not the time for this nonsense.'

Amalric ignored him. 'And your current duties? Have you been fulfilling them?'

Hugues swallowed nervously. He could not deny that his mind had been elsewhere. The nightmares were increasing in intensity, making him afraid to sleep and leaving him exhausted. He was a tormented man and the imprint of this torment was becoming evident in his dishevelled costume, the haunted expression on his face and the nervousness of his demeanour.

'Answer me, brother.'

'I have been troubled of late but it is a passing thing and now that Carcassonne has fallen, recovery will come quickly.

'A good answer brother,' said Amalric. 'I commend you on your loyalty. However, we have agreed that now is not the time to burden you with heavier duties. We are sending you to the Abbey of Saint-Michel de Cuxa, where you will have the opportunity to recuperate.'

It took a few moments for the message to sink in but when understanding came it did so in a rush and Hugues clenched his fists as the anger rose within him. Not only had he failed in his ambition to become Bishop but he had been demoted and banished from his beloved Carcassonne. Three punishments in one. Despite all his work, his obedience to the Church, his spotless lifestyle … the devil had found a way in and had brought him down. It was Roese's fault, and her mother's; two women in league with the dark side.

'You will leave this afternoon,' said Amalric. Seeing the expression on Hugues' face, he added more gently. 'It is for the best.'

'You should count yourself lucky,' growled Simon de Montfort. He pushed back his chair and strode purposefully from the room.

'Who then will be Bishop?' asked Hugues.

Amalric pointed at the third man, who thus far had remained silent. 'Bishop Bernard Raymond de Rochefort.'

Rochefort bowed his head slightly and smiled. 'I am pleased to meet you, my brother.'

Hugues own smile was more of a grimace. Finding himself lost for an appropriate reply, he simply bowed. 'I will prepare,' he said and turned towards the door

Outside, the heat hit Hugues like a solid force, the dust scouring his eyes and clogging his nose. He paused and looked out once more over Carcassonne, taking in every detail, letting it imprint itself on his memory. Appalled that he might never again see his beloved city, he closed his eyes and breathed deeply, despair overwhelming him.

To his alarm, when Hugues opened his eyes once more, he found himself in an unfamiliar room. It was cold, as if the seasons had changed in a moment. He looked around at the strange furnishings; one wall was lined with bookshelves, and an enormous desk was positioned by the window, a metallic looking object sitting on its top. It was only then that he noticed the stranger seated in an armchair and staring at him intently. He was old, his hair grey and thinning, and over his eyes he wore a strange contraption of what looked like thin metal and glass.

'Who are you?' shouted Hugues suddenly afraid. He leaped out of his chair, then sat down again quickly when he realised that he himself was not who he thought he was; in place of his flowing gown, he was clad in tight hose and a knitted over-shirt of some sort. Confused, he stared down at himself for a moment wondering if he had gone mad. With his hands he felt the unfamiliar contours of his face and then reached up to touch the hair which hung down the sides like a woman's. Terrified, he backed away from the stranger and began to pray, emitting a stream of Latin into the room.

'Fern?' The stranger's voice broke into his thoughts. 'Your name is Fern.'

Astonished, Hugues looked at the stranger. 'I am Hugues de … ' he stopped suddenly in mid-sentence.

Confused and still partly caught between worlds, Fern looked across at Jacques. 'What happened?'

'I am not sure but I think Hugues stepped for a moment into the future.' Jacques stood up and began pacing, clearly excited by what had unfolded. 'The question is, does he remember? And if he does, what form would that memory take? A dream perhaps? A vision?'

'And where was I while Hugues was here?'

Jacques stopped in his tracks. 'I do not know. Were you aware of yourself?'

Fern shook her head uncertainly. 'In the past, even when I've been in Hugues body, I've always had a sense of myself in the background, but this time he took over.' She looked up at Jacques, afraid. 'What if I lose myself?'

Jacques' hesitation was only momentary. 'You will not,' he said.

'I want to get this over with, Jacques. It's scaring me.'

'We will work harder then.' He lit a cigarette and sat down. 'Now tell me exactly what happened in the regression.'

Fern began relating the details to Jacques.

'This was clearly another pivotal point in Hugues' life,' he said when she had finished. 'The moment where all his hopes were broken.' Clearly excited, he began pacing the room. 'Now we know the connection with St Michel de Cuxa. It was almost certainly Hugues who spoke through you that day to beg forgiveness of the Virgin Mother … I have not seen this before.'

'Do you think we should check the records there?' asked Fern.

'If you like but I do not encourage people to become involved in the facts because in most cases it is the threads and themes of our lives rather than the historic detail that needs to be understood.'

'But it would be interesting to know,' persisted Fern.

Jacques shrugged. 'Perhaps. But what if you found no record of Hugues or if some of the details of his life differed from your memories? Would you then discount all the past life because of a few discrepancies?

'I don't know,' said Fern uncertainly. 'I guess not. I'm just curious.'

'Many people will mistakenly dismiss everything on the basis of a single error. When you regress into a past life, you immerse yourself in it and you experience it once more. Within this immersion lies the possibility of changing your perspective on the past and releasing your emotional ties to it. This cannot be done if an emphasis is given to the facts of the story.'

'Okay,' said Fern. 'I promise I won't go looking for Hugues. At least not in the real world.'

Chapter Thirty-Five

Fern was in the cell again watching the man she now recognised as Hugues pacing back and forth, his heart heavy with despair and the bitter anger that had become a permanent feature of his life. Standing close to the wall, she watched closely, as Hugues paced, noting the limp he had acquired and the grubbiness of his gown. He did not look more than thirty or so, yet he'd lost all sense of pride in his appearance. He was dishevelled and unwashed, his body emanating a fierce odour of rotting flesh which Fern assumed arose from the wounds he was inflicting on himself with the knotted rope that lay on the floor. There was a madness in him and he seemed to be sliding towards an abyss.

At the far wall, he spun around once more and resumed his pacing, only to stop suddenly and peer into the shadows where Fern stood. Alarmed, she backed further into the wall, trying to lose herself in the shadows as his eyes met hers. She didn't know what he was seeing but it was clear it frightened him. Perhaps his own fears and prejudices had turned Fern into a horned demon, a monstrous figure of sorts. Deciding to face his fear, Hugues picked up a crucifix, then holding it out in front of him he stepped toward her, reciting something as if she were a devil he could exorcise. Fern tried to speak but all that came out was a low growl and suddenly she was gasping for breath as an unfamiliar weight settled on her chest.

She woke from her dream but the relief she felt at finding herself in her own bed was short-lived. The bedroom was cold but not the cold of an October autumn night; this was the same uncanny cold she'd felt in the chapel. Felling the hairs lifting on the back of her neck, Fern tried to roll over, intending to switch on the light but the weight on her chest was too heavy, pinning her in place. Her eyes were drawn to the end of the bed where a figure was standing, gazing at her. For a terrified instant she thought Hugues must have followed her back through time and space but almost immediately Fern realised it was not Hugues. This figure was translucent. Through him and the darkness of the room she could just make out the edges of the chest of drawers, but even so there was enough detail for her to see that he was old and bent with white hair. Fern watched, appalled yet frozen to the spot as the 'hungry man' slowly faded then disappeared, the weight lifting from her chest simultaneously.

Free to move again, Fern quickly switched on the bedside lamp and scanned the room, searching the shadows and straining her ears for anything that might suggest he was still here, but there was nothing. Suddenly fearful for Freya, she jumped out of bed and raced down the hall but Freya was fast asleep in her bed, undisturbed, the night light banishing the worst of the dark. When Fern entered the room, Jeannie uncurled herself and arched her back, then stood her ground as Fern approached. They faced each other for a few moments, Fern uncertain how to deal with a hostile cat, and the cat fiercely protective of Freya. With a shock, Fern noticed Jacques' missing kitchen knife sitting on Freya's bedside table. It had not been there earlier when she'd read Freya a bed-time story.

As Fern stood staring at the knife, she felt her mind descend into a deep fog. She stepped closer to Freya's bed her eyes focussed on the sleeping child whose name she could no longer quite remember even though it was there on the tip of her tongue. As she watched the child, sleeping there so peacefully she felt a wave of bitterness wash through her and without any conscious decision on her part, her hand reached out to grasp the knife. When her fingers wrapped around its handle, it felt like a perfect fit, as if the knife and her hand had been made for this moment. Then the cat hissed and lashed out at her, one claw catching the skin on her arm and drawing blood. In an instant Fern was herself again. Horrified, she took the knife back to the kitchen and slid it into the drawer where it belonged.

When Fern returned to Freya's room she was still shaking with the shock. She had no idea what had happened. Had she acted of her own accord or been controlled by the ghost? Fern wanted to believe it was the ghost but even that explanation didn't comfort her because it could happen again at any time. Ahmed had told her that Freya was in danger but he hadn't hinted at the possibility that Fern herself could be the source of that danger.

Fern sat down in the armchair next to Freya's bed and watched her sleeping daughter, her heart filled with love for this beautiful child, a product of the love between her and Adam and yet so much more than that. Freya murmured in her sleep and rolled over, a smile flickering across her face as she did so, one hand landing on Jeannie who licked it dutifully. Amber was right, thought Fern. I have so much to be grateful for and yet … she shifted uncomfortably on the chair, aware that she was caught in a paradox of sorts. She needed to stop focussing on what she'd lost and what more she might lose but at the same time there were real reasons to worry about Freya's safety.

Feeling a wave of exhaustion wash over her, Fern leaned back in the armchair and closed her eyes. There'd been no disturbances for days so once again she'd allowed herself to believe the ghost had lost interest. Yet in the space of an hour everything had changed. The ghost had revealed itself to Fern and somehow acted through her to threaten Freya. On top of that each past life regression she did with Jacques was more intense than the previous one and Fern felt increasingly disturbed by the prospect of continuing with the sessions.

After 'the thing' with Kia, Fern had thought she and Freya would have to leave but after talking with Amber, she knew there was no need. Also, Jacques was becoming more enthusiastic about the past life regressions, wanting to push forward more quickly. To leave now would disappoint him. In a sense it would be a betrayal after all he'd done for her and Freya. On the other hand, there was no evidence that she and Freya were resolving whatever was between them; in fact, Freya was becoming increasingly distant. And then there was the ghost. In the end, Fern had to decide what was best for her and Freya, and after this episode with the knife that had become clear.

Having come to a decision, Fern closed her eyes and drifted into a fitful but dreamless sleep that was brought to an abrupt end a few hours later when Freya woke.

'Hello Mama.'

Startled, Fern opened her eyes and blinked in the sudden daylight. After a moment of confusion, she realised that she was still sitting on the chair in Freya's room. She stretched, wincing at the cramp in her arm and the pain in her neck where she'd slept crookedly.

Freya was sitting up in bed and looking at her curiously. 'What are you doing on the chair?'

Fern yawned. 'I don't know. I just fell asleep here.'

'Are you protecting me from the hungry man?'

Fern nodded, knowing there was no point trying to trick Freya. 'You know what? I'm missing Granny Iris and Uncle Micki. How about we go and visit them soon?'

Freya thought about it for a moment. 'Will the hungry man be there too?'

'No, he lives here.'

'Okay,' said Freya. 'But not until after Amber's party.'

Chapter Thirty-Six

As they walked down the drive to Amber's and Kia's house, there were butterflies in Fern's stomach. Amber had assured her there was nothing to worry about but Fern couldn't believe it would be as easy as that. The desire she'd felt towards Kia had gone, evaporated in an instant but even so she didn't relish the prospect of facing him again.

At the end of the drive, they were greeted with carved pumpkins wearing ghoulish glowing faces. Freya gasped and ran over to inspect them. There were already people milling around the giant unlit bonfire, drinking wine in paper cups and talking animatedly. Fern didn't recognise anyone, though Jacques nodded to a few people. She listened to the murmur of their voices; French was the predominant language but there was also Spanish, English and possibly Dutch. Fern wondered if they were all witches. She thought not. Amber and Kia had friends from all walks of life.

Freya's small hand suddenly slipped into hers and Fern instinctively squeezed it, the unexpected affection warming her heart. She looked down at Freya who had wanted to dress as a ghost, then protested when Fern suggested she wear a sheet, saying that ghosts didn't look like that. And witches don't look like this, Fern had said, showing her a picture of an ugly old crone with a wart on the end of her nose, it's just what people expect. In the end Freya had decided to be a monster and with a bit of imagination she and Jacques had managed to make her look monsterish.

Freya tugged at Fern's hand and pointed at the children playing excitedly in their costumes but she shook her head, suddenly shy, when Fern asked if she wanted to play with them. It was a clear night but cold and Fern shivered in the light dress she'd chosen for the occasion, realising she wasn't wearing enough even though she'd added leggings and her silk pashmina. The bonfire would be a welcome source of heat but even so, Fern looked at it with misgiving, remembering that last bonfire, two and a half years ago – for Adam's wake. The memory brought tears to her eyes and she had to look away.

Amber had set up tables which were already heavily laden with food as each guest brought something for the feast. Fern placed her own offering of sushi on the table and Jacques deposited next to it the four bottles of wine he had insisted on bringing, despite Fern's protests. 'An event like this requires a good deal,' he'd said. And that was that. He filled two paper cups with wine for himself and Fern, and one with lemonade for Freya who let go of Fern's hand and sipped it solemnly, her eyes never leaving the group of children.

When Jacques fell into conversation with the manager of the local patisserie, Fern took the opportunity to study Amber who was talking animatedly with a group of people nearby. There was nothing fine about Amber, nothing fragile. She was sturdy and beautiful, with a physical confidence that Fern envied. As the weather cooled, her standard shorts and T-shirt had been replaced by jeans and jumpers but tonight Amber had made an effort and she looked exquisite. She was dressed in a long emerald green velvet dress that was almost medieval in style, with a laced-up bodice and low front, a narrow waist and a skirt that draped languidly over her hips. Her hair was usually swept back but tonight it was loose and wild, the strands a gleaming fusion of red and blonde. She looked even more like a goddess than usual.

Spotting Fern, Amber waved and made her way over, weaving between the growing crowd. She gave Fern a hug, kissed Jacques on both cheeks and dutifully shrieked at Freya's costume. 'You've brought a monster. Perfect.'

Before Fern had time to worry about it, Kia suddenly appeared next to Amber and wrapped his arm loosely around her waist. When his eyes met Fern's she blushed, remembering the intimacy of their last meeting. Then Kia stepped forward and kissed Fern on both cheeks.

'Welcome my friend,' he said.

Immediately the tension dissipated and Fern felt at ease. 'Great bonfire. Did you build it?'

He nodded. 'It should burn well.'

Amber looked at them both and smiled. Then she took Freya's hand. 'Come. Let me introduce you to the other little monsters.' She looked back over her shoulder. 'Help yourself to more drinks. We're eating later, after the ceremony.'

Fern was already on her third drink by the time Kia announced he was lighting the bonfire.

The crowd watched as he held a flame to the kindling. He'd stacked the logs well, so it caught quickly, the flames rushing upwards in a strange whooshing sound that sucked in all the air around it. There was a communal gasp and many people stepped away, suddenly afraid of the heat the fire emitted and its power.

Fern remembered Freya's fear at Adam's funeral when the fire had been lit and hoped she wouldn't be afraid again tonight. Worried, she searched amongst the crowd before spotting the children standing huddled together, staring open mouthed at the fire. Sure enough, Freya was with them staring at the flames, her eyes filled with terror. Fern pushed her way urgently through the crowd and lifted Freya in her arms, effectively breaking the spell the flames had cast on her daughter.

Sobbing, Freya wrapped her legs around Fern and buried her face in Fern's chest.

'It's alright, sweetheart,' said Fern, kissing the top of Freya's head. 'It won't hurt you. And soon it will burn down to nothing.'

Fern carried her over to where Jacques was standing, and together they watched, entranced as the flames rose, sending sparks out into the blackness of the night. She felt a sudden dizziness as she saw the eyes of Roese staring steadily out of the fire at her. Then suddenly Fern was back in the thirteenth century, in the body of Hugues, unable to bear Roese's gaze yet incapable of turning away. It felt like an eternity but it must only have been seconds before Roese freed him from her spell, her eyes fixing instead on her mother, Madame de Bourgiers, whose face was riven with helpless grief. It was only then that Hugues realised the immensity of what he had done, or failed to do. While he was not responsible for putting Roese to death he had not helped her avoid it and for this he was culpable.

'This is the night when the gateway between our world and the spirit world is at its thinnest.' Amber's voice suddenly rang out into the night, breaking the silence that had fallen with the lighting of the fire and breaking Fern free of Hugues so suddenly she lost her balance and almost fell with Freya still in her arms.

Amber stood alone before the fire, her arms wide her palms facing forward.

'Tonight is a night to call out to those who came before us. Tonight we honour our ancestors. We call to you, the spirits of our ancestors, and welcome you to join us for this night. We know you watch over us always, protecting us and guiding us. And we thank you.'

The atmosphere became charged with energy. Guests sipped their drinks, some smiling and unbelieving, some looking around nervously, while others nodded solemnly, caught up in the ritual. Fern glanced at Jacques and was surprised to see how seriously he was taking this.

'I thought you found all this stuff silly,' she said.

Jacques raised an eyebrow. 'While I do not feel the path of witchery is a complete one there are some functional elements within it.'

'Such as?'

He pointed at the bonfire. 'Such as this, for example.'

'Halloween?'

Jacques scowled. 'Halloween has become an empty container filled only with sugar but this is an ancient ritual and if it is carried out with purpose then it still bears some function.'

'So witchery is a worthwhile path after all?' said Fern. 'Sage sticks and all.'

Jacques laughed. 'It is not my path but it is important to respect the ways of others.'

As Fern was wondering what exactly was Jacques's path, Amber's voice rang out again.

'It's time to make an offering to our ancestors. If you'd like to be part of this ceremony, please fill your cups.' She picked up her own cup and waited while some of the guests filled theirs.

'Would you like to make an offering Freya?' asked Fern. 'We could do a prayer for Daddy. What do you think?'

Freya nodded.

'Come on then. She put Freya down and together they went to fill their cups and collect soul cakes from an elderly woman who had taken on the role of bartender for the evening. Ready to make their offering, they returned to the bonfire, leaving a comfortable distance between themselves and the flames.

Amber lifted her cup high and everyone else who was taking part, followed suit. 'Repeat after me:

This is the cup of remembrance

We remember all of you

You are dead but never forgotten

And you live on within us. '

When it was done, Amber poured a portion of her drink onto the earth and then drank down the rest. 'If you want you can make an offering in your own way to your ancestors,' she said.

Jacques stared into the fire, his eyes glimmering with unshed tears as he connected once more with Madeleine. 'I will let you go my beloved Maddy,' he said, his voice cracking with emotion. Then he spoke to his dead son. 'Be free, Alain.' Still staring at the fire, Jacques took a big gulp of his wine, the tears running freely down his cheeks.

Freya reached out and took Jacques' hand for a moment and he smiled sadly down at her through his tears. Looking at them together like this, Fern felt a pang of sadness that they were leaving. When she'd told Jacques, he hadn't argued but it was clear he was disappointed and he would miss Freya immensely.

When Jacques' tears had stopped, Freya extracted her hand from his then poured some more of her drink onto the ground and nibbled at her biscuit. 'Dada,' she said with a quiet smile. Ritual over, she handed the rest of the biscuit to Fern and ran off to join the other children.

Fern poured a little more of her drink onto the ground and tried to focus her thoughts on Adam, all the time straining to reach through the veil to him. But she felt nothing, saw nothing and heard nothing. Perhaps he's angry with me for betraying him with Kia, she thought and turned away, frustrated and ashamed. It was then that she felt it, a wisp of breath caressing her face, the scent of sandalwood and a glimpse of fair hair. Instinctively she reached out her hand but he was gone; too quickly, far too quickly.

'Thank you,' she whispered. 'Thank you for loving me.'

Fern wiped her eyes and took a gulp of her wine, watching others complete their own rituals and move away, taking plates and filling them with food, milling about chatting or sitting down on blankets around the fire. Without Adam, Fern had no anchor to ground her at social gatherings like this and she didn't feel up to stepping across the divide between strangers. She took another gulp of wine and a dizziness rose within her making her wonder briefly if she'd drunk too much. But the air was shimmering in a familiar way and the prickling sensation on the back of her neck made her realise that something else was happening. She looked around expectantly and saw Petrona emerge from the crowd of guests who seemed unaware of her strange presence. It was good to see a familiar face, even an otherworldly one and Fern smiled as Petrona approached.

'You are ready,' said Petrona.

'What for?'

'The witch will tell you.' Then she disappeared before Fern could ask any questions.

Frustrated, Fern scanned the crowd hoping to catch another glimpse of Petrona but neither she or Amber were anywhere to be seen. Music started now and the atmosphere quickly became charged with a different energy as voices rose into a blur of sound broken only by sudden bursts of laughter and the occasional shout. Someone refilled Fern's cup with wine as people began to dance before the bonfire, swaying and swirling to the music. The children joined in too and Fern watched entranced as Freya danced with them, twirling around and around in the flickering light, her movements a spell of sorts for there was Beattie dancing next to her, laughing, eyes sparkling, the other children accepting her as if she had always been there. In that moment Fern fully grasped what others had tried to point out to her in the past; that Freya was separate from Fern and had her own life path to follow. Fern's role was to guide and protect her, but she'd mistaken guiding and protecting for controlling, and instead stifled Freya, not letting her make the mistakes she needed in order learn and grow.

Fern felt Adam brushing her again in a gentle affirmation. She smiled. 'Okay, I've got it,' she whispered.

'Your little monster's having fun,' said Amber, appearing at Fern's side. 'Phew, I'm out of breath from all that dancing.' She glanced at the soul biscuit in Fern's hand. 'You should eat that. Each one eaten represents a soul being freed from Purgatory.'

Fern obediently ate the cake which was sweet and laced with cinnamon and nutmeg. She washed it down with a mouthful of wine, wondering what soul she might be releasing. Was Adam in purgatory? With all her heart, she hoped not. The consensus seemed to be that Fern was holding herself back, but maybe she was holding Adam back too. She sighed, suddenly tired.

'Petrona said I was ready.'

'Good,' said Amber, putting on a petulant tone. 'Maybe you'll believe *her*.'

'Ready for what? asked Fern.

'For a ritual separation from ancestral trauma.'

Fern took another sip of her wine and looked at Amber blankly. She was drinking on an empty stomach so it wasn't surprising that the world around her was beginning to spin and her mind refusing to grasp what was happening.

'Remember the conversation we had a few weeks ago?' said Amber.

'Ah that,' said Fern, struggling to remember. 'Why would I want to separate from them?' she asked, suddenly confused. 'People worship their ancestors.'

'You're not turning your back on them only from their suffering which is what stops you from living well.'

'Their suffering! This is ridiculous,' said Fern, suddenly angry. 'What about my suffering? I've got to release Adam and Hugues and get rid of Jacques' ghost and now you're telling me I have to release my bloody ancestors too. I'm tired. I haven't got the energy to worry about them.'

'Perfect. Let's get on with it then,' said Amber.

'Here?' Fern looked around at the crowd of people. Some were still dancing in front of the bonfire, others were sitting quietly eating. One man was curled up asleep, warmed by the flames. 'It's not really a good time.'

'It's the best time of the year. The ancestors are here. They're listening and they want your help.'

'How does severing me from their suffering help them?'

'It's a kind of domino effect, echoing through every generation past and future. It's not just a healing for you it also releases their suffering.'

Fern stared at Amber for a moment, trying to understand the implications of what she was saying. She remembered Amber telling her about epigenetics, how traumas were carried by all the descendants, effecting the way each one lived their lives. If that were true then it was hard to believe that a simple ritual could do all that. If she asked, Amber would tell her that it wasn't so easy. She would say that you had to be ready. That all the work lay in the preparation. Fern knew this but even so she wondered. Am I ready now?

She took another gulp of her wine. 'Okay. If there's so much hanging on this let's do it.'

Amber took Fern's cup away and led her to a quieter spot, but still close enough to the bonfire to warm them. They sat on the earth facing each other.

'You don't have to do anything,' said Amber. 'Depending on how sensitive you are you may not even notice it happening.'

She studied Fern for a few moments. 'Okay. I'm getting the belief coming up. It's what I expected. *I have to suffer on behalf of my Ancestors.* And there's a trapped emotion of anxiety keeping this in place. Trapped at conception,' she added.

There was a pause while Amber concentrated. 'There I've released it. Now let's change the belief to something more positive. Repeat after me. *It is time to release the suffering of my Ancestors. I can release my Ancestors suffering without having to suffer myself'*.

'And again,' said Amber, making Fern repeat the lines over and over. At first the words were just words and Fern wondered again how a few words could make any difference but then she felt the tone change. Suddenly she meant it.

'There,' said Amber. 'It's imprinted. Now we have to sever your ties to their suffering.' Amber looked closely at Fern. 'Have you had a sense of a heavy weight on your shoulders or tension of some sort?'

Surprised, Fern nodded. 'Like something's sitting on my shoulders pushing me into the ground.'

Amber studied Fern for a moment. 'There are strings coming from both of your shoulders and you look anguished! You're carrying negative emotions and energy on behalf of your Ancestors on both sides. I'll release them in a minute, once we've severed the strings.'

'What will happen?' asked Fern, suddenly alarmed.

'You'll fall.'

'Will it hurt.'

Amber laughed. 'No. You have support but still it will take a lot of trust. Try to relax and just allow the process to unfold.'

'Allow what?' asked Fern, frustrated at being excluded from her own drama. 'Why can't I see?'

Amber shrugged. 'I guess they don't want you to. There's enough going on in your life right now. They're making it easier for you.'

'That's kind of them,' said Fern, and not even she knew if she was being sarcastic.

'Ah,' said Amber. 'An angel has cut the strings and is floating you down to earth.' She smiled and gave Fern a hug. 'It's done.'

'Is that it?' asked Fern. She felt lighter somehow, the pressure eased from her shoulders but otherwise nothing had changed. 'What happens now?'

'Well, you'll need a while to integrate all this. But over time you'll have more intuition, more energy, you'll be more resilient and you'll feel as if you deserve to be here.' She yawned, then stood up and brushed down her dress. 'Guess I'd better go and play hostess.'

Fern stood up too and took Amber's hand. 'I'm sorry if I seem ungrateful. I'm just confused.'

'I'm not surprised,' said Amber, giving her a hug. There's too much happening at once. This should ease it a little and help you see your way through.'

'Thank you.'

Fern watched Amber, walk away, transforming seamlessly into another role and effortlessly shedding the past, like a duck, the water running off its feathers without penetrating. It was hard to believe that Amber could be so generous, so certain of the love in her heart that she could share Kia in the way she had. Fern was only just beginning to understand the value of their gift to her. And now Amber had given again, simply because she could.

Fern's thanks had been just a word but now gratitude flowed through her and she felt the full force of its expansive energy. Soon after she'd met Adam, Fern had promised herself that she would never let her heart close again. But despite her promise, when Adam died, her heart had slammed shut with a resounding thud. She'd broken her pact with life and treated it with disrespect. The people closest to Fern had tried to tell her this but words hadn't been enough. She'd needed to realise it for herself. And now she did. It was time to open her heart once more.

Fern looked around for Freya, only to find that most of the children had trickled away from the group and back to their parents. Freya was sitting on Jacques' lap and they were both eating from plates piled with food. Suddenly hungry Fern grabbed a plate, helped herself to a slice of quiche and some sushi, grabbed some hot chestnuts and sat down next to them.

The food helped soak up the effects of the alcohol and Fern felt more settled as she peeled a chestnut and handed the flesh to Jacques, then peeled another for herself. She was already beginning to feel the changes. There was a stronger sense of connection between the parts of her mind and a bigger picture was emerging again, as if she were a bird flying high, looking down on earth and seeing the patterns of things.

The music stopped and a silence descended on the gathering, each person mesmerised by the dying fire. Eventually someone began strumming a guitar in a gentle rhythm and the party shifted into another gear. One voice rang out and then another until people were singing together, their voices harmonising with the guitar. Fern wished she'd brought her pipe with her. She hadn't played it since that last time she'd seen Adam, at the forest camp but now it was time to reclaim her music. She joined in the singing, surrendering to the notes, her voice rising into the heavens as she arched her neck and looked up at the night sky, seeing fine lines connecting the stars and forming shapes she seemed to recognise. Excitement surged through her as she realised there was so much that she didn't know, mysteries beyond words that she was yet to discover.

Suddenly overwhelmed, Fern turned away from the heavens and looked at Freya, who had fallen asleep on Jacques' lap; Freya who always sought men out, who trusted them without question. So far her instincts had been impeccable and fingers crossed they would remain so. Fern looked at Jacques, his face red from the alcohol or the heat of the fire. His eyes were slightly glazed too and there was a sad expression on his face. She wondered if Madeleine was still in his thoughts and if he'd succeeded in letting her go as she'd asked him to.

As she gazed at Jacques, Fern's vision suddenly deepened and she saw colours emerge within and around him. Startled she broadened her gaze and saw colours around everyone else too, including the trees. It was beautiful, a magical reminder that the energy of living beings was not just contained within the physical boundaries of their bodies. Astonished, Fern watched the colours shift and change around her. She noticed Amber standing on the other side of the bonfire, her arm around Kia's waist. Their colours were connected in a special way. Were they soul mates she wondered, as she and Adam were? Fern saw the warmth of new life within Amber's womb and knew she was pregnant. Seeing her looking, Amber smiled. Fern returned the smile and blew a kiss before returning her attention to Jacques. The predominant colour around him was blue and there was a smattering of yellow but the greyness was there too, more localised, a spreading patch in his chest. More confirmation that Jacques was ill. Knowing how reluctant he was to seek help, she felt a surge of anxiety, and with that the colours around her were extinguished.

Chapter Thirty-Seven

Fern finished clearing one of the overgrown vegetable patches, turned the soil and fertilised it with organic compost. Despite winter setting in, the seedlings Amber had given them a few weeks earlier were thriving in their sunny patch sheltered by the stone wall. Amber had told her there was still time to plant carrots, garlic, onions and spring cabbage, as well as strawberry runners, so Fern had decided to plant out a second vegetable patch before they left, as a gesture of gratitude towards Jacques, who loved fresh produce but had no idea how to grow it.

'It's all about the terroir,' he'd told Fern then attempted a translation of a word that meant so much more than just soil. 'It's place also and weather and … ' He'd thrown his hands up in frustration. 'Madeleine understood this but I am an ignoramus.'

Today Fern and Freya had already planted carrot seeds and garlic heads and now they were working together to get the last of the strawberry runners in around the edge of the patch. Fern was digging her fingers into the soil and making little holes which Freya filled with water from her tiny watering can. When they'd finished the preparation, Fern separated the runners, before handing each one to Freya who carefully placed it in the hole then patted the earth down around it. Neither of them spoke, yet they seemed to know what each other wanted. They made a great team, Fern thought, wishing it could be like this all the time.

It was a cold morning but the sun was warming them in the walled garden. Since the ancestral ritual Amber had conducted at the party two days before, Fern had felt a new clarity; the fuzziness and anxiety had receded and the heavy weight on her shoulders had lifted. There were still glimpses too, of the colours she'd seen that night.

She paused for a moment and watched Freya contentedly planting the seedlings. Her overall feeling was one of relief. While there was still a lot to worry about, the ghost had been quiet for a few days and she'd avoided any more regressions with Jacques since telling him they were leaving. Freya seemed more settled too and was sleeping through the night again, which meant neither of them were exhausted. In fact, life seemed so normal that Fern could almost believe that the frightening events over the past few months had never happened.

She took the shovel and began digging a hole deep enough to plant the apricot tree Jacques had bought yesterday.

'Beattie wants to dig.' said Freya.

Fern nodded and handed over the spade. Freya set to work, issuing orders to Beattie and spraying the paving stones with dirt. Fern would have to clean it up later but it was worth it to see Freya so content. She sat down on the edge of one of the garden beds and watched, wanting this moment to go on forever. Despite his disappointment that they were leaving, Jacques seemed content too; he was standing on a ladder whistling as he pruned an almond tree.

'Finished,' said Freya and put down the spade.

'Okay,' said Fern. 'You put the tree in but we'll get Jacques to cover it with earth because it's his tree.'

Freya held the tree upright in the hole as they waited for Jacques to climb down the ladder. He was a little out of breath and as Fern handed him the spade she wondered if the pruning had been too much for him.

Jacques shovelled in the dirt, while Freya patted it down and mumbled some words Fern couldn't quite catch; most likely a blessing. Then Fen picked up the watering can and gave the sapling a good soaking to help it on its way.

'Right,' she said when they'd finished. 'I'll make us some hot chocolate.'

As Fern heated the milk, she was filled with a profound sadness that all this was coming to an end. In a week they would leave France and return to Tasmania. But for what? This was the question she kept asking herself. Freya's uncle and grandmother were there but although that might be enough for Freya, and although Fern loved them both dearly, she'd begun to wonder if living there would be enough for her. She'd always been plagued by a kind of restlessness that never allowed her to feel at home anywhere. Then when she'd met Adam, it no longer mattered because she belonged with him and his home became hers. But now she needed to make a home for herself and Freya. Somewhere they felt a connection with. Was it as simple as making a decision? she wondered. Or did a place speak to you? Fern pondered these questions as she spooned in the hot chocolate and watched it dissolve into the milk as she stirred.

'Mama,' called Freya, not loudly but there was a tone in it that alerted Fern. 'MAMA,' she called more loudly.

Fern rushed out to the garden to find Freya struggling to support Jacques. Quickly Fern took his other arm and together they settled him on a garden chair.

'What is it?' Fern asked as she studied Jacques. The greyness was still there. His face was pale too and his breathing was coming too quickly.

'It's nothing,' gasped Jacques between breaths. 'I stood up too quickly, that is all.' He rubbed his arm, then saw Fern looking and stopped. 'Poor circulation,' he said. 'I've always had that problem.'

'You're not well.'

'I'm fine.'

Fern shook her head. 'I'm going to call the doctor,' she said.

'I will not see a doctor.'

'You need to see one.'

'Since when have you become my mother?'

Defeated, Fern groaned. 'You're impossible,' she said, knowing that if something happened to Jacques, she would blame herself.

He sniffed. 'And you have burned the milk.'

Chapter Thirty-Eight

'What do you think?' asked Fern, laying out her design on the table. Amberosia, written in a simple font, with a sprig of rosemary curled around it.

'It's perfect,' said Amber. 'I love it.'

Fern breathed a sigh of relief. 'That can be the logo design but you'll still have to decide on the colours and the packaging … I can help,' she added, noting Amber's growing confusion. 'You're starting simple so I'd go for a small cardboard packet for the teas – two types to begin with, a plain one and a blend. And a glass jar with a narrow neck and a dropper for the tinctures. We can order them online today.'

Amber nodded gratefully. 'Thank you. It all feels so rushed though.' She reached out and took Fern's hand. 'I wish you weren't leaving us.'

Fern felt another stab of regret. 'Me too … But we can keep in touch.'

'It's not the same,' said Amber, her voice tinged with sadness.

The door opened, letting in a burst of cold air and Kia stepped inside. 'It's miserable out there,' he said, taking off his sodden coat and hanging it behind the door.

'Look what Fern's done,' said Amber.

Kia looked over Fern's shoulder at the design Amber had chosen. 'Great. That's perfect,' he said. 'Drink anyone?'

'Coffee please,' said Fern, knowing it was the last thing she needed. She was firing, her brain sparking ideas and connections. It hadn't happened like this for a long time and she was loving it. Right now, anything seemed possible.

'Coffee for me too,' said Amber.

'Peppermint tea for you,' said Kia, looking sternly at her.

Amber groaned. 'Just one coffee?' she pleaded. 'A weak one?'

Fern smiled, her suspicions confirmed. 'How long have you known?'

'Only a week. It's early days yet and I haven't told anyone. We have to be careful because I've already had two miscarriages.' She smiled and stroked her belly. 'But I feel good about this one. It's going to be okay.' She groaned again when Kia put a peppermint tea in front of her. 'Look what I have to put up with!'

Fern laughed. 'You'd hate the coffee anyway. I did when I was pregnant with Freya. It made me retch.'

They worked together for a couple more hours, planning which teas and tinctures to start the range with and ordering what was needed.

'You've made it so easy,' said Amber when they'd finished. 'You should be doing something like this for yourself.'

'There's too much up in the air at the moment. I don't even know where I want to live so I can't really run a business.'

'I thought you were going back to Tassie.'

'We are. At least for now. But I'm starting to wonder if I'd be better off leaving behind the memories and starting fresh. I love Tassie but it was always Adam's place not mine.'

'Stay here then. You can be godmother to this one,' Amber added, rubbing her belly.

'Godmother?' Fern was shocked.

'Yeah,' said Kia. 'We were going to ask but then you announced you were leaving.'

Struggling against tears, Fern turned away and stared through the window at the world outside, the heavy rain blurring its edges. There was no clarity out there, no warmth, just uncertainty. She shivered and drew her focus back to the safety of this kitchen with its crackling fire and the rich aroma of the lentil stew bubbling on the stove. Then she turned her gaze back to Amber and Kia. She was growing to love them both and it would be a wrench to leave but she'd made her decision.

'That would have been such an honour,' she said. 'And it means a lot to me.'

'Then stay.'

Fern shook her head sadly. 'It's all planned and Freya's excited about it. I can't change my mind now,' she said. 'And I can't live with Jacques' ghosts or my own. It's too hard.'

Fern was not in a good mood when she and Freya finally arrived back at Jacques' house. The rain had become heavier as the afternoon progressed, so Kia had dropped her off at the school. He'd offered to wait and drive both her and Freya home but she'd assured him that Jacques would collect them as he'd promised. She and Freya had waited, sheltering as best they could under the only tree in the school yard which had all but lost its leaves, then they'd finally given up and walked home in the rain. Now they were soaked through, tired out and bad tempered, and Fern had the beginnings of a bad headache, the pain shooting in bursts down the right side of her head.

Half way up the hill Freya had suddenly announced that she wanted to stay in France with her friends and with Jacques. When Fern had told her it was too late to change her mind, Freya had suggested Fern go back to Australia alone, then fallen into one of her sulks and refused to speak again. They'd walked the rest of the way in silence, both lost in their own thoughts.

As they stepped into the house, Fern could hear voices inside the chapel. Curious, she looked in to see Jacques sitting on the couch talking to a man whose back was facing the door. On the coffee table was a bottle of whiskey, already half empty and an ashtray half full. Jacques had lit the fire, making the chapel feel almost cosy, and Jeannie was curled up on the rug, soaking up the warmth. The late afternoon light, already dimmed by the blanket of heavy clouds was doing little to illuminate the room, though the fire itself was casting flickering shadows on the walls.

Freya forgot her dislike of the chapel and with a squeal of delight, raced over to the rug where she sat stroking the purring cat.

'You are back at last,' said Jacques smiling benevolently at Fern as she stood dripping in the doorway.

'We were waiting for you,' said Fern.

The smile fled quickly from Jacques' face. 'Mon dieu! I am sorry. I forgot my promise.' He gestured at the man who sat with his back facing the door. 'I have an unexpected visitor.'

At this, the man twisted around in the leather armchair to greet her.

Fern gasped. 'You know each other?' she asked.

'Mais oui,' said Jacques. We have known each other for a long time. This is the man who taught me to enjoy whiskey!'

'Another coincidence?' said Fern, looking pointedly at Jacques.

'Coincidence?' Jacques said, confused. It was clear he was unaware of Fern's connection with Ahmed.

Ahmed smiled. 'There is no such thing as a coincidence.'

'What are you doing here?'

Ahmed appeared unperturbed. 'I have come to see my friend,' he said, smiling at Jacques.

'It seems I have gone astray and this man has come to put me back on the straight line,' explained Jacques.

Fern shivered. Her clothes were sopping wet and needed changing, as were Freya's so she decided to leave explanations for later.

'Come on Freya,' she said. 'Let's get some dry clothes.'

Freya shook her head stubbornly.

'Don't be stupid. You'll catch a cold.'

Again, she shook her head.

'Have it your way,' said Fern. She stormed up to her room, peeled off her wet clothes and put on the only other warm things she had – jeans and an old cardigan of Jacques that was far too big for her. They'd not come to France prepared for cold weather. Stupid really, thought Fern. In Tassie just about every day encompassed all four seasons and she'd eventually learned to dress accordingly. In southern France, Fern had assumed it would be hot all the time, and now she was regretting it.

As Fern pondered the presence of Ahmed, her temper grew worse by the moment, as did her headache. What she didn't understand was why she felt so angry with him. She didn't like being manipulated and surely that was exactly what Ahmed had done. But there was more to it than that and she couldn't put her finger on it.

When Fern returned to the chapel, darkness had already descended. She switched on the light, flooding the room with a sudden brightness.

'Non,' barked Jacques, shielding his eyes. 'If you must have more light then use the candles.'

Fern sighed and switched off the light, then fetched the matches and much to Freya's delight, began lighting the candles that were dotted around the room. The effect was beautiful. When she'd finished, Fern sat down on the couch next to Jacques and looked closely at Ahmed who she'd only met on that one occasion, just before Adam's death. This time he was dressed more casually, in chinos and a knitted jumper, but even so there was something formal about him. He was a man who didn't stand out, and yet…

Unperturbed by Fern's stare, Ahmed smiled and offered her a whiskey.

She shook her head. 'Did you know?'

'Know what?'

'That Adam would die.'

'How could I know that?'

'You seemed to know everything else. 'Why didn't you warn me? Why didn't you stop it happening?'

'I am not a prophet,' said Ahmed. 'I am only aware of what is required.'

Clearly Adam wasn't required, thought Fern bitterly. 'The thing is … ' she paused, trying to work out what she needed to say. 'You told me I had to keep Freya safe.' When Ahmed nodded, she went on. 'It's evident that I was meant to come here and find out how, but I wouldn't have come if Adam hadn't died.'

'Perhaps not,' said Ahmed.

Fern's voice rose. 'We were happy together. We loved each other. We were soul mates! We didn't need you to … ' Seeing Freya staring at her, Fern stopped mid-sentence. 'Freya, why don't you get yourself a drink and some biscuits. To her surprise, Freya obediently got up and left the room, giving Fern a wary glance as she did so.

When she was sure Freya was out of earshot, Fern turned back to Ahmed. 'Was Freya the only purpose of my time with Adam?'

'There is rarely a single purpose for anything,' said Ahmed.

'Wouldn't it have been better if Freya had been brought up by us both?'

'Of course. A child requires two parents.'

'Then why did Adam have to die?'

'He did not have to die. That outcome would have been one of a great number of possible outcomes, each dependent on numerous choices and events. Life is not as straightforward as you might wish to believe it.'

Jacques was watching them both, astonished. 'It is apparent that you already know each other,' he said, when there was a pause in the conversation. He stood up. 'No doubt I will discover all at some point but until then I will drag my drunken self to the kitchen and prepare dinner.'

Ahmed smiled. 'Thank you, my friend. Some food would help soak up this whiskey.'

'If you had given me some warning I would have cooked up a feast but now you must make do with pasta.'

'Your company and a little pasta will be feast enough for me,' said Ahmed, smiling fondly at Jacques.

Fern's head was still pounding and she could feel a numb exhaustion creeping into her. The stresses of the past weeks were taking their toll, she thought, as she let her body fold into the couch's soft back. She couldn't blame Ahmed for what had happened, just as she shouldn't blame herself. But even so, she needed more information. She leaned forward again 'When we met that day you told me a bunch of things and I just nodded like an idiot.'

Ahmed smiled. 'You have questions?'

'You told me that before I could protect Freya, I had to fix what lay between us.'

'And so you do.'

'You suggested learning past life therapy and somehow I found myself here with a man you already know, investigating a past life of another man who lived in this area.'

Ahmed nodded. 'It is not surprising. You simply followed your nose.'

'But all these investigations are making it worse. Our relationship is crap. She doesn't trust me. And the deeper I go the worse it gets.'

Ahmed nodded again. 'Yes, that's true.'

'That's why I've stopped the investigation.'

'So you're running away.'

'No, I'm removing Freya from danger. It's too much. I can't control it.'

Ahmed swirled the whiskey in his glass, watching the golden liquid reflect the candle light, then took a sip and placed his glass down on the table. 'You should see it through.'

Fern sighed. This was the third person today who'd told her she should stay. 'It's too late. I've made my decision.'

'You might be able to leave this ghost behind, but you will carry the past life with you wherever you go. It is your decision but I strongly suggest that you stay and see through what you have begun.'

'Hear, hear,' said Jacques who had returned carrying a bottle of wine and three glasses. He poured them all a glass and held up his own. 'Let's toast to that.'

Still scowling, Fern took a sip of wine. 'If I'm carrying Hugues with me then why didn't I have a problem with him until I got here?'

'You did,' said Ahmed.

'I'd never heard of him.'

'And yet your life is lived in reaction to him and to other influences. If you want to be free then you must recognise this.'

Fern pondered Ahmed's words. Amber had said something like this when she'd helped Fern sever her responsibilities to her ancestors. Yet Hugues felt different. She wasn't just reacting to him, it was as if he were possessing her. Like a demon, she thought, shuddering.

'Is Hugues possessed by something?' she asked.

'You could describe it that way. A deformed shadow was cast upon him and a fragment of this continues to exist within you.'

'And how do I get rid of it?'

'That is Jacques' job,' said Ahmed, smiling at his friend who had appeared in the doorway.

'One that I am not doing well,' admitted Jacques. 'That Hugues is a stubborn man.'

Chapter Thirty-Nine

T he wind had blown last night's rain away and the morning was sunny and peaceful. Fern and Ahmed were sitting outside eating breakfast. There was a briskness to the air and a rug of yellow leaves lay around the base of the now bare fig tree next to them, but the walled garden was well protected and the sun still contained enough strength to warm them through. Unusually, Jacques had not yet appeared, even though Fern had already dropped Freya at school, picked up baguettes and pastries from the boulangerie and made a second breakfast for herself and Ahmed.

Ahmed drained his coffee and finished his pain au chocolat then leaned back in the seat. 'I am replete. Thank you.'

Fern reached for a second croissant. She felt plagued by indecision. Up until yesterday leaving had seemed the best way forward but now doubts had crept into her mind. Stay or go? The question replayed itself over and over in her head becoming more urgent as their departure day loomed closer.

'Decisions, decisions!' said Ahmed.

Fern looked at him sharply. 'I've already made up my mind.'

'But your mind is not yours. It is being ruled by fear.'

Fern opened her mouth to retort then closed it again. Perhaps Ahmed was right and she should consider her motivations more deeply.

Ahmed picked up the paper and began reading, his changing expression reflecting the concerns he found in the headlines. Fern's French still had a long way to go but, glancing at the paper even she could gather that the world was in turmoil, a pressure cooker letting out bursts of hot steam all over the place.

'What's happening?' she asked when Ahmed tutted loudly.

'Change is approaching.' He gestured at the newspaper. 'The old structures of our societies are failing, regimes are toppling like dominoes, the earth is shaking herself into a new position, sending wind and rain to cleanse herself of the pollution humanity has produced … It's a messy process but necessary and it must be achieved in a balanced way.'

Surprised, Fern stared at him for a moment. 'It doesn't seem balanced to me,' she said eventually, glancing again at the paper.

'Things are rarely as they seem.' Ahmed poured himself another coffee. 'This is a crucial time. If you like you can think of it as a battle for the soul of humanity. Will mankind become more angelic or more robotic?' He smiled. 'To be or not to be? That is the question.'

Fern pondered Ahmed's words, recognising something in them, a confirmation of her own thoughts. Each shift and change, each unpleasant truth uncovered, each new technology … all carrying the seeds to shift the world in one direction or the other and sometimes paradoxically in both directions at once.

Ahmed folded up the paper in disgust. 'There is so much that must be read between the lines that there is little point doing so. It is better to read the signs. As above so below. As within so without. The world is a reflection of greater forces.'

'Who are you?' asked Fern.

Ahmed smiled. 'Now that's not a straight forward question to answer.'

'Okay, what do you do for a living?'

'I am a company director.'

'How do you know Jacques?'

'I am his teacher.'

Fern felt her frustration building. 'Teacher of what?'

'Of a path that leads us home.'

Fern frowned. 'That tells me absolutely nothing.'

Ahmed smiled. 'It tells you a great deal.'

'So, a spiritual teacher?'

'If you like.'

'How can you be a company director and a spiritual teacher?'

'My teaching is not a profession it is a requirement. My profession is also a requirement, for each of us must stand on his own two feet in the world.'

'Why are you here now?'

'At any moment it is easy to step aside from the path, a nudge one way or another and we lose our way. My pupil has strayed.'

'You mean Jacques?'

'Yes. Like you he is burdened with guilt. A most destructive emotion.'

'Over Madeleine?' asked Fern.

Ahmed nodded.

'Why?'

'That is not my story to tell.'

'Jacques isn't well,' said Fern.

'Yes, I know.'

'I can't get him to see a doctor. If you're his teacher he'll listen to you.'

At that moment Jacques stepped out into the garden looking hung-over and exhausted. 'Why would I listen to Ahmed?' he asked.

'Ah my friend,' said Ahmed smiling up at Jacques. 'You are awake. Perhaps you could tell Fern why you won't see a doctor for your condition.'

Jacques scowled. 'So you wish me to bare my soul?' he said, his voice raspy from too many cigarettes. At Ahmed's almost imperceptible nod he reluctantly turned to Fern. 'Very well … My wife died because I did not take seriously her ill health. I tried to deny it because I am like an ostrich who puts his head in the sand and thinks that he is safe.'

'But surely your wife knew she was sick. Wasn't it up to her to see a doctor?'

Jacques' scowl deepened. 'Do not try to seek excuses for me.' He spun around and disappeared into the kitchen.

Ahmed smiled sadly. 'Guilt is a heavy weight to carry and one that we can easily become attached to. As you know too well.'

'Madeleine died two years ago,' said Fern. 'Why did you take so long coming?'

'Jacques is not a child. He has needed the opportunity to resolve this for himself. Ahmed glanced at the house. 'Given time and a gentle nudge he will.'

'Then why did you choose to come now?'

Ahmed smiled at Fern's probing. 'You are right. There were other factors and as so often happens they are interlaced.'

'Freya?'

'Yes, Freya, of course. But you too have need of guidance.'

'Me? Are you offering to teach me?'

'That is up to you.' Ahmed stood up, then paused and looked back at Fern. 'When you are faced with a decision as to which choice to make it can help to distinguish a different kind of knowing in relation to your choices. Choose the one that initially radiated certainty and brought with it a calm sense of peace. It is often replaced quickly with doubt but try not to forget the original feeling. It will help you find the best outcomes. Eventually you will reach a place where there is no choice. That is true freedom.'

'Now I must go and speak with Jacques before leaving,' he said. 'No doubt we will meet again.' With a wave he disappeared into the kitchen, leaving Fern pondering his advice.

Chapter Forty

F ern found Jacques in his office, typing furiously with two fingers onto his laptop. He looked even rougher than earlier; his face had that increasingly familiar greyness under the stubble he hadn't bothered to shave off.

'You look terrible.'

'I am fine,' he said, impatiently waving away her question. 'I am not used to drinking whiskey in such large quantities, that is all.

'Has Ahmed gone?'

'Oui.' He looked up from the screen and fixed his gaze on Fern. 'Why did you hold information back from me?'

'What do you mean?' Fern asked, surprised.

'You have not told me the truth about why you are here. You said you wanted to learn past life therapy but now I am told me that this is not the reason.'

'I do want to learn past life therapy,' protested Fern.

'But that is not why you came. You said something one evening; when the vase broke in Freya's room. You said that someone had told you there was a threat to Freya. But you did not explain and I did not pursue it.'

'It didn't seem important,' said Fern, knowing this was only a half-truth.

Jacques exploded. 'It is an insult to me that you would decide what is important and what is not. You entrusted yourself to me so that I could teach you but you did not give me the right tools. How am I to do my job if I do not know what is needed?'

'I'm sorry,' said Fern. 'Ahmed told me I needed to fix my relationship with Freya and to do that I had to step into the past. He didn't say come to you but somehow that's what happened. I don't know why I didn't say.' She paused searching for an explanation. 'I didn't know you and it just sounded so … unlikely.'

'That was for me to ascertain.'

Fern nodded. 'I see that now. I'm sorry. She paused, 'Since we arrived my relationship with Freya has got worse. That's why I wanted to leave.'

'Wanted?' barked Jacques.

'I've decided it would be best to stay on after all and see this through. I was just about to ask if that would be okay but I understand if you want us to leave now.'

The scowl on Jacques' face softened a little. 'No, no, you must stay. We have wasted time but it is not irretrievable.'

Fern smiled. 'Thank you.'

'We will change direction. That is all. But first we must finish with this Hugues of yours.' Fern nodded. 'Fair enough.'

'Good. We are at peace once again.' Jacques slammed shut his laptop. 'Now we shall do a regression.'

As Fern closed her eyes, she felt a sharp pain shooting down the right side of her head. Instinctively, she followed the pain into its source and found herself watching an old monk, back bent and shuffling slowly towards what appeared to be a well. To the left was the stone wall of a building, most likely a church. It was not well maintained; with moss growing on the walls and weeds running rampant in the paved outside area leading to the well.

Suddenly Fern slipped into the man's body and felt the bitter cold sweep into her bones, along with a familiar bitterness. It was Hugues, but he was much older now and weighed down with an aching weariness.

'It is her fault I am here,' muttered Hugues, the words fumbling in his almost toothless mouth as he bent over to draw water from the well. *If not for her* ... he thought. An image of Roese appeared in his mind and he reached out to stroke her hair but she remained just out of his reach, teasing him with her tantalising presence. He groaned, his torment overwhelming him. Wincing with pain Hugues let go of the bucket he had been hoisting up from below. As it splashed back into the water, he clenched his fist and shook it at the sky. 'Get away from me demon,' he shouted. 'Do you hear me? Be gone!' The effort exhausted him and he clutched his head as a fresh pain shot through it, sending him staggering backwards. 'Leave me in peace,' he whispered as he struggled to regain his balance.

A crashing sound snapped Fern back into Jacques' study and she opened her eyes, dazed and confused by the sudden shift in place and time.

'Mon dieu!' Jacques stood up abruptly. 'What was that?'

Struggling to return to the present, Fern followed Jacques into the chapel where Jacques' lantern lay broken on the floor.

'I was fond of this lantern,' he said sadly, bending over to pick up the shards of glass.

The phone rang and Jacques straightened up, wincing as he stood. 'What now?' he grumbled and headed into the hallway to answer it.

Fern sniffed, noting the lingering smell of the extinguished candle which neither she nor Jacques had lit. The hungry man was back and stronger than ever. Her instinct told her to run but suddenly fed up with her fear, instead she bent over to finish cleaning up the glass.

'I'm not afraid of you,' she whispered, hoping the words would be enough to make it true.

Moments later, Jacques reappeared in the doorway. 'Freya is not well. We must collect her.'

Chapter Forty-One

Freya was curled up on the couch in the kitchen, sniffling loudly while Fern and Jacques prepared pumpkin soup for lunch. Jacques had turned up his nose at the prospect but changed his mind when Fern told him it was Freya's favourite. 'Very well but we will do it the French way,' he'd insisted and sent Fern out to fetch rosemary, thyme and sage while he chopped the leeks. Now she was attacking the pumpkin with a large kitchen knife and wondering if the finished product would remotely resemble the soup Freya loved.

Freya sneezed loudly, sending a new surge of guilt through Fern. 'I should have insisted Freya change out of her wet clothes yesterday,' she said.

Jacques shrugged. 'You tried. She would not. There is no point feeling guilty.'

Fern stopped her chopping and glared at Jacques. 'You're not exactly in a good position to lecture me on guilt, Mr I blame myself for everything!'

'Okay, okay. I see your point … Here let me finish that,' he added, taking the knife.

The tension in the kitchen rose as Jacques barked orders at Fern, insisting that the timing was vital and sighing loudly when she grated the cheese badly and burnt the sliced baguettes under the grill.

Twenty minutes later, Jacques tasted the soup and pronounced it perfect, then proudly ladled it into bowls.

'Voila,' he said placing a tray on Freya's lap. On it sat a vast bowl of soup with toasted baguette slices floating on top. This soup hardly resembled the one Freya was familiar with – different texture, different colour, different flavours – and Fern was certain Freya would throw a tantrum.

Freya looked at it suspiciously. 'What's that?' she asked pointing at the top of the baguettes.

'Melted gruyere,' said Jacques. 'It is good. The flavour of the cheese balances with the soup and the texture of the baguette contrasts with it. It is very important.'

Freya stared at it for a moment longer then to Fern's surprise and relief she picked up her spoon and began eating.

Jacques smiled knowingly at Fern. 'You see, she is becoming a child of France.'

After lunch Freya fell asleep on the couch so Fern went upstairs to her room and began unpacking once again, wondering how many failed attempts they would make to leave this place. Freya's cold had reinforced Fern's decision to stay for a while longer and there was no point living out of bags. She'd already bought a few warm things for Freya but it was clear that she'd have to buy some for herself with the little money she had left.

As Fern reached into the side pocket of her pack, her fingers clasped the Tempest Stone she'd hidden there weeks ago. Not wanting to feel its power she quickly let go and instead grasped the owl carving that Michael had given her. Holding it to her nose, she sniffed the lovely scent of myrtle wood, letting it transport her back to Tasmania and to Michael. She missed his steady optimism, his bear-like hugs and his insights, particularly the way he'd helped her learn the herbs, showing her what was needed. She missed Iris too. And now she felt a tug of regret and guilt, because in choosing to stay here for longer, she'd disappointed them. Would she always be torn between people and places like this?

But something of Michael had come with her all this way because as she cradled the owl in both hands, she could feel his strength seeping into her. 'See in the dark,' he'd said when he'd carved it for her. And still she didn't know what he'd been trying to tell her. Perhaps he'd imbued this object with something, an energetic pattern of some sort. Perhaps it was just a carving. Nothing else. Either way she felt comforted with it close by so she slipped the tiny owl into her pocket, slid her empty pack under the bed and returned downstairs to see how Freya was going.

Jacques was sitting at the table reading the newspaper Ahmed had tossed aside with disgust that morning. 'She's still asleep,' he said, glancing up briefly.

Freya's face was a little flushed but she looked peaceful enough. Fern rested her hand momentarily on Freya's forehead; it was warmer than it should be but not burning hot. Sensing movement in the garden she looked up and smiled. 'Amber's here.'

Jacques grunted.

'You love her,' said Fern. She filled the kettle and switched it on just as Amber reached the door, carrying a large hessian bag.

'Hello. Thought I'd pop in and see how you are.'

Fern gave her a hug then gestured at Freya.

Amber pursed her lips then bent over and gave Freya a kiss on the forehead. 'Poor thing's not well.' She patted the cat which was curled up next to Freya. 'Pleased to see Jeannie's looking after her though.'

'You should keep away from the child. What if you catch a cold?'

Amber rolled her eyes. 'I'm pregnant Jacques, not an invalid.' She leaned over and gave him a kiss on the forehead too. 'But it's good to know you care.'

Jacques flushed, muttered something about Amber lacking any sense, and returned to his paper.

Amber tipped out the contents of the bag onto the table. 'I thought you might need something warm to wear.'

Fern stared at the pile of clothes. 'How did you know we were staying?'

Amber shrugged. 'Just a hunch I guess.'

'And the clothes?' asked Fern.

'You didn't exactly arrive equipped for winter. There's not much. It was difficult finding anything you wouldn't swim in.' She picked out a rust-coloured polar fleece jacket and held it up against Fern. Not too bad and it suits your colouring. There's also a couple of woolen sweaters that shrunk in the wash and a woolen skirt I've never worn.' She looked at it regretfully and shook her head. 'I love that skirt but it's always been too small. Nothing for sweetpea I'm afraid,' she added, glancing affectionately at Freya. 'But I have brought one more thing.' She reached in her bag and with a flourish pulled out a small carton. 'Amberosia peppermint tea!'

Fern took it and turned it over in her hands, inspecting the design printed simply on natural cardboard. It felt like a miracle that an idea could be turned into something actual like this and so quickly. 'It's perfect,' she said, giving Amber a hug. 'Congratulations!'

Amber smiled proudly. 'I thought you should be the first to taste it.'

Fern filled a pot with peppermint leaves and poured over boiling water. Letting the tea steep, she prepared a coffee for

Jacques who refused any hot drink without caffeine in it. She turned the pot three times each way as her mother used to do and then poured it in mugs, steam rising and filling the room with the sweetly pungent scent of mint.

'To new ventures,' said Fern, lifting her mug.

'To growing friendships,' said Amber, lifting her own.

'To peace and quiet,' growled Jacques, rustling his paper.

Amber nudged him with her elbow. 'Come on, admit it, you love having us around, attending to your every whim.'

Jacques smiled despite himself. 'It has some compensations.'

On the couch, Freya groaned in her sleep then sat up suddenly, face flushed and eyes staring into the distance as if she were in a trance. Alarmed, Fern jumped up, ready to comfort Freya, but when she tried to hug her, the child pushed her away.

'You will burn in hell,' she said, staring unseeing at her mother, and suddenly the atmosphere in the room filled with dread.

Chapter Forty-Two

'Mama. Help me Mama,' shouted Freya.

'It's alright sweetheart,' I'm here.'

'Mama!' she shouted again, throwing off her blankets.

Worried, Fern reached down to pick up the blankets. For the past three hours she'd been sitting by Freya's bed trying to get her to take something to bring her temperature down. Usually Freya liked the sickly, sweet pink liquid but tonight she kept pushing the spoon away, spilling it onto the sheets and making everything sticky. Fern picked up the wet flannel and wiped Freya's hot face with it then covered her with the blankets once again before returning wearily to the armchair next to the bed, where she sat watching her daughter tossing and turning.

She thought again about the awful pronouncement Freya had made that afternoon. They'd all decided it was the fever speaking but even so, a feeling of terror had settled into the pit of Fern's stomach and it was clear that both Amber and Jacques were shaken.

'Help Mama,' shouted Freya as she flung off the blanket again. 'It's burning.' In her scrabble to get away from whatever was tormenting her, Freya slipped over the edge of the bed. Fern grasped her quickly, breaking her fall and then held her in her arms, trying to comfort her.

Exhausted, Freya stilled for a moment before wiggling out of Fern's arms again. 'The fire … the fire,' she screamed, backing away towards the door.

Fern followed, trying to induce her back into bed but Freya shook her head stubbornly.

All at once she started shivering. 'I'm cold Mama.'

Fern scooped her up, put her back in the bed and piled extra blankets on top of her but the shivering continued, so in the end she climbed into the narrow bed and held her daughter close, hoping that her own warmth would seep into Freya. Gradually the shivering stopped and Freya fell into a fitful sleep, waking and protesting each time Fern tried to extricate herself. Eventually Fern gave up, and with one leg sticking out of the bed to make more room, she finally fell asleep too.

Wake up.

Fern slept on, the words failing to find their way through the veil of sleep.

Wake up. There is danger. The voice was quiet but insistent and it was this insistence that finally penetrated Fern's mind and woke her. Confused, she took stock for a moment then remembered she was in Freya's bed and still dressed in her jeans and jumper. Her left arm was numb, the circulation cut off by Freya's sleeping body. Her back was twisted and her neck itchy where the wool of the jumper Amber had given her was rubbing.

There is danger. Fully awake now, Fern glanced uncertainly around the semi-dark room, trying to identify the source of the words. There was no one there, aside from herself and Freya, who was sleeping soundly now that the fever had settled.

Danger. The voice came again, sending prickles of fear through Fern. It was a familiar voice … a woman … Then she had it. Petrona.

Wondering what Petrona meant, Fern slipped out of the bed, covered Freya with the blanket then looked around the room again, but there was nothing to suggest any danger and no sign of the old woman either. It was only when Fern stepped into the hallway that she smelled the smoke; just a trace at first and she wondered if it was coming from outside, perhaps from a chimney or a bonfire nearby. But as she descended the stairs the smoke grew thicker and it quickly became apparent that its source was inside the house. Panicking now, Fern rushed into the kitchen, assuming that Jacques had left something on the stove but there was nothing there. Suddenly Fern knew with a sinking certainty that it was coming from the chapel. Running into the room she found smoke and flames billowing from one of the curtains.

Shocked, Fern stood frozen for a moment, uncertain what to do first.

'Jacques,' she shouted, her voice resounding around the chapel walls but going no further. She approached the curtain, thinking that if she could pull it down and stamp on it, the fire would be easier to contain. But the heat of the flames was already too much and she was forced to back away.

Fern raced to the kitchen, pausing briefly at the base of the stairs to shout for Jacques again. In the kitchen she searched frantically for a water container, eventually finding a plastic tub under the sink. She turned the tap up high and waited impatiently for it to fill.

'Merde,' shouted Jacques, moments later as he stumbled through the door. 'I will call the fire brigade.'

Fern ran back to the chapel, the movement sending some of the water slopping over the edges of the container. She threw the remainder over the curtain but it made little difference. The flames were growing quickly and the fire beginning to spread into the wooden frames of the window. They needed a hose but the garden hose wouldn't reach this far so they'd have to make do until the fire brigade arrived.

With a shock, Fern remembered that Freya was asleep upstairs, and in danger of getting trapped by the fire if it spread. She had to get her. But as she turned toward the door, she distinctly heard laughter, a deep rolling sound that sent chills down her spine. Spinning around she found herself face-to-face with the hungry man, only this time he was so close she could smell his fetid breath. He was clothed in a ragged gown, his head hooded, his face crumpled with age, his eyes filled with hatred. Instinctively Fern recoiled, then remembering Freya she tried to step around it but found herself glued to the spot, the flames crackling behind her, the hungry man in front of her, holding her there, feeding himself on her energy. Then he laughed triumphantly and Fern felt a dark heavy weight as the hungry man slipped into her, still laughing, only now the laughter was coming from inside Fern.

'We are one,' he said. His words were almost drowned out by the roar of the flames, but even so, she felt the force of them and his gloating triumph.

Jacques ran in, carrying a bucket of water just as the burning curtain behind Fern began to fall. 'Move,' he shouted, seeing the danger, then watched horrified as Fern stood frozen in place.

'Watch out!' he shouted again, but Fern only laughed as it landed on her, knocking her off balance, and she laughed again as she fell to the floor encased in its flames.

Jacques leaped forward and pulled Fern free of the curtain then pushed her onto the thick woolen rug, rolling her over and over on it until he was certain the flames were extinguished. Then for good measure he poured the bucket of water over her.

The moment the water touched her, Fern felt the presence leave. Shocked and deflated, she lay on the rug, her clothes singed and saturated, her eyes stinging from the smoke and wet ash, the places where the flames had scorched her beginning to burn.

In the distance came the sound of an approaching fire engine, its siren blaring. Any minute now they'd be here. Fern breathed a sigh of relief. The curtain was burning itself out on the tiled floor but although the flames had taken hold in the window frame, the room was mostly stone and terracotta tiles so the fire wouldn't have a chance to spread to the main house where Freya was sleeping.

'Are you injured?' asked Jacques, his worried face appearing above her.

Her throat raw with smoke, Fern just shook her head.

'Bon,' said Jacques. But you cannot stay here, he added and reached down to help her up.

Fern took Jacques' hand and stood up shakily. 'I'm fine,' she whispered.

Jacques nodded, relieved, then raced back to the kitchen for more water.

Fern stood for a moment watching the flames as she waited for her head to stop spinning. Her wet jeans were clinging to her legs and the owl carving in her pocket was digging into her thigh. She reached in to retrieve it and as her fingers closed around the owl she saw Michael once again, his open face, the intensity of his look as he tried to make her understand. See in the dark, he'd told her. And suddenly she did. Fern felt her blood run cold as the realisation settled in. It didn't make sense but the pieces fitted together so easily it was hard to believe she hadn't seen it earlier.

Jacques returned with a fresh bucket of water and threw it on the curtain, dowsing more of the flames and sending out billows of smoke. They were both coughing as a group of firemen burst through the door and pulled them from the room.

Two hours later when the firemen were confident that the fire was completely extinguished, Jacques made them coffee and asked about the cause of the fire.

'A lit candle under the curtain,' said one of them, shaking his head. 'Either it was arson or a stupid mistake,' he said.

Jacques and Fern exchanged glances. 'It was a mistake of course,' Jacques said, knowing full well that no-one had used the chapel that evening.

The fireman drained his coffee and handed back the cup. 'Better get some batteries in those smoke alarms,' he said. 'You're lucky to be alive.'

'Yes, yes,' said Jacques as he saw them to the door. 'I will. And thank you. We are most grateful.'

Jacques shut the front door and stood for a moment surveying the mess in the chapel. 'It could be worse,' he said sadly as Fern joined him. 'Most of the damage is from the water and smoke,' he added, staring morosely at the singed and sodden couch.

He scowled at the half-finished coffee in his hand. 'It is time for something a little stronger I think.' Turning, he staggered slightly and Fern reached out to steady him. 'I do not need help,' he said, shaking his arm free.

Freya was asleep on the couch, placed there by a fireman who had slung the still sleeping child over one shoulder and carried her downstairs, the unusually compliant cat tucked under his other arm. Mercifully she'd missed all the drama, waking only briefly when Fern had covered her with a blanket. Her eyes had widened when she'd seen her mother's face, but she'd fallen straight back to sleep when Jeannie jumped up on the couch next to her and curled up purring.

Jacques sank into a kitchen chair, looking exhausted, his face pallid under the streaks of wet ash.

Wine? asked Fern wondering if she looked as awful as he did.

Jacques shook his head. 'Something even stronger is needed.'

Fern fetched the bottle of whiskey and poured him a generous portion. As she did so she caught a glimpse of herself in the mirror. The water had turned the ash to mud and sent it running in streaks down her face. One eyebrow was singed and so was much of her hair; she would need to cut it all off and start again. Sadly, she inspected her jumper; a gift from Amber earlier that day but now ruined.

'It is lucky you were wearing wool,' said Jacques. 'Without it you would have been badly burned.'

Fern hadn't exactly emerged unscathed but she knew what Jacques meant. The firemen had inspected her for burns and been surprised at how few there were. A few blisters on one hand and a small patch on her neck and eyebrow, both treated and bandaged but as time passed their stinging heat was getting worse.

Hoping it would help dull the pain, Fern poured a whiskey for herself too. Jacques was right, she was lucky but there was more to it than that. Amber had delivered a woolen jumper only hours before the fire, Freya had insisted Fern sleep with her, not giving her a chance to change into her pyjamas and then Petrona had warned her. Was this luck or something else? Fern wondered.

'Thank you,' said Jacques, when she handed him a glass. 'And thank you for raising the alarm. I do not like to think what might have happened otherwise.'

'It would probably have burned itself out.'

'Even so, it would have done much more damage.' Jacques took a sip of whiskey. 'Ahh, that is good medicine.'

'You drink too much,' said Fern.

'And you can talk?' said Jacques, gesturing to her glass.

Fern smiled and took a sip, then grimaced and put the glass down. 'Perhaps you should do as the firemen suggested and put some batteries in your smoke detectors.'

'Yes. I will,' said Jacques. 'I have learned my lesson but even so, I do not like them. They always go beep and disturb me.'

'It was the ghost,' said Fern.

Jacques looked up sharply. 'Are you sure. Could there be no other reason?'

'I'm sure. I saw him.'

'Oui.' Jacques nodded, reluctantly accepting Fern's word. 'I did not see it, however I saw that you were not yourself.'

'He was in me,' said Fern, shuddering at the memory.

Jacques looked concerned. 'He has become very strong then.' He hesitated, clearly battling with his conscience. 'I was wrong to ask you both to stay.'

Fern laughed. 'Don't tell me you're suggesting I leave… Not now I know who the ghost is.'

Jacques froze, his drink halfway to his mouth. 'You know?'

'It's Hugues.'

Jacques looked puzzled for a moment then surprised as the implications set in. 'Hugues?' He took a gulp of his whiskey then shook his head. 'Impossible.'

'I saw him in the chapel earlier. Much older and practically unrecognizable, and he said something I didn't understand until afterwards. He said "We are one."'

'But what would he be doing here?'

'I'm not sure but I think that chapel must be where he spent the last years of his life.'

Jacques stared at her for a moment, pondering her words then shrugged. 'I do not think there is enough evidence but I am too tired to think in a clear manner about your theory.' He stood up, swayed precariously then steadied himself on the back of the chair. 'I am going to bed.'

Chapter Forty-Three

Two days had passed since the fire and much of that time had been spent cleaning out the chapel and airing out the acrid smell of smoke from the house. Fern had visited a hairdresser and now her hair was short and wispy, making her look like a pixie, according to Kia who had come over the day before to help remove the furniture in the chapel.

Freya had almost recovered from her cold so Fern had promised she could return to school the next morning. She'd been a model patient, happy to curl up on the couch and read picture books or watch a movie. In contrast, Fern had been trying unsuccessfully to get Jacques to rest because he was clearly exhausted. With the cleaning over and the new furniture ordered, she hoped he would slow down but the weather had shifted another gear into winter with a forecast for frost the following morning. Now he was worrying about the potted lemon and lime trees.

'They do not like the ice,' he said. 'I must bring them in for the winter.'

'Where will they go,' asked Fern.

Here on the terrace.' Jacques grabbed the side of a terracotta pot and began to tug at it. 'It is time to pull the glass shutters across and enclose the verandah. That will keep the frost from them and make this area a pleasant place to sit in the winter.' He tugged again at the giant pot but only succeeded in moving it a few centimetres.

'Here, let me,' said Fern. She tried to pull it toward her but it wouldn't budge.

'They're heavy,' said Jacques. 'We will need to do this together.'

'Why don't we wait and ask Kia to help when he comes over next?' suggested Fern, worried that despite the cold, Jacques' face was damp with perspiration.

'We have four hands between us,' said Jacques scathingly. He reached down and tugged again, heaving and straining until the pot began to move. Fern quickly joined in, grabbing the other side and pushing until they had the pot in its new resting place.

When Jacques straightened up, he was breathing in quick shallow pants.

'You should rest,' said Fern.

'I'm fine,' he retorted and turned to the second pot.

Helpless to stop him, Fern joined in once again but halfway across the tiles, Jacques' hands suddenly slipped from the side of the pot and he fell to the floor, hands clutching his chest.

Fern knelt down beside him. 'Can you hear me, Jacques?' she asked trying to keep her voice calm.

Jacques nodded almost imperceptibly, his face pallid but his eyes open and alert.

'I'm going to call an ambulance.'

Jacques shook his head then paused a moment gathering his strength. When he spoke, his voice was a whisper. 'Just help me up. I'll be fine.'

'I'll help you off these cold tiles and then I'm going to call an ambulance.' She heaved him into a sitting position then called Freya and asked her to clear her things off the couch. Freya glanced at Jacques with wide eyes but quickly did as she was told, returning to help Fern pull Jacques up from the floor and heave him onto the couch where he lay, panting and pale. Fern covered him with a blanket, then called an ambulance, managing to provide the details in broken French.

When she returned, a little colour had returned to Jacques' face and his breathing had settled.

'The ambulance is on its way,' said Fern.

'No need, no need. You are making too much fuss.' He struggled to sit up then admitting defeat, sank back down once more. 'It is cold,' he said, shivering suddenly.

Fern grabbed a second blanket from the cupboard in the hallway and draped it over him. 'I'll make you some tea,' she said. 'No, not coffee, you need something soothing.'

When Fern returned with the tea, Freya was perched on the side of the couch holding Jacques' hand. 'Don't be scared, Jacqui,' she was saying. 'I'm here.'

Fern helped Jacques sit up a little and then handed him his tea. He took a sip and grimaced at the flavor. 'English muck, he said weakly but took another sip before returning the mug to Fern and sinking back onto the cushions. When Freya tucked him in and informed him that the siren he could hear in the distance was his ambulance he managed only a weak smile.

Fern focused on Jacques, trying to still her mind so that she could get a better sense of what was going on inside him. The colours she'd seen at Samhain had faded for the most part but she could still sense what needed attention. It was his heart. She was certain of it, but all the certainty in the world wouldn't fix it for him. A surge of helpless fear ran through her as she waited impatiently for the ambulance to arrive.

In the morning, Fern dropped Freya off at school before catching the bus to the hospital in Prades where the ambulance officers had taken Jacques the previous evening. They'd mixed light-hearted banter with a serious intent, making even Jacques feel comfortable. He'd still protested when they said they were taking him to hospital but the protests were half-hearted and he'd been reasonably polite about it.

Fern yawned as the bus wound its way down the mountain road. She'd spent most of the night awake, worrying about Jacques. The ambulance officers had explained they were concerned about his heart but that was all they could tell her so she'd called the hospital a few times but all she'd been able to find out was that he would be staying there overnight.

In Prades she got off the bus and made her way to the hospital, where she asked directions to his ward. Jacques was sitting up in bed, his chest covered with sensors and wires connected to a machine above him. It was a familiar sight and the reminder of Adam's final hours brought a fresh wave of anxiety, which Fern struggled to mask as she stepped into the room.

Seeing Fern, Jacques rolled his eyes and tried to look contrite. 'Yes, yes. You were right and I am an idiot. It seems my heart is in need of maintenance.'

'You're stubborn,' said Fern, relieved that he seemed himself again. 'Was it a heart attack?'

'Non. I have been lucky, they tell me. Ha. Lucky!'

'Then what's wrong with your heart?' asked Fern, surprised.

He shrugged. 'They have given me pills and soon I must have an operation to clear the arteries.'

'Did your son ring?'

'Oui,' Jacques smiled. 'He said your French was magnificent.'

'Yeah, right,' said Fern. Her French had been far from magnificent but Edmond had rescued her from her misery and switched to almost perfect English. 'Is he coming?'

'Yes, in a few days. He will not allow me to have the operation here. He thinks only Parisian hospitals are competent. So, he and Alexis will collect me and drive me to Paris where I will be given the best treatment.'

'Good.' Fern was relieved there would be someone else to nag Jacques about his health now. 'How long do you have to stay here?'

Jacques smiled. 'Your journey was in vain. They are sending me home today.'

A shadow crossed his face and the smile disappeared. 'Edmond has given me a scolding. I think that is the word you use. He has accused me of not wishing to live, since the deaths of Alain and of Madeleine. He reminded me how selfish I was being. Apparently, I should wish to live for his sake,' Jacques added drily.

Fern nodded. 'And so you should.'

'Yes, yes, he is right, of course. It is strange. Since Madeleine died, I have welcomed the thought of death but now I discover there is much to live for after all.'

Chapter Forty-Four

As promised, Jacques returned in the afternoon with strict instructions that he should rest. Instructions he grudgingly followed until the next morning.

It was a cold morning so after dropping Freya at school and stocking up at the market, Fern stoked the fire in the kitchen, unpacked the shopping and settled down at the table with a pot of Amber's peppermint tea and a book.

Jacques appeared in the doorway looking grumpy. He glanced at the wall clock above the sink. 'It is after ten o'clock. You are late.'

'For what,' asked Fern, surprised.

'We have a regression to do.'

'You're not well enough, Jacques.'

'Rubbish. I'm perfectly well.'

'But you're not supposed to stress yourself.'

'There will be no stress. At least not for me.' He looked at Fern. 'Nor for you, I hope. Today will be a release.'

Fern looked unconvinced. 'Why do you think it will be so easy?'

'No doubt you can feel the difference in the house.'

Fern nodded. Until the night of the fire the house had been holding its breath but somehow the fire had released it and now it was breathing regularly again. 'The tension has gone from the atmosphere,' she said.

Jacques nodded. 'I have thought about this a good deal. Surely we should be more concerned after that episode in the chapel but we are not. Or at least I am not.'

'You've had other things to think about.'

'Even so,' said Jacques. 'I believe the ghost has vented its fury and now waits to be released.'

Fern thought about it for a moment. 'How do we do that?'

Jacques sat down at the table opposite Fern. 'I have also thought about your notion that the ghost and Hugues are the same. I should not have dismissed it so quickly. It is not something I have encountered in the past but with consideration I can see that the pieces sit together. We must make use of the connection you have already made. We regress you and take Hugues through his death once again. In so doing we will release him from you and from this house where he is caught.'

Fern nodded. 'Okay, but I still don't get how Hugues can be a ghost if he's my past life. How can he be in more than one place at once?'

'Oui, I have thought about this. Perhaps a ghost is not a complete person but rather an aspect of a soul that has become trapped elsewhere and cannot or will not release itself. In you, Hugues manifests as a repeated pattern and as a part of your soul that is wounded or absent. In this house?' Jacques paused and considered for a moment. 'If Hugues died here in torment, then that part of him is trapped and that means a part of you is also trapped, so it's even more urgent that we release him.'

'But if Hugues is a part of me what will happen to me when he goes to the light?'

'You will feel a release too but you will not lose yourself. The opposite will occur and the effect will be beneficial. It will mean the return to you of something that has been lost.'

'What if I don't want this part of myself?'

'You will not become Hugues. The emotions associated with him will be released, and eventually the patterns of behaviour will subside too. You will simply feel more complete and more able to live well in the world.'

Fern pondered this for a moment. 'Okay,' she said, but we should do the regression in the chapel.'

'Ah, of course, that is sensible. The chapel is the oldest part of this building and that is where we first felt the effects of this ghost.'

'And I'm pretty sure that's where he died,' said Fern.

'Come then,' said Jacques.

Fern followed him out of the kitchen, her fear of re-immersing herself in Hugues or vice versa, battling with her eagerness to be free of him.

The chapel was still not a welcoming space but this time it was because the smell of stale smoke still pervaded the atmosphere. The airing of the chapel had also removed its last vestiges of warmth and now the room was terribly cold.

'No doubt this will make Hugues feel at home,' grumbled Jacques as he lit the fire.

The new couch hadn't arrived yet so Fern fetched a couple of chairs from the kitchen and placed them close to the fire. They perched on them, shivering in the cold air; the newly lit fire looked nice but it wasn't emitting much warmth.

'Now,' said Jacques, 'I want you to try and find Hugues at the end of his life. Remember the sensations in your last regression. The pain in your head would be a good entry point.'

Fern began concentrating on the pain but it remained evasive, still there in the distance but receding out of reach when she tried to engage with it. Her thoughts were getting in the way, the fury and manic laughter she'd encountered only a few nights ago, the flames catching on her clothes, the acrid smell of singed hair and wool, her helpless fear, his gloating triumph, the two becoming one … She shuddered and opened her eyes. 'I can't do it.'

'Yes you can.'

Fern stared at the fire which was blazing now, its heat licking at their legs. 'I can't bear the thought of being part of him again.'

All your life he has been part of you. This is an exorcism. You are liberating yourself from him. It must be done.' Jacques paused and sniffed. 'Can you smell that?'

'The smoke?'

'No, something else.'

Fern sniffed the air and identified the heady perfume. 'Incense.'

'Yes. It is an invitation. Let it transport you across time to Hugues.'

Concentrating on the incense, Fern closed her eyes and almost immediately found herself

shuffling slowly across the chapel, her bones aching with the cold, her joints swollen and screaming with pain, her robe tattered, the hem swishing along the floor, sweeping it as she walked. Hugues glanced through the window. It was daylight still but the sky visible through the window was heavy and tinged with a green hue. It would snow soon. No doubt it was waiting until he stepped outside in search of wood to for the fire.

As Hugues passed, he noted that the incense stick at the altar had almost burned itself out. He sighed, knowing he should light another. But there were few sticks left and he had no idea when he might replenish them. Perhaps he could forego it. There was no-one here to take note of his sins and certainly God had forsaken him long ago. These days there was little money and ever fewer donations of candles, oil or incense so he was forced to ration them, slipping into his hard pallet earlier each night as winter cut minutes and hours from the daylight. He would lie there for twelve hours, sometimes more, wrapped in his thin blankets, his knees curled up into his chest for warmth, shivering and hungry, the scant food in his stomach serving only to fill him with the craving for more.

Pulling his hood tighter around his head, Hugues stepped outside. Immediately the wind hurled itself at him, clawing its way through his garments. Knowing he would not be able to withstand it for long, he hurried across the sodden ground to the woodlands nearby where he gathered what kindling he could carry. It was wet wood and there was no time to dry it so most likely the twigs would do little more than fill the room with smoke. Returning, he placed the kindling next to the chapel door and went to collect a log from the dwindling wood pile. His heart sank as he surveyed the few remaining logs, for Hugues no longer had the strength to cut wood and the boy from the village who had done this chore for him in the past had succumbed to disease a few weeks earlier. Without heat Hugues knew he would not last long.

Hugues picked up a log then straightened and stood for a moment gazing at the jagged silhouettes of the Pyrenees, coated in snow. If only, he thought. If only he had never met her. He'd been so close to the pinnacle. Tantalisingly close. He could have reached out his hand and touched it. For precious moments he allowed himself to remember that feeling, the hope he had carried with him and the ambition too, the pride he'd felt in his success, the care he'd taken with his robes. And now, he was nothing. As the first flakes of snow began to fall, Hugues stumbled and nearly dropped the log. It is not fair, he thought bitterly as he readjusted his balance and tightened his grip, grimacing with the pain in his knuckles.

His luck had left him with the fall of Carcassonne to Simon de Montfort, pulled from under his feet by the power and greed of others. The crusade against the heretics had quickly become a scrabbling for power amongst men who cared nothing for who they cut down before them, Catholics and Cathars alike. He too had once confused politics with God but at least he no longer made that mistake. In contrast, these men still bickered over their trophies and bartered for power, seeking ever greater cuts and while they did so the country slipped further into degradation and lawlessness. Few pilgrims passed this way these days and for good reason. Bandits, disease and hunger were rife, leaving little time for the worship of God. Even here in the sanctity of the church he found himself tossing and turning at night, one ear listening out for thieves. Still, if he were murdered it would put him out of his misery.

It was a small compensation for Hugues that the majority of the Cathars had been eliminated in the Crusade but he was tormented by the certainty that some had slipped the net. He could smell their heresy; wafts of it still clung to the countryside. He blamed them for his plight; the heretics and the woman whose name he could no longer bear to speak, a heretic too for all her denials. His luck might have left him with the fall of Carcassonne but the cracks had appeared earlier. Since her death he'd fallen again and again, landing in ever more shameful situations, until this final banishment to this godforsaken chapel where he'd become a hermit priest, shunned by many and respected by few; his single duty to maintain the chapel for the few pilgrims who passed by.

He'd found some peace here at first, away from the ambitions that were rife in the Abbey and the daily reminders that he was no longer a player in their games. He'd found solace in cultivating the garden and living a simpler life, foolishly believing he had left the past behind. But it was not long until *she* sought him out and began her torments, once again turning his life into a living hell. It is not fair, he thought again. Not fair.

A blinding pain shot down the side of Hugues head, stopping him in his tracks. It had appeared for the first time a few days earlier and he was becoming used to the way it came and went as it saw fit. In its intensity the disabling pain drew him into its centre so that he could not focus on anything else. Then as before, it passed a few moments later. Hugues shook his head, trying to free himself from the residue of the pain, then slowly made his way back to the chapel entrance, where he paused again, clenched his fist and shook it at the statue of Mary Magdalene, perched above the door. 'A curse on you, whore,' he shouted at the stone carving. What irony that I should be given the task of safekeeping a chapel dedicated to that woman, he thought as he stepped through the door, not bothering to brush the mud from his feet or the snow from his shoulders.

Back in the little side room off the chapel that served as his living quarters, Hugues built up the fire but held scant hope it would catch. When he had done all he could, he sat down in the almost darkness to draw his breath and try to regain some strength in his limbs. What little daylight that was left was struggling to find its way through the solitary window so if the fire didn't catch soon and send its flickering light through the room, he would need to light the precious lantern. Hoping against hope, he waited and watched the pitiful fire for some time, poking and prodding the kindling, but despite his ministrations it refused to emit anything but smoke.

Sighing, Hugues stood up again, groaning at the pain in his knees then doubled over as a cough emerged from deep within him, sending his lungs into painful spasms. He waited for it to pass then limbs trembling with fatigue, he lit the lantern with a smouldering stick. In the flickering light the room felt more welcoming but the light itself created shadows and it was in the darkest of these shadows that Hugues' torment lay. Shuddering, he forced his mind to practical matters and decided to replenish the incense after all, for the scent would bring him comfort.

In the chapel he noted with relief that a bowl of food had been left for him. Hugues lifted the cover and sniffed at the thin stew. Just lentils and a few vegetables but it smelled wholesome. No doubt it was from the old woman who lived further down the river. Another heretic, he thought contemptuously; a Cathar most likely by the vegetarian fare she left, and most certainly a witch. She rarely showed herself, usually sending her daughter on the errands. But he'd come face-to-face with her once and introduced himself. 'Petrona,' she had said in return, then simply smiled when he asked her why she didn't worship in the chapel. Still, she was kind. Kinder than she needed to be, for it was clear she did not hold the Church in high esteem. Hugues had little doubt that her generosity was aimed at the whore who stood guard over the chapel, not at him. He knew he should not consort with the witch but he no longer had the liberty to be proud or cautious; fate had seen to that. Tonight he would eat the woman's food with gratitude and leave the pot out for her daughter to collect in the morning.

The pain returned suddenly, sucking the breath from him and making him drop the lid he was holding. It clattered on the stone floor and broke into pieces. As he watched the shards radiating outwards from the spot it had landed, the pain intensified, shooting down his neck and sending him stumbling towards the altar. His legs folded from under him and he fell heavily on his front, the impact driving the air out of his chest and leaving him struggling for breath. Vaguely he heard the lantern clatter onto the stone floor beside him, and his rosary snap, the beads scuttling across the floor. Then he felt rather than saw the darkness descend.

When Hugues returned to consciousness, he could not tell where he was at first. He opened his eyes and searched the darkness for something which would help anchor him. His gaze settled on the window above him and he stared at the night sky for a time, knowing it might be his last glimpse before death captured him. Clouds formed a heavy blanket above the earth, warming the night but not the chapel where he lay. The silence outside was broken by the howling of a wolf and then another, and Hugues shuddered, thanking God that he had closed the chapel door for he had always feared being torn limb from limb by those accursed beasts.

Hugues took stock. His left leg was twisted under him and there was a numbness spreading down his right side. The pain in his head and neck had subsided but been replaced by a stabbing and throbbing pain in his chest. Each breath was agonising and he surmised that he had broken some ribs. Keeping his breath shallow, Hugues tried to lift himself up from the floor but soon realised he had no strength left to do so. Groaning with pain, he released his muscles and sank helplessly back to the ground, his mind desperately seeking a solution but finding only two certainties: he would not be rescued and he could not save himself.

Hugues awaited death both impatiently and fearfully, wanting oblivion but afraid of hell. For a time, the cold of the stone floor crept into his body, making him tremble and agitating the pain in his chest. Then the cold withdrew, leaving him numb all over. His eyes had become used to the darkness in the chapel and he could now make out the altar and the arched roof. It should have been comforting but as always, with vision came shadows and these were darker and deeper than ever before. Roese appeared suddenly before him and he was shocked to see that her face was no longer beautiful. Instead, the flesh was blackened, the mouth fixed in a scream of pain. The only intact part of her was her eyes which stared into him unblinking. He tried closing his eyes but still this vision of her penetrated behind his eyelids. Terrified, he began to pray, begging God to have mercy on him.

'Help me,' whimpered Hugues.

'Tell me what is happening,' said Jacques.

'I am lying on the floor, I've fallen and I can feel nothing but death won't come. It is punishing me. It is not fair that even at death I am to be tormented.'

'It will come soon,' promised Jacques. 'Fern, try to make yourself known to Hugues.'

Deep inside herself Fern heard Jacques and began to concentrate on separating from Hugues. Suddenly she was no longer lying on the floor but instead, standing before him looking down at his prostrate figure. Then just as suddenly she was back inside Hugues looking out. Only this time she could see a figure standing before her. A demon thought Hugues, shrinking away in fear, only to look again and see that it did not resemble anything from his knowledge of demons. This strange figure was evidently female yet dressed in a hose and a woollen vest, her hair cut short. Hugues felt a vague stirring of recognition. He had seen this figure before somewhere. Perhaps in a dream.

Fern tried to speak but the atmosphere was thick and sluggish just as if it were a nightmare, making each movement of her mouth an immense effort. There was much to say but in the end she could manage only three words. 'You are loved.'

At this Hugues felt a new pain in his chest as if his heart were tearing open. He began to cry silently, letting the tears flow freely for the first time in many years and with this release a weight lifted from him as the shadows fled.

Death arrived in the coldest part of the night just before dawn. Hugues' breath slowed as he felt its approach. Then after a sudden gasp his breath stopped altogether.

'It is time,' said Jacques, noting Fern's gasp. 'Hugues, you must go to the light. You are free now.'

At Jacques' words, Hugues' spirit lifted out of his body and looked back down on itself, lying sprawled on the chapel floor, alone in death as in life. Confused, he looked beyond the chapel which had been his prison for years of his life and then held a part of his soul for centuries. The light beyond was bright, almost dazzling and within it he could see figures gathering to welcome him; people he had once loved who should by all rights have despised him. His eyes settled on his mother, who smiled a welcome. He searched her face but there was no sign of the disappointment he knew she'd felt at his fall from grace. And his beloved mentor, Bishop Berenger was holding his hands out towards Hugues, his eyes shining with kindness. *Come. It is time.* He searched for Roese and found her, standing next to her mother, beautiful as ever, not disfigured as he'd last seen her. She looked at him, her eyes gentle, no trace of his betrayal reflected in them. *It is over.* She held out her hand and, in that moment, Hugues understood that in letting go he was leaving behind the hell he'd created for himself. He took one step and then another, pausing only a moment to look back at his prison, the container of his body lying crumpled on the tiles below. Breathing a deep sigh of relief, he reached his hand out to Roese and clasped her fingers.

Chapter Forty-Five

W hen Fern returned to herself her spirit felt lighter somehow and yet more complete. She opened her eyes and
looked at Jacques. 'It's over.'

He reached across and grasped her hand. 'Yes, it is. Finally!'

'Now I am free.' Fern smiled as the idea began to settle into
reality. 'And so are you.'

'From what?' asked Jacques, momentarily confused.

'The ghost.'

'Ah, yes, that is a cause for celebration. We will have no
more mischief in this house.' He glanced at the fire then picked
up a metal rod and poked at the burning log, sending sparks up
into the chimney. 'However, there is something more you must
do.'

'What?' asked Fern, suddenly suspicious.

'You have released much today and there will be a natural
time of integration and understanding as you identify the patterns
and parallels between your life and Hugues' life. However, it is
important that you also understand who Roese is.'

'Roese?' Fern felt a sinking feeling growing within her.
'Why?'

'In this case it is important. Do you have no idea?'

Fern shook her head then paused, suddenly uncertain.
Closing her eyes she conjured Roese's face once again and began
sifting through the many expressions she'd seen in those eyes: a

sparkling mischief, intelligence, trust, terror, hurt and the steady look Roese had given Hugues as she waited for the fire to take hold. A look that gave nothing away and yet penetrated into the depths of his conscience, a look that was remarkably familiar.

'Freya! … I should have known… It's obvious now. I should have seen it.' She paused. 'But I was looking at everything the wrong way.'

'Most things are obvious in retrospect,' said Jacques. 'If you had told me the entire story, then perhaps I would have understood earlier.' He frowned. 'But I should have been more alert because it is common for a small group of souls to incarnate together in various roles. An old enemy becomes a parent in a new life, a lover becomes a brother, a child becomes a boss … Sometimes the roles change over many lifetimes until the karmic residue is resolved.'

'What is wrong?' he asked, noticing Fern's worried expression. 'You should be pleased to have the opportunity to begin once more with your daughter.'

Fern sighed. 'How can knowing this help my relationship with Freya? If anything, it will make it worse.'

'It will not. Freya feels negative emotions around her relationship with you but does not understand why. When she understands she will not hold a grudge. Children are quick to accept these things.'

'You're not suggesting we should tell her?'

'Why not?'

'If I've released Hugues that should be enough for our relationship to change.'

'It will help most certainly but Freya might be holding on to psychic debris from her life as Roese. If we talk to her about the past it might help to make the way forward clearer.'

'Isn't she too young?'

Jacques nodded. 'She is too young to undergo a regression but children that age often instinctively understand about past lives so it is possible to have a conversation and find out what she might already know.' When Fern didn't look convinced, Jacques went on. 'Does Freya have history of nightmares?'

'Night terrors,' said Fern.

'Is she afraid of fire?'

'You know the answer to that.'

'Then she is already aware at some level. Children move more easily through the veils than adults and Freya is a sensitive child.' Jacques stood up. 'Do not worry, I will not have a conversation with her without your consent. Think about it and tell me when your mind is made up.' He smiled and rubbed his stomach. 'For now, I am hungry so I will be a good patient and allow you to make lunch.'

That afternoon, Fern walked down the hill to collect Freya, grateful all over again for the heavy jacket Amber had given her and the woollen scarf Jacques had donated. Even so, her fingers were so cold she had to stuff them deep into her pockets. Around her the peaks of the mountains were disappearing one by one as heavy low clouds began building in the sky, their slightly green hue suggesting it might snow.

Fern's realisation that Freya and Roese were the same person had been a shock but on reflection it was also a relief. Now she could at least understand why Freya had never properly trusted her and why this distrust had deepened when they'd arrived at Jacques' house and begun digging into the past. She could also understand why Ahmed had been so keen for Fern to resolve what was between her and Freya.

Fern turned into the school yard and stood waiting for Freya. Since the regression that morning she'd felt different although it wasn't something she could pin down. However, Freya was highly sensitive so Fern wasn't surprised when she gave her an appraising look in the school ground before slipping her hand into Fern's.

As they walked back up the hill the first flakes began to fall.

'It's snowing Mama, squealed Freya. She stuck out her hand and tried to catch the flakes but they quickly melted.

In minutes the snow began to fall heavily and was soon settling on the ground. Fern pulled up Freya's hood then tightened her own scarf in an effort to stop the snowflakes finding their way down the back of her neck. Within moments her hair was covered with melting flakes and Fern wished she'd been less vain and accepted the awful hat Jacques had offered.

When they arrived at the front of the house, Freya gathered up some snow, worked it into a ball and threw it at Fern, laughing. Fern responded with one of her own and Freya shrieked with delight. Soon they were having an all-out war in the front garden, joined by Beattie.

'Look Jaqui,' Freya shouted, when he appeared at the door. 'It's snowing.'

'Ah,' said Jacques, as a snowball landed on his chest. 'Aside from watermelon pip spitting, snowball fights are my favourite thing but for now I am banned from them.' He ducked as another snowball flew through the air, only just missing him. 'I am returning to the safety of the kitchen where there is a hot chocolate and orange gateau waiting for you.'

'Yay,' shouted Freya and raced inside, dripping snow as she went.

Before entering the house, Fern paused and looked up at the statue of Mary Magdalene above the door, feeling a surge of inexplicable gratitude. Without thinking, she crossed herself.

Above her, Mary Magdalene seemed to smile at the gesture and then the features of her stone carved face shifted and changed and Fern found herself looking instead at Petrona.

'Learn well and serve well,' said Petrona, her words gentle as a kiss.

Fern smiled. 'I'll do my best. I promise.'

Petrona's features blurred and Mary Magdalene emerged once again, the stone figure gazing down at Fern as she brushed the snow from her face and shoulders then stepped gratefully into the warmth of Jacques' house. Inside, she helped Freya peel off her wet shoes and socks and replaced them with the slippers she'd bought a few days before.

'Here,' said Jacques putting mugs of hot chocolate in front of them. You can warm your hands on this … Yes, yes, I have had a rest,' he added when Fern looked at him suspiciously. 'It takes little energy to boil milk.'

Fern laughed and took a sip of the drink. 'Thank you.'

'Should I?' asked Jacques, glancing at Freya.

Fern nodded.

He turned to Freya who was holding the mug in both hands and blowing on the warm milk. 'I have a question for you Freya.'

Freya looked up, surprised by Jacques' suddenly serious tone.

'Have you heard of the name Roese?'

To Fern's astonishment Freya nodded solemnly. 'I was Roese before I was me. I died in a big fire.'

'How do you know that?' asked Jacques, clearly surprised.

Freya hesitated. 'I saw the fire in Mama's stone.'

Jacques glanced at Fern, a question in his eyes.

'The tempest stone. Freya was holding it the day she fell over and hit her head.'

Jacques nodded, remembering. 'And you thought it best not to mention this?'

'It didn't seem important.'

Jacques gave Fern a withering look before turning back to Freya. 'Do you know why you died in the fire?'

'They were liars. They said I was a heretic but I wasn't. I was following the Way of Love. Just like Ramon.' Freya's eyes flashed with anger and for a moment she looked much older than her five-year-old self.

Fern was shocked. 'How do you know these words?'

Freya shrugged and took a bite of her orange cake.

'Children often use words they would not normally use when they describe a past life. Just as you did in your regressions with Hugues.' He turned back to Freya. 'Tell me more about Ramon?'

'Freya's lips trembled suddenly. 'I lost Ramon. I miss him.'

'Ramon was waiting in the light. Do you remember going into the light after the fire?'

Freya shook her head and took another bite of her cake, then began licking the icing off her fingers.

Jacques glanced quickly at Fern before addressing Freya once more. 'And what about Hugues?'

A shadow crossed Freya's face. 'He was a man in a long dress who didn't like Roese very much. Beattie says he was a bad man but I don't think he was.'

She jumped up. 'I want to play in the snow.'

Jacques glanced at Fern who nodded. 'D'accord,' said Jacques, 'but I have one more question. Who is Hugues now?'

Freya looked puzzled for a moment. Then her brow cleared as she understood. 'He's Mama.' She retrieved her still damp jacket, pulled on her rubber boots and dashed outside.

'So she knew all along,' said Fern as the door banged shut behind Freya.

'Some of it most certainly but I imagine she has pieced together the rest just as we have, only with less effort. As I have told you before, the veils are thinner for children. In a few years she will most likely have forgotten, just as she will forget her invisible friend.'

Fern nodded sadly. 'What I don't understand is why she never mentioned it.'

Jacques shrugged. 'Perhaps she did not think it necessary. Children are often practical in their dealings with past lives. Matter-of-fact, I think you English say. Unlike many adults,' he added, casting a pointed look in Fern's direction.

'Okay, point taken,' said Fern.

They sat in silence for a time, watching Freya playing happily outside in the snow, chatting contentedly to Beattie.

'I wonder what effect all this will have on her,' said Fern.

'It is hard to tell. Some of the heaviness within Freya must be associated with her grief at losing Ramon. But Freya is too young to regress so I cannot help her with her grief.'

'What about the burning?' asked Fern, remembering with a shudder the terror in Freya's face as she held the tempest stone that day.

'That fear should ease now. And because you have released Hugues, we should see a difference in Freya's relationship with you.' Jacques smiled. 'I think we are already seeing a difference,' he added as Freya, sensing their gaze, paused for a moment and waved.

Eyes sparking with mischief, she screwed up her face and pressed it against the glass door then backed away, laughing. Fern laughed too and returned the smile but tears were forming in her eyes and a lump growing in her throat. She'd been wondering whether or not to speak more with Freya about the past but now she could see it wasn't necessary. Everything Fern needed to know was contained in Freya's expression.

Chapter Forty-Six

Fern was sitting in Jacques' wicker chair on the verandah which was now enclosed by glass doors, the lemon and lime trees safely ensconced inside. Beneath her feet, the flagstones that had soaked up the sun all day were releasing their heat so it felt warm for now despite it being so cold outside. Through the glass she could see that the moon was full, illuminating the clear night sky and revealing the rugged contours of Canigou and the mountains around it. She still found it strange to think that she'd lived and died here so long ago, that in a sense she was part of this land. And Freya too, was connected to this landscape where she'd once lived, and where she'd died a violent and agonising death, not at the hand of Hugues but with his blessing. For the hundredth time, Fern reminded herself that there was no point holding onto a guilt that was centuries old. It wouldn't do to keep allowing the past to curse her and the people she loved.

Cautiously she shifted one leg and then the other, flexing her feet in the hope of easing the pins and needles tingling through them. She didn't want to disturb Freya who was curled up asleep on her lap, or the cat which was curled up by her feet. The house was quiet around them; no wind buffeting the shutters, no creaks within and no ghost creating tension in the atmosphere. Earlier, she and Freya had made eggs on toast and eaten their dinner watching television, smiling at the thought of Jacques shaking his head in disapproval. His operation in Paris had gone well but he would be staying with Edmund and Alexis for a few weeks to recuperate, and Fern had agreed that she and Freya would stay at least until he returned and take care of the house for him.

Freya shifted slightly in her sleep and Fern gently stroked her head, noting once again the similarities with Adam that were becoming more noticeable as she grew. The fine fair hair that tangled so easily, the way she shook her head to clear strands of it from her eyes, and there was more; a hand gesture here, an emphasis there, things Fern couldn't always put her finger on. However, for the first time since Adam's death, she was able to note these similarities with gratitude and sadness rather than a disabling grief. Adam's death had broken something inside her, sending her spiralling into a vast shadow-filled chamber and she was only just realising how hard that must have been for Freya.

Despite her concern about Jacques' health, Fern was pleased that she and Freya had the opportunity to spend some time alone together. They were still eyeing each other warily, not sure how best to relate, but that was gradually changing. Where there had once been a chasm between them, a bridge was forming and they were becoming mother and daughter again, without the ghosts of the distant past complicating things.

Freya smiled in her sleep and Fern's heart opened to her, wider than she'd ever thought possible. She lifted the sleeping child in her arms and carried her upstairs to bed, the cat padding along quietly behind them. When Fern pulled up the bedcovers, Freya opened her eyes for a sleepy moment and smiled at her mother with a tenderness and trust that made Fern catch her breath.

'Best Mama,' she said happily.

Caught up in Freya's smiling face, Fern felt her chest expand and something enter her, a force so powerful that for a moment it seemed as if her heart might burst, but then it softened and she felt it flowing gently through her, permeating her cells. Turning her attention inwards. she became aware of an inner vastness that encompassed the world and the universe beyond, connecting her to the past and to the future, a complicated map with lines drawn from one life to another in a glorious evolutionary pattern. For what seemed an eternity but must only have been an instant, Fern gazed transfixed through an all-perceiving eye that revealed life on its grandest and broadest scale.

Freya's eyes closed as she slipped back into sleep and Fern's gaze turned outwards once more. Overwhelmed by an immense sense of gratitude, she leaned over to kiss Freya goodnight.

'Sweet dreams best daughter,' she whispered.

Acknowledgements

I am grateful for the financial support of Arts Tasmania; without it my writing journey would have been a good deal bumpier. I'm also deeply grateful to my children who continue to believe in me; my husband, Tim for his patience and love; my writing group and community. And finally, my gratitude goes to the mystery behind inspiration. My thanks as always, to the giver.

Flight

standalone prequel to *Between Worlds*

'That one will be the death of her father …
mark my words, the death of him.'

So says the prophecy that accompanies Fern's birth. Her mother, fearing the wrath of the baby's father, is forced to give Fern up for adoption.

Twenty years later, Fern is haunted by the feeling that something is very wrong. Her family and friends think she is losing her mind but Fern is convinced that someone is after her.

Seeking to unlock the mystery, Fern takes flight onto the streets of Sydney, where she meets two unlikely allies: Cassie, a woman cursed with the gift of clairvoyance, and Adam, an ex-soldier tormented by his past. As danger looms, Fern and Adam embark on an adventure which takes them far into the labyrinthine depths of the Tasmanian wilderness, where Fern must finally confront her demons.

With modern gothic undertones and interwoven with myth and metaphor, *Flight* is a metaphysical thriller and a love story, compelling and original, sometimes eerie, sometimes earthy, always spellbinding.

'An adventure story that encapsulates both a physical and spiritual journey … interesting and original with some startling contrasts between the ordinary and extraordinary.'

Bookseller + Publisher

'A mesmerising tale of the real, unreal and surreal… '

Weekend Gold Coast Bulletin

Gathering Storm

'You'll be swept a long by this journey of
discovery. A great road movie of a novel.
Katherine Scholes

English artist Storm Cizekova grew up believing that her mother
died when she was born. But then Storm finds a photo of herself
in the heart of the Australian desert – and in her mother's arms.

Haunted by unanswered questions, Storm embarks on a journey of self-discovery that will challenge everything she holds
dear: her family history, her art, even her relationship with her
partner Max. Who is she really, and where does she belong?

Her search will take her from the snow-covered Malvern
Hills in England to the rich red heart of the Australian outback.
Retracing her mother's footsteps through the stark beauty of the
desert landscape, Storm hopes to find the courage to confront
some shocking truths from her past and the strength to face her
future.

Gathering Storm is an exploration of identity and dislocation
in a personal sense, through family history and genetic inheri-
tance, but also from a broader cultural perspective, in relation
to nationhood and citizenship. It explores the nature of truth, the
power of lies and the damage they leave in their wake. But probably, most importantly, Gathering Storm is about identifying and
breaking free of negative patterns, by turning around and facing
the monsters in one's life and taking the journey from anger to

forgiveness and compassion – it's about becoming oneself and living one's life in relation to that, instead of through the wounds that can be inherited from one's ancestors, from one's culture, and created through the experience of living.

'… A bit of a Heart of Darkness Apocalypse Now tale. It is part thriller, part hippie road story and part rite-of-passage trip in search of identity. Above all it is a compelling, stylish and well-paced read. Frightening at times and searching in its awareness of landscape and family secrets, this is a fine debut.'

Weekend Australian

'A deeply moving fiction debut in which Dub examines the virtue of truth, the harm of lies, the pain of secrets, the desire for belonging and the difficulty of confronting ones past to ensure the future.'

Weekend Gold Coast Bulletin

'A gritty sandblown kind of story that once begun gets into your consciousness with compelling insistence. Yes, it's a page-turner and yes, it's a thriller-cum-rite-of-passage tale… The strength of Dub's ability to tell a story and hold an audience is clear in this first novel of hopefully many more. It is a book of many pathways to the heart and soul, of not only a country but families who deny the truth of who they are and what they strive to protect…'

Sunday Tasmanian

'Here we have a Tasmanian writer with a first novel that grabs you from the very first page. Well written, it is a compelling story that takes the protagonist on a journey of self discovery… We will hear more from Rosie Dub; well done.'

Tasmanian Life